MADONNA
OF THE
SEVEN HILLS

Also by JEAN PLAIDY

THE MURDER IN THE TOWER
DAUGHTER OF SATAN
THE GOLDSMITH'S WIFE
EVERGREEN GALLANT

The Charles II Trilogy

THE WANDERING PRINCE
A HEALTH UNTO HIS MAJESTY
HERE LIES OUR SOVEREIGN LORD

The Tudor Novels

MURDER MOST ROYAL
THE SIXTH WIFE
ST. THOMAS'S EVE
THE SPANISH BRIDEGROOM
GAY LORD ROBERT
THE THISTLE AND THE ROSE

The Mary Queen of Scots Series

ROYAL ROAD TO FOTHERINGAY
THE CAPTIVE QUEEN OF SCOTS

Jean Plaidy

MADONNA
OF THE
SEVEN HILLS

G. P. Putnam's Sons
New York

FIRST AMERICAN EDITION 1974

Copyright © 1958, 1974 by Jean Plaidy

SBN: 399–11456–4

Library of Congress Catalog

Card Number: 74–13502

PRINTED IN THE UNITED STATES OF AMERICA

CONTENTS

AUTHOR'S NOTE   7

THE BIRTH OF LUCREZIA   9

THE PIAZZA PIZZO DI MERLO   21

MONTE GIORDANO   40

ALEXANDER VI   58

SANTA MARIA IN PORTICO   66

LUCREZIA MARRIED   89

PESARO   129

CESARE   172

SANCHIA OF ARAGON   184

ROMAN CARNIVAL   207

SAN-SISTO   241

THE SECOND BRIDEGROOM   299

AUTHOR'S NOTE

I HOPE THAT my readers will bear in mind the proverb *Altri tempi, altri costumi,* and adjust their mental vision to the fifteenth century when Popes took their vows of celibacy merely as a form, and when murder was so commonplace that an old Tiber boatman on seeing the body of the Pope's son thrown into the river did not think it necessary to report it because he saw bodies thrown in every night.

Only by judging the Borgias against their own times can they arouse our sympathy, and only if they arouse our sympathy can they be understood.

Below are some of the books which have been of great help to me:

Lucrezia Borgia: A Chapter from the Morals of the Italian Renaissance. Ferdinand Gregorovius.

The Life and Times of Lucrezia Borgia. Maria Bellonci. Translated by Bernard Wall.

Lucrezia Borgia. Joan Haslip.

The Life of Cesare Borgia. Raphael Sabatini.

Lucretia Borgia, The Chronicle of Tebaldeo Tebaldei, Renaissance Period, Commentary and Notes by Randolph Hughes. Algernon Charles Swinburne.

Life and Times of Roderigo Borgia, Pope Alexander VI. The Most Rev. Arnold H. Mathew, D.D.

Chronicles of the House of Borgia. Frederick Baron Corvo.

Hadrian the Seventh. Frederick Rolfe (Frederick Baron Corvo).

Alma Roma. Albert G. MacKennon, M.A.

Cesare Borgia. Charles Yriarte. Translated by William Stirling.

Cesare Borgia. William Harrison Woodward.

An Outline of Italian Civilization. Decio Pettoello.

History of the Italian Republics in the Middle Ages. J. C. L.
Sismondi. (Recast and Supplemented in the light of
historical research by William Boulting.)

*Memoirs of the Dukes of Urbino : Illustrating the Arms, Arts
and Literature of Italy from 1440 to 1630.* (3 Vols.) James
Dennistoun of Dennistoun.

J.P.

THE BIRTH OF LUCREZIA

I T WAS COLD in the castle, and the woman who stood at the window looking from the snowy caps of the mountains to the monastery below thought longingly of the comfort of her house on the Piazza Pizzo di Merlo sixty miles away in Rome.

Yet she was content to be here for it was Roderigo's wish that their child should be born in his mountain castle; and she could feel nothing but delight that he should care so much.

She turned her back on the majestic view and looked round the room. The bed was inviting, for her pains were becoming more frequent. She hoped the child would be a boy, since Roderigo could do so much more for a boy than for a girl.

Already she had given him three handsome sons, and he doted on them, particularly, she believed, on Cesare and Giovanni; but that was because Pedro Luis the eldest had been sent away. It was sad to lose him but it was a wonderful future which would be his: education at the Spanish Court, where he was to receive the dukedom of Gandia. And there would be equally grand opportunities for the others – for Cesare, for Giovanni, and the unborn child.

Her women were hovering. Madonna should lie down now, they advised, for the child would surely soon be born.

She smiled, wiping the sweat from her forehead, and allowed them to help her to the bed. One touched her forehead with a sweet-smelling unguent which was cool and refreshing; another put a goblet of wine to her lips. They were eager, these women, to serve Vannozza Catanei, because she was beloved by Roderigo Borgia, one of the greatest Cardinals in Rome.

She was a lucky woman to have become so dear to him, for he was a man who needed many mistresses; but she was the chief one, which in itself was something of a miracle since she was no longer young. When a woman was thirty-eight she must indeed be attractive to hold the attention of such a one as Cardinal Roderigo Borgia. Yet she had done it; and if there were times when she wondered whether he came to see their children rather than for the purpose of making love to her, what of that? Sons such as Pedro Luis, Cesare and Giovanni could make a stronger bond than passion; and if, in the future, there were younger and more beautiful women to charm him, she would still be the one who had given him his favourite children.

So she would be contented – when the pains were over and the child born; she was sure the baby would be healthy and handsome; all her children were. They had all inherited her golden beauty and she hoped the new child would, for it delighted their father. So she must be pleased that he had insisted on bringing her here to his castle at Subiaco, even though the journey had been long and tedious and the wind was fierce in the Apennines. He wished her to have their child in his palace, and he wished to be near her when it was born. That would have been less simple to achieve in Rome, for Roderigo was after all a man of the Church sworn to celibacy, and here in the mountain fastness of the Subiaco castle he could give way to his joy with an easier mind. So she would soothe herself while she waited by thinking of her beautiful house on the Piazza Pizzo di Merlo in which, due to the bounty of Roderigo, she lived so graciously. She delighted in the Ponte quarter in which there was always so much going on. It was one of the most populous districts of the city, and merchants and bankers abounded there. It was favoured by the most notorious and prosperous of the courtesans, and dominated by the noble family of Orsini who had their palace on Monte Giordano, and whose castle, the Torre di None, was part of the city's wall.

Not that Vannozza considered herself a courtesan. She was faithful to Roderigo and regarded him as her husband, although of course she knew that Roderigo, being a Cardinal, could not marry, and that if he had been able to he would have been obliged to look for a wife in a different stratum of society.

But if Roderigo could not marry her he had been as considerate as any husband. Roderigo, thought Vannozza, was surely the most charming man in Rome. She did not believe she was the only one who thought this, although a man such as Roderigo would certainly have his enemies. He was made for distinction; his eyes were on a certain goal, the Papacy, and those who knew Roderigo well would surely feel that he had an excellent chance of achieving his ambition. No one should be deceived by those gracious manners, that enchantingly musical voice, that attractive courtesy; they were so much a part of Roderigo, it was true, but beneath the charm was a burning ambition which would certainly carry him as far as he intended it should.

Roderigo was a man whom Vannozza could adore, for he had all the qualities which she admired most. Therefore she prayed now to the saints and the Virgin that the child which she was about to bear should have charm and beauty (for Roderigo, possessing the former to such a degree, was very susceptible to the latter) and that should she, herself a matron of thirty-eight, fail to arouse his sexual desire she could continue to bask in his gratitude for the children she had borne him.

How long would the children be kept under her roof? Not long, she imagined. They would depart as Pedro Luis had departed. Roderigo had fine plans for the boys; and Vannozza, beloved of the Cardinal though she might be, had little social standing in Rome.

But he would remember that part of her lived in those children, and she would continue in her charming house, the house which he had given her. It was the sort of house which was possessed by the nobles of Rome, and she delighted in it. She had enjoyed sitting in the main room of the house, the whitewashed walls of which she had decorated with tapestries and a few pictures; for she had wanted to make her house as luxurious as that of the great families – the Orsinis and the Colonnas. Her lover was generous and had given her many presents; in addition to her tapestries and paintings she had her jewellery, her fine furniture, her ornaments of porphyry and marble, and – most treasured of all – her *credenza*, that great chest in which she stored her majolica, and her gold and silver goblets and drinking vessels. The *credenza* was a sign of social standing, and Vannozza's eyes shone every time she looked at hers. She would walk about her beautiful house, touching her beautiful possessions and telling herself in the quiet coolness she enjoyed behind its thick walls that she had indeed been a fortunate woman when Roderigo Borgia had come into her life and found her desirable.

Vannozza was no fool, and she knew that the treasures which Roderigo had given her were, in his mind, as nothing compared to those she had given him.

Now the pain was gripping her again, more insistently, almost continuously. The child was eager to be born.

In another wing of his castle of Subiaco the great Cardinal also waited. His apartments were far from those of his mistress for he did not wish to be distressed by the sound of her cries; he did not wish to think of Vannozza's suffering; he wished to think of her as she had always taken pains to be in his presence – beautiful, light-hearted and full of vitality, even as he was himself. In childbirth Vannozza might fail to be so and he preferred to remember her thus, as he was a man who hated to be uncomfortable; and Vannozza in pain would render him so.

Therefore it was better to shut himself away from her, to wait in patience until the message came to him that the child was born.

He had turned from the shrine before which he had been kneeling. The lamp which burned constantly before the figures and pictures of the saints had shone on the serene face of the Madonna, and he had fancied he had seen reproach there. Should he, one of the mightiest of Cardinals, be praying for the safe delivery of a child he had no right to have begotten? Could he expect the Madonna to grant him a son – a beautiful healthy boy – when, as a son of the Church himself, he was sworn to celibacy?

It was an uncomfortable thought and as Roderigo always turned hastily from such, he allowed himself to forget the shrine and looked instead at the emblem of the grazing bull which adorned the walls, and which never failed to inspire him. It was the emblem of the Borgias and one day it would be, so determined Roderigo, the most feared and respected symbol in Italy.

Ah yes, it was comforting to contemplate the bull – that creature of strength, peacefully grazing yet indicative of so much that was fierce and strong. One day, pondered the Cardinal, the Borgia arms should be displayed all over Italy, for it was the dream of Roderigo that the whole of Italy would one day be united, and united under a Borgia. Another Borgia Pope! Why not? The Vatican was the centre of the Catholic world; certainly the Vatican should unite a divided country, for in unity there was strength, and who more fitted to rule a united Italy than the Pope? But he was not yet Pope, and he had his enemies who would do all in their power to prevent his reaching that high eminence. No matter. He would achieve his ambition as his uncle Alfonso had achieved his when he had become Pope Calixtus III.

Calixtus had been wise; he had known that the strength of a family was in its young members. That was why Calixtus had adopted him, Roderigo, and his brother Pedro Luis (after him he had named Vannozza's eldest boy), that was why he had enriched them and made them powerful men in the land.

Roderigo smiled complacently; he had no need to adopt children; he had his own sons and daughters. The daughters were useful when it came to making marriages which would unite eminent families with the Borgias; but sons were what an ambitious man needed and, praise be to the saints, these were what he had, and he would forever be grateful to the woman, who was now in childbed in this very castle, for providing them. Pedro Luis in Spain would ensure that country's benevolence towards his father; dashing young Giovanni – for him Roderigo had the most ambitious plans, for that best loved of his sons should command the armies of the Borgias; and Cesare, that bold young scamp (Roderigo smiled with pleasure at the memory of his arrogant little son), he must perforce go into the Church, for, if the Borgias were to achieve all that Roderigo planned for them, one of them must hold sway in the Vatican. So little Cesare was destined to follow his father to the Papal Chair.

Roderigo shrugged his shoulders, and smiled gently at himself. He had yet to achieve that position; but he would; he was determined that he would. The gentle smile had faded and for a few moments it was possible to see the man of iron behind the pleasant exterior.

He had come far and he would never go back; he would prefer death rather. He was as certain as he was that a child was being born in his castle of Subiaco that one day he would ascend the Papal throne.

Nothing ... nothing should stand in his way, for only as Pope could he invest his sons with those honours which would enable them to work towards that great destiny which was to be the Borgias'.

And the new child? 'A boy,' he prayed, 'Holy Mother, let it be a boy. I have three fine sons, healthy boys, yet could I use another.'

He was all gentleness again, thinking of the nursery in the house on the Piazza Pizzo di Merlo. How those two little ones delighted in the visits of Uncle Roderigo! It was necessary at present that they should think of him as 'uncle'; it would be quite inconceivable that he – a Holy Cardinal – should be addressed as Papa. 'Uncle' was good enough for the present; one day those little boys should know who they really were. He looked forward to his pleasure in telling them. (Roderigo enjoyed bringing pleasure to those whom he loved but if there was any unpleasant task to perform he preferred others to do it.) What glorious fate awaited them because he, the illustrious Cardinal, was not merely their uncle, but their father! How Cesare's eyes would flash – the arrogant and delightful little creature! How Giovanni would strut – dear, best-beloved Giovanni! And the new child ... he too would come in for his share of honours.

What were they doing now? Disagreeing with their nursemaid, very likely. He could imagine the threats of Cesare, the sullen anger of Giovanni. They were brimming with vitality – inherited from Vannozza as well as from their father, and each knew how to achieve his desires. They would get the better of twenty nursemaids – which was what he must expect. They were the sons of Roderigo Borgia, and when had he failed to get his way with women?

Now he was thinking of the past, of the hundreds of women who had pleased him. When he had first gone into the Church he had been dismayed because celibacy was expected of him. He could laugh at his naïvety now. It had not taken him long to discover that Cardinals, and even Popes, had their mistresses. They were not expected to lead celibate lives, only to appear to do so, which was quite a different matter. Not continence but discretion was all that was asked.

It was a solemn moment when a new life was about to begin; it was even more solemn to contemplate that, but for an act of his, this child would not have been preparing to come into the world.

He sat down and, keeping his eyes on the grazing bull, recalled those incidents in his life which had been of greatest importance to him. Perhaps one of the earliest and therefore the most important, for if it had not happened, all that had followed would not have been possible, was when his uncle Calixtus III had adopted him and his brother Pedro Luis and promised that he would treat them as his own sons if they would discard their father's name of Lanzol and called themselves Borgia.

Their parents had been anxious that the adoption should take place. They had daughters – but Pope Calixtus was not interested in them, and they knew that no better fate could befall their sons than to come under the immediate patronage of the Pope. Their mother – the Pope's own sister – was a Borgia, so it merely meant that the boys should take their mother's name instead of their father's.

That was the beginning of good fortune.

Uncle Alfonso Borgia (Pope Calixtus III to the world) was Spanish and had been born near Valencia. He had come to Italy with King Alfonso of Aragon when that monarch had ascended the throne of Naples. Spain – that most ambitious Power which was fast dominating the world – was eager to see Spanish influence throughout Italy, and how could this be better achieved than by the election of a Spanish Pope?

Uncle Alfonso had the support of Spain when he aspired to the Papacy, and he was victorious in the year 1455. All Borgias were conscious of family feeling. They were Spanish, and Spaniards were not welcome in Italy; therefore it was necessary for all Spaniards to stand together while they did their best to acquire the most important posts.

Calixtus had plans for his two nephews. He promptly made

Pedro Luis Generalissimo of the Church and Prefect of the City. Not content with this he created him Duke of Spoleto and, in order that his income should be further increased, he made him vicar of Terracina and Benevento. Pedro Luis was very comfortably established in life; he was not only one of the most influential men in Rome – which he would necessarily be, owing to his relationship with the Pope – he was one of the most wealthy.

The honours which fell to Roderigo were almost as great. He, a year younger than Pedro Luis, was made a Cardinal, although he was only twenty-six; later there was added to this the office of Vice-Chancellor of the Church of Rome. Indeed, the Lanzols had no need to regret the adoption of their sons by the Pope.

It had been clear from the beginning that Calixtus meant Roderigo to follow him to the Papacy; and Roderigo had made up his mind, from the moment of his adoption, that one day he would do so.

Alas, that was long ago, and the Papacy was as far away as ever. Calixtus had been an old man when he was elected, and three years later he had died. Now the wisdom of his prompt action in bestowing great offices on his nephews was seen, for even while Calixtus was on his death-bed, there was an outcry against the Spaniards who had been given the best posts; and the Colonnas and the Orsinis, those powerful families which had felt themselves to be slighted, rose in fury against the foreigners; Pedro Luis had to abandon his fine estates with all his wealth and fly for his life. He died shortly afterwards.

Roderigo remained calm and dignified, and did not leave Rome. Instead, while the City was seething against him and his kin, he went solemnly to St Peter's in order that he might pray for his dying uncle.

Roderigo was possessed of great charm. It was not that he was very handsome; his features were too heavy for good looks, but his dignity and his presence were impressive; so was his courtly grace which rarely failed to arouse the devotion of almost all who came into contact with him.

Oddly enough those people who were raging against him parted to let him pass on his way to St Peter's while benignly he smiled at them and gently murmured: 'Bless you, my children.' And they knelt and kissed his hand or the hem of his robes.

Was that one of the most triumphant hours of his life? There had been triumphs since; but perhaps on that occasion he first became aware of this great power within him to charm and subdue by his charm all who would oppose him.

So he had prayed for his uncle and had stayed with him at his bedside while all others had fled; and although his magnificent palace had been sacked and looted, he remained aloof and calm, ready to cast his deciding vote at the Conclave which would follow and which assured Aeneas Sylvius Piccolomini of becoming, as Pius I I, the successor of Calixtus.

Pius must be grateful to Roderigo, and indeed he was.

Thus Roderigo came successfully through the first storm of his life and had assured himself that he was able to stand on his own feet, as poor Pedro Luis had not been able to do.

Roderigo collected his brother's wealth, mourned him bitterly – but briefly, for it was not in Roderigo's nature to mourn for long – and found himself as powerful as he had ever been, and as hopeful of aspiring to the Papal throne.

Roderigo now wiped his brow with a perfumed kerchief. Those had been times of great danger, and he hoped never again to see the like; yet whenever he looked back on them he was aware of the satisfaction of a man who has discovered that the dangerous moment had not found him lacking in shrewd resourcefulness.

Pius had indeed been his good friend, but there had been times when Pius had found it necessary to reprove him. He could recall now the words of a letter which Pius had sent to him, complaining of Roderigo's conduct in a certain house where courtesans had been gathered to administer to the pleasures of the guests. And he, young handsome Cardinal Roderigo, had been among those guests.

'We have been informed,' wrote Pius, 'that there was unseemly dancing, that no amorous allurements of love were lacking, and that you conducted yourself in a wholly worldly manner.'

Roderigo threw back his head and smiled, remembering the

scented garden of Giovanni de Bichis, the dancing, the warm perfumed bodies of women and their seductive glances. He had found them irresistible, as they had him.

And the reproof of Pius had not been serious. Pius understood that a man such as Roderigo must have his mistresses. Pius merely meant: Yes, yes, but no dancing in public with courtesans, Cardinal. The people complain, and it brings the Church into disrepute.

How careless he had been in those days, so certain was he of his ability to win through to his goal. He had determined to have the best of both ways of life. The Church was his career, by means of which he was going to climb to the Papal throne; but he was a sensualist, a man of irrepressible carnal desires. There would always be women in his life. It was not an uncommon foible; there was hardly a priest who seriously took his vows regarding celibacy, and it had been said by one of the wits of Rome that if every child came into the world with its father's clothes on, they would all be dressed as priests or Cardinals.

Everyone understood; but Roderigo was perhaps more openly promiscuous than most.

Then he had met Vannozza, and he had set her up in a fine house, where now they had their children. Not that he had been faithful to Vannozza; no one would have expected that; but she had remained reigning favourite for many years and he adored their children. And now there was to be another.

It was irksome to wait. He, who was fifty, felt like a young husband of twenty, and if it were not for the fear of hearing Vannozza's crying in her pain he would have gone to her apartment. But there was no need. Someone was coming to him.

She stood before him, flushed and pretty, Vannozza's little maid. Even on such an occasion Roderigo was aware of her charms. He would remember her.

She curtseyed. 'Your Eminence . . . the child is born.'

With the grace and agility of a much younger man he had moved to her side and laid beautiful white hands on her shoulders.

'My child, you are breathless. How your heart beats!'

'Yes, my lord. But . . . the baby is born.'

'Come,' he said, 'we will go to your mistress.'

He led the way. The little maid, following, realized suddenly that she had forgotten to tell him the sex of the child, and that he had forgotten to ask.

The baby was brought to the Cardinal who touched its brow and blessed it.

The women fell back; they looked shame-faced as though they were to be blamed for the sex of the child.

It wás a beautiful baby; there was a soft down of fair hair on the little head, and Roderigo believed that Vannozza had given him another golden beauty.

'A little girl,' said Vannozza, watching him from the bed.

He strode to her, took her hand and kissed it.

'A beautiful little girl,' he said.

'My lord is disappointed,' said Vannozza wearily. 'He hoped for a boy.'

Roderigo laughed, that deep-throated musical laugh which made most people who heard it love him.

'Disappointed!' he said. 'I?' Then he looked round at the women who had come closer, his eyes resting on them each in turn, caressingly, speculatively. 'Disappointed because she is of the feminine sex? But you know . . . every one of you . . . that I love the soft sex with all my heart, and I can find a tenderness for it which I would deny to my own.'

The women laughed and Vannozza laughed with them; but her sharp eyes had noticed the little maid who wore an expectant expression as Roderigo's glance lingered upon her.

She decided that, as soon as they returned to Rome, that child should be dismissed and, if Roderigo should look for her, he would look in vain.

'So my lord is pleased with our daughter?' murmured Vannozza, and signed to the women to leave her with the Cardinal.

'I verily believe,' said Roderigo, 'that I shall find a softer spot in my heart for this sweet girl even than for those merry young rogues who now inhabit your nurseries. We will christen her Lucrezia; and when you are recovered, Madonna, we will return to Rome.'

And so on that April day in the Borgia castle at Subiaco was born the child whose name was to be notorious throughout the world: Lucrezia Borgia.

THE PIAZZA PIZZO DI MERLO

HOW DELIGHTED VANNOZZA was to be back in Rome! It seemed to her during those months which followed the birth of Lucrezia that she was the happiest of women. Roderigo visited her nurseries more frequently than ever; there was an additional attraction in the golden-haired little girl.

She was a charming baby – very sweet-tempered – and would lie contentedly in her crib giving her beautiful smile to any who asked for it.

The little boys were interested in her. They would stand one on either side of the crib and try to make her laugh. They quarrelled about her. Cesare and Giovanni would always seize on any difference between them and make a quarrel about it.

Vannozza laughed with her women, listening to their bickering: 'She's *my* sister.' 'No, she's *my* sister.' It had been explained to them that she was the sister of both of them.

Cesare had answered, his eyes flashing: 'But she is more mine than Giovanni's. She loves me – Cesare – better than Giovanni.'

That, the nursemaid told him, will be for Lucrezia herself to decide.

Giovanni watched his brother with smouldering eyes; he knew why Cesare wanted Lucrezia to love him best. Cesare was aware that when Uncle Roderigo called it was always Giovanni who had the bigger share of sweetmeats; it was always Giovanni who was lifted up in those strong arms and kissed and caressed before the magnificent Uncle Roderigo turned to Cesare.

Therefore Cesare was determined that everyone else should love him best. His mother did. The nurserymaids said they did; but that might have been because, if they did not, he would have his revenge in some way, and they knew that it was more unwise to offend Cesare than Giovanni.

Lucrezia, as soon as she was able to show a preference, should show it for him. He was determined on that. That was why he hung about her crib even more than Giovanni did, putting out his hand to let those little fingers curl about his thumb.

'Lucrezia,' he would whisper. 'This is Cesare, your brother. You love him best . . . best of all.' She would look at him with those wide blue eyes, and he would command: 'Laugh, Lucrezia. Laugh like this.'

The women would crowd round the crib to watch, for strangely enough Lucrezia invariably obeyed Cesare; and when Giovanni tried to make her laugh for him, Cesare would be behind his brother pulling such demoniacal faces that Lucrezia cried instead.

'It's that demon, Cesare,' said the women to one another, for although he was but five years old they dared not say it to Cesare.

One day, six months after Lucrezia's birth, Vannozza was tending her vines and flowers in her garden. She had her gardeners but this was a labour of love. Her plants were beautiful and it delighted her to look after them herself for her garden and her house were almost as dear to her as her family. Who would not be proud of such a house with its façade, facing the piazza, and the light room with the big window, so different from most of the gloomy rooms in other Roman houses. She had a water cistern too, which was a rare thing.

Her maid – not the one whom Roderigo had admired; she had long since left Vannozza's service – came to tell her that the Cardinal had called, and with him was another gentleman; but even as the girl spoke Roderigo stepped into the garden, and he was alone.

'My lord,' cried Vannozza, 'that you should find me thus. . . .'

Roderigo's smile was disarming. 'But you look charming among your plants,' he told her.

'Will you not come into the house? I hear you have brought a guest. The women should have attended to you better.'

'But it was my wish to speak to you alone . . . out here while you worked among your flowers.'

She was startled. She knew that he had something important to say, and she wondered whether he preferred to say it
out of doors because even in well-ordered houses such as hers
servants had a habit of listening to what they should not.

A cold fear numbed her mind as she wondered if he had
come to tell her that this was the end of their liaison. She was
acutely conscious of her thirty-eight years. She guarded her
beauty well, but even so, a woman of thirty-eight who had borne
several children could not compete with young girls; and there
could scarcely be a young girl who, if she could resist the
charm of the Cardinal, would be able to turn away from all that
such an influential man could bring a mistress.

'My lord,' she said faintly, 'you have news.'

The Cardinal lifted his serene face to the sky and smiled his
most beautiful smile.

'My dear Vannozza,' he said, 'as you know, I hold you in
the deepest regard.' Vannozza caught her breath in horror. It
sounded like the beginning of dismissal. 'You live here in this
house with our three children. It is a happy little home, but
there is something missing; these children have no father.'

Vannozza wanted to cast herself at his feet, to implore him
not to remove his benevolent presence from their lives. They
might as well be dead if he did. As well try to live without the
sun. But she knew how he disliked unpleasant scenes; and she
said calmly: 'My children have the best father in the world. I
would rather they had never been born than that they should
have had another.'

'You say delightful things . . . delightfully,' said Roderigo.
'These are my children and dearly I love them. Never shall I
forget the great service you have done me in giving them to me,
my dearest love.'

'My lord. . . .' The tears had come to her eyes and she
dashed them away, but Roderigo was looking at the sky, so
determined was he not to see them.

'But it is not good that you should live in this house – a
beautiful and still young woman, with your children about you,
and only the uncle of those children to visit you.'

'My lord, if I have offended you in some way I pray you tell
me quickly where I have been at fault.'

'You have committed no fault, my dear Vannozza. It is but to make life easier for you that I have made these plans. I want none to point at you and whisper; "Ah, there goes Vannozza Catanei, the woman who has children and no husband." That is why I have found a husband for you.'

'A husband! But, my lord . . .'

Roderigo silenced her with an authoritative smile. 'You have a young baby in this house, Vannozza; she is six months old. Therefore you must have a husband.'

This was the end. She knew it. He would not have provided her with a husband if he had not tired of her.

He read her thoughts. But it was not entirely true that he was weary of her; he would always have some affection for her and would continue to visit her house, but that would be mainly to see his children; there were younger women with whom he wished to spend his leisure. There was some truth in what he was telling her; he did think it wise that she should be known as a married woman, for he could not have it said that his little ones were the children of a courtesan.

He said quickly: 'Your husband's duties will be to live in this house, to appear with you in public. They will end there, Vannozza.'

'Your lordship means?'

'Do you think that I could mean anything else? I am a jealous lover, Vannozza. Have you not yet learned that?'

'I know you to be jealous when you are a lover, my lord.'

He laid his hand on her shoulder. 'Have no fear, Vannozza. You and I have been together too long to part now. It is solely for the sake of our children that I take this step. And I have chosen a quiet man to be your husband. He is a good man, a man of great respectability, and he is prepared to be the only sort of husband I could content myself with giving you.'

She took his hand and kissed it.

'And your Eminence will come and visit us now and then?'

'As ever, my dear. As ever. Now come and meet Giorgio di Croce. You will see that he is a mild-tempered man; you will have no difficulty with such a one, I do assure you.'

She followed him into the house, wondering what inducement had been offered to this man that he had agreed to marry her. It was not difficult to guess. There would be scarcely a man in Rome who would refuse to marry a woman whom the influential Cardinal had selected for him.

Vannozza was uneasy. She did not care to be bartered thus, as though she were a slave. She would certainly keep Giorgio di Croce in his place.

In her room which overlooked the piazza he was waiting. He rose as they entered and the Cardinal made the introductions.

The mild-tempered man took her hands and kissed them; she studied him and saw that his pale eyes gleamed as he took in her voluptuous charm.

Did the Cardinal notice? If so, he gave no sign.

From the loggia of her mother's house Lucrezia looked out on the piazza and watched with quiet pleasure the people who passed. The city of the seven hills outside her mother's house fascinated her, and it was her favourite pleasure to slip out to the loggia and watch people passing over the St Angelo Bridge. There were Cardinals on white mules whose silver bridles gleamed in the sunshine; there were masked ladies and gentlemen; there were litters, curtained so that it was impossible to see the occupants.

Lucrezia's wide wondering eyes would peer through gaps in the masonry as her fat little fingers curled about the pillars.

She was two years old but life with her brothers had made her appear to be more. The women of the nursery loved her dearly for, although she was like her brothers in appearance, she was quite unlike them in character. Lucrezia's was a sunny nature; when she was scolded for a fault, she would listen gravely and bear no malice against the scolder. It was small wonder that in that nursery, made turbulent by the two boys, Lucrezia was regarded as a blessing.

She was very pretty, and the women never tired of combing or adorning that long hair of the yellow-gold colour which was so rarely seen in Rome. Lucrezia was already, at two – like her brothers she was precocious – aware of her charm, but she accepted this in quiet contentment as she accepted most things.

Today there was a hush over the house, because something

important was happening, and Lucrezia was aware of the whispers of serving men and maids, and of the presence of strange women in the house. It concerned her mother, she knew, because she had not been allowed to see her for a whole day. Lucrezia smiled placidly as she looked on the piazza. She would know in time, so she would wait until then.

Her brother Giovanni came and stood beside her. He was six years old, a beautiful boy with auburn hair like his mother's.

Lucrezia smiled at him and held out her hand; her brothers were always affectionate towards her and she was already aware that each of them was doing his best to be her favourite. She was coquette enough already to enjoy the rivalry for her affections.

'For what do you watch, Lucrezia?' asked Giovanni.

'For the people,' she answered. 'See the fat lady with the mask!'

They laughed together because the fat lady waddled, said Giovanni, like a duck.

'Our uncle will soon be here.' said Giovanni. 'You are watching for him, Lucrezia.'

Lucrezia nodded, smiling. It was true that she always watched for Uncle Roderigo. His visits were the highlights of her life. To be swung in those strong arms, to be held above that laughing face, to smell the faint perfume which clung to his clothes and watch the twinkling jewels on his white hands and to know that he loved her – that was wonderful. Even more wonderful than being loved so much by her two brothers.

'He will come today, Lucrezia,' said Giovanni. 'He surely will. He is waiting for a message from our mother.'

Lucrezia listened, alert; she could not always understand her brothers; they seemed to forget that she was only two years old, and that Giovanni who was six and Cesare who was seven seemed like adults, grand, large and important.

'Do you know why, Lucrezia?' said Giovanni.

When she shook her head, Giovanni laughed, hugging the secret, longing to tell yet reluctant to do so because the anticipation of telling so pleased him. He stopped smiling at her suddenly and Lucrezia knew why. Cesare was standing behind them.

Lucrezia turned to smile at him, but Cesare was glaring at Giovanni.

'It is not for you to tell,' said Cesare.

'It is as much for me as for you,' retorted Giovanni.

'I am the elder. I shall tell,' declared Cesare. 'Lucrezia, you are not to listen to him.'

Lucrezia shook her head and smiled. No, she would not listen to Giovanni.

'I shall tell if I want to,' shouted Giovanni. 'I have as much right to tell as you. More . . . because I thought to tell first.'

Cesare had his brother by the hair and was shaking him. Giovanni kicked out at Cesare. Cesare kicked back, Giovanni yelled and the two boys were rolling on the floor.

Lucrezia remained placid, for such fights were commonplace enough in the nursery, and she watched them, content that they should be fighting over her; she was nearly always the cause of these fights.

Giovanni was yelping with pain; while Cesare shrieked with rage. The maid-servants would not come near them while they fought thus. They were afraid of those two boys.

Giovanni who was being held down to the floor by Cesare, shouted: 'Lucrezia . . . our mother is . . .'

But he could say no more because Cesare had his hand over his brother's mouth. His eyes looked black with rage and his face was scarlet. 'I shall tell. It is my place to tell. Our mother is having a baby, Lucrezia.'

Lucrezia stared, her eyes wide, her soft babyish mouth open in astonishment. Cesare, watching her amazement, was placated. She was looking at him as though he were responsible for this strange thing. She made him feel powerful, as she had ever since she had been a baby and he had hung over her crib and watched her little fingers curl about his thumb.

He released Giovanni and both boys got to their feet. The fight was over; it was one of many which took place every day in the nursery. Now they were ready to talk to their little sister about the new baby, to strut before her and boast of all that they knew concerning the great events which went on outside their nursery.

Vannozza lay waiting for the Cardinal to visit her. A boy this time, but she was uneasy.

She had good reason to be.

The Cardinal had continued his visits during the two years of her marriage, but they had been less frequent and she had heard a great deal of gossip about the charming young women in whom he was interested.

Giorgio was a good man, a meek man, as the Cardinal had declared him to be; but even the meekest men are yet men, and Vannozza was possessed of voluptuous and irresistible charm. There had been long summer evenings – the cool of the evening was the best part of the day – when they supped in her lovely vineyard in the Suburra, when they had talked and grown drowsy and afterwards gone into the house, each feeling stimulated by the presence of the other.

After all, they were married, and Roderigo's visits were so infrequent.

It was to be expected, of course, even though the rule had been laid down that Giorgio was merely to share the public rooms of her house.

Could Roderigo blame her? She did not think he would. But if there was a question of the child being his, he might feel less inclined to do for it what he planned to do for the others.

When a woman held a child in her arms, a child of a few hours, how could she help it if for a short while that child seemed more precious to her than anything else on Earth? Cesare would always hold first place in her affections; but at this time as she lay exhausted in her bed the little newcomer – her Goffredo – being the most helpless of her brood, must, she decided, have the same opportunities as his brothers.

He looked exactly as the others had; indeed it might be little Lucrezia who lay in her arms now, a baby a few hours old; and there was no doubt who her father was. Goffredo might be Roderigo's son. With such a lover and a husband living under her own roof, even Vannozza could not be sure. But she must do all in her power to make the Cardinal sure he was the child's father.

He was coming to her bedside now. Her women stepped back in awed reverence as he approached.

'Vannozza, my dear!' His voice sounded as tender as ever, but he rarely showed anger, and she could not tell what his feelings were towards the child.

'A boy this time, my lord. He is very like Lucrezia ... and I fancy I see Your Eminence in that child every day.'

A plump white hand, sparkling with gems, touched the baby's cheek. It was a tender, paternal gesture, and Vannozza's spirits rose.

She picked up the child and held him out to the Cardinal who took him from her; she saw his face soften in a look of pride and joy. It was small wonder, she thought then, that many loved Roderigo; his love of women and children made them eager to please and serve him.

He walked up and down with the child, and in his eyes was a faraway look as though he were seeing into the future. Surely that meant that he was making plans for the new-born boy. He did not suspect. He must have compared himself with Giorgio and asked himself how any woman could consider the little apostolic clerk, when she must compare him with the charming and mighty Cardinal.

He put the baby back into her arms and stood for a while smiling benignly down at her.

Then he said slyly; 'Giorgio? He is pleased?'

There was a period in Lucrezia's life which she would remember until the day of her death. She was only four years old, yet so vivid was the memory that it was imprinted for ever on her mind. For one thing it was the beginning of change.

Before that time she had lived the nursery life, secure in the love of her mother, looking forward to the visits of Uncle Roderigo, delighting in the battle of her brothers for her affection. It had been a pleasant little world in which Lucrezia lived. Each day she would take her stand on the loggia and watch the colourful world go by, but all that happened beyond her mother's house seemed to her nothing more than pictures for her idle pleasure; there was an unreality about all that happened on the other side of the loggia and Lucrezia was safe in her cosy world of love and admiration.

She knew that she was pretty and that no one could fail to notice this because of her yellow hair and her eyes which were light blue-grey in colour; her eyelashes and brows were dark and inherited from her Spanish ancestors, it was said; and it was this combination which, partly because it was so unusual, was so attractive. She had the arresting looks of one who was only part Italian, being also part Spanish. Her brothers also possessed this charm.

The serving-maids could not help embracing her, patting her cheeks or stroking her lovely hair. 'Dearest little Madonna,' they would murmur, and they would whisper together about those enchanting *occhi bianchi* which were going to make a seductress of their little Madonna.

She was happy in their affection; she would snuggle up to them, giving love for love; and she looked forward to a career as a seductress with the utmost pleasure.

Little Lucrezia up to that time believed that the world had been made for her pleasure – her brothers had the same feeling in regard to themselves – but because Lucrezia was by nature serene, ready to be contented, and could only be pleased herself when she pleased others, her character was quite different from those of her brothers. Cesare and Giovanni's young lives were darkened by their jealousy of each other; Lucrezia knew no such jealousy. She was the Queen of the nursery, certain of the love of all.

And so, up to her fourth birthday the little girl remained shut in her world of contentment which wrapped itself about her like a cosy cocoon.

But with the fourth birthday came the first indication that life was less simple than she had believed it to be, and that it did not go on for ever in the same pleasant pattern.

At first she noticed the excitement in the streets. There was much coming and going across the bridge. Each day great Cardinals, their retinues with them, came riding into Rome on their mules. People stood about in little groups; some talked quietly, some gesticulated angrily.

All day she had waited for a visit from Uncle Roderigo, but he did not come.

When Cesare came into the nursery she ran to him and took his hands, but even Cesare had changed; he did not seem as interested in her as before. He went to the loggia and patiently she stood beside him, like a little page, humble, waiting on his pleasure as he liked her to; yet he said nothing, but stood still, watching the crowds in the streets.

'Uncle Roderigo has not come to us,' she said wistfully.

Cesare shook his head. 'He will not come, little sister. Not today.'

'Is he sick?'

Cesare smiled slowly. His hands were clenched, she saw, and his face grew taut as it did so often when he was angry or determined about something.

She stood on the step which enabled her to be as high as his shoulder, and put her face close to his that she might study his expression.

'Cesare,' she said, 'you are angry with Uncle Roderigo?'

Cesare caught her neck in his strong hands; it hurt a little, this trick of his, but she liked it because she knew that it meant: See how strong I am. See how I could hurt you, little Lucrezia, if I wished to; but I do not wish to, because you are my little sister and I love you because you love me . . . better than anyone in the world . . . better than our mother, better than Uncle Roderigo, better, certainly better, than Giovanni.

And when she squealed and showed by her face that he was hurting – only a little – that meant: Yes, Cesare, my brother. You I love better than any in the world. And he understood and his fingers became gentle.

'One is not angry with Uncle Roderigo,' Cesare told her. 'That would be foolish, and I am no fool.'

'No, Cesare, you are no fool. But are you angry with someone?'

He shook his head. 'No. I rejoice, little sister.'

'Tell me why.'

'You are but a baby. What could you know of what goes on in Rome?'

'Does Giovanni know?' Lucrezia, at four, was capable of sly

diplomacy. The lovely light eyes were downcast; she did not want to see Cesare's anger; like Roderigo she turned from what was unpleasant.

The trick was successful. 'I will tell you,' said Cesare. Of course he would tell. He would not allow Giovanni to give her something which *he* had denied her. 'The Pope, who you know is Sixtus IV, is dying. That is why they are excited down there; that is why Uncle Roderigo does not come to see us. He has much to do. When the Pope dies there will be a Conclave and then, little sister, the Cardinals will choose a new Pope.'

'Uncle Roderigo is choosing; that is why he cannot come to see us,' she said.

Cesare stood smiling at her. He felt important, all-wise; no one made him feel so wise or important as his little sister; that was why he loved her so dearly.

'I wish he could choose quickly and come to see us,' added Lucrezia. 'I will ask the saints to make a new Pope quickly . . . so that he can come to us.'

'No, little Lucrezia. Do not ask such a thing. Ask this instead. Ask that the new Pope shall be our Uncle Roderigo.'

Cesare laughed, and she laughed with him. There was so much she did not understand; but in spite of the threatening strangeness, in spite of the gathering crowd below and the absence of Uncle Roderigo, it was good to stand on the loggia, clinging to Cesare's doublet, watching the excitement in the square.

Roderigo was not elected.

The excitement, watched by the children, persisted throughout the city. The scene had changed. Lucrezia heard the sounds of battle in the streets below, and Vannozza, in terror, had barricades put about the house. Even Cesare did not know exactly what it was all about, although he and Giovanni, strutting around the nursery, would not admit this. Uncle Roderigo only visited the house briefly to assure himself that the children were as safe as he could make them. His visits now were merely to see the children; since the birth of little Goffredo he had ceased to regard Vannozza as his mistress, and now there was another baby, Ottaviano, whom Vannozza made no pretence of passing off as his. As for little Goffredo, Roderigo was enchanted by the child, who was turning out to be in every way as beautiful as his elder brothers and sister. Roderigo, having need of sons and being susceptible to beautiful children, was more often than not inclined to give Goffredo the benefit of the doubt, and the attention he bestowed on the others was then shared by the little boy. Poor little Ottaviano was an outsider, ignored by Roderigo, though dearly loved by Vannozza and Giorgio.

But during those weeks there was little time even to regret Roderigo's absence; the children could only look out on the piazza with amazement at the changing scene.

Innocent VIII had become Pope and he had allowed Cardinal della Rovere, who was the nephew of the deceased Sixtus, to persuade him to make war against Naples. The powerful Orsinis who, with the Colonnas, dominated Rome, were friends and allies of the Neopolitans, and this gave them an excuse for rising against the city. They put Rome almost into a state of siege and their old enemies, the Colonnas, lost no time in going into battle against them. Therefore, the streets of Rome, during that period which followed the death of Sixtus and the election of Innocent were the scenes of many a fierce battle.

The children – Cesare, Giovanni and Lucrezia – watching behind the barricades saw strange sights in the city of Rome. They saw the fierce Orsinis coming out in force from Monte Giordano to attack the equally fierce and bloodthirsty Colonnas. They watched men cut each other to pieces in the piazza immediately before their eyes; they saw the way of lewd soldiery with the girls and women; they smelt the hideous smells of war, of burning buildings, of blood and sweat; they heard the cries of victims and the triumphant shouts of raiders.

Death was commonplace; torture equally so.

Little Lucrezia, four years old, looked on at these sights at first with wonder and then almost with indifference. Cesare and Giovanni watched with her and she took her cue from them.

Torture, rape, murder – they were all part of the world outside their nursery. At four years of age children accept without surprise that which is daily paraded before their eyes and Lucrezia was to remember this time of her life not as one of horror, but of change.

The fighting died down; life returned to normal; and two years passed before there was another and this time a more important change for Lucrezia, a change which marked the beginning of the end of childhood. She was nearly six, a precocious six. Cesare was eleven and Giovanni ten; she had been so much their companion that she had learned more than most children know at six years of age. She was as serene as ever, perhaps a little more eager now to provoke that rivalry between her brothers than she had been, understanding more than ever what power it gave her, and that while each sought to be her favourite, she could be the most powerful person in the nursery.

Certainly she was serene, for she was wise; she had come to her power through her brothers' rivalry and all she had to do was award the prize – her affection.

She remained the darling of the nursery. The maids could be sure that there would be no tantrums from Lucrezia; she was kind to little Goffredo whom his brothers scarcely deigned to notice on account of his youth; and she was equally kind to little Ottaviano whom her brothers would not notice at all. They knew something about Ottaviano which made them despise him, but Lucrezia was sorry for him, so she was particularly kind.

Lucrezia enjoyed her life; it was amusing to play one brother off against the other, to worm their secrets from them, to use this rivalry. She liked to walk in the gardens, her arms about Giovanni, being particularly loving when she knew Cesare could see her from the house. It made her feel warm and cosy to be loved so much by two such wonderful brothers.

When Uncle Roderigo came she liked to climb over him looking close into his face, perhaps putting out a delicate finger to touch the nose which seemed gigantic, to caress the heavy jowls, to bury her face in his scented garments and to tell him that the smell of him reminded her of her mother's flower gardens.

Uncle Roderigo loved them all dearly, and came often with presents; he would have them stand round him while he sat on the ornamental chair which their mother kept for him, and he would look at them all in turn – his beloved children whom, he told them, he loved beyond all things on Earth; his eyes rested most fondly of all on Giovanni. Lucrezia was aware of this; and sometimes when she saw the dark look it brought to Cesare's face she would run to Uncle Roderigo and throw herself at him in order to turn his attention from Giovanni to herself.

She was often successful, for when Uncle Roderigo's long fingers caressed her yellow hair, when his lips touched her soft cheek, there would be a special tenderness which he could only give to her. He would hold her more tightly to him and kiss her more often.

'My enchanting little one,' he would murmur. 'My little love.'

Then he ceased to watch Giovanni so devotedly and that pleased Cesare who did not mind Uncle Roderigo's loving Lucrezia. It was only Giovanni who aroused his jealousy.

Then Vannozza might appear at the door holding little Goffredo by the hand, pushing him forward; and Goffredo would break from his mother and run shrieking with joy, shouting: 'Uncle Roderigo, Goffredo is here.' He would be dressed in his blue tunic, which made him look as beautiful as a painted angel in one of the pictures which their mother cherished; and Uncle Roderigo would hesitate – or pretend to hesitate – for one second before he picked up the beautiful little boy. But only when Vannozza had gone would he smother him with kisses and take him on his knee and let him pull gifts from the pockets of his robes, while he called him 'My little Goffredo.'

Ottaviano never came. Poor Ottaviano, the outsider; he was pale and delicate and he coughed a great deal. He was very like Giorgio, who was kind but who must be, so Cesare commanded, ignored by them all, since he had nothing to do with them.

But it was through Ottaviano and Giorgio, those two who were regarded as insignificant by the three children in the nursery, that change came into their lives.

They grew listless, both of them. The weather was sultry and it was said that there was pestilence in the air. Giorgio grew paler and thinner each day until he took to his bed and there was quiet throughout the house.

Vannozza wept bitterly, for she had come to love her meek husband, and when he died she was very sad. It was not long afterwards that little Ottaviano, suffering in the same way as his father had, took to his bed and died. Thus in a few months the household had lost two of its members.

Lucrezia wept to see her mother unhappy. She missed little Ottaviano too; he had been one of her most faithful admirers.

Cesare found her crying and wanted to know why.

'But you know,' she said, her light eyes wide and wondering. 'Our father is dead and our little brother with him. Our mother is sad and so am I.'

Cesare snapped his fingers angrily. 'You should not weep for them,' he said. 'They are nothing to us.'

Lucrezia shook her head and for once she would not agree with him. She had loved them both; she found it easy to love people. Giorgio had been so kind to her, Ottaviano had been her dear little brother, so she would insist on weeping even though Cesare forbade her.

But Cesare must not be crossed. She saw the dark angry look come into his eyes.

'Lucrezia, you shall not cry for them,' he insisted. 'You shall not, I say. Dry your eyes. Look here is a kerchief. Dry them and smile. Smile!'

But it was not possible to smile with all her grief upon her. Lucrezia tried, but she remembered the kindness of Giorgio and how he had carried her on his shoulder and looked so pleased when people had admired her yellow hair; she remembered how little Ottaviano had a habit of creeping close to her and slipping his little hand in hers; she remembered how he used to lisp her name. She could not smile, because she could not forget that she would never see Giorgio and Ottaviano again.

Cesare seemed as though he were finding it difficult to breathe, which meant he was very angry. He took her by the neck, and this time there was more anger than tenderness in the gesture.

'It is time you knew the truth,' he said. 'Have you not guessed who our father is?'

She had not thought of possessing a father until Giorgio came into the house, and then, as Vannozza called him husband, she had thought of him as father, but she knew better than to say that Giorgio was their father; so she was silent, hoping Cesare would relax his hold on her neck and let the tenderness return to his fingers.

Cesare had put his face close to hers; he whispered: 'Roderigo, Cardinal Borgia, is not our uncle, foolish child; he is our father.'

'Uncle Roderigo?' she said slowly.

'Of a certainty, foolish one.' Now his grip was tender. He laid his lips on her cool cheek and gave her one of those long kisses which disturbed her. 'Why should he come here so often, do you think? Why should he love us so? Because he is our father. It is time you knew. Now you will see that it is unworthy to cry for such as Giorgio and Ottaviano. Do you see that now, Lucrezia?'

His eyes were dark again – not with rage perhaps, but with pride because Uncle Roderigo was their father and he was a great Cardinal who, they must pray each day, each night, might one day be Pope and the most powerful man in Rome.

'Yes, Cesare,' she said, for she was afraid of Cesare when he looked like that.

But when she was alone she went into a corner and continued to weep for Giorgio and Ottaviano.

But even Cesare was to discover that the death of those whom he had considered insignificant could make a great difference to his life.

Roderigo, still solicitous for the welfare of his ex-mistress, decided that, since she had lost her husband, she must be provided with another; therefore he arranged a marriage for her with a certain Carlo Canale. This was a good match for Vannozza since Carlo was the chamberlain of Cardinal Francesco Gonzaga, and a man of some culture; he had encouraged the poet, Angelo Poliziano, in the writing of *Orfeo*, and had worked with distinction among the humanists of Mantua. Here was a man who could be useful to Roderigo; and Canale was wise enough to know that through Roderigo he might acquire the riches he had so far failed to accumulate.

Roderigo's notary drew up the marriage contracts and Vannozza prepared to settle down with her new husband.

But as she had gained a husband she was to lose her three eldest children. She accepted this state of affairs philosophically for she knew that Roderigo could not allow their children to remain in her house beyond their childhood; the comparatively humble home of a Roman matron was not the right setting for those who had a brilliant destiny before them.

Thus came the greatest change of all into Lucrezia's life.

Giovanni was to go to Spain, where he would join his eldest brother, Pedro Luis, and where his father would arrange for honours to fall to him; and those honours should be as great as those which he had given to Pedro Luis. Cesare was to stay in Rome. Later he was to train for a Spanish Bishopric, and to do this he must study canon law at the universities of Perugia and Pisa. For the time being he was with Lucrezia but they were soon to leave their mother's house for that of a kinswoman of their father's; therein they would be brought up as fitted their father's children.

It was a staggering blow to Lucrezia. All that had been home to her for six years would be home no longer. The blow was swift and sudden. The only one who rejoiced in that household on the Piazza Pizzo di Merlo was Giovanni, who strutted about the nursery, wielding an imaginary sword, bowing in mock reverence before Cesare whom he called my lord Bishop. Giovanni, intoxicated with excitement, talked continually of Spain.

Lucrezia watched Cesare, his arms folded across his breast, his face white with suppressed anger. Cesare did not rage, did not cry out that he would kill Giovanni; for once Cesare was beaten.

The first important change of their lives had been reached and they all had to accept the fact that however much they might boast in the nursery, they had no alternative but to obey orders.

Only once, when he was alone with Lucrezia, did Cesare cry out as he thumped his fist on his thighs so violently that Lucrezia was sure he was hurting himself: 'Why should he go to Spain? Why should I have to go into the Church? I want to go to Spain. I want to be a Duke and a soldier. Do you think I am not more fitted to conquer and rule than he is? It is because our father loves him better than he loves me that Giovanni has cajoled him into this. I will not endure it. I will not.'

Then he took Lucrezia by the shoulders, and his blazing eyes frightened her.

'I swear to you, little sister, that I shall not rest until I am free . . . free of my father's will . . . free of the will of any who seek to restrain me.'

Lucrezia could only murmur: 'You will be free, Cesare. You will always do what you want.'

Then he laughed suddenly and gave her one of those fierce embraces which she knew so well.

She was anxious about Cesare, and that meant that she did not worry so much about her own future as she might otherwise have done.

MONTE GIORDANO

ADRIANA OF THE house of Mila was a very ambitious woman. Her father, a nephew of Calixtus III, had come to Italy when his uncle became Pope, because it seemed that under such benign and powerful influence there might be a great future for him. Adriana was therefore related to Roderigo Borgia, who held her in great esteem, for she was a woman not only of beauty but of intelligence. It was owing to these qualities that she had married Ludovico of the noble house of Orsini, and the Orsini was one of the most powerful families in Italy. Adriana had a son who had been named Orsino; this boy was sickly and, having a squint, rather unprepossessing, but on account of his position – as the heir to great wealth – Adriana hoped to make a brilliant marriage for him.

The Orsinis had many palaces in Rome but Adriana and her family lived in that on Monte Giordano, near the Bridge of St Angelo. And it was to this palace that Lucrezia and Cesare were taken when they said good-bye to their brothers and their mother.

Here life was very different from what it had been in the house on the Piazza Pizzo di Merlo. With Vannozza there had been light-hearted gaiety, and the children had enjoyed great freedom. They had been allowed to wander in the vineyards, or to enjoy trips on the river; they had often visited the Campo di Fiore where it had given them great delight to mingle with all kinds of people. Cesare and Lucrezia realized that life had indeed been changed.

Adriana was awe-inspiring. She was a beautiful woman but always dressed in ceremonial black, insisting constantly that it must not be forgotten that this was a Spanish household even though it was in the heart of Italy. With its great towers and crenellations dominating the Tiber, the palace was gloomy; its thick walls shut out the sunshine and the gaiety of the Rome which the children had known and loved. Adriana never laughed as Vannozza had laughed, and there was nothing warm and loving about her.

She had many priests living in the palace; there were constant prayers, and consequently Lucrezia believed in those first years in the Orsini palace that her foster-mother was a very virtuous woman.

Cesare chafed against the discipline, but even he was unable to do anything about it, even he was overawed by the gloomy palace, the many prayers and the feeling that the palace was a prison in which he and Lucrezia had been incarcerated while Giovanni had been allowed to go in pomp and splendour to Spain and glory.

Cesare brooded silently. He did not rage as he had in his mother's house; he was sullen and sometimes his quiet anger frightened Lucrezia. Then she would cling to him and beg him not to be sad; she would cover him with kisses and cry out that she loved him best of all . . . better than anyone else in the whole world, that she would love him today, the next day and for ever.

Even this declaration could not appease him, and he remained brooding and unhappy, but sometimes he would turn to her and seize her in one of those fierce embraces which hurt her and excited her. Then he would say: 'You and I are together, little sister. We'll always love each other . . . best in the world . . . best in the whole world. Swear it to me.'

And she swore it. Sometimes they would lie together on her bed or his. She would go there to comfort him, or he would come to her for comfort. Then he would talk of Giovanni and how unfair life was. Why did their father love Giovanni? Cesare would demand. Why should not Cesare have been the one who was chosen to go to Spain? Cesare would never go into the Church. He hated the Church, hated it . . . hated it.

His vehemence frightened her. She crossed herself and reminded him that it was unlucky to talk thus against the Church. The saints, or perhaps the Holy Ghost might be angry and come to punish him. She was afraid, she said; but she said it to give him the chance of comforting her, to remind him that he was great Cesare, afraid of none, and she was little Lucrezia who was the one to be protected.

Sometimes she made him forget his anger against Giovanni. Sometimes they laughed together and remembered the fun they had had on their jaunts to the Campo di Fiore. Then they would swear that no matter what happened they would always love each other best in the world.

But during those first months the children felt that they were prisoners.

Roderigo visited them at Monte Giordano.

In the early days Cesare asked that they might go home, but Roderigo, fond father though he was, could be firm when he felt himself to be acting for the good of his children.

'My little ones,' he said, 'you have been running wild in the house of your mother. But to run wild is for little children, not for big ones. It is not meet that you should pass your time in that humble house. A great future awaits you both. Trust me to judge what is best for you.'

And Cesare knew that when his father's face was set in those lines there was nothing to be done about it. He had to obey.

'Very soon,' Roderigo told Cesare, 'you will be leaving this house. You will be going to the university. There you will have great freedom, my son; but first I would have you know how to act like a nobleman, and although there is discipline here such as you have never encountered before, this is necessary to make you worthy of what you will become. Have patience. It is but for a little while.'

And Cesare was mollified.

The head of the house of Orsini was Virginio, one of the great soldiers of Italy, and when he was at Monte Giordano, the palace resembled a military camp. Virginio shouted orders to all, and the serving men and maids scurried hither and thither, in fear of displeasing the great commander.

Strangely enough Cesare, who so longed to be a soldier, had no objection to this stern rule; and for the first time in her life Lucrezia saw her brother ready to bend to the will of another. Cesare rode behind Virginio, straight as a soldier, and Virginio would often watch him and do his utmost to hide the smile of approval which touched his lips. He would watch Cesare, bare to the waist, learning to wrestle with some of the best teachers in the whole of Italy; the boy gave a good account of himself.

'That boy for the Church!' said Virginio to Adriana and Ludovico her husband. 'He's made for a military career.'

Adriana answered: 'Careers in the Church, my dear Virginio bring a man more profit than those of soldiering.'

''Tis a tragedy to make a prelate of him. What is Roderigo Borgia thinking of?'

'His future . . . and the future of the Borgias. That boy is destined to be Pope, I tell you. At least that is what Roderigo Borgia plans to make him.'

Virginio swore his soldier's oaths and set the boy more arduous tasks, shouted at him, bullied him and Cesare did not object. He dreamed of being a great soldier. Virginio approved of his dreamings, and even went so far as to wish the boy was his son.

Thus that year was made tolerable for Cesare and, such was Lucrezia's nature that, seeing her brother reconciled, she could become reconciled too.

But by the end of the year Cesare had left the Orsini palace for Perugia, and Lucrezia wept bitterly in her loneliness. Then she suddenly began to realize that with Cesare absent she enjoyed a certain freedom, a certain lack of tension; she found that she could begin to consider what was happening to herself irrespective of Cesare.

Lucrezia was growing up and her religious education must not be neglected, since that formed the background of the education of all Italian girls of noble birth. Most of them went into convents, but Roderigo had given much anxious thought to this matter, for the behaviour in convents was not always above reproach and he was determined to protect his Lucrezia. The Colonnas sent their daughters, it was true, to San Silvestro in Capite, and the convents of Santa Maria Nuova and San Sisto he believed were equally worthy; so he decided that it should be San Sisto's on the Appian Way to which Lucrezia should go for religious instruction. She was to stay there only for brief periods though, and she returned often to Monte Giordano where she was instructed in languages –

Spanish, Greek and Latin – as well as painting, music and fine needlework.

It was not necessary, Roderigo had pointed out to Ádriana, that his little daughter should become a virago (a term which in those days simply meant a learned woman). He wished his Lucrezia to be highly educated that she might be a worthy companion for himself. It was vital that she should be instructed in deportment, that she should acquire the airs and graces of a noblewoman and be able to take her place among Kings and Princes; he wished her to be modest in her demeanour. Her serenity of character gave her a charming graciousness which was apparent even at the age of seven, when she began this course of grooming; that, Roderigo wished to be preserved, for, as he saw his little daughter growing in beauty every day, he was becoming more and more ambitious on her account.

The nuns of San Sisto quickly learned to love their little pupil, not only for her pleasant looks and charming manners, but because of that eager desire within her to please everybody and be their friend; and perhaps also they remembered it was rumoured that she was indeed the daughter of the great Roderigo Borgia, the richest of Cardinals and one who, it was said in high places, had every chance of one day becoming Pope.

When Lucrezia had been three years at Monte Giordano, Ludovico, Adriana's husband, died and the palace was plunged into mourning. Adriana covered herself with black veils and spent much time with her priests, and Lucrezia told herself then that Adriana was a very good woman.

One day when Lucrezia had returned from San Sisto's to Monte Giordano and sat at table with Adriana and Orsino she thought how sad it was that she and Orsino should eat and drink from silver utensils while Adriana, because she was a widow, mourning her husband in the Spanish manner, must do so from earthenware.

Lucrezia leaned on the table, the top of which was made of marble and coloured pieces of wood, and said: 'Dear Madonna Adriana, you are still very unhappy because you are a widow. I know, because my mother was unhappy when Giorgio di Croce died. She wept and talked of her unhappiness, and then she felt better.'

Adriana straightened the long black veil which flowed over her shoulder. 'I would not talk of my grief,' she said. 'In Spain we say it is ill-mannered to show one's grief to the world.'

'But we are not the world – Orsino and I,' persisted Lucrezia. 'And my mother . . .'

'Your mother was an Italian woman. It will be well if you forget your Italian birth. In Spain to share a pleasure is a good thing because in sharing what is good one gives something worth having. To share one's sorrow is to beg that one's burden shall be partly carried by another. Spaniards are too proud to ask favours.'

The matter was closed. Lucrezia blushed over her plate. She had much to learn, she realized. She was sorry she had spoken, and now she looked pleadingly at Orsino for comfort; but he was not looking at her. Orsino was one of the few people who did not admire her yellow hair and pretty face. She might have been one of the ornamental chairs, of which there were so many in the principal rooms of the palace, for all the notice he took of her.

Adriana was looking severe, and Lucrezia feared that she would always disappoint her because she was such a good woman and thought always of doing what was right.

Later that day, as she and Adriana sat together working on an altar cloth, Adriana said: 'You will soon have a companion to share your dancing and music lessons.'

Lucrezia dropped the gold thread and waited breathlessly.

'I am to have a daughter,' said Adriana.

'Oh, but . . . a daughter! I thought . . .' Lucrezia at nine years of age was knowledgeable. She had seen certain sights from the house on the piazza; she had listened to the talk of her brothers and the servants. It seemed incredible that the pious widow could have a daughter.

Adriana was looking at her in surprise, and Lucrezia flushed again.

'My son is of a marriageable age,' said Adriana coldly. 'His bride will soon be coming here. She will live with us as my daughter until the marriage takes place.'

Lucrezia picked up her needle and began to work, hoping to hide her embarrassment. 'That will be pleasant, Madonna Adriana,' she said, but she felt sorry for the girl who would be married to Orsino.

'Orsino,' said Adriana as though reading her thoughts, 'is one of the best matches in Rome.'

'Is Orsino happy?' asked Lucrezia. 'Is he dancing with joy because he is to have a bride?'

'Orsino has been brought up as a Spanish nobleman. They, my dear Lucrezia, do not jump for joy like any Italian shepherd on the Campo di Fiore.'

'Assuredly they do not, Madonna Adriana.'

'He will be happy. He knows his duty. He must marry and have sons.'

'And the bride . . . .'

'You will soon see her. I shall teach her as I do you.'

Lucrezia continued to stitch, thinking of the companion she was to have. She hoped the bride would not mind too much . . . having to marry Orsino.

Lucrezia waited in the great dark room in which, because this was a special occasion, the tapestries had been hung.

They were gathered to greet the girl who was being brought to her new home, and Lucrezia wondered how she was feeling. She would quickly try to reassure her for she would be a little frightened perhaps. Lucrezia herself knew how alarming it could be to be taken from one's home to an entirely different place.

Orsino stood beside his mother. Adriana had talked severely to him of his duty and poor Orsino looked more sallow than ever in his Spanish black, and not at all like a bridegroom-to-be; his squint was more distressing than ever; it always seemed more pronounced at times of stress, and his mother's cold gaze was continually admonishing him.

Lucrezia was also in black, but there was gold and silver embroidery on her gown. She wished that they did not always have to follow the Spanish customs. The Spanish were fond of black for all ceremonial occasions and Lucrezia loved bright

scarlet and gold and particularly that shade of deep blue which
made her hair look more golden than ever. But black made a
happy contrast to her light eyes and fair hair, so she felt she
was fortunate in that.

And as she waited, Giulia Farnese entered the room. Her
brother, Alessandro, a young man of about twenty, had
brought her. He was proud, distinguished-looking and splendidly clad; but it was Giulia who held Lucrezia's attention
and that of all those assembled, for she was beautiful, and her
hair was as golden as Lucrezia's. She was dressed in the Italian
fashion in her gown of blue and gold, and she looked like a
Princess in a legend and far too beautiful for this world among
the sombrely clad Orsinis.

Lucrezia felt a twinge of jealousy. All would be saying:
This Giulia Farnese is more beautiful than Lucrezia.

The girl knelt before Adriana and called her 'Mother'. When
Orsino was pushed forward, he came shambling, and was
fumbling and ungracious in his greeting. Lucrezia watched
the lovely young face for a sign of the revulsion she must
surely be feeling, and she forgot her jealousy in her pity for
Giulia. But Giulia showed no emotion. She was demure and
gracious – all that was expected of her.

They quickly became friends. Giulia was vivacious, full of
information, and very ready to give her attention to Lucrezia
when there were no men about.

Giulia told Lucrezia that she was nearly fifteen. Lucrezia was
not quite ten; and those extra years gave Giulia a great advantage. She was more frivolous than Lucrezia and not so
ready to learn, nor so eager to please. When they were alone
she told Lucrezia that she thought Madonna Adriana too
strict and solemn.

'Madonna Adriana is a very good woman,' insisted Lucrezia.

'I don't like good women,' retorted Giulia.

'Is that because they make us all feel so wicked?' suggested
Lucrezia.

'I'd rather be wicked than good,' laughed Giulia.

Lucrezia looked over her shoulder at the figure of the Madonna and child with the lamp burning before it.

'Oh,' laughed Giulia, 'there's plenty of time to repent. Repentance is for old people.'

'There are some young nuns at San Sisto's,' Lucrezia told her.

That made Giulia laugh. 'I'd not be a nun. Nor would you. Why, look at you! See how pretty you are . . . and you'll be prettier yet. Wait until you're as old as I am. Mayhap then, Lucrezia, you'll be as beautiful as I am, and you'll have lovers, many of them.'

This was conversation such as Lucrezia enjoyed. It brought back echoes of a past she could scarcely remember. It was four years since she had left the gaiety of her mother's house for the strict etiquette and Spanish gloom of Monte Giordano.

Giulia showed Lucrezia how to walk seductively, how to brighten her lips, how to dance. Giulia possessed secret knowledge which she allowed Lucrezia to coax from her.

Lucrezia was a little worried about Giulia; she was afraid that, if Adriana discovered what she was really like, she would send her away and this exciting companion would be lost to her.

They must not let Adriana see the carmine on their lips. They must not appear before her with their hair in the loose coiffure into which Giulia had arranged it. Giulia must never wear any of the dazzling but daring gowns which she had brought with her. Giulia giggled and tried to be prim before her prospective mother-in-law.

Orsino never troubled them, and Lucrezia noticed that he seemed more afraid of his bride than she was of him.

Giulia had a sunny nature; she told Lucrezia that she would know how to deal with Orsino when the time came. It was clear that all the low-cut dresses, the attention to her appearance which seemed to absorb Giulia, were not for Orsino's benefit.

Lucrezia felt that Giulia must be very wicked.

I believe, though, she said to herself, I also like wicked people better than good ones. I should be desolate if Giulia went away, but I should not care very much if Madonna Adriana did.

There was excitement in the Orsini palace. It was one of

those special days when Lucrezia must be more sedate than usual, when she must behave as a Spanish lady, and walk with the utmost grace, for Cardinal Roderigo Borgia was coming to Monte Giordano to visit his daughter, and Adriana was eager that he should not be disappointed in her.

Lucrezia wore her hair parted in the centre and falling demurely over her shoulders. Giulia watched her Spanish maid prepare her, with great interest.

'Is he very solemn, the great Cardinal?' she asked.

'He is the most important man in Rome,' boasted Lucrezia.

'Then,' said Giulia, 'you will have to pull down your lips in a sour expression because, when you do not, you look too happy, and you will have to be quiet and speak only when spoken to.'

'My father likes to see me happy,' said Lucrezia. 'He likes me to smile, and he likes me to talk too. He is not in the least like Adriana. But she will be watching and I shall have to remember all she has taught me, since, as he sent me here to be taught by her, that is surely what he wished me to learn.'

Giulia grimaced; and Lucrezia left her and went down to the intimate and pleasant little room where Roderigo was waiting for her.

The tapestries were hanging on the walls and the finest silver goblets had been brought out for this occasion.

Adriana stood by Roderigo while Lucrezia bowed in the Spanish fashion. Roderigo laid his hands on her shoulders and kissed her cheeks and then her forehead.

'But how she grows, my little one,' he said tenderly. 'Madonna Adriana has been telling me of your progress.'

Lucrezia looked askance at Adriana whose expression was grim.

'It has not been as good as you hoped?' said Lucrezia timidly.

'My dear, who of us reaches perfection? You please me. That will suffice.' Roderigo looked at Adriana, who bowed her head. He was asking that they be left alone.

When Adriana had gone she took all restraint with her, and Lucrezia threw herself into her father's arms telling him how wonderful it was to see him.

He kissed her with tenderness and passion, and brought a bracelet from his pocket, which he put on her wrist. She kissed it and he kissed it. He was always passionately sentimental when they were alone. He wanted to tell her of his love and to be assured of hers.

When these assurances were made they talked of Vannozza and of Cesare and Giovanni.

'Cesare does well at the university,' said Roderigo. 'I am proud of his scholarship and his prowess at sport. It will not be long, I swear before he becomes a Cardinal. And Giovanni does very happily in Spain. My Lucrezia is growing into a beautiful lady. For what more should I wish?'

'And Goffredo?'

'He grows in strength and beauty every day. Ah, we shall have to make plans for him ere long.'

Over her father's shoulder Lucrezia saw the door open slowly. Giulia, her face flushed, was peering round it.

Lucrezia shrank in horror. This was an unforgivable breach of etiquette. Giulia could not realize how very important the Cardinal was. To dare to come peeping thus . . . it was unthinkable. Giulia would be dismissed, and the marriage arrangements would be broken off, if Adriana discovered she had done such a thing.

Roderigo had sensed his daughter's dismay; he turned sharply and Giulia was caught.

'And who is this?' asked Roderigo.

'Giulia, you must come in now,' said Lucrezia, 'and I will present you to the Cardinal.'

Giulia came, and to Lucrezia's consternation she was not wearing her most modest gown, and her lips were faintly carmined. Lucrezia prayed the Cardinal would not notice.

Giulia, reckless as she was, flushed and with her golden hair falling in tumbled curls about her shoulders, looked a little apprehensive as she came slowly towards them.

'My father,' said Lucrezia quickly, 'this is Giulia who is to marry Orsino. She meant no harm, I do assure you.'

The Cardinal said: 'I believe she did mean harm. She looks full of mischief.'

'Oh no . . .' began Lucrezia; and then she stopped, realizing that her father was not at all angry.

'Come, my child,' he said, 'you do not need my daughter to speak for you. I pray you, speak for yourself.'

Giulia ran to him and knelt. She lifted those wonderful blue eyes of hers to his face, and she was smiling that confident smile which said clearly that she did not believe anyone could really be annoyed with her, if only because of her enchanting presence.

'So you are to marry Orsino,' said the Cardinal. 'My poor child! Do you love the young man?'

'I love Rome, Your Eminence,' said Giulia, 'and the people I meet in Rome.'

The Cardinal laughed. To Lucrezia's great relief she knew now that, far from being angry, he was pleased.

'On these occasions when I visit Lucrezia,' he explained to Giulia as though she were one of his family, 'there is no ceremony. I will have it thus. Come, you shall sit on one side of me, Lucrezia on the other, and we will talk to each other of Rome ... and the people we meet in Rome....'

'You are gracious to me, Your Eminence,' said Giulia with a demureness which did not ring true. 'I fear I have behaved very badly.'

'My child, you are charming enough to dispense with that etiquette which others less fortunate must sustain.'

Lucrezia noticed, as they sat together laughing and talking, that her father turned more often to Giulia than to herself.

She was too astonished to feel jealousy.

And it was thus that Adriana found them.

Strangely enough Adriana did not appear to be angry, and much to Lucrezia's relief and astonishment nothing was said about Giulia's alarmingly bold action.

Giulia herself seemed to change subtly; she was more subdued and, when Lucrezia tried to talk to her about Roderigo, Giulia seemed less communicative than usual. Yes, she replied to Lucrezia's insistence, she did think the Cardinal was a very fine man. The finest man she had ever seen? demanded Lucrezia, who always enjoyed hearing compliments about her family. It might well be so, admitted Giulia.

She would say no more than that and, during the whole of that day, she seemed to withdraw herself from Lucrezia so that the little girl could not help feeling uneasy.

And when on the following day, hearing the sound of horses' hoofs, she looked out from her window, and saw the Cardinal riding away from the palace, her first impulse was to call him, but that of course would be undignified. He had come alone, which was unusual, and he had not seen *her* which was more unusual still. For what reason would he come to Monte Giordano if it were not to see his little daughter?

It was bewildering. Then Lucrezia thought she understood. Certainly he could not allow Giulia's boldness of the previous day to go unpunished. Because he was gentle by nature and hated to be present when it was necessary to punish, he had not scolded Giulia but had pretended to be pleased by her company. That was entirely due to his courteous manners; but now he had come back to talk seriously to Adriana; he had come to complain and ask how such a minx as Giulia could possibly be a fit companion for his daughter.

Lucrezia's bewilderment turned to misery. She felt sure that very soon she would be deprived of Giulia's bright company.

Giulia was gay. She was wearing a new necklace set with emeralds and rubies.

'But it is exquisite workmanship,' cried Lucrezia. 'You possessed such a treasure and did not show it to me before!'

'It is certainly exquisite,' agreed Giulia; 'and I should never have kept it from you for a day, sweet Lucrezia, if I had had it to show you. I have just received it.'

'A gift! From whom?'

'That would be to tell, and to tell is somewhat unwise.'

Giulia had seemed to grow up in a few hours. Full of coquetry, she seemed more like a girl of eighteen than one of fourteen. Her laughter was high and infectious; she sang gay Italian songs about love; and she was tantalizingly secretive. There was also the mystery of the necklace.

But Giulia was too young, too excited to keep up the secrecy for long. She wanted to share confidences; she wanted to flaunt her experience before Lucrezia. Lucrezia demanded:

'What has happened? Why are you so pleased? You do not care that the Cardinal complained to Madonna Adriana of your forwardness – which may well mean that you will be sent away.' Then Giulia laughed and retorted; 'I shall not be sent away. And the Cardinal did not complain. I'll tell you something, Lucrezia. I have a lover.'

'Orsino . . .'

'Orsino! Do you think I should ever take Orsino for a lover? Would you?'

'I . . . but I would never . . .'

'Mayhap you *are* over-young yet. For myself I shall be fifteen soon . . . and married to Orsino. Therefore what is there for me to do but take a lover?'

'Oh, have a care,' begged Lucrezia. 'What if Madonna Adriana should hear you talk thus? You would be sent away.'

'I shall not be sent away. Oh no . . . no . . . no!'

Giulia laughed so much that the tears came to her eyes. Lucrezia gazed at her puzzled.

The Cardinal's visits to Monte Giordano became very frequent and he did not always come to see Lucrezia.

Giulia would dress very carefully before his visits – not in her most modest gowns – and sometimes Lucrezia would hear Giulia's high-pitched laughter when she was alone with the Cardinal. It was disconcerting.

But he always came to see *me*! Lucrezia told herself.

And then she began to understand.

Giulia had many rich presents. She was the loveliest girl in Rome, Lucrezia had heard the servants say. They had named her *La Bella*, and referred to her more often by that name than her own. The rich presents came from a rich lover, a lover whom Giulia was entertaining in the formal household of the Orsinis. It was some time before Lucrezia would allow herself to believe who that lover was.

Then she could keep her suspicions to herself no longer.

One night she slipped from her bed, took her candle, and went to Giulia's bedchamber. Giulia was asleep, and the light from Lucrezia's candle showed her the beauty of that perfect face. Giulia was indeed *La Bella*.

The candlelight playing on Giulia's face awoke her and she started up, staring in alarm at Lucrezia.

'What is wrong?' she demanded.

'I have to know,' said Lucrezia. 'The Cardinal is your lover, is he not?'

'Did you wake me up to tell me what everybody knows?' demanded Giulia.

'So it is true!'

Giulia laughed. 'Think of it,' she said, sitting up and hugging her knees. 'He is fifty-eight and I am not yet fifteen. Yet we love. Is that not miraculous? Who would have thought a man so old could make me love him?'

'With him,' said Lucrezia solemnly, 'all things are possible.'

That made Giulia emit one of her secretive laughs. 'It is true,' she said. 'And I am happy.'

Lucrezia was silent, looking at Giulia, seeing her afresh, trying to remember what she had been like before this astonishing thing had happened to her.

Then she said slowly: 'If Madonna Adriana heard of this, she would be very angry.'

Giulia laughed again, recklessly it seemed to Lucrezia.

'What you are doing should be kept secret,' persisted Lucrezia. 'I know we do not like Madonna Adriana, but she is a good woman and she would never allow you to live in her house if she knew.'

Giulia stopped laughing and looked intently at Lucrezia.

'You will be cold, standing there,' she said. 'Come into my bed. You are no longer a child, Lucrezia. Why, you will soon be ten. You will soon have lovers of your own. There! That is better, is it not? Now, let me tell you this. The Cardinal is my lover. He says I am the most beautiful woman in the world. *Woman*, you understand, Lucrezia. And soon I shall marry Orsino. But who cares for Orsino! Not I. Nor the Cardinal.'

'Madonna Adriana cares for him.'

'Yes. Indeed yes. That is why she is contented that I should please the Cardinal. My family is contented also, Lucrezia.'

'Contented! But how can that be when you are to marry Orsino?'

'Yes, yes. And it is a good match. The Farnese and the Orsini

will be united, and that is good. One cannot marry a Cardinal
... alas ... alas!'

'If Cardinals could marry, my father would have married
my mother.'

Giulia nodded. Then she went on: 'You must not be *sorry*
for Orsino. I told you his mother is contented that I am the
Cardinal's mistress. I told you that, did I not?'

'But she is a good woman. We have thought her harsh, but
we must admit that she is good.'

'Lucrezia, you live in a world of childhood and it is time you
left it. Adriana is *glad* that the Cardinal loves me. She helps
me dress when he is coming, helps to make me beautiful. And
what does she say when she helps me dress? She says: "Do
not forget that you will be Orsino's wife ere long. Get the
Cardinal to agree to advance Orsino. He has great influence
at the Vatican. Make sure that you squeeze the greatest good
from this ... for yourself and Orsino." '

'So she is pleased that you and my father are lovers?'

'Nothing could delight her more. She makes everything
easy for us.'

'And you so soon to marry her son!'

Giulia laughed. 'You see, you do not know the world. If I
were to have a love affair with a groom ... ah, then I should be
beaten. I should be in disgrace, and he, poor fellow, would
doubtless have a sword run through him one dark night, or be
found in the Tiber with a stone about his neck. But my lover is
a great Cardinal and when men of influence love as he loves me
then all gather round to catch some of the prizes. That is life.'

'Then Adriana with all her prayers and sternness, all her
righteousness, is not a good woman after all!'

'Good and bad, little Lucrezia, what are they? It is only little
children who have sentimental notions such as yours. The
Cardinal is happy to love me; I am happy to be his mistress.
And Orsino's family and my family are happy because of the
great good I can bring to them. Orsino? He does not count,
but one might say even he is happy because it means that he
will not have to make love to me, which – unnatural monster
that he is – I do not believe he is at all eager to do!'

Lucrezia was silent for a while, thinking more of Adriana

than anyone else: Adriana solemnly on her knees before the Madonna and the lamp; Adriana, lips pursed, murmuring, 'One must do this because, however unpleasant, it is one's duty'; Adriana, who made one feel that the saints were continually on the watch, recording the slightest fault to be held against one at the day of Judgment, the good woman, who was willing to allow the illicit love affair, between a man of fifty-eight and her prospective daughter-in-law of fourteen, to be conducted in her house, and moreover connived at it and encouraged it because it could bring honours to her son.

Honours! It was necessary, Lucrezia realized, to make a reassessment of words and their meanings.

She was indeed a child; there was much that she had to learn; and she was very eager to grow out of childhood, a state in which it seemed innocence was synonymous with folly.

Giulia had married Orsino, and the ceremony had taken place in the Borgia palace, the first of the witnesses to sign the marriage documents being Roderigo Borgia.

The married couple returned to Monte Giordano and life went on as before. The Cardinal paid frequent visits to the Orsini palace and no one now made any secret of the fact that he came chiefly to visit his mistress.

He was delighted to see his daughter also, and seemed content to spend a great deal of time in the company of the two young girls.

Giulia was exerting her influence on Lucrezia who was growing more and more like her. Giulia talked of the love between herself and the Cardinal and of many more trivial matters. She told Lucrezia that she knew how their hair could retain its bright yellow colour; she had a recipe which would make it shine like pure gold with the sun on it. They washed their hair, tried the concoction, and congratulated themselves that their hair was more golden than ever.

Lucrezia began to long for the time when she would have a lover, for, always ready to be influenced by those who were near her, she was modelling herself on Giulia.

When she heard that her eldest brother, Pedro Luis, had died and that Giovanni was to become Duke of Gandia and marry the bride who had been selected for Pedro Luis, it seemed hardly important, apart from the fact that she wondered how Cesare would receive this news. He would surely want the dukedom of Gandia; he would surely want Pedro Luis' bride.

She was eleven when the Cardinal called at the palace and, after embracing her, told her that he was arranging a match for her.

It was to be a Spanish match because he believed Spain, which was fast rising to a power of first magnitude determined on the domination of the world, had more to offer his daughter than Italy.

Her bridegroom was to be Don Cherubino Juan de Centelles who was the lord of Val d'Ayora in Valencia, and it was a grand match.

Lucrezia was a little alarmed, but her father hastily assured her that, although the nuptial contract was drawn up and would soon be signed, he had arranged that she should not leave Rome for a whole year.

That was comforting. A year seemed a very long time to the young Lucrezia.

Now she could discuss her coming marriage with Giulia and it delighted her to do so, particularly as that event seemed so very far away in the distant future.

She was beginning to know the world, to accept with the utmost calm the relationship between her father and Giulia; to accept the mingling piety and callous amorality of Adriana.

That was life as it was lived in that stratum of society into which Lucrezia had been born.

She had learned this much; and it meant that she had left her childhood behind her.

DURING THE FOLLOWING year Lucrezia really did grow up, and afterwards it seemed to her that before Giulia had come into her life bringing enlightenment she had indeed been an innocent child.

Giulia was her dearest friend. Together they made many journeys to the Cardinal's palace where Roderigo petted them both, delighting that it was Lucrezia who brought him Giulia and Giulia who brought him Lucrezia.

And why should Lucrezia question the rightness of such conduct? She, Giulia and Adriana were all guests at the wedding of Franceschetto Cibo, a grand occasion when the whole of Rome had rejoiced and there were bonfires on all of the seven hills; Franceschetto was openly acknowledged as the son of Innocent VIII, and the Holy Father made no secret of this, for he was present at the banquet and caused the fountains to run with wine; moreover Franceschetto's bride was the daughter of the great Lorenzo de' Medici; so that it was not only Romans who honoured the Pope's bastard.

So naturally it did not occur to Lucrezia to do anything but accept the conditions in which she lived.

Goffredo had now come to live at Monte Giordano, and she was happy to have her young brother with her. He wept a little to leave his mother, but Vannozza, while missing him sadly, was very glad to let him go for she saw in the arrangement an admission by Roderigo that he accepted Goffredo as his son.

It was during that year that Roderigo decided that Don Cherubino Juan de Centelles was not a satisfactory match for his daughter. It may have been the brilliant marriage of Franceschetto Cibo which decided him. It was true Franceschetto was the son of a Pope, but Innocent was ageing fast and who knew what the next months might bring forth? No! He would find a better match for his daughter.

He blithely dissolved the previous contract and made another more suited to his ambitious plans, choosing Don Gasparo di Procida, the count of Aversa, for Lucrezia's betrothed. This was because Don Gasparo was a connexion of the House of Aragon which now ruled in Naples.

Lucrezia accepted the change placidly. As she had seen neither of her prospective bridegrooms she had no feelings in the matter. She had Roderigo's happy nature which made her believe that everything would come out well for her.

And then, in that August of the year 1492 when Lucrezia was twelve years old, there occurred that event which was to prove so important to the rest of her life.

Innocent was dying and there was tumult throughout Rome. The question on every lip was: Who shall succeed Innocent?

There was one man who was determined to do so. Roderigo was sixty. If he were going to achieve his life-long ambition he must do so soon. When he heard the news that Innocent was on his death-bed he determined, as he never had before, that he would be the next Pope.

Roderigo, gentle, courteous, seeming malleable, was a man of iron beneath the gentle exterior. Nothing was going to stand in his way. Unfortunately there must be a Conclave, and the Pope must be elected. Those days were days of real stress for Roderigo. He did not visit his mistress or his daughter during that period of decision, but the thoughts of everyone in the Orsini palace were with him at that time. They all prayed that the next Pope would be Roderigo.

Lucrezia was in a state of turmoil. Her father seemed to her godlike; tall, powerful; she could not understand why there should be any anxiety. Why did not everyone understand that there was only one thing they could do, and that was elect Cardinal Roderigo Borgia as their Pope?

She talked to Giulia, who was as tense and anxious as herself, for although it was exciting to be the mistress of the richest Cardinal in Rome, how much more so to be the mistress of the Pope. So Giulia shared Lucrezia's excitement, her enthusiasm and her fears. Little Goffredo sought to understand, and added his prayers to theirs; and Adriana saw a glittering future wherein she might cast aside her mourning and accompany her daughter-in-law to the Vatican; there she might live in state ... if only Roderigo were elected Pope.

The heat was fierce in Rome during that fateful August. Each in his separate cell, the great Cardinals went into Conclave. Crowds were gathered in the streets, clustering about the Vatican, and there was continued and heated speculation as to the results.

In the beginning no one thought very highly of Roderigo's chances.

There were great rivalries, for Italy was at this time a country divided into small states and dukedoms, with the result that there were continual differences between them. Innocent had been weak but he had enjoyed the advice of his great ally, Lorenzo de' Medici, and it was largely due to this that the peninsula had been enjoying a period of peace. But Lorenzo had died and trouble was looming.

Ludovico Sforza, Regent of Milan, and Ferrante of Aragon, King of Naples, were the great rivals who threatened to plunge Italy into a state of war. The reason for this was that Ludovico's nephew, Gian Galeazzo, was the true heir of Milan; but Ludovico held this young man a prisoner and made himself Regent. His excuse was that the young Duke was not fit to rule; he, Ludovico, had brought about this unhappy state of affairs by arranging that the boy should be demoralized both mentally and physically with debaucheries which were arranged at Ludovico's instigation. Gian however had married an energetic princess of Naples, Isabella of Aragon, who was granddaughter of Ferrante. This was the cause of the trouble between Naples and Milan which threatened at this time to flare up into a war which could have involved all Italy.

Both Naples and Milan were afraid that the French would seek to invade their territory, for the French declared that they had a claim both to Naples and Milan – to Naples through the House of Anjou, and to Milan through the house of Orléans.

This meant that it would be very important for Ludovico and Ferrante to have a Pope at the Vatican who would favour them.

Rivalry was intense. Ascanio Sforza, brother of Ludovico,

was the hope of Milan. Ferrante supported Giuliano della Rovere.

Roderigo, like a sly fox, waited.

He knew he had little to fear from Ascanio, as he was only thirty-eight and if he became Pope it would be the death-knell to the hopes of almost every living Cardinal. With such a young man elected, unless he died very young, there would be little hope of another Conclave for years. Moreover it was hardly likely that Ludovico's party would have much support. The Regency of Milan was known throughout the length and breadth of Italy as a usurper.

This was not the case with della Rovere, but although he was eligible, he had a bitter tongue which offended people. He might have supporters, but he also had many enemies.

The favourite was perhaps the Portuguese Cardinal Costa, who was eighty years of age. At such a time it was often felt to be advisable to elect a very old man, to give a short breathing space before there was another Conclave. If Cardinal Costa were elected, it would not be such a tragedy as the election of della Rovere or – the saints forbid it – Ascanio Sforza.

But Roderigo was determined that none should be elected but himself.

There was also among the several candidates Cardinal Oliviero Carafa whom Ascanio – feeling that on account of his youth he himself had a poor chance – was supporting because Carafa was an enemy of Ferrante.

Another candidate – Roderigo Borgia – did not seem to be in the running; but Roderigo was standing quietly, slyly waiting.

Roderigo was the richest of the Cardinals, and he knew what an important factor wealth was at such times. A little bribe here, a fat one there, a promise of gold and silver, a hint of what a man of his wealth could pay for votes – and who knew, the Papal throne might well be his while the others were wrangling amongst themselves.

The Cardinals were walled-up and the Conclave began. It was a period of intense strain for Roderigo yet he managed to conceal his feelings. As he attended morning Mass and Communion he was considering how he could win the votes he needed. At this time it seemed a hopeless task which lay before him, yet as he made his way to the Sistine Chapel lighted in readiness with candles on the altar and on the desk before each of the thrones, he seemed perfectly calm. He looked about him at his fellow Cardinals in their rustling violet robes and white *rochets*, and he knew that within none of them did the fire of ambition burn as fiercely as it did in him. He must succeed.

It seemed to him that the procedure was slower than it had ever been, but eventually the Cardinal-Scrutators were elected and he was sitting at his desk. There was no sound in the chapel but the scratching of many pens as each Cardinal wrote: 'I, Cardinal .... elect to the Supreme Pontificate the Most Reverend Lord my Lord Cardinal . . .'

Oh why, fumed Roderigo, could one not vote for oneself!

He rose with the rest and joined in the ceremonial walk to the altar. He knelt and murmured: 'I attest before Christ who is to be my judge, that I chose him whom I think fittest to be chosen if it is according to God's will.'

They placed their ballot papers on the shallow dish which covered the chalice, and tipped the paten until the paper slid into the chalice; then slowly and solemnly, each purple-clad figure returned to his throne.

At the first counting of votes Roderigo had seven, but Carafa had nine, Costa and Michiel, the Cardinal of Venice, also had seven, and della Rovere five. As for Ascanio Sforza he had none, and it was clear from the beginning that none of the Cardinals was ready to see a man so young on the Papal throne.

This was deadlock, for there must be a majority of two-thirds for one candidate before he was elected.

A fire was made and the papers burned; and all those waiting in St Peter's Square to hear the result of the election, seeing the smoke, excitedly called each other's attention to it and knew that the first scrutiny had been ineffectual.

Roderigo now decided that he must act quickly. In his own cell he laid his plans and when he mingled with his fellow Cardinals, he lost no time in getting to work.

He began with Ascanio Sforza, begging him to walk with him in the galleries after the siesta. Ascanio, realizing he had no chance of being elected, hinted that he was ready to gain what he could. Roderigo could offer him bigger bribes than any.

'If I were elected Pope,' Roderigo promised, 'I would not forget you. Yours should be the Vice-Chancellorship and I would also give you the Bishopric of Nepi.' It was a good consolation prize, and Ascanio wavered only a little before he agreed. And as with Ascanio, so with others who quickly realized that they were out of the running yet could come out of the Conclave richer men than when they went into it.

So while Rome sweated and waited for the results, that sly fox Roderigo worked quietly, stealthily and with the utmost speed within the Conclave. He had to. He had made up his mind that this time he must succeed, for how could he tell when there would be another chance.

It was August 11th, five days after the Conclave had begun. In the Piazza San Pietro people who had been waiting all through the night watched, their eyes on the walled-up window.

As the dawn lightened their eager faces there was a sudden shout and excitement was at fever-pitch for the bricks had begun to fall from the walled-in window.

The election was over. After the fourth scrutiny there had been an unanimous choice.

Roderigo Borgia had been elected Pope, and from now on he would be known as Alexander VI.

Roderigo stood on the balcony listening to the acclaim of the people. This was the greatest moment of his life. The crown, for which he had fought ever since his uncle, Calixtus III, had adopted him and his brother, was now his. He felt powerful as he stood there, capable of anything. Who would have believed five days ago that he would be the chosen one? Even his old enemy, della Rovere, had given him his vote. It was wonderful what a little persuasion could do, and who could resist persuasion such as a rich abbacy, the legation of Avignon and the fortress of Ronciglione? Not della Rovere. A great deal to pay for a vote? Not at all. He had bought power with the wealth he had accumulated over the years, and he was going to make sure that it became unlimited power.

He held out his hands and for a few seconds there was complete silence among the multitude.

Then he cried: 'I am the Pope and Vicar of Christ on Earth.'

There was loud acclamation. It was of no importance how he had reached this eminence. All that mattered was that it was his.

The Coronation of Alexander VI was the most magnificent Rome had ever seen. Lucrezia, watching from a balcony of a Cardinal's palace, was overwhelmed with pride and joy in this man who – apart from Cesare, whom she had not seen for so long – she loved best in the world.

This was her father, this handsome man, in his rich robes, sitting so straight on his white horse, blessing the multitudes who crowded about him, the centre of all the pageantry, this man was her father.

Alexander was fully aware that there was nothing the people enjoyed more than pageantry, and the more brilliant, the better they liked it; and the more splendid it was, the greater would be the respect they had for him. Therefore he was determined to outdo all previous coronations. No expense must be spared, he had commanded; nor was it. The people of Rome were going to rejoice that day because Alexander VI was their Pope.

His Papal guards were so splendidly attired that even great Princes looked drab beside them; their long lances and shields glittered in the sunshine, and they looked like gods. Cardinals and high dignitaries who took part in the procession with their retinues, were all determined to outdo each other in their splendour, and so long was the procession that it took two hours for it to pass from St Peter's to St John Lateran. And in the centre of it all was the Pope on his snow-white horse, the sixty-year-old Pope who seemed to have the vigour of a man of twenty. It was small wonder that the people – even as Lucrezia did – believed the new Pope to be more than human.

The procession was stopped here and there that Alexander's admirers and supporters – who now comprised the whole of Rome, it seemed – might pay their homage.

'*Vive diu bos, vive diu celebrande per annos,*
Inter Pontificum gloria prima choros,' chanted one handsome

boy on behalf of his noble family who wished to show they were wholeheartedly in support of the new Pope.

Others strewed flowers before him and cried: 'Rome raised Caesar to greatness – and now here is Alexander; but one was merely a man, the other is a god.'

Alexander received all this homage with a charm and courtesy which won the hearts of all who saw him.

What a moment of triumph! Everywhere was the emblem of the grazing bull. Alexander lifting his eyes saw it; he also noticed the golden-haired girl on the balcony, the only one of his children to witness this triumph. There was Giovanni in Spain, Cesare in his university of Pisa, and little Goffredo (whom he accepted partly because he loved the boy, partly because sons were so necessary to him) was too young to make an appearance. His children! They would all have their parts to play in his dream of power. Little Lucrezia standing there, eyes wide with awe and wonder, accepting him, as did these people in the streets this day, as a god among them, was the representative of his children.

The homage of the people, the shouts of acclamation, the intoxicating sense of power, they were the narcotic which lulled a man to sleep in which he dreamed of greatness; and all greatness must first take its shape in dreams.

'Blessings on the Holy Father!' cried the crowd.

Aye! thought Alexander. Let the blessings of the saints fall upon me, that I may realize my dreams and unite all Italy under one ruler; and let that ruler be a Borgia Pope.

SANTA MARIA IN PORTICO

L UCREZIA SOON UNDERSTOOD how much more gratifying it was to be the daughter of a Pope than that of a
Cardinal.

Firmly on the Papal throne, Alexander made no secret of
his intentions. Giovanni was to return from Spain that Alexander might put him in charge of the Papal armies; Cesare
was to be made Archbishop of Valencia; as for Lucrezia she
was to be given a palace of her own – that of Santa Maria in
Portico. Lucrezia was delighted with this honour, and especially
so because she might now move from the gloomy fortress of
Monte Giordano into the centre of the City.

Alexander had a double purpose in giving Lucrezia this
palace; it adjoined the Church of St Peter's and there was a
secret passage which connected it with the church and continued into the Vatican. Adriana and Giulia were to be of
Lucrezia's household; Orsino would accompany them, but of
course he was of no account.

Lucrezia looked forward to the new life with zest. It was
wonderful to be grown up. Her brother Giovanni would soon be
in Italy and Cesare, so her father had told her, was to be recalled to Rome. He was only being kept away for a short while
because Alexander did not want the people to think he was
continuing his policy of nepotism since, before his election,
he had promised to abandon it. Cesare was already an Archbishop, and Alexander knew that if his son were in Rome it
would become very difficult not to shower more honours upon
him. So, for the moment, Cesare should remain at Pisa – but
it would only be for the present.

Lucrezia had a great deal to look forward to. She saw her
father often, saw him in the midst of all his pomp and ceremony, and thus he seemed to grow more splendid, more
magnificent.

All day she would hear the bells of St Peter's; and while she worked at her embroidery or sat at her window watching the passing pageants, the scent of incense and the sound of chanting voices came to her seeming to promise her a wonderfully exciting future.

Adriana had put off her mourning and was as respectful to Lucrezia as she was devoted to Giulia, who had even more influence at the Vatican than Lucrezia had.

Lucrezia understood why. She was not surprised if, looking in on Giulia's bedchamber, she found the young girl absent. The sound of footsteps, late at night or in early morning, in that corridor from which led the secret passage to the Vatican, did not surprise her.

She agreed with Adriana that Giulia was indeed fortunate to be loved by one so magnificent as Alexander.

Many important visitors – ambassadors and other dignitaries from the various states – called at the palace of Santa Maria and, under Adriana's guardianship, Lucrezia knew how to receive them. None came without bringing gifts – some for Lucrezia, some for Giulia.

'How kind they are!' said Lucrezia one day when she was examining a beautiful set of furs. 'None comes empty-handed.'

Giulia laughed at her simplicity. 'Do not be quite so grateful, dearest Lucrezia,' she advised. 'They only give because they hope to get in return something which means far more to them.'

Lucrezia was reflective. 'It spoils the gift,' she said. 'Indeed it makes no gift at all.'

'Of course it is no gift. It is a payment for favours they hope to receive.'

'The furs no longer seem so beautiful,' sighed Lucrezia.

Giulia looked at her fondly and thought what a long time it took for her to grow realistic. If Lucrezia had been born poor what a good-hearted little simpleton she might have been!

Was she not aware that, as the Pope's beloved daughter, she had great influence with him?

Lucrezia did know, for she was quickly made aware of this. Adriana believed that Alexander did not want a simpleton for a daughter, therefore this simplicity, this generous open-heartedness of Lucrezia must be checked. Such qualities were foolish.

It was necessary for her to have many rich possessions, Adriana implied. Did she mean to rely entirely on her father for them? No, let her be subtle. Let her use her own shrewdness, so that the Pope realized that he had a clever little daughter and could be proud of her.

Did she love fine clothes? None more. Lucrezia had always been a little vain of her beauty, and what could show it to better advantage than beautiful furs and fine brocades? Then let her make those who sought her favours aware of this. Let them know that, if they made her presents which pleased her, she would show her gratitude by begging her father to give them the help they needed.

'Why,' said Adriana, 'Francesco Gonzaga will be coming to see you soon. He greatly desires that his brother Sigismondo should become a Cardinal.'

'He comes to ask me this?'

'A word to your father from you would help his cause.'

'But how could I who know so little of such matters influence my father?'

'Your father wishes you to show yourself to be a Borgia. He would be pleased to do what you ask of him, and he would like Gonzaga to know in what esteem he holds you. If Gonzaga brought you a valuable present and you could say to your father; "See what Gonzaga has brought me!" why then His Holiness would be pleased at the honour done you and would be ready, I doubt not, to grant favours to one who had shown he knew how to pay for them.'

'I see,' said Lucrezia. 'I did not know that these matters were arranged thus.'

'Then it is time you learned. You love pearls, do you not?'

Lucrezia's eyes sparkled. She did love pearls. They suited her fair skin; when she put on the beautiful necklace which Giulia had been given by Alexander she was sure she looked as beautiful as Giulia.

'I will tell Gonzaga that you are excessively fond of pearls,' said Adriana, smiling knowledgeably.

And it surely would be wonderful, thought Lucrezia, to possess pearls like Giulia's.

So this was the way a Pope's daughter lived. It was wonderfully exciting and very profitable. Who was Lucrezia – rather lazy Lucrezia, who more than most girls loved fine clothes and becoming ornaments – who was she to disagree with this mode of living?

Alexander received his daughter in his apartments at the Vatican; with her, as companion, came Giulia. Alexander still doted on the latter and could scarcely let a day pass without seeing her.

When Alexander received these two beloved ones he liked to do so in the utmost intimacy, so he dismissed all his attendants when they arrived, and had the girls sit, one on either side of him that he might put an arm about each.

How beautiful they were, he thought, with their young smooth skins and their shining golden hair – surely two of the loveliest girls in Rome. Life seemed good when he at sixty had the vigour of a young man, and he was certain that Giulia was making no pretence when she showed so clearly that her passion for him was as great as his for her, and that her poor little squint-eyed husband, young as he was, had no charm for her.

Lucrezia nestling against her father was admiring the splendour of his apartments. The ceiling was gilded and the walls of delicate colours; there were oriental carpets on the floor, and the great artist Pinturicchio had begun the murals; but these did not yet cover the walls, and below them were hangings of the finest silk. There were many chairs, stools and cushions of silk and velvet in brilliant colours; and dominating all was the glory of the Papal throne.

All this belonged to this godlike person who, it seemed impossible to believe, was her tender and loving father, and who when he was alone with his beloved girls would seem to imply that his greatest joy in life was pleasing them.

'I have sent for you this day because I have something to tell you, daughter,' he said. 'We are going to cancel the arrangements we have made for your marriage to Don Gasparo di Procida.'

'Is that so, Father?' she asked.

Giulia laughed. 'She does not mind. She does not mind in the least.'

The Pope caressed his daughter's cheek, and Lucrezia was reminded of the pleasure she had derived from Cesare's caresses.

'Father,' she cried, 'when shall I see Cesare?'

Giulia and the Pope laughed together and exchanged glances.

'You see I am right,' said Giulia. 'Poor Lucrezia! She has never had a lover.'

It was hardly a frown which crossed the Pope's face; he rarely showed displeasure with his loved ones, but Giulia was aware that her remark had disturbed him. She was however too sure of her power to be afraid of displeasing. 'It's true,' she said almost defiantly.

'One day,' said Alexander, 'my daughter will find great joy in love, I doubt not. But she will wait until the time when she is ready.'

Lucrezia took her father's hand and kissed it.

'She cares more for her father and brothers than for any others,' said Giulia. 'Why, she says of every man she sees: "How insignificant he is beside my father . . . or Cesare or Giovanni!"'

'Lucrezia is a Borgia,' said Alexander, 'and Borgias see great virtue in Borgias.'

'They are not the only ones,' said Giulia, laughing and holding his arm aganst her. 'I pray you, beloved and Holy Father, tell us who will now be Lucrezia's bridegroom.'

'A man of great importance. His name is Giovanni Sforza.'

'Is he an old man?' asked Giulia.

'What has age to do with love?' demanded the Pope, and this time there was reproach in his voice.

But Giulia was quick with her soothing reply. 'It is only gods who have the gift of remaining for ever young. Giovanni Sforza, I'll swear, is but a man.'

Alexander laughed and kissed her. 'It is a good match. My

beloved daughter will bless me for arranging it. Come, Lucrezia, are you not going to show your pleasure?'

Lucrezia kissed him dutifully. 'But I have been betrothed so many times. I will wait until I see him and then until I am married to him before I am too grateful.'

The Pope laughed. They amused him with their chatter and he was sorry to have to send them away because official matters must be settled.

Surrounded by their attendants they left the Vatican, and as they were crossing the square an unkempt vagabond peered at Giulia insolently and cried out: 'Why, 'tis the bride of Christ!'

Giulia's eyes flashed, but the man lost no time in running as fast as his legs could carry him, and had disappeared before Giulia could send anyone after him.

'You are angry, Giulia,' said Lucrezia, 'angry at the words of a beggar.'

'I do not care to be insulted,' retorted Giulia. 'You know what he meant.'

'That you are my father's mistress. That is no insult. Think of all those who come to pay court to you because of that!'

'The common people consider it an insult,' said Giulia. 'I wish I could have that man put in prison. I'd have him punished.'

Lucrezia shivered. She knew that often men who insulted those in high places had their tongues cut out.

She would not think of that. Perhaps she would have to learn to contemplate such things with indifference, as she had had to learn to accept the relationship between her father and Giulia and pious Adriana's acceptance of it, and as she had had to accept the fact that she must make herself rich and important by taking bribes. She doubted not that in time she would grow as indifferent as others to these matters; but there was a softness within her which made it difficult for her.

She must conform. She must be like those who lived about her. But for the time being she would refuse to think of the cruel things which could happen to men and women, merely because they spoke too freely.

She wanted to be happy; therefore she would not think of anything that might make her otherwise.

She turned to Giulia. 'Perhaps I shall marry this man, this Giovanni Sforza. I like the sound of him. He has the same name as my brother.'

'There are many Giovannis in Italy,' Giulia reminded her.

'But I doubt not that something will happen to make my father choose another husband for me. Giulia, would it not be strange if I never married . . . because no sooner am I betrothed to one than I must marry someone who will be more grand, more suitable?'

'You will surely marry one day.'

'Then I shall have a lover . . . even as you have.'

'Husbands are not always lovers, my dear. And you have a long way to go before you are as I am.'

Giulia put her face close to Lucrezia's and smiled her most secretive smile. 'I will tell you a secret. The Pope is more than my lover. He is the father of the child I carry within me.'

'Oh, Giulia! So you are to have a child!'

Giulia nodded. 'That was why I was so angry when that vagabond said what he did. I believe it is becoming known. That means that some of our servants are more inquisitive than they should be . . . and too talkative.'

'Do not punish them for that, Giulia,' said Lucrezia. 'It is natural that they should be so.'

'Why should you care whom I punish?'

Lucrezia said: 'I do not want to think of punishments. The sun shines so beautifully on the piazza, does it not, and were not my father's apartments quite beautiful? Cesare and Giovanni will soon be home, and I shall have a husband. There is so much to make me happy. It is merely that I do not wish to think of anyone's not being pleased.'

'There are times,' said Giulia, 'when you seem so simple; and there are times when you seem so very difficult to understand.'

Lucrezia was in her apartment at the Palace of Santa Maria, and her slaves and women were helping her to dress. One fastened the ribbon of her gown while another set a jewelled ornament in her hair.

The arrangements for her marriage had advanced considerably; Don Gasparo, the rejected suitor had, been placated with a gift of three thousand ducats; and the whole of Italy was talking of the Borgia-Sforza alliance. Some saw in this a threat to their security, and della Rovere had decided he would be safer out of Rome. Ferrante of Aragon was disturbed by the alliance and waited apprehensively for what it would bring forth.

There was no doubt in Lucrezia's mind that this betrothal had reached a stage which none of the others had, and it seemed almost certain that she would marry Giovanni Sforza.

So, when a page knocked for admission and told one of her attendants that a noble gentleman had arrived at the palace and was asking to see her, Lucrezia immediately thought that Giovanni Sforza had come.

This was wrong of him, of course. He should not come informally; there would be a ceremonial procession into the city; the Pope's daughter and her betrothed husband could not meet like any serving man and maid; but it would be pleasant and so romantic to do so. She smoothed the folds of her brocade gown and looked at her reflection in the polished metal mirror. She was beautiful; she longed to partake of that sort of love about which Giulia talked.

She said: 'Tell him I will receive him.'

But even as she turned, the visitor stood in the doorway and the sight of him made Lucrezia forget the romantic longing she had had to see her future husband.

'Cesare!' she cried, and forgetting all ceremony she ran to him and threw herself into her brother's arms.

She heard his low laughter, laughter of triumph, of passion, of something she did not understand but loved. She took his hand and kissed it many times.

'You are happy to see me, Lucrezia?'

'It has been a long time,' she cried.

'You thought of me now and then?'

'Every day, Cesare, every day of my life. I never knelt

before the Madonna in my room without mentioning your name.'

Cesare was looking impatiently at the women ranged about her. It was as though a new element was in the room, dominating all others; the women looked different; they stood like creatures who had been turned to stone. Yet they almost cringed. Lucrezia remembered how, long ago in the nursery in their mother's house, the slaves and serving men and women had been afraid of Cesare.

She said: 'Leave us. My brother and I have much of which we wish to talk, and that is for our ears alone.'

They did not need to be told twice.

Brother and sister twined their arms about each other and Cesare drew her to the window. 'I would look at you,' he said. 'Why, you have changed, my Lucrezia.'

There was anxiety in her eyes. 'Cesare, you are not displeased with the change?'

Cesare kissed her. 'It delights me,' he said.

'But you must tell me of yourself. You have been out in the world. You are an Archbishop. That sounds strange. My brother Cesare, Archbishop of Valencia. I shall have to be very demure when I am with you. I must remember that you are a holy man of the Church. But Cesare! You do not look like an Archbishop! This doublet of yours! I declare it is stitched with gold. And what a little tonsure. A simple priest has more than that.'

His eyes blazed suddenly; he clenched his fists, and Lucrezia saw that he was shaking with rage.

'Do not talk of these matters! Lucrezia, I demand that you stop. Archbishop of Valencia! Do I look like an Archbishop? I tell you, Lucrezia, I will not be forced to continue this life. I was never meant for the Church.'

'No, Cesare, you were not, but . . .'

'But one of us must go into the Church. One of us, and that one must be myself. I am the eldest but I am the one who must stand aside for my brother. *He* will soon be home. One imagines the preparations there will be for him. Giovanni, Duke of Gandia! Our father cares more for his little toe than for the whole of my body.'

'It is not true,' she cried, distressed. 'It is not true.'

'It is true.' His eyes seemed murderous as they were turned upon her. 'Do not contradict me, child, when I tell you it is true. I will not remain in the Church, I will not. . . .'

'You must tell our father,' said Lucrezia soothingly.

'He will not listen. By all the saints, I swear it.' He went to the shrine and, lifting his hands as one who was about to take a solemn oath, he cried: 'Holy Mother of God, I swear I will not rest until I am free to lead the life I wish. I will allow no one to bind me, to lead me. I, Cesare Borgia, am my own master from this day on.'

He had changed, Lucrezia realized; he had grown more violent, and she was afraid of him.

She laid her hand pleadingly on his arm. 'Cesare,' she said, 'you will do what you wish. No one shall lead you. You would not be Cesare if you allowed that.'

He turned to her and all the passion seemed to have left him; but she saw that he still shook with the violence of his emotion.

'My little sister,' he said, 'we have been long separated.'

She was anxious to turn the subject away from the Church. 'I have heard news of you from time to time, how you excelled in your studies.'

He touched her cheek gently. 'Doubtless you have heard many tales of me.'

'Tales of daring deeds.'

'And foolish ones?'

'You have lived as men do live . . . men who answer to none.'

He smiled tenderly. 'You know how to soothe me,' he said. 'And they will marry you to that oaf from Pesaro, and doubtless they will take you away from me.'

'We shall visit often, Cesare . . . all of us, you, Giovanni . . . Goffredo. . . .'

His face darkened. 'Giovanni,' he cried with a sneer. 'He will be on his brilliant campaigns, subduing all Italy with his armies. He will have little time to be with us.'

'Then you will be happy, Cesare, for you always hated him.'

'And you . . . like the rest . . . worshipped him. He was very handsome, was he not? Our father doted on him – so much that he forces me to go into the Church when that is where Giovanni should go.'

'Come, tell me about your adventures. You were a gay young man, were you not? All the women of Perugia and Pisa were in love with you, and you, by all accounts, were not indifferent to them.'

'There was not one of them with hair as golden as yours, Lucrezia. There was not one of them who knew how to soothe me with sweet words as you do.'

She laid her cheek against his hand. 'But that is natural. We understand each other. We were together when we were little. That is why, of all the men I ever saw, there was not one as beautiful in my eyes as my brother Cesare.'

'What about your brother Giovanni?' he cried.

Lucrezia, remembering the old games of coquetry and rivalry, pretended to consider. 'Yes, he was very handsome,' she said; then, noticing the dark look returning to Cesare's face, she added quickly: 'At least I always thought so until I compared him to you.'

'If he were here, you would not say that,' accused Cesare.

'I would, I swear I would. He'll soon be here. Then I'll show that I love you best.'

'Who knows what gay manners he has picked up in Spain! Doubtless he will be irresistible to the whole world, as he now is to my father.'

'Let us not talk of him, Cesare. So you have heard that I am to have a husband?'

He laid his hands on her shoulders and looked into her face.

He said slowly: 'I would rather talk of my brother Giovanni and his beauty and his triumphs than of such a matter.'

Her eyes were wide and their innocence moved him to a tenderness which was unusual with him.

'Do you not like this alliance with the Sforzas?' she asked. 'I heard that the King of Aragon is most displeased. Cesare, perhaps if you are against the match and have good reason . . . Perhaps if you speak to our father . . .'

He shook his head.

'Little Lucrezia,' he said quietly, 'my dearest sister, no

matter whom they chose for your husband, I should hate him.'

It was hot June and everywhere throughout the city banners fluttered. The Sforza lion was side by side with the Borgia bull, and every loggia, every roof, as well as the streets, was filled to see the entry into Rome of the bridegroom whom the Pope had chosen for his daughter.

Giovanni Sforza was twenty-six, and a widower who was of a morose nature and a little suspicious of the bargain which was being offered him.

The thirteen-year old child who was to be his bride meant nothing to him as such. He had heard that she was beautiful, but he was a cold man, not to be tempted by beauty. The advantages of the match might seem obvious to some, but he did not trust the Borgia Pope. The magnificent dowry which had been promised with the girl – thirty-one thousand ducats – was to be withheld until the consummation of the marriage, and the Pope had strictly laid down the injunction that consummation was not to take place yet because Lucrezia was far too young; and should she die childless, the ducats were to go to her brother Giovanni, the Duke of Gandia.

Sforza was no impetuous youth. He would wait, before congratulating himself, to see whether there was anything about which to be congratulated.

He had a natural timidity which might have been due to the fact that he came of a subordinate branch of the Sforzas of Milan; he was the illegitimate son of Costanzo, the Lord of Cotignolo and Pesaro, but he had nevertheless inherited his father's estate; he was impecunious, and marriage with the wealthy Borgias seemed an excellent prospect; he was ambitious, and that, could he have trusted the intentions of Alexander, would have made him very happy with the match.

But he could not help feeling uneasy when trumpets and bugles heralded his approach as he came through the Porta del Popolo, whither the Cardinals and high dignitaries had sent important members of their retinues to greet him and welcome him to Rome.

In that procession rode two young men, more magnificently, more elegantly attired than any others. They were two of the most strikingly handsome men Sforza had ever seen, and he guessed by their bearing who they must be. He was thankful that he could cut a fine figure on his Barbary horse, in his rich garments and the gold necklaces which had been lent to him for the occasion.

The younger of these men was the Duke of Gandia, recently returned from Spain. He was very handsome indeed, somewhat solemn at the moment because this was a ceremonial occasion and he, having spent some years at a Spanish Court, had the manners of a Spaniard. Yet he could be gay and lighthearted; that much was obvious.

But it was the elder of the men who demanded and held Sforza's attention. This was Cesare Borgia, Archbishop of Valencia. He had heard stories of this man which made him shudder to recall them. He too was handsome, but his was a brooding beauty. Certainly he was attractive; he would dominate any scene; Sforza was aware that the women in the streets, who watched the procession from loggia and rooftop, would for the most part focus their interest on this man. What was it about him? He was handsomely dressed; so was his brother. His jewels were glittering; but not more so than his brother's. Was it the manner in which he held himself? Was it a pride which excelled all pride; a certainty that he was a god among men?

Sforza did not care to pursue the subject. He only knew that if he had a suspicion of Alexander he felt even more uneasy regarding his son.

But now the greeting was friendly; the welcome warm.

Through the Campo di Fiore went the cavalcade, the young men in its centre – Cesare, Sforza and Giovanni – across the Bridge of St Angelo to pause before the Palace of Santa Maria in Portico.

Sforza lifted his eyes. There on the loggia, her hair shining like gold in the glittering sunshine, was a young girl in crimson satin decorated with rubies and pearls. She was gripping a pillar of the loggia and the sunlight rested on her hands adazzle with jewels.

She looked down on her brothers and the man who was to be her husband.

She was thirteen and those about her had not succeeded in robbing her of her romantic imaginings. She smiled and lifted her hands in welcome.

Sforza looked at her grimly. Her youthful beauty did not move him. He was conscious of her brothers on either side of him; and he continued to wonder how far he could trust them and the Pope.

The Palace of Santa Maria was in a feverish state of excitement; there was whispering and shouting, the sound of feet running hither and thither; the dressmakers and hairdressers filled the anteroom; Lucrezia's chaplain had been with her for so long, preparing her spiritually, that those who must prepare her physically were chafing wth impatience.

The heat was intense – it was June – and Lucrezia felt crushed by the weight of her wedding gown heavily embroidered with gold thread and decorated with jewels which had cost fifteen thousand ducats. Her golden hair was caught in a net ornamented with glittering precious stones. Adriana and Giulia had personally insisted on painting her face and plucking her eyebrows that she might appear as an elegant lady of fashion.

Lucrezia had never felt so excited in the whole of her life. Her dress may have been too heavy for comfort on this hot day, but she cared little for that, for she delighted in adorning herself.

She was thinking of the ceremony, of the people who would crowd to see her as she crossed from the Palace to the Vatican, of herself, serenely beautiful, the heroine of this splendid occasion, with her pages and slaves to strew garlands of sweet-smelling flowers before her as she walked. She gave scarcely a thought to her bridegroom. Marriage was not, she gathered from what she had seen of those near her, a matter about which one should concern oneself overmuch. Giovanni Sforza seemed old, and he did not smile very often; his eyes did not flash like Cesare's and Giovanni's. He was different; he was solemn and looked a little severe. But the marriage was not to be consummated and, Giulia had told her, she need not be bothered with him if she did not want to be. She would continue to stay in Rome – so for Lucrezia marriage meant merely a brilliant pageant with herself as the central figure.

Giulia clapped her hands suddenly and said: 'Bring in the slave that Madonna Lucrezia may see her.'

√ The servants bowed and very shortly a dwarf Negress was standing before Lucrezia. She was resplendent in a gold dress, her hair caught in a jewelled net, and her costume was an exact replica of her dazzlingly beautiful mistress's. Lucrezia cried out in delight, for this Negress's black hair and skin made that of Lucrezia seem more fair than ever.

'She will carry your train,' said Adriana. 'It will be both amusing and delightful to watch.'

Lucrezia agreed and turning to a table on which was a bowl of sweetmeats, she picked up one of these and slipped it into the Negress's mouth.

The dark eyes glistened with the affection which most of the servants – and particularly the slaves – had for Madonna Lucrezia.

'Come,' said Adriana sternly, 'there is much to do yet. Madalenna, bring the jewelled pomanders.'

As Madalenna made for the door she caught her breath suddenly, for a man had entered, and men should not enter a lady's chamber when she was being dressed; but the lord Cesare obeyed no rules, no laws but his own.

'My lord . . .' began Adriana, but Cesare silenced her with a frown.

'Cesare, what do you think of my dress?' cried Lucrezia. 'Tell me whether you admire me now.'

Cesare ignored her and, looking straight at Adriana, said: 'I wish to speak to my sister . . . alone.'

'But, my lord, the time is short.'

'I wish to speak to her alone,' he repeated. 'Do I not make my meaning clear?'

Even Adriana quailed before this arrogant young man of eighteen. Rumours of his life at the universities of Perugia and Pisa had reached her, and the strangeness of the stories had made her shudder. Accidents often happened to those who opposed this arrogant son of the Pope and she was not so powerful that she could risk offending him.

'Since you ask it, it shall be,' she temporized, 'but my lord, I beg of you remember that we must not arrive late at the Vatican.'

He nodded his head, and Adriana signed to all the attendants to leave with her.

When they had gone Lucrezia cried: 'Cesare, there is little time. I should be prepared. . . .'

'You should be prepared to give me a little of your time. Have you forgotten, now that you have a bridegroom, how you swore that you would never love any as you loved me?'

'I do not forget, Cesare. I never shall.' She was thinking of herself crossing the square, imagining the cries of admiration; she could smell the incense and the scent of flowers.

'You are not thinking of me,' said Cesare. 'Who does? My father thwarts me, and you . . . you are as light-minded as any harlot.'

'But Cesare, this is my wedding day.'

'It is little to rejoice in. Sforza! Do you consider him a man? Yet I would rather see you married to him, than to some, for I swear he is little more than a eunuch.'

'Cesare, you must not be jealous.'

Cesare laughed. He came to her and gripped her neck in the gesture she remembered so well. She cried out in alarm because she was afraid for her jewelled net.

'The marriage shall not be consummated.' He laughed. 'I made our father see the wisdom of that. Why, who knows, if the scene changes these Sforzas may not be worthy of our friendship, and then it may well be that the Holy Father will wish he had not been so eager to get his daughter married.'

'Cesare, why are you upset about this marriage? You know I have to marry, and it makes no difference to my love for you. I could never love any as I love you.'

He continued his hold on her neck; his fingers would mark it – they always did – and she longed to beg him to release his hold, but she dared not. She enjoyed being with him as she always did, but now, as ever, that excitement which he aroused

had its roots in a certain fear which she did not understand
and which repelled her while it enticed.

'I believe that to be so,' he said. 'No matter what happens
to you or to me ... there will always be this bond between us.
Lucrezia and Cesare ... we are one, little sister, and no husband of yours, nor wife of mine could ever change that.'

'Yes, yes,' she said breathlessly. 'It is true. I know it is true.'

'I shall not be at the supper party after the ceremony,' said
Cesare.

'Oh, but you must, brother. I so look forward to dancing
with you.'

Cesare looked down at his Archbishop's robes. 'It is not
meet, sister, that men of the Church should dance. You will
be dancing with your brother, the Duke of Gandia. He will
make a splendid partner, I doubt not.'

'Cesare, you will surely be there!'

'At your nuptial celebration. Certainly I shall not. Do you
think I can bear to see you making merry at such a time?'

'Giovanni will be there, and mayhap Goffredo. . . .'

'One day, sister, you will understand that my feeling for you
is stronger than anything Giovanni could feel for anyone.'

There were shouts in the square and Cesare strode to the
window.

Lucrezia stood beside him, but she could no longer feel the
same pleasure in all the pomp which was being prepared for
her, because she was deeply aware of the clenching and unclenching of Cesare's hands and the angry expression on his
face.

'He comes,' said Cesare. 'The handsome Duke of Gandia.'

'He is to conduct me to the Vatican,' said Lucrezia. 'I
should be ready by now. Oh, we shall be late. Cesare, we must
bring back Adriana and Giulia. Giovanni is here and I am not
ready.'

But Adriana, hearing the sounds of Giovanni's approach,
decided that it was necessary for her to risk Cesare's anger,
and she came into the room followed by Giulia and Lucrezia's
attendants.

'The Duke is here,' she said. 'Come now, let me see if your
net is in place. Ah yes, and where is the black dwarf? Here,

dwarf. Take Madonna Lucrezia's train and stand there. . . .'

Cesare watched the preparations frowning, and Lucrezia aware of him felt that his jealousy was clouding this happy day.

Giovanni entered.

He had changed a great deal since he had gone to Spain. Tall and very elegant, he had led a life of debauchery but at seventeen this had left very little mark on his face. He wore a golden beard which softened the sensual cruelty of his mouth, and his eyes, pale, transparent and so like Lucrezia's own, though beautifully shaped and dark-lashed, lacked the serene gentleness of his sister's and were in contrast cold and hard. But he had that Borgia fascination which he had inherited from his father, and in his fine colourful garments, which consisted of a Turkish robe *à la Française* so long that it swept the floor, made of curling cloth of gold with immense pearls sewn into the sleeves and a cap adorned with an enormous gem, he was a magnificent spectacle. Jewels sparkled on his person and about his neck was a long necklace entirely composed of rubies and pearls.

Lucrezia caught her breath as she looked at him.

'Why, Giovanni,' she cried, 'you look magnificent.'

For a moment she forgot Cesare glowering there. To him it seemed symbolic of his father's wish to humiliate him. Here before Lucrezia stood her two brothers, the rivals; and one, through the grace and bounty of their father, could come like a prince while the other must wear the comparatively drab garments of the Church.

Cesare felt one of those moods of rage sweeping over him. When they possessed him he wanted to put his hands about the throats of those who fostered these moods, and squeeze and squeeze that he might soothe his hurt vanity by their screams for mercy.

He could not squeeze that elegant throat. There had been a hundred times in his life when he had longed to. One must not touch the Pope's beloved. One day, he thought, I shall be unable to restrain myself.

Giovanni, understanding the mood of his brother, looked slyly from him to Lucrezia. 'Ah, my little sister, my beloved Lucrezia, you say I look magnificent, but you . . . you are like a goddess. I do not believe you can be my pretty little sister. No human being could possess such beauty. How you sparkle! How you glitter! Even my lord Archbishop looks the brighter for your closeness to him. I hear you are not coming to our father's party, brother. Mayhap it is as well. The sombre garb of you men of the Church is apt to have a sobering effect, and there must be naught but gaiety this night.'

'Silence!' cried Cesare. 'Silence, I say!'

Giovanni raised his eyebrows and Adriana cried: 'My lord, we must go. As it is, we shall be late.'

Cesare turned and strode out of the room. His attendant, who had been waiting outside the apartment, prepared to follow him. Cesare turned to the boy – he was little more. 'You smile,' he said. 'Why?'

'My lord?'

Cesare had the boy by the ear. The pain was almost unbearable.

'Why?' screamed Cesare. 'I asked why.'

'My lord . . . I do not smile.'

Cesare knocked the boy's head against the wall. 'You would lie then. You have been listening, and what you overheard amused you.'

'My lord . . . my lord!'

Cesare took the boy roughly by the arm and pushed him towards the staircase. The boy lifted his hands as he fell and Cesare heard his screams as he tumbled headlong down the stairs. He listened, his eyes narrowed, his mouth slightly turned down. The cries of others in pain never failed to soothe the pain within himself, the pain born of frustration and fear that there were some in the world who did not recognize him as of supreme importance.

Led by her brother Giovanni, Lucrezia entered the Pope's new apartment at the Vatican. The apartments were already crowded by all the most important people of Rome and representatives from the courts of other states and dukedoms.

Lucrezia had forgotten Cesare in the excitement of crossing the square, from the Palace to the Vatican; the shouts of the people were still in her ears and she could still smell the scent

of the flowers which had been strewn in her path. And here on
the Papal throne was her father, magnificent in his white and
gold vestments, his eyes shining with love and pride as they
rested upon her. Those eyes, however, quickly strayed to his
beloved and beautiful Giulia who stood on one side of Lucrezia;
on the other was another beautiful young girl, Lella Orsini,
who had recently married Giulia's brother Angelo Farnese.

The bridegroom came forward. He looked almost shabby
compared with the glory of that other Giovanni, the bride's
brother. Giovanni Sforza, conscious of lacking the Spanish
elegance of the Duke of Gandia, was remembering that even
the necklace he wore about his neck was borrowed.

As for Lucrezia, she was scarcely conscious of him. To her,
this marriage was nothing more than a brilliant masque.
Sforza must be there because without him she could not play
her part, and since there was to be no consummation for a
long time she knew that life was going on exactly as it always
had.

They knelt together on a cushion at the feet of Alexander and
when the notary asked Sforza if he would take Lucrezia as his
wife, the bridegroom answered in loud and ringing tones: 'I
will with a good heart!' And Lucrezia echoed his words. The
Bishop put the rings on their fingers while a nobleman held a
naked sword over their heads; and after that the Bishop
preached a touching sermon concerning the sanctity of marriage, to which neither Lucrezia nor her husband paid a great
deal of attention.

Alexander himself was impatient. There were too many such
ceremonies in his life, and he was eager to proceed with the
merrymaking.

Now celebrations began, and there were many churchmen
present who wondered at the ease with which the Pope could
cast aside his role of Holy Father and become the jocular host
who is determined that all shall rejoice at his daughter's wedding.

None laughed more heartily than the Pope at the somewhat
bawdy jokes which were circulated and which were considered
to be a necessary part of wedding celebrations. A comedy was

performed for the enjoyment of the company, obscene songs were sung; riddles were asked and answered, and all these had a sly allusion to the married state. Hundreds of pounds of sweetmeats were distributed among the guests – the Pope and all the Cardinals being served first, followed by the bride and bridegroom, the ladies, the prelates and the remaining guests. The fun was hilarious when the sweets were dropped down the bodices of the women's gowns and there were shrieks of delight as these were retrieved. When the company was tired of this game the remains of the sweetmeats were thrown from the windows and the crowds who were waiting below scrambled for them.

Later the Pope gave a dinner-party in the pontifical hall and, when the company had feasted, the dancing began.

The bride sat beside her husband, who glowered at the dancers; he disliked such entertainments and was longing for this one to end. Not so Lucrezia; she longed for her husband to take her hand and lead her in the dance.

She glanced sideways at him. He seemed very old, she thought, very stern. 'Do you not like to dance?' she asked him.

'I do not like to dance,' he answered.

'But does not the music inspire you to do so?'

'Nothing inspires me to do so.'

Her feet were tapping, and her father was watching her; his face was a little flushed with so much feasting and merry-making, and she knew that he understood how she was feeling. She saw him glance at her brother Giovanni, who had interpreted the glance. In a moment he was beside her.

'Brother,' he said, 'since you do not partner my sister in the dance, I will do so.'

Lucrezia looked at her husband, thinking that perhaps now she would have to ask his permission; she was a little apprehensive, knowing that neither of her brothers would allow any to stand in the way of what they wanted to do.

She need not have worried. Giovanni Sforza was quite indifferent as to whether his wife danced or stayed at his side.

'Come,' said the Duke of Gandia. 'A bride should dance at her wedding.'

So he led her into the very centre of the dancers and holding her hand, he said: 'Oh, my sister, you are the fairest lady of the ball, which is as it should be.'

'I verily believe, dear brother,' she said, 'that you are the handsomest of the men.'

The Duke bowed his head and his eyes gleamed at her, amused and passionate as they had been in the nursery days.

'Cesare would be beside himself with envy if he saw us dance together.'

'Giovanni,' she said quickly, 'you should not provoke him.'

' 'Tis one of the joys of my life,' he murmured, 'provoking Cesare.'

'Why so, Giovanni?'

'Someone must provoke him, and everyone else, except our father, would seem to be afraid to.'

'Giovanni, you are not afraid of anything.'

'Not I,' said Giovanni. 'I would not be afraid of your bridegroom if he, being jealous to see his bride look so lovingly at me, should challenge me to a duel.'

'He will make no such challenge. I fancy he is glad to be rid of me.'

'By the saints, then perhaps I should run him through for his neglect of my lovely sister. Oh, Lucrezia, how happy I am to be with you once more! Have you forgotten the days in our mother's house ... the quarrels, the dances? Ah, those Spanish dances. Do you remember them?'

'I do, Giovanni.'

'And do you not think them more inspiring, more full of meaning than these of Italy?'

'Yes, Giovanni.'

'Then we will dance them, you and I. ...'

'Giovanni, dare we?'

'We Borgias dare anything, sister.' He drew her to him and there was light in his eyes which reminded her of Cesare's. 'Do not forget,' he went on, 'that though you have married a Sforza, you are a Borgia ... always a Borgia.'

'No,' she answered, and she was breathless with sudden excitement. 'I shall never forget it.'

One by one the other dancers fell away from them, so that after a while there was none dancing but the Duke of Gandia and his sister. The dances were those of Spain – throbbing with passion, the sort of dances which a bride and bridegroom might have performed together, portraying love, desire, fulfilment.

Lucrezia's long hair escaped from its net in the abandonment of the dance; and there were many who whispered: 'How strange that the sister and brother should dance thus while the bridegroom looks on!'

The Pope watched with benign affection. These were his best-loved children, and it did not seem strange to him to see them dance thus: Lucrezia expectant, on the brink of womanhood, and Giovanni with the light of a demon in his eyes, and a malicious glance over his shoulder for the dull bridegroom – and for another perhaps, another who wished he was present to watch this almost ritual dance with their sister.

Giovanni Sforza yawned in his indifference. Yet he was less indifferent than he seemed. Not that he had any deep feelings for the golden-haired child who was his wife; but it had occurred to him that the Borgias were a strange family, alien to Rome; their Spanish blood made them that; and he felt faintly uneasy sitting there, and although he was in a semi-stupor through too much food and wine, too much heat, too many celebrations, he was conscious of a warning voice within him: 'Beware of these Borgias. They are a strange, unnatural people. One must be prepared for them to do anything ... however startling, however strange. Beware. ... Beware of the Borgias!'

LUCREZIA MARRIED

THOSE WEEKS WHICH followed her wedding were full of
pleasure for Lucrezia. She saw little of her husband, and
her brothers were constantly with her. The old rivalry was
revived and, although Lucrezia was aware that there was now
an even more dangerous element in this than there had been
in nursery days, she could not help being stimulated by it.

It was an unusual situation; the bride and bridegroom
indifferent to each other, while the bride's brothers strutted
before her, as though they were trying to woo her, each trying
to persuade her that he was a better man than the other.

The brothers invaded Lucrezia's apartments day and night;
each planned spectacles in whch he played the leading part
and Lucrezia that of honoured guest.

Adriana protested, but Giovanni ignored her, and Cesare's
eyes blazed with anger. 'The insolence of the woman is beyond
endurance!' he cried, and there was a threat in his words.

Giulia remonstrated with Lucrezia.

'This is a strange mode of behaviour,' she declared. 'Your
brothers attend you as though you were something more than a
sister.'

'You do not understand,' Lucrezia explained. 'We were
together in the nursery.'

'Brothers and sisters often are.'

'Our childhood was different. We sensed the mystery which
surrounded us. We lived in our mother's house, but we did not
then know who our father was. We loved each other . . . we
were necessary to each other, and then we were parted for so
long. That is why we love more than most families.'

'I would rather see you take a lover.'

Lucrezia smiled gently; she was too good-hearted to tell
Giulia that she understood the reason for her concern; the
Pope still doted on her and she remained his favourite mistress,
but all lovers of members of the Borgia family must be jealous

of that family's feelings for its own members. Giulia was thinking that, now Cesare and Giovanni were in Rome, the love their father bore them and his daughter far exceeded that which he had for herself, and she was frankly jealous.

Lucrezia was fond of Giulia; she understood her feelings; but the bond between herself and her brothers could not be broken by anyone.

Meanwhile the weeks passed. She would go to the Campo di Fiore to watch Giovanni joust; then Cesare staged a bull-fight in that same spot, himself acting as the brave matador. He arranged that there were crowds to watch, and in the place of honour, where she might miss nothing, was Lucrezia, to tremble when she saw him face death, to exult when she saw him triumph.

All her life Lucrezia would never forget that occasion; the moment of fear when she saw the bull charge and heard the deep sigh of the crowd; she herself had almost swooned with fear, in one terrible second visualizing a world without Cesare. But Cesare was supreme; light as a dancer he had stepped aside as the angry bull thundered past. How handsome he looked! How graceful! He might, thought Lucrezia, have been dancing the old *farraca*, that dance in which a man mimed his play with the bull, so unconcerned did he seem. She would never dance the *farraca* herself nor see others dance it without recalling this moment of fear and exultation; she would always remember the hot sun in the Campo di Fiore and the realization that Cesare was to her the most important person in the world.

She had sat there seemingly serene, yet she was praying all the time: 'Madonna, keep him safe. Holy Mother of God, do not let him be taken from me.'

Her prayers were answered. He killed his bull and came to stand before his sister, that all present should know that it was for her he fought.

She took his hand and kissed it and her eyes had lost their mildness as she raised them to his. She had never seen him look quite so happy as he did then. He had cast aside all resentment; he had forgotten that he was an Archbishop and Giovanni a Duke. The crowd was acclaiming him, and Lucrezia was

telling him of the depth and breadth of her love for him.
Lucrezia planned a ball in honour of her brave matador.
'And what of the hero of the joust?' demanded Giovanni.
'For him also,' said Lucrezia fondly.

She wanted them to be together; it was only when she was
conscious of their intense rivalry that she could feel she was
back in her childhood.

So at the ball she danced with Giovanni while Cesare
glowered, and with Cesare while Giovanni looked on with
smouldering jealousy. Often the Pope would be present on such
occasions and there was astonishment among the spectators
that the Holy Father could look on smiling while his sons and
daughter danced the strangely erotic Spanish dances, and that
he could witness the jealous passion of these two brothers –
and the sister's pleasure in it – with such tolerant amusement.

Lucrezia would be seen riding between her brothers to
Monte Mario to watch the noblemen trying out their falcons,
laughing, laying wagers as to which of the birds would win the
prize.

As for Giovanni Sforza, he lived like an outsider in this
strange household. The marriage was not yet to be consummated. At that he shrugged his shoulders. He was not a man
deeply interested in such pleasures, and his needs could be
supplied by the occasional summoning of a courtesan. But
there were occasions when he resented the continual presence
of those two overbearing young men, and on one of these he
ventured to protest to his wife. She had returned with her
brothers from riding and when she went to her apartment he
followed her there; he turned and waved a dismissal at her
attendants. They obeyed the signal and did not enter the room.

Lucrezia smiled tentatively at him. Wishing to live on good
terms with all, she was always polite to her husband.

Sforza then said to his wife: 'This is a strange life you lead.
You are constantly in the company of one of your brothers –
or both.'

'Is it strange?' she asked. 'They are my brothers.'

'Your conduct is talked of throughout Rome.'

Lucrezia's eyes were wide with surprise.

'Do you not understand what is being said?'

'I have not heard it.'

'One day,' said Sforza, 'you will be my wife in very truth. I would have you remember that that day must surely come. I would ask you to see less of your brothers.'

'They would never allow it,' said Lucrezia. 'Even if I wished it.'

There was a sound of laughter from without and the brothers entered the room. They stood side by side, legs thrust apart, and it was not their obvious strength and vigour which sent a twinge of alarm through Sforza. He felt then that there was something to fear which was as yet unseen, and that any normal man who made an enemy of them must certainly go in fear of his life.

They were not scowling, and Sforza felt it might have been better if they were. They were smiling, and Lucrezia and her husband might not have been in the room, for all the notice the brothers took of them.

Giovanni said, as his hand rested lightly on his sword: 'This man our sister has married . . . it has come to my ears that he resents our presence in her house.'

'He should have his tongue cut out if he has made such a monstrous suggestion,' drawled Cesare.

'And doubtless will,' added Giovanni, half drawing his sword from its sheath and letting it fall back again. 'Who is this man?'

'A bastard son of the tyrant of Pesaro, I have heard.'

'And Pesaro, what is Pesaro?'

'But a small town on the Adriatic coast.'

'A beggar . . . little more, eh? I remember he came to his wedding in a borrowed necklace.'

'What should we do to such a one if he became insolent?'

Giovanni Borgia laughed softly. 'He will not become insolent, brother. Beggar he may be, bastard he is, but he is not such a fool as all that.'

Then they laughed and turned to the door.

Lucrezia and Sforza heard them shouting and laughing as they went out. Lucrezia ran to the window. It was a strange sight to see the Borgia brothers walking together like friends.

Sforza was still standing where he had been when the door

had opened. During the time when the brothers had been speaking he had felt unable to move, so strongly had he been aware of an overwhelming sense of evil.

Lucrezia had turned from the window and was looking at him. There was compassion in her gaze and the compassion was for him; for the first time since she had seen him Lucrezia was aware of some feeling for him, and he for her.

He knew that she too was conscious of that evil which had seemed to emanate from her brothers.

As the brothers walked away they knew that Lucrezia was at the window watching them.

Cesare said: 'That will doubtless make the fool think twice before he speaks slightingly of us again.'

'Did you see him quail before us?' said Giovanni with a laugh. 'I tell you, brother, it was all I could do to prevent myself drawing my sword and giving him a prick or two.'

'You showed great restraint, brother.'

'You also.'

Giovanni glanced sideways at Cesare. Then he said: 'Strange looks come our way. Have you noticed?'

'We have rarely been seen walking thus amicably together. That is the reason.'

'Before you begin to scowl at me, Cesare, let me say this: There are times when you and I should stand together. All Borgias must do this sometimes. You hate me as my father's favourite, for my dukedom and the bride I shall have. The bride is no beauty, if that is any consolation to you. She has a long horse-face. You would fancy her no more than I do.'

'I would take her and the dukedom of Gandia in exchange for my Archbishopric.'

'That you would, Cesare, that you would. But I will keep her, and my dukedom. I would not be an Archbishop even though the Papal throne was to be mine in the future.'

'Our father has a long life before him.'

'I pray Heaven that it is so. But, Archbishop . . . nay, do not glower so . . . Archbishop, let us continue this friendship just for one hour. We have our common enemies. Let us consider them as we did the Sforza a short while ago.'

'And these enemies?'

'The accursed Farnese. Is it not a fact that that woman, Giulia Farnese, demands what she will of our father and it is granted her?'

' 'Tis true enough,' murmured Cesare.

'Brother, shall we allow this state of affairs to continue?'

'I agree with you, my lord Duke, that it would be well to put an end to it.'

'Then, my lord Archbishop, let us put our heads together and bring about that happy state of affairs.'

'How so?'

'She is but a woman, and there are other women. I have in my suite a nun from Valencia. She has beauty, grace and the charm of a nun. She has given me great pleasure. I think I shall put her to the service of my father. I have a Moorish slave also, a dusky beauty. They make a satisfactory pair – the nun and the slave; the one all vestal reluctance, the other . . . insatiably passionate. We will go to our father, you and I, and we will tell him of the virtues of these two. He will wish to share . . . and sharing, who knows, he may forget the beautiful Giulia. At least she will not be the sole playmate of his leisure hours. There is safety in numbers; it is when there is one – and rarely any other – that one sees danger ahead.'

'Let us visit him now. Let us tell him of your nun and your slave. He will at least be eager to see them and, if they are all you say . . . well, it might be that we can loosen the hold of the Farnese on our Holy Father.'

The two young men went across the square to the Vatican while many eyes followed them, marvelling at this new friendship.

It was said in the streets that one marriage begot another, and this was indeed the case. Giovanni was to make a Spanish marriage; Cesare was for the Church and could have no marriage; Lucrezia was married to Giovanni Sforza; now it was the turn of little Goffredo.

Vannozza, happy with her husband, Carlo Canale, was dizzy with joy. Often her children came to see her and nothing delighted her more than to give intimate little parties for their entertainment. Her talk was mostly of her children; my son, the Duke, my son, the Archbishop, my daughter, the Countess of Pesaro. And now she would be able to talk equally proudly of her Goffredo. He would be a Duke or a Prince very shortly as the Pope was to make a grand marriage for him.

This showed clearly, thought Vannozza, that Alexander no longer doubted that Goffredo was his son. But this was not so; Alexander continued to doubt. Yet he was of the opinion that the more brilliant the marriages he could make for his children, the better for the Borgias generally; he wished he had a dozen sons; therefore it was expedient to thrust aside all doubt and, at least in the eyes of the world, accept Goffredo as his.

The moment was propitious to arrange a new Borgia marriage. Ferrante, the King of Naples, had watched with concern the growing friendship between the Vatican and the Sforzas of Milan.

Alexander, sensualist though he was, was also a clever diplomat. He preferred to be on good terms with the rival houses of Milan and Naples. Moreover, Spain was naturally favourable to the ruling house of Naples, which was Spanish in origin and maintained the Spanish customs at the Court.

Ferrante was aware of the Pope's desire for friendship and had sent his son, Federico, to Rome with proposals to lay before the Holy Father.

Ferrante's elder son, Alfonso, who was heir to the throne of Naples, had a natural daughter, Sanchia, and Ferrante's suggestion was that Sanchia should be betrothed to the Pope's youngest son. That Goffredo was but eleven years and Sanchia sixteen was no handicap; nor was her illegitimacy, for illegitimacy was not considered an important stigma in fifteenth-century Italy, although of course legitimate children took precedence over natural ones. Goffredo himself was illegitimate; therefore it seemed a good match.

Little Goffredo was delighted. He came hurrying to Lucrezia, as soon as he heard the news, to impart it to her.

'I, sister, I too am to be married. Is not that great good news? I am to go to Naples and marry a Princess.'

Lucrezia embraced him and wished him happiness, and the

little boy ran about the apartment dancing with an imaginary bride, going through the ceremony which he had seen Lucrezia perform with her husband.

Cesare and Giovanni called on their sister, and Goffredo ran to them and told them the news. Lucrezia knew that they had already heard; she was aware of this because of Cesare's sullen looks. This was another reminder that he was the only one of them who must remain unmarried.

'What a bridegroom you will be!' said Giovanni. 'An eleven-year-old bridegroom of a sixteen-year-old bride who is, unless rumour lies . . . but no matter. Your Sanchia is a beauty – a great beauty, my brother – so whatever else she may be she will be forgiven.'

Goffredo began to walk about the apartment on his toes to make himself look taller. He stopped suddenly, his eyes questioning; then he looked towards Cesare.

'Everybody is pleased,' he said, 'except my lord brother.'

'You know why he is ill-pleased, do you not?' cried Giovanni. 'It is because as a holy man of the Church there can be no bride for him.'

Goffredo's face puckered suddenly, and he went to Cesare. 'If you wish for a bride, my lord,' he said, 'I would give you mine; for I should find no pleasure in her if by possessing her I should cause you pain.'

Cesare's eyes glinted as he looked at the boy. He had not known until that moment how firmly Goffredo admired him. The little boy standing there clearly implied that he thought Cesare the most wonderful person in the world; and with Lucrezia and his young brother, to admire him thus, Cesare felt suddenly happy.

He did not care for Giovanni's taunts. He gloried in his rivalry with Giovanni because he had made up his mind that one day Giovanni was going to pay for every insult, just as any other man or woman would.

'You are a good boy, Goffredo,' he said.

'Cesare, you believe I am your brother . . . entirely your brother, do you not?'

Cesare embraced the boy and assured him that he did; and Lucrezia watching saw all the cruelty and the hardness leave her brother's face. Like that, she thought, my brother Cesare is surely the most beautiful person in the world.

Lucrezia longed for peace between them all. They were all together now, and Cesare was delighted by the artless words of the boy. If Giovanni would only join then in their happy circle, they could dispense with rivalry; they could be as she longed to see them, in complete harmony.

'I will play wedding songs on my lute, and we will sing,' she cried. 'We will pretend we are already at Goffredo's wedding.'

She clapped her hands and a slave brought her lute; then she sat on cushions, her golden hair falling about her shoulders; and as her fingers touched the lute she began to sing.

Goffredo stood behind her, and laying his hands on her shoulders sang with her.

The brothers watched them, listening; and for a short while peace was with them all.

Now there was more merrymaking at the Vatican in honour of the formal betrothal of Goffredo and Sanchia of Aragon which took place in the Pope's apartments, Federico, Prince of Altamura and uncle of the bride, taking her place. This was conducted in the presence of the Pope with all the ceremony of a true marriage.

There was a great deal of merriment because little Goffredo as the husband looked so incongruous beside the Prince who was taking the place of the bride, and ribald comments soon broke out; nor were these checked by the presence of the Holy Father who in fact laughed more heartily than anybody and even added to the quips.

There was nothing Alexander liked better than what he called a good joke, and by good he meant bawdy. Federico, finding himself the butt of all the amusement and being something of an actor, then began to amuse the company by playing the part of bride with such fluttering of eyelashes and coy gestures that what took place in the Vatican was more like a masque than a solemn ceremony.

Federico continued with his acting at the feasting and balls which followed; it was a joke of which no one seemed to tire, and the fun was increased when a member of Federico's retinue took an opportunity of whispering to the Pope that he would be even more amused if he had seen Sanchia.

'How so?' asked Alexander. 'I have heard she is a beauty.'

'She has beauty, Holiness, to make all others seem plain beside her. But our Prince behaves as a coy virgin. There is nothing coy about Madonna Sanchia . . . and nothing of the virgin either. She has had a host of lovers.'

The Pope's eyes glistened with merriment. 'Then this makes the joke even better,' he said. He called Cesare and Giovanni to him. 'Did you hear that, my sons? Did you hear what was said of Madonna Sanchia, our coy virgin?'

The brothers laughed heartily at the joke.

'I deeply regret,' said Giovanni, 'that young Goffredo is to go to Naples, and that Sanchia will not join him here.'

'Ah, my son, I should not give much for poor Goffredo's chances if she set eyes on you.'

'We should be rivals for the lady,' said Cesare lightly.

'A pleasant state of affairs indeed!' said the Pope. 'Mayhap since she is such an obliging lady she would be wife to three brothers.'

'And to their father mayhap,' added Giovanni.

This amused the Pope immensely, and his eyes rested fondly on Giovanni.

Cesare decided then that if ever Sanchia came to Rome she should be his mistress before she was Giovanni's.

Then his eyes narrowed and he said sharply: 'So our little Goffredo is to be a husband. I myself am to be denied that pleasure. It is strange that Goffredo should be married before you, brother.'

Giovanni's eyes flashed hatred, for he immediately understood Cesare's meaning.

Alexander was saddened. He turned to Giovanni. 'Alas,' he said, 'you must soon return to Spain for your marriage, my dear son.'

'My marriage will wait,' said Giovanni sullenly.

'Ah, my son, time does not stand still. I shall be well pleased when I hear that your wife is the mother of a fine boy.'

'In time . . . in time,' said Giovanni shortly.

But Cesare was smiling secretly. Alexander's mouth was

set along firm lines. When his ambition was concerned he could be adamant, and as Cesare had been forced to the Church so Giovanni would be forced to go to his Spanish wife. It seemed to Cesare an even better joke than Federico's miming of Madonna Sanchia. Once he had longed to be in Giovanni's shoes that he might go to Spain to receive great honours including a Spanish dukedom; he had been forced to stay behind and enter the Church. Now Giovanni wanted nothing so much as to stay in Rome, and he would be forced to leave as certainly as Cesare had been forced into the Church. Cesare laughed inwardly as he watched his brother's sullen looks.

Giovanni was angry. Life in Rome suited his temperament far better than the Spanish mode of living. In Spain a man of rank was stifled by etiquette; and Giovanni had no fancy for the pallid, long-faced bride, Maria Enriques, whom he had inherited from his dead brother. It was true that Maria was a cousin of the King of Spain and that marriage with her would forge a strong link with the Spanish Royal house and secure for him royal protection. But what did Giovanni care for that? He wanted to be in Rome, which he thought of as home.

He would rather be recognized as the son of the Pope than cousin, by marriage, to the King of Spain. He had felt homesick while he was away. He had imagined himself riding about Rome, and, cynic though he was concerning most things, tears would come to his eyes when he thought of entering the Porta del Popolo and watching the races to the Piazza Venezia in Carnival week. There seemed nothing like it in Spain – the Spanish were a melancholy people compared with the gay Italians. He had found great pleasure and sadness in thinking of the crowds, in the grand stand in the Piazza del Popolo, who had assembled to watch the race of riderless horses. How he had enjoyed those races, how he had shouted with glee to see the frightened beasts let loose, with pieces of metal tied to them to make a noise and frighten them still further as they galloped, the devilish type of spurs fastened midway between withers and shoulders, leaded and pear-shaped, the heavy end having seven spikes which prodded the horse at every step! The terrified horses, as they thundered along the Corso, provided a sight not to be missed. Yet in Spain he had sadly missed it. He had longed to wander along the Via Funari where the rope-makers lived, and the Via Canestrari where the basket-makers lived, to the Via dei Serpenti; to gaze at the Capitol and think of the heroes of Rome who had been crowned with glory there, and to see the Tarpeian Rock from which guilty men were thrown; to laugh at the old saying that glory was but a short way from disgrace, and to answer it with: Not for a Borgia; not for the son of the Pope!

All this was Rome, and Rome was where he belonged; yet he was so unfortunate as to be sent away from it.

He sought to postpone the hour of his departure. He threw himself madly into pleasure. He roamed the streets with a band of selected friends, and there was not a beautiful young woman – or man – who was safe, once Giovanni had set eyes on her or him.

He favoured the most notorious of the courtesans. He roamed the Ponte district in their company. He liked courtesans; they were experienced, as he was; he liked also very young girls, and one of his favourite pastimes was seducing or forcing young brides before their marriage took place. Giovanni, he himself knew, would never be a brave soldier, and instinct told him that Cesare, who was no coward, was aware of that streak of cowardice in him, and that Cesare exulted because of it whilst raging at the unfairness which had made Giovanni a soldier and himself a man of the Church.

Giovanni sought to hide that streak of weakness within him, and how could he do this better, he thought, than by inflicting cruelty on those who could not retaliate? If he abducted a bride about to be married, who could complain against the beloved son of an all-powerful Pope? Such adventures lulled his fear of inadequacy and, he felt, made him appear as a lusty adventurer.

There was one person in whose company he found great delight. This was a Turkish Prince whom the Pope was holding as hostage in the Vatican. Djem was of striking appearance; his Asiatic manners amused Giovanni; his Turkish costume was picturesque and he was more cunning and more coldly barbarous than anyone Giovanni had ever known.

Giovanni had struck up a friendship with Djem and they were often seen about the city together. Giovanni appeared in Turkish costume; it suited him, and Djem with his dark looks made a striking contrast to the golden beauty of Giovanni. They were together in Alexander's cortège when it travelled from church to church; and it seemed strange to the people of Rome to see two prominent figures on a pair of matched horses, both dressed in turbans and colourful oriental costume.

Most people were horrified to see the Turk in this procession for the Turk was an infidel; but Giovanni insisted that his friend accompany them, and the Turk smiled at the horrified looks of the people in his slow indolent way which everyone knew was a veil to hide his barbarism. From him they looked to the handsome Duke of Gandia whose keen eyes were on the look-out for the most beautiful young women, marking the spot where they could later be found, and pointing them out to Djem, who would be planning that night's adventures.

In this Asiatic, who was capable of devising strange orgies of calculated cruelty and extraordinary eroticism, Giovanni had found a congenial companion.

Here was another reason why he had no wish to leave Rome.

As for Alexander, he knew of the complaints against Giovanni; he knew that the people were shocked by the appearance of the Pope's son in Turkish costume; but he merely shook his head and smiled indulgently.

'He means no harm,' he said. 'He is young yet, and it is merely high spirits which cause him to play his merry pranks.'

And Alexander was as loth to let his beloved Giovanni leave Rome as Giovanni was to go.

Lucrezia sat with Giulia; there was a piece of embroidery before her and she was smiling at it. She enjoyed working the beautiful pattern on silk in gold, scarlet and blue threads. Bending over the work she looked, thought Giulia, like an innocent child, and Giulia felt slightly impatient. Lucrezia was now a married woman, and though the marriage had not been consummated she had no right to look such a baby.

Lucrezia, thought Giulia, is different from the rest of us. Lucrezia is apart. She is like her father, yet lacking his wisdom and understanding of life; she has the same way of turning away from the unpleasant and refusing to believe in its existence; and she has a tolerance besides. I believe she makes excuses for the cruelty of people, almost as though she understands what makes them act cruelly; and that is part of her strangeness, for Lucrezia is never cruel herself.

All the same Giulia felt impatient in her company, for Giulia was uneasy. She hated Cesare and Giovanni; they had always made her uncomfortable, but now she knew that they were deliberately trying to oust her from her position. Sexually she was out of reach. She was, after all, their father's mistress and the bond between Giulia and the Pope was a strong one as he did not feel towards her as he would towards any light love of a night or so. Therefore his sons, while desiring her as they would desire any beautiful woman, were forced to respect her; consequently they were piqued about this, and it was part of their arrogance that they should dislike any who brought home to them the fact that they could not have all their own way in all directions. The Pope towered above his sons; he was the fount from whom all blessings flowed; and although he was the most indulgent of fathers, the most generous of benefactors, there were some bounds beyond which even they might not go.

Giulia's was a case which underlined this fact, and they resented her because of it. Accordingly they endeavoured to destroy her influence.

She knew that they sought the most beautiful young people in Rome, and that they introduced the girls to their father. (Alexander had never been interested in their young male friends.) The Pope had been greatly taken with a certain Spanish nun whom Giovanni had brought with him in his retinue. The result was that the Holy Father had been too busy to see Giulia for some days. Giulia was furious, and she knew whom to blame.

Impetuous as she was, she wanted to storm into the Papal apartments and denounce Giovanni; but that would be folly. Much as the Pope liked to please his beautiful young mistress, and indeed found it difficult to refuse the request of any pretty young woman, there was one for whom he cared more than any woman – his precious Giovanni.

And if the Spanish nun was proving very delectable he might feel just a little more impatient than he would otherwise have done, if Giulia railed against Giovanni. Alexander might love various women in various degrees, but his love for his children never faltered.

Now Giulia, looking at the fair young face bent over the embroidery, said slyly: 'Lucrezia, I am worried about Giovanni.'

Lucrezia's innocent eyes were wide with surprise. 'You are worried about him? I thought you did not like him.'

Giulia laughed. 'We banter . . . as brother and sister might. I would not say that I loved him as you do. I would never have that blind adoration for a brother which you have for yours.'

'I think you are very fond of your brother Alessandro.'

Giulia nodded. It was true. She was fond of Alessandro to the extent that she was determined to secure for him his Cardinal's hat before long. But that was different from this passionate attachment which seemed to exist between the Borgia brothers and their sister.

'Oh, fond enough,' she said lightly. 'But I was talking of Giovanni. There is a great deal of gossip in the streets concerning him.'

'There is always gossip,' murmured Lucrezia lightly, picking up her needle.

'That's true, but this is a time when gossip could be very harmful to Giovanni.'

Lucrezia lifted her head from her work.

'On account of his marriage,' went on Giulia impatiently. 'I have heard it said, by friends who have come from Spain, that there is talk at the Court there of Giovanni's wild behaviour, of his friendship with Djem, and how they spend their time. There is some displeasure in quarters where it could prove harmful to Giovanni.'

'Have you told my father this?'

Giulia smiled. 'If it came from me he would feel I was

jealous of Giovanni. He knows that I am aware of the affection between them.'

'Yet he should know,' said Lucrezia.

Giulia was well pleased. It was easy to lead Lucrezia the way in which one wanted her to go.

'Indeed he should.' Giulia looked out of the window to hide the sly smile playing about her lips. 'If it came from you it would carry weight.'

Lucrezia rose. 'Then I shall tell him. I shall tell him at once. He would be distressed if aught should happen to prevent Giovanni's marriage.'

'You are wise. I have it from a very reliable source that his future father-in-law is considering the annulment of the betrothal, and that if Giovanni does not claim his bride within the next few months another husband will be found for her.'

'I will go to my father at once,' said Lucrezia. 'He should know of this.'

Giulia followed her. 'I will accompany you,' she said, 'and if the Holy Father feels disposed to see me, there I shall be.'

Alexander wept as he embraced his son.

'Father,' cried Giovanni, 'if you love me as you say, how can you bear that I should leave you?'

'I love you so much, my son, that I can let you go.'

'Could not there be a more worthwhile marriage for me here in Rome?'

'No, my son. We have the future to think of. You forget you are Duke of Gandia and that when you are married to Maria you will have the might of Spain behind you. Do not underestimate the importance of this tie with the Spanish royal house.'

Giovanni sighed, but the Pope put his arm about him. 'Come, see what wedding presents I have for you and your bride.'

Giovanni looked almost sullenly at the furs and jewels, and the chests which were decorated with beautiful paintings. In the last weeks all the best jewellers of Rome had been busy buying the best stones, and resetting them in exquisite ornaments for the Duke of Gandia. Alexander opened a

chest and showed his son sables and ermine and necklaces
of pearls and rubies until he made the young man's eyes
glisten with eagerness to wear them.

'You see, my son, you will go to Spain in all the splendour
of a Prince. Does not that delight you?'

Giovanni admitted grudgingly that it did. 'But,' he added,
'there is still much I regret leaving.'

The Pope embraced him. 'Be assured, my beloved, that you
do not hate going more than I hate to see you go.' Alexander
put his face close to his son's. 'Marry your Maria,' he said; 'get
her with child. Get yourself an heir . . . and then, why should
you not come back to Rome? Rest assured none here will
scold you for not remaining once you have done your duty.'

Giovanni smiled. 'I will do it, Father,' he said.

'And remember, Giovanni, while you are in Spain you must
behave as a Spaniard.'

'They are so solemn.'

'On ceremonious occasions only. I ask nothing more of you
but this, my dearest boy: Marry, get an heir and conduct
yourself in a manner not to offend the Court of Spain. Apart
from that . . . do as you will. Enjoy your life. Your father
would have you happy.'

Giovanni kissed his father's hand and left him to join
Djem who was waiting for him.

They rode out into the City on one of their adventures, more
gay, more bizarre than ever. Giovanni felt he must cram as
much excitement as possible into the short time left to him.

When his son had gone, the Pope sent for two men: Ginès
Fira and Mossen Jayme Pertusa.

'You are making your preparations?' asked the Pope.

'We are ready to leave for Spain at a moment's notice, Most
Holy Lord,' answered Ginès.

'That is well. Keep close to my son and report to me everything that happens to him; however insignificant, I wish to
hear of it.'

'We are your servants, Holiness.'

'If I should discover that you have withheld any detail—
however small – I shall excommunicate you, and you may
look forward to eternal damnation.'

The men grew pale. Then they fell to their knees and swore that, as far as it was in their power, they would report every detail of the life of the Duke of Gandia; they had no wish on Earth but to serve his Holiness.

Lucrezia had been riding out to Monte Mario to watch the falcons and, as she returned to the Palace, a slave ran to her to tell her that Madonna Adriana was looking for her.

Lucrezia made her way to the apartment where she found Adriana somewhat disturbed.

'The Holy Father wishes you to go to him,' she said. 'There is news of some sort.'

Lucrezia's eyes widened and her lips fell slightly apart, a characteristic expression which, with her receding chin, made her look more like a girl of ten than one approaching fourteen.

'Bad news?' she asked, fear creeping into her eyes.

'It is news from Spain,' said Adriana. 'I know nothing else.'

News from Spain must involve Giovanni. Indeed during the last months no one had been able to forget Giovanni. Alexander was preoccupied at all times by thoughts of his beloved son.

When bad news came from Spain he shut himself away and wept, and he would be quite unhappy for perhaps a day – which was a long time for him to grieve; then he would brighten and would say: 'One cannot believe all one hears. Such a magnificent Prince must naturally have enemies. '

The news had always been bad, so Lucrezia was fearful as she heard of the summons to go to her father.

She said: 'I will take off my habit and go to him at once.'

'Do so,' said Adriana; 'he is impatient for you.'

She went to her apartments and Giulia followed her there. Giulia was pleased because she had regained all her old power over the Pope. She had learned that she must shrug aside his light preference for Spanish nuns or Moorish slaves; such desires passed. Lucrezia had told her of her mother's attitude towards her father's lighter loves; Vannozza had laughed indulgently, and he had always cared for Vannozza; he had given her two husbands, and Canale was treated as a member of the family; even Cesare had some regard for him out of respect for their mother. And look how the Pope had loved Vannozza's children, showering on them such loving care that could not have been exceeded even if he had been able to marry Vannozza and they were his legitimate offspring.

Lucrezia was right; and Giulia was determined that her little Laura should be treated with the same loving care. Alexander certainly doted on the little girl, and as a sign of his love of her mother had promised to bestow the Cardinal's hat on Alessandro Farnese. Her family could not tell her often enough how they admired her and depended on her.

But now Giulia wondered about this news which the Pope wished to impart to his daughter. In the old days she would have been rather piqued that he had not told her first, but now she was able to adapt herself and hide any resentment she felt.

'My father awaits me,' said Lucrezia as her slave helped her to take off her riding habit.

'I wonder what fresh trouble there has been,' said Giulia.

'It may not be trouble,' said Lucrezia. 'It could be good news.'

Giulia laughed at her. 'You do not change at all,' she said. 'You have been married nearly a year and yet you are the same as you were when we first met.'

Lucrezia was not listening; she was thinking of all the preparations previous to Giovanni's departure. She knew how important Giovanni was to Alexander; she knew that he had gone to the utmost trouble to ensure that his son should please the Spanish Court; she knew about the Bishop of Oristano, into whose care the Pope had put Giovanni from the moment he stepped on to Spanish soil; she knew of the orders which had been issued to Ginès Fira and Pertusa. Poor men, how could they prevent Giovanni from disobeying his father's orders!

And poor Giovanni! Not to go out at night. Not to play at dicing. To keep his wife company and sleep with her every night until a child was conceived. To wear gloves all the time he was at sea because salt was harmful to the hands, and in Spain a nobleman was expected to have soft white hands.

And Giovanni, of course, had disobeyed his father. Letters came from Fira and Pertusa telling of these matters, and those letters plunged the Pope into gloom – temporary gloom, it was true – before he roused himself and said that in spite of everything he knew his dearest son would do all that was expected of him.

There had been gloomy letters from Giovanni. His marriage had taken place at Barcelona, and the King and Queen of Spain had been present, which was a great honour and showed in what esteem they held Maria; but wrote Giovanni, he had no taste for his wife; she was dull and her face was too long; she repelled him.

Lucrezia tried not to think of that day the letter came from Fira and Pertusa saying that Giovanni had refused to consummate the marriage and that, instead of sleeping with his bride, he took a few companions and prowled about the town at night looking for young girls to seduce or rape.

This was terrible, for if the Pope made excuses for his son, the King of Spain would not, and Giovanni's bride was of the royal house and must not be humiliated thus.

For the first time Alexander wrote angrily to Giovanni, and bade Cesare write on the same lines to his brother; this Cesare was only too eager to do.

Lucrezia was saddened by this state of affairs. She knew that her father was as worried as he possibly could be; it was not as much as most parents would have been, of course, but Lucrezia loved him so dearly that she could not bear to think of his being even mildly distressed.

She had wept in his presence and he had embraced her and kissed her passionately. 'My darling, my darling,' he had cried. 'You would never hurt your father in this way, my sweet, sweet girl.'

'Never, Father,' she had assured him. 'I would die rather than hurt you.'

He had held her against him, called her his dear, dear love, and he could scarcely bear her to be out of his sight for a whole day.

But the storms passed and Alexander was soon his gay benign self again, for there was a letter from Giovanni declaring that by writing as he had his father had caused him great unhappiness – the greatest he had ever suffered.

At which Alexander wept and reproached himself.

He read Giovanni's letter aloud to Lucrezia, having sent for her on receipt of it.

' "I cannot understand how you can believe in such sinister reports which were written by malicious people who have no regard for the truth. . . ." '

'You see?' Alexander had cried jubilantly. 'We have misjudged him.'

'Then,' said Lucrezia, 'Fira and Pertusa have lied?'

Lights of fear came into the grey-blue eyes to disturb their mildness. She was afraid for those two men who had done, she knew, what the Holy Father had asked of them, and who might have to be punished to prove Giovanni right.

Alexander waved his hand. 'No matter. No matter,' he said. He did not want to discuss the two men whom he trusted to tell him the truth; he did not want to have to admit that he knew Giovanni's words to be lies. It was so much pleasanter to make believe that they were true.

'His marriage has been more than consummated,' cried the Pope, continuing to read the letter. He burst out laughing. 'Indeed it has. I know my Giovanni!'

Alexander went on reading:

' "If I have prowled at night, oh my Father, I did so with my father-in-law, Enrico Enriques, and other friends of His Most Catholic Majesty. It is the custom to take a stroll by night in Barcelona." '

Then Alexander had walked about the apartment, talking about Giovanni, telling Lucrezia that he was always certain that his children would never fail him; but Lucrezia had been conscious of an uneasiness. And so, when this message came, she was afraid that there was further alarming news about her brother.

When she reached her father's presence she knew that she had been worrying unduly; she was taken into his arms and kissed fervently.

'My dearest daughter,' cried the Pope; 'here is the best possible news. We shall celebrate this with a banquet this very night. Listen to what I have to say, my darling: Your brother is soon to be a father. What do you say to that, Lucrezia? What do you say to that?'

She clasped her arms about him. 'Oh Father, I am so happy; I can think of no words to express my joy.'

'As I knew you would be. Let me look at you. Oh, how your eyes shine and sparkle! How beautiful you are, my daughter! I knew the joy this would give you; that is why I would let no other impart the news to you. I would tell none until you knew first.'

'I rejoice for Giovanni,' said Lucrezia. 'I know how happy this will make him; and I rejoice also for your Holiness, because I believe the pleasure it gives you is even greater than that which it will bring to Giovanni.'

'So my little daughter cares deeply for her father?'

'How could it be otherwise?' demanded Lucrezia, as though astonished that he should ask.

'I loved you dearly since the first day when I held you in my arms, a red-faced baby with a gleam of silvery down on your head; and I have loved you steadily since. My Lucrezia . . . my little one . . . who would never willingly cause me a moment's anxiety!'

She took his hand and kissed it. ' 'Tis true, Father,' she said. 'You know me well.'

He put his arm about her and led her to a chair.

'Now,' he said, 'we will see that all Rome rejoices in this news. You and Giulia must put your lovely heads together and devise a banquet to outdo all banquets.'

Lucrezia was smiling when she returned to her apartments. She was surprised to find her husband there.

'My lord?' she said.

He laughed. 'It is strange to see me here, I know,' he answered grimly. 'It should not be, Lucrezia. You are my wife, you know.'

Sudden fear seized her. She had never seen Sforza thus. There was something in his eyes which she did not understand.

She waited apprehensively. 'You have been with his Holiness?' he asked.

'Yes.'

'I guessed it. Your radiant looks tell me and I know how matters stand between you.'

'Between my father and myself?'

'The whole of Rome knows that he dotes upon you.'

'The whole of Rome knows that he is my father.'

Sforza laughed; it was an unpleasant laugh, but mildly so; everything was mild about Sforza. 'It is because all Rome knows him to be your father that this affection . . . this more than doting . . . is so strange,' he countered.

She stared at him, but already he had turned and was striding out of the apartment.

Cesare came to the Palace of Santa Maria in Portico. He was in a strange mood, and Lucrezia was unsure what it implied. Was he angry? Certainly he must be. Giovanni was now to be a legitimate father, and that was something, Cesare would be telling himself, that he could never be. How sad, thought Lucrezia, that the happiness of her father over Giovanni's wife's pregnancy must be a further cross for Cesare to bear.

She knew that he had never forgotten the vow he had made before the Madonna to escape from the Church; and she knew that he was as determined now to fulfil it as he had been when he had made it.

So now when he strode in, she wondered what could be the meaning of that glittering expression in the eyes, that tight tension of the lips.

She had heard rumours of his life at the universities. It was said that no vice was too degrading for Cesare to indulge in, if only experimentally. It was said that his father's money and influence had enabled him to set up a little court of his own and that he ruled his courtiers like a despotic monarch; one look was enough to subdue them and, if any failed to do his bidding, accidents quickly befell those people.

'Cesare,' said Lucrezia, 'has anything happened to anger you?'

He took her by the neck and bent back her head. He kissed her lips lightly. 'Those beautiful eyes see too much,' he murmured. 'I want you to come riding with me.'

'Yes, Cesare; with the utmost pleasure. Where shall we ride?'

'Along by the river mayhap. Through the city. Let the people see us together. They enjoy it. And why should they not? You are pleasant enough to look at, sister.'

'And you are the handsomest man in Italy.'

He laughed. 'What,' he said, 'in my priest's robes!'

'You add dignity to them.. No priest ever looked like you.'

'A fact which doubtless makes all the Bishops and Cardinals rejoice mightily.'

He is in a good mood, she thought. I was mistaken.

As they rode out another rider joined them. This was a lovely red-haired girl, magnificently, indeed over-dressed, glittering with jewels, her long red hair falling about her shoulders.

'Fiametta knows you well, sister,' said Cesare, looking from the red-haired woman of the world to the golden innocence of Lucrezia. 'She declares that I speak your name far too frequently when I am in her company.'

'We are a devoted family,' Lucrezia explained to the girl.

'Indeed it is so,' said Fiametta. 'The whole of Rome talks of your devotion – one to another; and it is hard to say who loves Madonna Lucrezia more, her brothers or her father.'

'It is comforting to be so loved,' said Lucrezia simply.

'Come,' said Cesare, 'we will ride together.'

He rode between them, the sardonic smile playing about his lips as they went. People in the streets walked past them with lowered eyes but, when they had passed, stopped to stare after them.

Cesare's reputation was already such that none dared give him a hostile or critical look which he might see; but they could not help staring at him, riding through the streets with his sister and the other woman.

Cesare knew full well that he was shocking them by riding in daylight with one of the most notorious courtesans in Rome together with his sister; he knew that an account of this would be taken to his father and that the Pope would be displeased. It was what Cesare intended. Let the people look; let them gossip.

Fiametta was enjoying the jaunt. She was delighted that the citizens should know that she was the latest mistress of Cesare Borgia. It was a fillip to her reputation; and the longer she remained in favour with him, the better, for surely that must show that she was superior in her profession to her fellows.

They rode to the ancient Colosseum which never failed to fascinate Lucrezia and yet to fill her with horror as she thought of the Christians who had been thrown to the lions and killed for their faith.

'Oh,' she cried, 'it is so beautiful, and yet . . . disturbing. They say that if one comes here at night and waits among the ruins one hears the cries of the martyrs and the roar of the wild beasts.'

Fiametta laughed. ' 'Tis a tale that is told.'

Lucrezia turned questioningly to Cesare.

'Fiametta is right,' he told her. 'What you would doubtless hear would be someone taking away the stones and marbles to build him a house. These stories of ghosts are told in order to keep those away from the Colosseum who might disturb the thieves.'

'Perhaps that is what it is. Now I no longer feel alarmed.'

'But I pray you,' said Cesare, 'do not come here at night, sister. It is not for such as you to do so.'

'Would you come here at night?' Lucrezia asked Fiametta.

Cesare answered for her: 'At night the Colosseum is the haunt of robbers and prostitutes.'

Fiametta flushed slightly, but she had learnt to show no anger to Cesare.

Lucrezia, seeing her discomfiture and understanding its cause – for she realized to what profession Fiametta belonged – said quickly: 'Pope Paul built his palace from these blocks of travertine. Is it not wonderful to contemplate that all those years ago the same marble, the same stone, was used and, although all the people who built it and lived in it are dead, fourteen hundred years later houses can still be built of the same material?'

'Is she not enchanting, my little sister?' said Cesare, and threw a kiss to her.

They galloped among the ruins for a while and then turned

their horses back towards the Palace of Santa Maria in Portico.

Cesare told Fiametta that he would come to visit her later that day and went into Lucrezia's palace with her.

'Ah,' he said, when they were alone – and whenever Cesare visited Lucrezia, her attendants always understood that he wished to be alone with her – 'now you are a little shocked, confess it, sister.'

'The people stared at us, Cesare.'

'And you do not like poor Fiametta?'

'I liked her. She is very beautiful . . . but she is a courtesan, is she not; and should she have ridden in our company through the streets?'

'Why not?'

'Perhaps because you are an Archbishop.'

Cesare brought his fist down upon his thigh in a well remembered gesture.

'It is precisely because I am an Archbishop that I rode through the streets with that red-headed harlot.'

'Our father says . . .'

'I know what our father says. Have your mistresses – ten, twenty, a hundred, if you must. Amuse yourself as you will . . . in private. But in public remember, always remember that you are a son of Holy Church. By all the saints, Lucrezia, I have sworn that I will escape from the Church, and I will behave in such a way that our father will be forced to free me.'

'Oh, Cesare, you will make him so unhappy.'

'And what of the unhappiness he causes me?'

'It is for your own advancement.'

'You listen to him rather than to me. I see that, sister.'

'Oh no, Cesare, no. I would have you know that if there were aught I could do to free you from the Church, willingly would I do it.'

'Yet you grieve for your father. You say with such sympathy: "He would be made unhappy." Not a word about my unhappiness.'

'I know you are unhappy, dearest brother, and I would do everything in my power to put an end to that unhappiness.'

'Would you, Lucrezia? Would you?'

'Anything . . . anything on Earth.'

He took her by the shoulder and smiled down at her. 'One day I may ask you to redeem that promise.'

'I shall be waiting. I shall be ready, Cesare.'

He kissed her ardently.

'You soothe me,' he said. 'Did you not always do so? Beloved sister, there is no one on Earth whom I could love as I love you.'

'And I love you too, Cesare. Is that not enough to make us happy, even if we have other trials to bear?'

'No,' he cried, his eyes ablaze. 'I know my destiny. It is to be a King . . . a conqueror. Do you doubt that?'

'No, Cesare, I do not. I see you always as a King and a conqueror.'

'Dear Lucrezia, when we were riding with Fiametta you looked at those old ruins and you thought of days long ago. There is one man glorious in our history. He conquered great countries. He lived before the Colosseum was built and he is the greatest man who – as yet – has come out of Rome. You know of whom I speak.'

'Of Julius Caesar,' she said.

'A great Roman, a great conqueror. I picture him, crossing the Rubicon and knowing that all Italy lay at his feet. That was forty-nine years before Christ was born, and yet there has never been another like him – as yet. You know what his motto was, do you not? *Aut Caesar, aut nullus.* Lucrezia, from this moment I adopt that as mine.' His eyes were brilliant with megalomania; he was so certain of his greatness that he made her believe him. 'But see, did they not call me Cesare! That was no mere chance. There was one great Caesar. There shall be another.'

'You are right!' she cried. 'I am sure of it. In years to come people will talk of you as they do of great Julius. You will be a great general. . . .'

Now his expression was ugly.

'And my father will make a Churchman of me!'

'But you will be Pope, Cesare. One day you will be Pope.'

He stamped his foot with fury. 'A Pope rules in shadow; a King in the full light of day. I do not wish to be Pope. I wish to be King. I wish to unite the whole of Italy under my banner and rule . . . myself and none other. That is the task of a King, not a Pope.'

'Our father must release you.'

'He will not. He refuses. I have begged. I have implored. But no, I am for the Church, he insists. One of us must be. Giovanni has his long-faced mare in Barcelona. Goffredo has his harlot of Naples. And I . . . I am to be wedded to the Church. Lucrezia, was there ever such crass folly? I feel murderous when I contemplate it.'

'Murderous, Cesare! Against him!'

Cesare put his face against hers. 'Yes,' he said grimly. 'I feel murderous . . . even towards him.'

'He must be made to understand. He is the best father in the world, and if he but knew your feelings . . . oh Cesare, he would understand them. He would see that something was done.'

'I have explained my feelings until I am weary. He loses all his benign looks then. I never saw a man so set on one thing as our father is when I talk of leaving the Church. He is determined that I shall stay.'

'Cesare, what you have said causes me much pain. I cannot be happy knowing that you harbour such thoughts of our father.'

'You are too soft, too gentle. You must not be so, child. How do you think the world will use you if you continue so?'

'I had not thought of how the world would use me. I think of you, dear brother, and how it has used you. And I cannot bear that there should be ill-feeling between you and our father. And Cesare . . . oh, my brother . . . you spoke of murder!'

Cesare laughed aloud. Then he was tender. 'Set your fears at rest, *bambina*. I would not murder him. What folly! From him come all our blessings.'

'Do not forget it, Cesare. Do not forget it.'

'I am a man who is full of rage, but not of folly,' he answered. 'I revenge myself in my own way. Our father insists that I go into the Church, and I insist on showing how unsuitable I am for that calling. That is why I roam the streets with my red-headed courtesan – in the hope of making our father realize that he cannot force me to continue this life.'

'But Cesare, what of the rumours we have heard concerning your marriage with a Princess of Aragon?'

'Rumours,' he said wearily. 'Nothing more.'

'Yet our father seemed to be considering this at one time.'

'It was diplomacy to consider it, child. Naples suggested it in order to alarm the Sforzas of Milan, and our father encouraged it for political reasons.'

'But he gave such a warm welcome to the ambassador, and everyone knew that he had arrived here to discuss a possible marriage between you and the Princess.'

'Diplomacy. Diplomacy. Waste no time on considering it. I do not. My only hope is to show our father how unsuitable I am for the Church, or to find a way of forcing him to release me. But there is little hope. Our father has determined to make me a Cardinal.'

'A Cardinal, Cesare! So that is the reason for your anger.' She shook her head. 'I am thinking of all those who bring presents to me and to Giulia because they hope we will influence our father in giving them the Cardinal's hat. And you . . . on whom he longs to bestow it . . . want none of it. How strange life is!'

Cesare was clenching and unclenching his hands. 'I fear,' he said, 'that once I am in my Cardinal's robes there will be no escape.'

'Cesare, my brother, you will escape,' she told him.

'I am determined,' said the Pope, 'that you shall become a Cardinal.'

Cesare had once more broached the subject of release and because he felt that his sister might have a softening effect on their father, he had insisted that she accompany him into his presence.

'Father, I implore you to release me from the Church before you take this step.'

'Cesare, are you a fool? What man in Rome would refuse such honours?'

'I am as no other man in Rome. I am myself and myself alone. I refuse this . . . this questionable honour.'

'You can say this . . . before Almighty God!'

Cesare shook his head impatiently. 'Father, you know, do you not, that once I am a Cardinal it will be more difficult to release me from my vows?'

'My son, there is no question of releasing you from your vows. Let us discuss this no more. Lucrezia, my love, bring your lute. I should like to hear you sing that new song of Serafino's.'

'Yes, Father,' said Lucrezia.

But Cesare would not allow her to sing and, although the Pope regarded his son with mild reproach, he did nothing more.

'You cannot make me a Cardinal, Father,' said Cesare triumphantly. 'I am your son, but your illegitimate son, and as you know full well no man can become a Cardinal unless he is of legitimate birth.'

The Pope brushed aside his argument as though it were not more than a wasp which provided a temporary irritation.

'Now I understand your anxiety, my son. It is for this reason that you have been reluctant. You should have spoken of your fears earlier.'

'So, Father, you see that it is impossible.'

You . . . a Borgia to talk of the impossible! Nonsense, my dear boy, nothing is impossible. A little difficulty, I'll admit; but have no fears, I have thought of ways of overcoming such.'

'Father, I implore you to listen to me.'

'I would rather listen to Lucrezia's singing.'

'I will be heard! I will be heard!' shrieked Cesare.

Lucrezia began to tremble. She had heard him shout thus before, but never in their father's presence.

'I think, my son,' said the Pope coolly, 'that you are overwrought. It is due to riding in the sun in company unfitted to your state. I would suggest you refrain from such conduct which, I assure you, my dearest boy, brings distress to those who love you, but could bring greater harm to yourself.'

Cesare stood, biting his lips, clenching and unclenching his hands.

There was a moment of fear when Lucrezia thought he was about to strike their father. The Pope sat, smiling benignly, refusing to accept this as a major difference between them.

Then Cesare seemed to regain his control; he bowed with dignity and murmured: 'Father, I crave leave to depart.'

'It is granted, my son,' said Alexander gently.

Cesare went, and Lucrezia stared unhappily after him.

Then she, who was sitting on a stool at her father's feet, felt his hand on her head.

'Come, my love, the song! It is a pleasant one and sounds best on your sweet lips.'

As she sang, the Pope caressed his daughter's golden hair, and they both temporarily forgot the unpleasant scene which Cesare had created; they both found it very easy to forget when it was comforting to do so.

In the Pope's private apartments Cardinals Pallavicini and Orsini sat with him.

'A simple matter,' said the Pope, smiling benignly, 'and I am sure it will present no difficulty to you . . . this little formality of proving that he who is known as Cesare Borgia is of legitimate birth.'

The Cardinals were astonished, for the Pope had openly acknowledged Cesare as his son.

'But, Most Holy Lord, this is surely an impossibility.'

'How so?' asked the Pope with bland surprise.

Orsini and Pallavicini looked at each other in bewilderment. Then Orsini spoke. 'Holy Father, if Cesare Borgia is your son, how could it be that he is of legitimate birth?'

Alexander smiled from Orsini to Pallavicini as though they were two simple children.

'Cesare Borgia,' he said, 'is the son of Vannozza Catanei, a woman of Rome. At the time of his birth she was a married woman. That dispenses with Cesare's illegitimacy, for a child born in wedlock is legitimate, is he not?'

'Holiness,' murmured Pallavicini, 'we were unaware that the lady was married at the time of his birth. It is generally believed that it was not until after the birth of her daughter Lucrezia that she married Giorgio di Croce.'

'It is true that the marriage with Giorgio di Croce took place after the birth of Lucrezia, but the lady was married before that. Her husband was a certain Domenico d'Arignano, who was an official of the Church.'

The Cardinals bowed. 'Then that proves Cesare Borgia to be legitimate, Holiness.'

'It does indeed,' said the Pope, smiling at them. 'Let a bull be made stating his parentage and his legitimacy.' His expression was regretful; it saddened him to deny his son; yet such denial there must be in the name of ambition. He added: 'Since I had taken this young man under my patronage I allowed him to adopt the name of Borgia.'

The Cardinals murmured: 'We will immediately obey your wishes, Most Holy Father.'

But when they had left him the Pope immediately set about drawing up another bull in which he declared that he was the father of Cesare Borgia. It saddened him a little that this bull must be a secret one – for a while.

Cesare raged up and down Lucrezia's apartment, and in vain did she try to soothe him.

'Not content,' cried Cesare, 'with forcing me into the Church my father now allows it to be said that I am the son of a certain Domenico d'Arignano. And who is Domenico d'Arignano, I beg you tell me. Who has ever heard of Domenico d'Arignano?'

'They will hear of him now,' said Lucrezia gently. 'The whole world will hear of him. His claim to fame will be that he was named as your father.'

'Insult after insult!' cried Cesare. 'Humiliation after humiliation! How much longer must I endure this state of affairs?'

'My dearest brother, our father but wishes to advance you. In his opinion, it is necessary that you become a Cardinal, and this is the only way in which he can make you one.'

'So he denies me!'

'It is only for a while.'

'Never,' cried Cesare, beating his fists on his chest, 'will I forget that my father has denied me.'

Meanwhile Alexander had called together a Consistory, that Cesare might be declared legitimate.

He had chosen this moment because so many had left Rome. The weather was hot and sultry and there had been reports of plague in various quarters. When pestilence crept into the city those who could invariably made an excuse to escape to their estates and vineyards in the country. This was such a time.

Alexander knew that there had been a great deal of opposition among the Cardinals on account of the favours he had bestowed on his family and friends; the matters he had to lay before them now concerned not only his son but the brother of his mistress, for although he had promised Giulia that her brother should have his Cardinal's hat it had not yet been bestowed upon him.

There were few Cardinals present at the Consistory, which pleased Alexander. Better to deal with a few opponents than many. But those who were present were suspicious because they understood that this was a preliminary move and they feared what was to come. Alexander carried nepotism too far, they said to one another. It would not be long before every man in any position of importance was one put there to serve the Pope.

And their suspicions increased when Alexander folded his beautiful hands, smiled his most benign smile and declared: 'My Lord Cardinals, make the necessary preparations. To-morrow we elect the new Cardinals.'

Then all was clear. Cesare had been declared legitimate that he might be made a Cardinal.

There was a faint murmur throughout the assembly, and many eyes were turned to Cardinal Carafa who had on previous occasions shown himself bold enough to oppose the Pope.

'Most Holy Lord,' said Carafa, 'has your Holiness given due consideration to the usefulness of making these nominations?'

Again that bland smile. 'The question of creating these Cardinals concerns me alone.'

'Holiness,' said a voice from the assembly, 'there are many among us who feel that it is not necessary to make new Cardinals at this time.'

The smile disappeared from the face of the Pope, and for a moment all those assembled caught a glimpse of an Alexander who usually remained hidden.

Carafa boldly went on: 'The point is, Holiness, that we know some of those names which you intend to propose, and we do not think they are suitable for the office, nor would we wish them to be our colleagues.'

This was a direct reference to Cesare's reputation and a reminder that he had been seen in the city in the company of the courtesan, Fiametta. Cesare had deliberately flaunted his friendship with the woman, anticipating a scene such as this.

It was characteristic of Alexander that his anger should be not against Cesare but the Cardinals.

He seemed to grow in stature. The Cardinals trembled before him, for there was a legend in Rome that no man of Alexander's age could possess such virility, such amazingly good health, unless he was superhuman. Those Cardinals felt that legend to be true as now their Pope faced them in his unaccustomed anger.

'You must learn who Alexander VI is,' he cried. 'And if you persist in your intransigence I shall annoy you all by making as many new Cardinals as I wish. You will never drive me from Rome, and any who try to, or oppose me in any way, will be very foolish men. You should really ponder on how foolish they will be.'

There was a short silence while Alexander looked angrily at the crestfallen Cardinals before him.

Then with the utmost dignity he went on: 'Now we will nominate the new Cardinals.'

And when the assembly saw that at the head of the list were the names of Cesare Borgia and Alessandro Farnese, and that all the thirteen proposed were men who could be trusted to work for the Pope against his enemies, they realized that there was nothing they dared do but agree to their election.

Alexander smiled at them, and the benevolent look had returned to his face.

When the Cardinals had left the Pope's presence they discussed the situation.

Della Rovere, who always looked upon himself as a leader, recovered his belligerence although in the presence of the Pope he had been as subdued as the rest.

His one-time enemy Ascanio Sforza supported him. How long were they to endure the outrageous nepotism of the Pope? they asked each other. Not content with making a Cardinal of his illegitimate son, he had done the same for his mistress's brother. All the new nominees were his pawns. Soon there would be scarcely a man in an influential position to raise his voice against Alexander.

And what was Alexander's policy? To enrich his own family and friends? It seemed so.

There were rumours in the city that men were dying mysteriously. Cesare Borgia's evil reputation was growing; it was now said that he was interested in and made a study of the art of poisoning; and that he had many malignant recipes which came from the Spanish Moors. But from whom would Cesare have learned this lore? From his father?

'Beware of the Borgias!' Those words were becoming more and more frequently heard throughout the city.

Alexander was aware of what was happening and, fearing a schism, he acted with his usual vigour. He made Ascanio Sforza almost a prisoner in the Vatican; and seeing what had happened to Sforza, della Rovere made haste to leave Rome.

Lucrezia's husband apprehensively watched the growing unrest. His relative and patron, Ascanio Sforza, was powerless in the Vatican. Moreover Giovanni Sforza knew that the Pope was less pleased with the marriage of his daughter than he had been, and that already he was on the look-out for a bridegroom who could bring him more profit.

The marriage had never been consummated; the dowry had never been paid. What sort of marriage was this?

He was beset by fears on all sides. He could not sleep easily for he was sure that he was spied on in the Vatican. He was afraid of the Orsinis who were allies of Naples and had always been the enemies of Milan. Would they, he wondered, now that he was out of favour at the Vatican, feel it to be a good opportunity to dispose of him? If he wandered across the bridge of St Angelo, would they come sweeping down from Monte Giordano and run a knife through his body? And if they did, who would care?

Giovanni Sforza was a man who was sorry for himself; he always had been. His relatives cared little for him – as did the new connexions he had acquired through his marriage.

His little bride – she seemed a gentle creature, but he must not forget that she was one of them – was a Borgia, and who would trust a Borgia?

He wished though, during that time, that he and Lucrezia had been husband and wife in truth. She had a sweet and innocent face, and he believed he could have trusted her.

But it was too late to think of that now.

There was a great spectacle taking place in Rome at this time. This was the departure of little Goffredo for Naples where he was to marry Sanchia of Aragon.

Cesare and Lucrezia watched their little brother set out for Naples; he was accompanied by an old friend of Cesare's, Virginio Orsini, who had made the boy's first year at Monte Giordano tolerable, and who was now Captain-General of the Aragonese army. Goffredo's tutor also accompanied the party to Naples; this was Don Ferrando Dixer, a Spaniard; and the Pope to show he did not forget the country to which he belonged, entrusted two caskets of jewels – presents for the bride and bridegroom – to this Spaniard.

And so the auburn-haired Goffredo, aged eleven, rode out of Rome to his bride, to be made Prince of Squillace and Count of Coriata and to receive the order of the Ermine, the motto of which was 'Better die than betray.'

There was one who watched the departure with mingling pride and sorrow. The maternal Vannozza's dream had come true. Her little Goffredo was accepted as the son of Alexander; he was to be a Prince, and she was happy.

But there were times when she wished that she were a humble

Roman mother with her children about her; there were times when she would have given up her vineyards and her house with the water cistern to be that.

Giovanni Sforza's anxiety was increased by the new friendship between Naples and the Vatican which the marriage of Goffredo and Sanchia must foster.

He was afraid to show himself in the streets for fear of enemies of his family; he was afraid of enemies within the Vatican circle. He had a beautiful wife but he was not allowed to live with her; he was lord of Pesaro, a town on the Adriatic coast which seemed to him, particularly at this time, a very peaceful spot, shut away from all strife by the mountains which protected it and blessed by the cool waters of the Foglia River. With the sea on one side and the mountains on the other Pesaro offered a freshness in contrast with the fetid air of Rome; and Sforza longed for Pesaro.

He sought audience of the Pope, because he felt he could no longer stay in Rome.

'Well, Giovanni Sforza,' said Alexander, 'what have you to say to me?'

'Holy Father, everyone in Rome believes that Your Holiness has entered into agreement with the King of Naples who is an enemy of the state of Milan. If this is so, my position is a difficult one since, as a captain of the Church, a post in which through your benevolence I have been installed, I am in the pay of Your Holiness, and also in that of Milan. I do not see how I can serve two masters without falling out with one of them. Would Your Holiness, out of your goodness, define my position, that I may serve you as I am paid to do yet not become an enemy of my own blood?'

Alexander laughed. 'You take too much interest in politics, Giovanni Sforza. You would be wise to serve those who pay you.'

Giovanni writhed before the calm gaze of the Pope and wished with all his heart that he had never agreed to marry with the Borgias.

'Your questions are answered, my son,' continued Alexander. 'Leave me now, and I beg of you do not concern yourself overmuch with politics. They do not touch your duty.'

Giovanni went away and immediately wrote to his uncle, Ludovico of Milan, telling him of what he had said to the Pope and declaring that he would sooner have eaten the straw under his body than have entered into the marriage. He was casting himself upon his uncle's mercy.

But Ludovico was not prepared to offer him asylum. Ludovico was intently watching the growth of the friendship between Naples and the Vatican; he was not convinced that the bond between those two was of such importance as might be thought in Naples; the Pope was wily and Ludovico preferred to remain aloof.

Giovanni was impatient.

The plague was increasing throughout Rome, and his fears increased with it. In the position he held at the Vatican he was free to leave Rome if he wished.

One day, surrounded by some of his men, he rode out of the city bound for Pesaro.

Lucrezia did not miss him in the least. She had seen little of him, and it was only at special functions that they had appeared together.

Giulia laughed at her as they played with Giulia's little daughter Laura, who was now nearly two years old.

'One would think you had gained a lover rather than lost one,' said Giulia.

'A lover! He was never that.' Lucrezia was wistful. One grew up, and she was fourteen now. Giulia had been fourteen when she had become Alexander's mistress.

'Well, do not show your pleasure in his departure quite so openly,' advised Giulia.

'Is my Holy Father coming to see me?' asked little Laura, tugging at her mother's skirts.

Giulia picked up the child and smothered her with kisses. 'Soon, I doubt not, my darling. He could not stay away long from his little Laura, could he?'

Lucrezia watched them, still wistful, thinking of those days when the same father had delighted other children whose nursery he had visited. Alexander – as tender a father to little

Laura as he had been to her and Cesare, Giovanni and Goffredo – remained as young as he had been when she and her brothers were in the nursery. Now they were no longer children, and it seemed that wonderful and exciting things happened to them all except herself. She had been married, but hers was no real marriage; and she could be glad because her husband had now run away. Whether he had run away from the plague or from her, it mattered not. Whatever he ran away from he was a coward. Yes, she was sure he was a coward.

She had dreamed of a lover as magnificent as her father, as handsome as her brother Giovanni, as exciting as Cesare – and they had given her a small man, a widower, a cold man who made no protest because the marriage was not consummated; they had married her to a coward who ran away from the plague and did not attempt to take her with him.

Not that she wanted to go. But, she told herself, if Giovanni Sforza had been the sort of man who insisted on taking me, I should have wanted to go.

'Giulia,' she said, 'do you think that, now Giovanni Sforza has left me, my father will arrange a divorce?'

'It will depend,' said Giulia, smoothing her daughter's long fair hair from her forehead, 'on how useful the Holy Father considers the marriage.'

'Of what use could it be . . . now?'

Giulia left her little daughter and going to Lucrezia laid her hand on her shoulder.

'No use at all,' she said. 'Depend upon it the marriage will be dissolved and then you will have a fine husband . . . a husband who will declare he will have none of this marriage which is no marriage. Moreover, you grow up, Lucrezia. You are old enough now for marriage. Oh yes, it will be a handsome husband this time. A true marriage.'

Lucrezia smiled. 'Let us wash each other's hair,' she said; and Giulia agreed. It was a favourite occupation, for their golden hair must be washed every three days because after that time it darkened and lost something of its bright colour, so they spent a great deal of time washing each other's hair.

And while they washed they talked of the handsome husband who would be Lucrezia's when the Pope had freed her from

Giovanni Sforza. Lucrezia saw herself in a gown of crimson velvet sewn with pearls. She was kneeling on a cushion at the feet of her father and saying: 'I will with a good heart.' And the man who knelt beside her was a shadowy figure, but he combined the presence of her father and the qualities she so admired in her brothers.

It seemed to her as though it were a Borgia who knelt beside her.

Lucrezia quickly ceased to dream, because when her father became aware that Giovanni Sforza had left Rome he was angry and recalled him at once.

But safe in Pesaro among his own subjects, far from the conflict of politics and the threat of plague, Giovanni could be bold. He ignored the orders.

There were threats and promises, for Alexander was afraid of what this son-in-law might do, once he was out of his control.

And then finally the Pope declared that if Giovanni Sforza would return to Rome his marriage should be consummated and the dowry paid.

All waited eagerly to see what Sforza would do then; Lucrezia waited . . . in trepidation.

PESARO

EVEN WITH SUCH baits held out to him, Giovanni Sforza was reluctant to return to Rome.

There was unrest throughout Italy, and Sforza was fully aware of this. This time it was not warring states of the peninsula which cast a shadow over the land; there was a mightier enemy.

The King of France had renewed his claims to the throne of Naples and had informed Alexander that he was sending a mission to the Vatican that the matter might be discussed.

Alexander, with his clever diplomacy, received the French mission graciously; and his reception of them was viewed with such disfavour throughout Italy that there were rumours that before long Alexander would be deposed. Della Rovere was alert; he was determined that next time the Papal throne was empty he would sit on it.

Alexander however was not perturbed. He had infinite belief in himself and was sure that he could make the best of a situation however ominous it seemed. Ferrante of Aragon had died and his son Alfonso was now King. Alfonso determined at all costs to keep the Papal friendship, and offered great bribes to Alexander in order to cement it. It was not in Alexander's nature to refuse the bribes, so he now allied himself with Alfonso; meanwhile the French were dissatisfied and threatened invasion.

In his retreat at Pesaro Giovanni Sforza watched what was going on but could not make up his mind which road to take. Ludovico of Milan had shown him quite clearly that he could not be trusted to help his relative in an emergency. The Pope was obviously strong since Alfonso of Naples was suing so ardently for Papal friendship. Therefore Giovanni Sforza decided that he would return to Rome.

Lucrezia was waiting. Her hair had been freshly washed, her body perfumed. At last she was to be a bride.

The Pope had welcomed his son-in-law as though his absence had been a natural one. He had embraced him warmly and declared that he was glad to receive him and that his nuptial couch was waiting for him.

There were banquets and the usual crude jokes. It was almost like another wedding, but Lucrezia could not enjoy the celebrations so lightheartedly as she had the real wedding. That had been a masque with herself in the principal part; this was reality.

Her husband's attitude had changed towards her; she sensed that. He took her hand and she felt his breath on her face. At last he had noticed that she was beautiful.

So they danced together, the dances of Italy, not the Spanish dances which she had once danced with Giovanni on that occasion which was so like this and yet so different.

And then to that nuptial couch.

He was quiet and said little. She was prepared for what must take place – Giulia had prepared her – but she knew that it was going to be very different from Giulia's experience.

She was a little frightened, but serene as always, and she knew that if she did not experience the ecstasy for which she had longed, at least she would be able to endure it.

When they were alone in the great bed she said to him: 'Tell me one thing first, Giovanni. Why did you wait so long before you came back?'

'It would have been foolish to return,' he mumbled. 'There was plague and . . . matters were uncertain.'

He turned to her, impatient after all the months of waiting, but she held aloof with the faintest sign of fear in her big light eyes.

'Did you come back for the consummation . . . or for the dowry?'

'For both,' he answered.

It was strange, bewildering, as Giulia had said; and yet it was not as Giulia had said. She was aware of excitement, of the discovery of a new world which seemed to be opening before her, of delights undreamed of. She knew that with another it would have been different; but even with this man it was adequate.

Yet with some . . .
She lay back smiling.

She had grown up overnight. Alexander and Giulia, who had
noticed it, discussed it together.

'I am sorry for her,' mused Giulia. 'My own experience was
so different. Poor Lucrezia with that cold and nervous creature!
Holiness, you should dissolve the marriage and give her a real
man.'

Alexander clicked his tongue playfully. 'Such ways to talk of
marriage! Oh, she is young yet. She has her whole life before
her. I do not however shelve the idea of arranging a divorce,
but divorces are not easy to arrange. The Church abhors them.'

'But if the Holy Father decided, the Church would fall in
with his wishes,' Giulia reminded him.

'Ah, wicked one, you mock. I must devise a punishment for
you.'

'I will say ten "I love yous" and throw myself in worship
at your feet, and cry "Do with me as you will, Holy Father,
for my body and soul belong to you." '

'My Giulia . . . my little love. What should I do without
you! But you will look after my Lucrezia, will you not? You
will advise her, wise woman that you are!'

'How to take lovers and deceive her husband. As I did.'

' 'Twas no deceit. Poor little Orsino, he was willing that it
should be so – most willing.'

They laughed together while she assured him that she loved
Lucrezia as a sister and that she would look after her as such.

Giulia wished though to discuss other matters. She was
eager that the Pope should arrange a grand marriage for Laura,
since she wanted all Italy to know that the little girl was
accepted as his daughter.

'I will do it. Dearest little Laura shall have as fine a husband
as you could wish.'

He kept her with him. He needed the relaxation his relationship with her could give him. There were dark clouds over
Rome at this time and he did not care to think of them. So he
would be gay with his Giulia; he would make love as a young
man while they both rejoiced in his virility.

That was the very best antidote to trouble, he had discovered.

They were in Lucrezia's apartment – Lucrezia and Giulia. Their hair was loose about their shoulders. Giulia's reached to her feet, and Lucrezia could sit on hers. They had been washing it once more.

'There is sun on the balcony,' said Giulia. 'Let us go there and dry it. Drying it in the sun should make it more golden than ever.'

'Should we go on to the balcony?'

'Why not?'

'Could not infection reach us there?'

'Oh, Lucrezia, are you not tired of being shut in the Palace? We must not go out . . . not even for a minute. I am weary of it all.'

'It would be more wearying still if we caught the plague.'

'I suppose so. I shall be glad when the hot weather has gone. Perhaps it will take the pestilential air with it.'

Giulia rose and shook out her damp hair. 'I shall go on to the balcony.'

'Did you not promise the Holy Father that you would not?'

Giulia grimaced. 'I did not mention the balcony. I said I would not go out.'

'He may have meant the balcony.'

'Then let us pretend he did not. I am going out there now. I am going to sit in the sun and dry my hair.'

'No, Giulia, you should not.'

But Giulia had already gone.

Lucrezia sat down thoughtfully, looking at the figure of the Madonna and the lamp before it.

'Holy Mother,' she prayed. 'Let all be well soon.'

There was much that was wrong, she knew. It was not only the plague; that was a frequent visitor. There were ugly rumours about her father. She had heard the servants whispering; she had not told anyone she had heard, because servants might be whipped or even more terribly punished for saying some of the things which she had overheard. They had said that the Pope's position was insecure and that there were

many who wanted him to be removed and a new Pope set up
in his place. Invasion was threatened by the French, and there
were some who said that the Pope was a secret ally of Italy's
enemy.

All these matters made her very uneasy. She did not know
much about her husband's political feelings. They shared their
bed now and she was in truth a wife, but a vaguely dissatisfied
one. Giulia had said that he was cold; she had discovered that
she herself was by no means so. She did not understand herself; desire – vague desire for someone unknown – was aroused
in her, but it was not satisfied by Giovanni. She would lie beside him listening to his snoring and long to feel a lover's arms
about her. Not Giovanni's. But there were times when she
began to believe that any lover was better than none.

The love she experienced was very different from that which
Giulia knew, but then Giulia's lover was that incomparable
man, Alexander.

Somewhere in the world there would be the lover she
desired, for there must be other men in the world who had the
qualities of the Borgias.

But these were her own affairs and Lucrezia was rarely
selfish, so that the affairs of others invariably seemed of as
great importance – if not greater – to her than her own.

She could find time to think of poor Cesare, more furious
than ever because now danger threatened and he was unable to
act. He longed to have his own *condotta* in the army; here was a
chance for military glory, and he was denied it. Adriana had
become very pious again and spent a lot of time on her knees,
so it was clear that she was very worried.

She heard shouting from the piazza and as she ran to the
balcony to see what was happening, Giulia fell almost fainting
into her arms.

There was blood on Giulia's forehead.

'What happened?' She looked from Giulia to the balcony.

'Do not go out there,' said Giulia. 'Am I bleeding? They
saw me there. A crowd gathered in no time. Did you hear
what they said of me?'

'I heard the shouting. Please sit down. I will bathe your
forehead.'

She clapped her hands and a slave came running.

'Bring me a bowl of water and soft cloths,' she cried, 'and tell none why you bring them.'

Giulia looked at Lucrezia earnestly. 'They called me lewd names,' she said. 'And they mentioned the Holy Father.'

'They . . . they dare not!'

'But they *dared*, Lucrezia. That means that something more than we realize is happening in the city.'

'Do you think they mean to depose him?'

'He'll never allow them to do that.'

The slave came in with the water. Lucrezia took it and Giulia said: 'I fell as I stepped on to the balcony and I have grazed my forehead.'

The slave bowed and went away, but she did not believe Giulia.

They know of this trouble, thought Lucrezia. They know more than we have been allowed to.

It was impossible to keep secret the news that stones had been thrown at the Pope's mistress who was on a balcony of Lucrezia's palace. When Alexander heard of it he came hurrying to them.

In spite of the dangerous position in which Alexander knew himself to be, his greatest concern at that moment was the safety of his mistress and daughter.

He embraced them tenderly and for the first time since the war clouds had appeared over his head he showed anxiety.

'But, my darling, let me see this wound. We must make sure there is no infection. Holy Mother of God, it might have been your eye. But the saints have preserved you, my precious one, and the wound is not great. And, Lucrezia, oh, my precious little daughter, you were unhurt. I thank the Virgin for that.'

He held them both against him as though he would never let them go, and as each looked up into his face, she was aware of the conflict there.

'You must not be anxious, dearest Father,' said Lucrezia. 'We will take the greatest care. We will not venture on to the balcony until all this trouble is over.'

The Pope released them and went thoughtfully to the figure

of the Madonna. He stood beside it, his lips moving slightly. He was praying, and they were both aware that he was urging himself to make a decision.

Slowly he turned to them, and he was the old firm Alexander again.

'My darlings,' he said, 'I now have to do something which grieves me as nothing else could. I am going to send you away from Rome.'

'Please do not do that, Father,' begged Lucrezia. 'Let us stay with you. We will promise *never* to go out. But to be away from you would be the worst that could befall us.'

He smiled and laid a hand on her head.

'And my Giulia, what has she to say?'

Giulia had thrown herself at his feet and taken his hand. Giulia was thinking: Something more terrible than even the plague is threatening Rome. The French armies may invade us . . . they will set up a Pope of their own choosing, and who knows what will happen to Alexander?

Giulia had found Alexander a very satisfactory lover, accomplished and experienced; she did not doubt that she had been fortunate in having the best tutor in Rome. But part of Alexander's attraction had been his power; the knowledge, first that he was the richest Cardinal in Rome, and later the Pope himself. Such was Giulia's nature that all this had added to her pleasure. To imagine him without his glory, perhaps a humiliated prisoner of the French, made him appear a different person from the all-powerful, ever-indulgent and generous lover by whom it was an honour to be loved.

Giulia was therefore not entirely dismayed by the thought of retirement to a safe place until it had been settled whether or not Alexander was to retain his power.

She gave no sign of this; and Alexander who would have immediately detected duplicity in a statesman, was unaware of it in his mistress. This was partly due to that constant desire to see only that which he wished to see.

He was as devoted to Giulia as ever. The gap in their years made her seem, even now that she was a mother, a young and artless girl. Her passion had always seemed spontaneous; her joy in him as great as his in her. Therefore he believed that she would be as heartbroken to leave him as he would be to lose her.

'We will not leave you,' said Giulia. 'We will face anything, Holy Father, rather than do so. I would rather die of the plague or at the sword of foreign soldiers than . . .'

'Stop, I beg you,' said Alexander wincing. 'You know not what you are saying.'

Giulia had recovered herself; she stood up and her face was as guileless as Lucrezia's. She said: 'Tis true, is it not, Lucrezia? We would rather face . . . anything . . . anything . . .' She paused that Alexander might visualize the utmost horrors. . . . 'Yes,' she continued, 'anything rather than leave you.'

Lucrezia threw her arms about her father. 'It is true, dearest Father,' she cried; and she meant it.

'My darling girls!' murmured Alexander, and his voice was broken with emotion. 'But it is because I love you as I do that I must be relentless in this matter. I cannot allow you to stay. I cannot imagine how dark my life will be without you; all I know is that it would be even darker if aught happened to you through my selfishness in keeping you here. The French are gathering their forces. They are a strong nation, and determined to have Naples. But they will not be content with Naples. Who can tell, we may see foreign soldiers in Rome. And my beloved, my Giulia, you think of death at the hands of foreign soldiers, but it is not always as simple as that. You are so young . . . so very beautiful. There were never two more lovely creatures in the world. And what would your fate be if you were to fall into the hands of brutal soldiery, think you? I will not think of it. I dare not think of it. I prefer to lose the brightness of your presence rather than think of it.'

'Then let us go away for as short a time as is necessary to ease your mind,' soothed Giulia.

'I hope it will not be too far from Rome,' added Lucrezia wistfully.

'Rest assured, my precious ones, that as soon as it is safe for you to be here, I shall hold you in my arms again.'

He embraced them both and continued to hold them against him.

'These are my plans, my dearest girls. Lucrezia shall visit her husband's domain of Pesaro. It is to Pesaro that I propose to send you both.'

There was one who was filled with delight at the prospect of leaving Rome, and that was Giovanni Sforza. He assured the Pope that his first care should be the two girls whom the Holy Father was placing under his protection, and he fervently agreed with His Holiness that Rome in this May of the year 1494 was no place for them.

So on a beautifully sunny day there was gathered in St Peter's Square a crowd of babbling servants and excited slaves to complete the cortège which was to journey to Pesaro. Giulia declared that she could not travel without her hairdressers, dressmakers, and all the servants necessary to her comfort; Lucrezia, knowing how those of her retinue would grieve if left behind, was equally insistent that hers should accompany her. In vain did Giovanni Sforza point out that they would have less need of all their fripperies in quiet Pesaro; the girls would not listen; and Giovanni, eager only to escape from Rome as quickly as possible, gave way.

Adriana, with her priests and servants, was also in the procession; and the Pope stood on his balcony watching until he could see the last of those two golden heads which brought so much pleasure into his life.

When they had gone he retired to his apartments and shut himself away to mourn their absence. He gave himself up to the study of the political stiuation, determined that he would employ every ounce of energy he possessed to make Rome a safe place, so that he might bring back his beloved girls to brighten his life.

As they left Rome behind them Lucrezia was surprised to see how Giulia's spirits rose.

'One would think,' she said, 'that you are glad to leave the Holy Father.'

'It is no use harbouring melancholy which can do nothing but make further melancholy. Let us forget we are in exile from our Holy Father and our beloved city. Let us make the most of what we have.'

'That will not be easy,' said Lucrezia. 'Did you not notice how sad he was?'

'He is the wisest man in Rome,' Giulia assured her. 'He will very soon cast off his sorrow. It is he who has taught me my philosophy of life. He'll soon be making merry. Therefore let us also make as merry as we can.'

'That is certainly his philosophy,' agreed Lucrezia.

'Then let us be gay . . . I wonder what kind of city this Pesaro is.'

On they went northwards across the leg of Italy, and through every town they passed the people turned out to see the strangers from Rome. They marvelled at the two golden-haired beauties in their rich dresses; they stared at little Laura, who was with her mother, and marvelled because they had heard rumours that this child, like the golden-haired Lucrezia, was the Pope's own daughter.

They hung out banners of welcome, and the lords of the various towns through which they passed entertained them royally. Such entertainments amused the people and, as no one was sure yet that Alexander would be deposed, it would be unwise to offend, at this stage, one who, legend had it, was endowed with superhuman powers.

Giovanni Sforza's spirits rose as the distance between himself and Rome increased. He took on new stature; he even became something like the lover of whom Lucrezia had dreamed; and she, always ready to be contented, found that, as far as her married life was concerned, she had never been happier.

How Giovanni glowed with pride to see the banners displayed in their honour, to be treated as an equal by some of the lords such as those of Urbino who had previously thought themselves far above him.

Giovanni was realizing at last the honour which could come to him through his union with the Borgias, and that made him tender towards his wife and very eager to please her; and since she was ready to be pleased, the harmonious relationship between them continued all through that journey.

Sforza sent notice of their impending arrival to Pesaro and instructed his servants there that he wanted a welcome such as they had never given before; he wished flowers to be strewn in the streets and banners to be set up; he wanted verses to be written so that on their arrival they might be recited to him and his bride.

And so he was delighted as they made the arduous journey across the Apennines, and he congratulated himself on having a wife who was not only easy to arouse to ardour, who was not only a beauty, but the daughter of a man who, even if his power was threatened, most would agree, was the mightiest in Italy.

So he prepared for the triumphant entry into Pesaro.

Lucrezia and Giulia had not failed to wash their hair the night before the day of the entry. Lucrezia was to wear a rich gown embroidered with gold, and her golden hair was to be caught up in a net set with many jewels.

She lay beside her husband thinking of the next day, sleepily remembering the passion he had shown during the journey, passion of which she had not thought him capable. She wished that he would wake up and that there might be more love-making.

Then she wondered what was happening in Rome and whether her father had recovered from his unhappiness. Giulia did not seem to regret very much that they had left him, although it was certain that he would have found comfort with another woman.

Strange that Giulia did not care. But perhaps it was as well, for if Giulia had cared she would be unhappy, and as the Pope would undoubtedly find means of comforting himself, it was fortunate that Giulia should be reconciled to the parting.

The wind was rising, and she could hear the rain beating down.

She hoped the sun would be shining in the morning.

'Giovanni,' she murmured, 'do you hear the wind rising?'

He was not very handsome; he was not like the lover of whom she had dreamed; but she had always been ready to compromise. She would endow him with beauty and with qualities he did not possess, and think of him as she wished him to be, rather than as he was.

She touched his cheek lightly with her finger. His face twitched and he put up a hand as though to brush away a fly.

'Giovanni,' she whispered.

But he only snored.

They rode into Pesaro in heavy rain and violent storm.

From the windows hung bedraggled banners; some had been blown down and lay neglected on the ground. The Lord of Pesaro had commanded that there should be banners, and banners his subjects provided; but the wind was cruel and obeyed no lord; so the entry into Pesaro was not the triumphal affair which its Lord had planned.

Giulia was angry; the rain had saturated her lovely hair so that it looked dark yellow instead of gold. Her beautiful dress was ruined.

'A curse on Pesaro!' cried Giulia, and wished herself in Rome.

Adriana murmured prayers as they rode. Her clothes were clinging to her uncomfortably, and the wind caught at her hair beneath its net; she felt undignified thus, and her dignity meant much to Adriana. Still she was calm and there was a certain triumph in her face. She was telling herself: 'Anything will be better than Rome at this time.'

Lucrezia's beautiful dress was ruined and her hair in the same state as Giulia's. One of her servants had found a large cape which she wrapped about her mistress so that all her glory was hidden to those few who had endured the wind and rain to watch the entry of the new Countess.

'I doubt not,' she said to Giulia, 'that the sun will shine tomorrow.'

'As doubtless we shall be in bed, nursing fevers, that will matter little to us,' grumbled Giulia.

They came to the Sforza palace and here, as ordered, were the poets waiting to read their verses of praises to their Lord and his bride.

So they must all stand in the rain and the wind whilst, huddled beneath the arches, the shivering poets read their verses welcoming their Countess to her home in sunny Pesaro.

Giulia sneezed, while Adriana silently prayed that the poets had kept their verses short, and Lucrezia, her beauty hidden by the great cloak, and her golden hair falling about her face in strands like dull yellow serpents, smiled as was expected of her, but her relief was obvious when the address was over.

What joy to be inside the palace, to dry and warm themselves by the great fire, to eat hot food and giggle with Giulia about the terrible journey to Pesaro which they would enjoy recalling because it was over.

But with the next day came the sunshine, and there was Pesaro before them in all its beauty.

Lucrezia, looking at the lovely expanse of Adriatic on which the town stood, the green hills surrounding it in a charming semi-circle at each end of which were the tall mountains of Accio and Ardizio, was delighted with her new home.

'Here,' she told Giulia, 'one feels shut away from the rest of the world.'

'That is why we were sent here, to be safe until the conflict passes.'

'I believe I could be happy,' said Lucrezia, 'if my father and my brothers were with me.'

'O, Lucrezia, you will have to learn to be happy without your father and your brothers.'

During the next days Lucrezia tried to be.

Giovanni's subjects had done their best to entertain their Countess in such a way that she would know how pleased they were to have her among them. There were banquets, dances, and carnival. The little streets of the town were full of laughing people, of clowns in grotesque costumes, and jugglers who had their tricks to perform in honour of Madonna Lucrezia. There had never been such gaiety in Pesaro, declared the people, and it was all in honour of the new Countess.

Lucrezia appeared among them and won their hearts, not only with her golden beauty, but with her obvious appreciation of all that they were doing for her.

Giulia and Lucrezia put their heads together and devised a programme of merrymaking, determined to make the people of Pesaro see such magnificence as they had never seen before. They brought out their most splendid dresses that they might dazzle the provincials and give them a glimpse of how splendid Roman society was.

They were determined to outshine a local beauty, Caterina Gonzaga di Montevecchio, of whom they had heard so much, but they were a little apprehensive, as the fame of this woman's beauty had travelled as far as Rome.

They washed their hair, put on their jewelled nets, each assuring the other that she had never looked more beautiful; the dresses of silk and brocade set with gems which they were wearing were such as they would have worn for a state occasion in Rome. Thus magnificently dressed they set out, with Giovanni as their escort, for the Gonzaga ball.

It was an evening of triumph. They studied the far-famed beauty and discovered that although she had a beautiful skin and figure, her nose was fat, her teeth ugly and her hair was insignificant beside the long gold tresses of Guilia and Lucrezia.

Giulia became hilariously gay; Lucrezia more serenely joyous; and as soon as they arrived back at the Sforza palace they sat down to write to the Holy Father and tell him all about it, describing the appearance of Caterina, because they knew His Beatitude may have had the impression that she was more beautiful than she really was.

Giulia added that Lucrezia was satisfied with her new home and that she was in good health. The people of Pesaro were devoted to Sforza, she wrote, and there had been continual festivities, dancing, singing, and masques. As for herself, being absent from His Holiness, on whom all her happiness depended, she was unable to take any delight or satisfaction in the gaiety. Her heart was with one who was the treasure of her life. She trusted that His Holiness would not forget them but soon bring them back to him.

Such letters delighted the Pope. He demanded that they should write every day, and assured them that every detail of their lives was of the utmost importance to him.

This appeared to be so because, although the French were about to invade Italy and his enemies within the peninsula were seeking to depose him, he was quite happy when he received letters from his beloved girls.

And when some weeks later news reached him that Lucrezia was confined to her bed with a fever, he was thrown into an agony of fear for her life. He shut himself into his apartments, would see no one, blamed himself for allowing her to go away from him while he made feverish plans for bringing her back despite the dangers.

He wanted them with him. He could not enjoy life without them. He wrote that absence from Giulia aroused within him a demon of sensuality which could only be placated by her; of all his children, he realized now there was none he cared for as for his golden-haired little beauty. How could he have thought that the love he bore his sons could compare with that which a man such as he was must feel for one as delicately formed, as exquisitely beautiful, as his Lucrezia. They must return. They must not be parted again. Whatever the dangers they must face them together.

'Donna Lucrezia, my beloved daughter,' he wrote in anguish. 'You have given us days of deepest misery. There was evil news in Rome, bitter and terrible news that you were dead or that there was no hope for your life. You will understand the sorrow caused us on account of the great love we bear you which is greater than that which we have for anyone else on Earth. We thank God and our Glorious Lady that they have removed you from danger, but we shall not be happy until we see you in person.'

So the letters travelled back and forth between Rome and Pesaro and, although it seemed to many that Alexander was on the edge of disaster, he refused to acknowledge this and declared that he would give all he had for the return of his darlings.

Giovanni Sforza wanted nothing so much as to stay in Pesaro; there he believed he was sheltered from the disasters of invasion; the French would surely not cross the Apennines to take possession of such an insignificant Dominion. Moreover Lucrezia, removed from the influence of her father, was a contented and loving wife. Why should they not stay in Pesaro for the rest of their lives?

There was one drawback to this. On account of his post in the Church he was in the pay of the Pope; and although as a Sforza he worked for Milan, his kinsman Ludovico, preparing for invasion of which he knew he must be one of the first victims, had little time or money to spare for Giovanni. Therefore Giovanni's income from Milan had not been paid for some time and, if he disobeyed the Pope by keeping his daughter from him, how could he expect his income from the Papacy to be paid?

Giovanni was a perplexed man during those weeks of festivities when Lucrezia and Giulia were flaunting their fine clothes and splendour at his provincial court.

Alexander understood his son-in-law perfectly. A meek man, a coward of a man, thought Alexander; the kind of man whom he despised. He knew that Giovanni was cowering in Pesaro, far from the impending conflict, and hoped to stay there keeping Lucrezia from her father.

That should not be; and, since if Giovanni decided to keep his wife at his side it would be a most delicate matter for the Pope to demand her return, Alexander arranged that Giovanni Sforza should be given a Neapolitan Brigade, and sent orders to Pesaro that he should at once set out to take over his command.

When Giovanni received this communication he was dumb-founded.

He strode into Lucrezia's apartment and demanded that she read the despatch from Rome.

'To leave at once . . . for Naples,' read Lucrezia. 'You . . . Giovanni . . . to go to Naples? But your family and the Nea-politans have always been enemies.'

'That is so,' cried Giovanni. 'What is your father planning? Does he wish to destroy me?'

'How could he wish to destroy my husband when he declares his greatest pleasure is in pleasing me?'

'Perhaps he thinks that by destroying me he would not displease you.'

'Giovanni!' Lucrezia's wide eyes were imploring him to say no more. She greatly feared scenes such as this.

'Oh yes,' stormed Giovanni. 'He wants you back with him. He cannot exist without you. Is that not what he says? Do you think I do not understand why? Do you think I am a fool?'

'He is my beloved father, it is true.'

Giovanni laughed aloud. 'Your beloved father! That is

amusing. The whole of Italy laughs. The Pope is the beloved
father of Madonna Lucrezia, and he yearns to shelter her
beneath the apostolic robe.'

'Giovanni, you are hysterical.'

It was true. Giovanni was terrified. He saw himself caught
in the Papal web. His relatives in Milan had no time for him;
his father-in-law, the Pope, wished him out of the way; therefore he was to be sent to the enemies of his family. What would
become of him?

'I shall refuse to obey the Pope's commands,' he said. 'Does
he think I do not see what they mean?'

'Oh, Giovanni,' said Lucrezia, 'you would be ill-advised to
disobey my father.'

'You would advise me to obey, would you not! You would
say "Go to the Neapolitans. Accept this command with them.
You are a Sforza and sworn enemy of the Neapolitans, but go,
go ... because my father wishes you out of the way, so that I
may return to him... and that I may live close to him, and the
rumours may grow and grow ... and grow...." '

He began to laugh, but his face was twitching with fear.

She sought to calm him; but he only shouted: 'I shall not go
– do you hear me? I shall not go.'

There was further trouble. News came from Capodimonte,
Giulia's native town, that her brother Angelo was very ill and
the family believed that he could not live.

Giulia was distraught. She was very fond of her family,
particularly her brothers Angelo and Alessandro.

She came to Lucrezia, and never in the course of their
friendship had Lucrezia seen Giulia so distressed.

'It is news from my home,' Giulia explained.

'My dearest Giulia, how sorry I am!' cried Lucrezia. 'We
must pray that all will be well.'

'I must do more than pray,' Giulia told her. 'I shall go to
him. I cannot let him die without seeing him again.'

'You remember my father's orders .... We were not to
leave Pesaro without his consent.'

'My brother is dying, do you understand? What if Cesare
or Giovanni were dying? Would you not go to them?'

'But it is not Cesare, nor Giovanni,' said Lucrezia calmly.
'It is only Angelo.'

'He is as much my brother as Cesare and Giovanni are
yours.'

But Lucrezia could not concede that. Giulia did not understand the bonds which bound the Borgia family. And the
Pope would be angry if Giulia left Pesaro to go to her
family.

'Why,' pointed out Lucrezia, 'Orsino is at Bassanello, and
that is not very far from Capodimonte. You know how my
father dislikes you to be anywhere near your husband.'

'I need not see Orsino.'

'But he might come to you. Oh, Giulia, if you value my
father's love, do not go to Capodimonte.'

Giulia was silent. She was torn between her desire to see her
brother and her wish to please the Pope.

Giovanni left for Naples. Lucrezia said farewell to him
without any great regret. During the last days she had seen
what a weak man she had married, and she longed for the
strength which she had always admired in her father and
brothers.

Giovanni, furious and humiliated, had decided that as he
could not serve the enemies of his family he would pretend to
do so and send information to his family as to the moves made
by the Neapolitan army. He would be doing dangerous work,
and if he were discovered, as a spy he would be in acute danger.
But what could he do? How else could he reconcile himself
with his family? He was a small ruler of a small community;
he was a provincial lord who could not live without the support
of his family and the Pope.

Gloom descended on the palace after Giovanni had left.
There were no more entertainments; the girls had no inclina-
tion for them. They would sit in the apartment, Lucrezia
amusing Laura while Giulia watched at the window for a
messenger from Capodimonte.

There came a day when that messenger arrived, and the news
he brought was grave. Angelo Farnese was on his death-bed;
there was no doubt of that; he had expressed a desire to see his

beloved sister Giulia who had brought so many honours to the family. That decided Giulia.

She turned to Lucrezia. 'I am leaving at once for Capodimonte,' she said. 'I am determined to see my brother before he dies.'

'You must not go,' insisted Lucrezia. 'My father will be displeased.'

But Giulia was firm, and that day she, with Laura and Adriana, set out for Capodimonte.

Giovanni, Giulia, Laura and Adriana had gone.

What changes, pondered Lucrezia, as she was left in loneliness at Pesaro, were taking place all around her.

In the Orsini castle at Bassanello, Orsino Orsini was brooding.

Like Giovanni Sforza, he was a weak man. Giovanni could never forget that he belonged to a small branch of the Sforza family and was despised by his wealthier relations; Orsino could not forget that he was small in stature, that he squinted, and that not even humble serving girls were eager for his attentions.

Often he brooded on the way he was treated. It seemed that they had mocked him even more than was necessary by marrying him to one of the most beautiful women in Italy, one who had already become the Pope's mistress before she was his wife.

It was as though they said; 'Oh, but it is only Orsino, and Orsino is of no account.'

His mother even had played a prominent part in his humiliation. 'Don't be silly, Orsino,' she had reproved him. 'Think what favours Giulia can make the Pope bestow on you. Riches! Land! They are more profitable than a wife. In any case if it's women you want there will be many at your disposal.'

La Bella Giulia! She was notorious throughout Italy. The Pope's mistress! Mother of the Pope's child! And she was married to Orsino who was never allowed to go near her for fear of offending the Pope!

Orsino swore an oath.

'This is an end to my humiliation. She has left the Pope. She is at Capodimonte and, by all the saints, I swear she shall be my wife in truth. I swear to take her from her lover.'

From his castle he looked out on the little village clustered about the old church with its campanile, six stories high; he gazed at the quiet valley through which the Tiber flowed. About him, all seemed at peace. But if he did what they expected of him he would not long enjoy peace. His family were firm allies of the Neapolitans and he was in command of a brigade. Soon he would have to leave this place and join the Neapolitan camp. Then he would be far away from Giulia and, if the Pope heard she had come to Capodimonte to visit her dying brother, he would not be so disturbed as he would be if he knew that Orsino Orsini was in the neighbourhood.

But why should one placate the Pope? Why was it so necessary now? The French were on the way with a mighty army, and it was said that one of their objects would be to depose Alexander. Well then, was there the same need to placate the Pope?

'By the saints, I will have what is mine!' vowed Orsino.

He sent for one of his captains, and when the man came to him he said: 'You will take the troops to Umbria. I have orders that they are to proceed there.'

The man acknowledged the order but Orsino saw the astonished look which came into his eyes.

'I am feeling unwell,' Orsino explained. 'I feel a fever creeping upon me. I cannot accompany you. I must remain behind for a while.'

He was smiling slyly as he dismissed the captain.

Now he had taken the first step.

The Holy Father was about to lose a mistress, and he, Orsino Orsini, was about to gain a wife.

When his men had left he set out for Capodimonte where both his mother and Giulia were surprised to see him.

'But what means this?' cried Adriana. 'Should you not be with your men in camp?'

'I will be where I wish to be,' said Orsino.

Giulia cried: 'But we understood you had orders.'

Orsino regarded her intently. It was not for nothing that she was known as La Bella throughout Italy. He was suddenly tortured by a hundred images of what her love-making with that connoisseur of love, the Holy Father, must have been; and he was maddened by mingled anger and desire.

He answered her: 'The time has come when I have decided to order my own life.'

'But . . .' began Giulia.

'And yours,' said Orsino.

'This is madness,' retorted Giulia. She looked at her mother-in-law, but Adriana was silent. She was thinking quickly. She did not believe that Milan would stand up against the onslaught of the French. She believed that very soon the foreigners would be in Rome. If they reached Rome, then Alexander's days as Pope were numbered. A women as shrewd as Adriana did not go on placating a man about to fall. If Italy were invaded it would be families such as the Orsinis and Colonnas who would survive; and Orsino, squint-eyed though he might be, was a powerful Orsini. Let him show a little spirit and his physical deformity would be forgotten.

Adriana lifted her shoulders. 'He is your husband when all is considered,' she answered.

And she left them together.

Giulia, startled, faced Orsino.

'Orsino, do not be foolish,' she said.

He had approached her, and seized her by the wrist.

'You know,' she cried, 'that the Pope has forbidden you to come near me.'

He laughed, and gripping her by the shoulders shook her roughly. 'Has it not occurred to you that it might be my place to forbid the Pope to come near you?'

'Orsino!'

'La Bella,' he said, 'you have brought great profit to your family. You have considered all the demands they have made upon you.' His eyes were on her smooth white neck on which she wore the sparkling diamond necklace which had been a gift from her lover. He pulled the necklace and the clasp snapped. He flung it from him without looking where it fell. And it was as though, as his hands touched her warm flesh, he made a decision. There would be no more prevarication. Not even for a moment.

'If you touch me,' she cried, 'you will have to answer to . . .'

'I answer to none,' he said. 'I would remind you of something which you seem to have forgotten . . . now, as when you married me. You are my wife.'

'Think carefully, Orsino.'

'This is not the time for thinking.'

She pressed her hands against his chest; her eyes were imploring; the lovely golden hair escaped from its net.

'Now!' he said. 'This moment . . . .'

'No,' she cried. 'I will not. Orsino . . . I hate you. Let me go. At a time like this! My brother dying . . . and . . . and . . .'

'There should have been other times,' he said. 'A hundred times . . . a thousand times. I've been a fool, but I'm a fool no longer. Those times have passed. This shall not.'

She was breathless, determined on escape. But he was equally determined; and he was the stronger of the two.

After a while she gave up struggling.

Angelo was dead. He had embraced his sister for the last time and told her that she must always thank the Virgin for her beauty and remember that through it she was able to lay the foundations of her family's greatness.

He did not know what was happening beyond the palace walls. He did not know what was happening within them. She was never free from Orsino. He was full of demands; he insisted on his rights; and he would take no refusal.

She herself was a sensual woman and as such was beginning to find a certain excitement in her encounters with Orsino.

Alexander would be furious, but she was powerless. She was a prisoner in Capodimonte at the mercy of a husband who had been kept away from her for years. Alexander was an accomplished lover, Orsino something of a boor, but the boor provided a stimulating change; and it amused her to submit to what was almost rape and yet was legitimate behaviour for a married pair.

She was sorry Lucrezia was not with her, so that she might have confided in her.

As for the Orsini family, they naturally supported their kinsman. Orsino was within his rights in his demands, they declared. Her lover? They could laugh now at an old man in decline. He would not last long.

Adriana had changed too. 'I must support my son,' she declared. 'It is the most natural thing in the world that he should insist on his wife's living with him.'

News of what had happened eventually reached Alexander. Never had anyone seen him so furiously angry as he was at that time. He paced up and down his apartments, threatening excommunications right and left. He would not leave Giulia in the hands of that boor, that cross-eyed idiot. She must be brought back to Rome at once.

Why had she been allowed to leave Pesaro? What of his daughter? Was she conniving at this plot against him?

He wrote to Lucrezia. It was bad enough, he wrote, that a daughter should be so lacking in filial love that she showed no wish to return to her father, but that she should disobey him passed all understanding. He was bitterly disappointed in one whom he had loved beyond everything on Earth. She was deceitful and indifferent to him, and the letters she was writing to her brother Cesare were not written in the same sly way as were those she wrote to him.

When Lucrezia heard thus from her father she was desperately unhappy.

There had always been quarrels between Giovanni and Cesare, but never between her and the other members of her family. And that her father should write to her in this way wounded her deeply.

Desperately lonely, she fell into a mood of melancholy. What had happened to the beloved family? They were all separated now. No wonder there was misunderstanding. Giovanni was in Spain, and Goffredo in Naples. Cesare was in Rome, wrapped up in his bitterness particularly now that war threatened. And most dire tragedy of all, her father loved her so little that he could vent his anger, at Giulia's betrayal, on her, his daughter Lucrezia.

She could only try to ease her sorrow by writing to her father. She implored him to believe that she had been unable to prevent Giulia's leaving Pesaro, and that she had done all in her power to stop her going. Her letters to him were as loving, as tender and as truthful as those she wrote to Cesare. He could always be sure of her love and devotion. 'I long to be,' she wrote,'at the feet of Your Beatitude, and I long to be worthy of your esteem, for if I am not I shall never know satisfaction and have no wish to live.'

When Alexander received this letter, he wept and kissed it tenderly.

'Why did I doubt my beloved girl?' he asked. 'My Lucrezia, my little love. She will always be faithful to me. It is others who disobey and deceive.'

But what an unhappy man he was! The 'demons of sensuality' were gnawing at him, and he could not shut out of his mind pictures of Giulia and the cross-eyed Orsino together.

The French fleet had a speedy victory over the Neapolitans at Rapallo. The French armies crossed the Alps and the Italians found themselves outmatched from the start. These armies under the white banners of the Valois were advancing through Italy. At Pavia Charles VIII found the poor half-demented Gian Galeazzo, the true Duke of Milan; and when his beautiful young wife Isabella threw herself at the feet of little Charles, the French King was so moved, because she was beautiful and had suffered so much, that he promised that he would do all in his power to restore her husband. However, Ludovico's friends hastily administered a posset to the young Duke, and within a few days he was dead. Ludovico was then declared Duke of Milan.

The news was bad for the Italians. Ludovico decided not to fight, and welcomed the French invaders as they swept through his land. The great captain Virginio Orsini also put up no fight, but issued the command that all were to give way to the invaders.

There was only one who seemed prepared to take a stand against the French: Alexander, the Pope.

He was contemptuous of the Italians. 'They are despicable,' he cried. 'Good for nothing but parading in fine uniforms. The only weapons the French need to conquer Italy are pieces of chalk, that they may mark their billets.'

He was determined that he would stand out alone if necessary against all his enemies.

Once again, as he had at the time of the death of Calixtus, Alexander showed the world the stuff of which he was made. No one could but admire that calm dignity, that assurance that he could not fail though all the world came against him.

The French King, *Re Petito* as the Italians called him, for he was deformed and made a strange sight riding in the midst of his stalwart troops, was a little disturbed about attacking a man who had the courage of Alexander. It seemed to him that there was a touch of divinity about the Pope after all. He therefore turned aside from the repeated prayers of Alexander's enemies in Italy to go ahead and depose him.

Harm must not come to the Pope from him, Charles decided; if it did, he might have the whole of Catholic France and Spain against him.

Cardinal della Rovere, Alexander's old enemy, who had allied himself with the French King, riding beside him and declaring that the French had come to deliver Italy from the yoke of Alexander, was dismayed. He saw once again that his plans to step into Alexander's shoes were to be foiled.

The French must pass through Rome on their way to the south, but Charles decided that all he would ask for in Rome was the Pope's permission for transit through the Papal states.

Meanwhile Alexander remained firm. He would resist the French demands, he said; a tremor of fear ran through all those who had been assuring themselves that Alexander's days of power were over. Adriana and the Orsinis in Capodimonte were the first to falter.

Adriana upbraided her son for disobeying the Holy Father, and other members of the Orsini family joined with her and urged Orsino to leave at once for his brigade and not risk infuriating Alexander further.

Consequently Giulia awoke one morning to find that the masterful manners of her husband had been only temporary, and that he had fled.

There came a letter for Giulia from the angry Pope.

'Perfidious and ungrateful Giulia! You tell us you cannot return to Rome without your husband's permission. Though now we know both the wickedness of your nature and those who advise you, we can only suppose that you wish to remain where you are so that you may continue relations with that stallion of a husband.'

Giulia read the letter in alarm; the Pope had never written to her in quite the same manner before; her family were beginning to criticize her for having turned against her lover for her husband's sake, and the husband, who had been so bold, had fled at the first sign that Alexander's power was unshaken.

Trembling she held her daughter to her.

'We should never have left Rome,' she said.

'Shall we go to see my father?' asked the little girl. She had refused to call the squint-eyed Orsino, Father; Father, to her, was a glorious god-like creature, tall, commanding, in beautiful robes with a deep sonorous voice, caressing hands and comforting affection.

'We shall,' said Giulia, determination shining in her eyes. She laughed suddenly. After all, she was La Bella, she could win back all she had lost.

She sent a slave to ask Adriana to come to her at once.

'I am leaving for Rome,' she told her mother-in-law as soon as she appeared.

'For Rome! But the roads are unsafe. The French invaders may be anywhere . . . before we reach Rome.'

But Adriana was looking intently at her daughter-in-law, and Giulia realized that, dangerous as the road might be, it was even more dangerous to remain under the shadow of Alexander's displeasure.

So Giulia, Adriana and a small retinue set out from Capodimonte on their journey to Rome.

Giulia was in high spirits; so was Laura. Giulia was wondering how she could have been momentarily excited by the

sudden masterful ways of Orsino who at the first hint of alarm
had taken to his heels and fled. She was longing for reunion with
her lover. Laura was prattling about going home and seeing her
father again; Adriana was silently praying that the Holy Father
had not been so angry towards herself and Giulia that he
would never have the same feelings for them again. They were
all eagerness to reach Rome.

The journey was long and tedious; the weather was not good,
as it was November; but the gaiety of Giulia was infectious, and
it was a merry party which travelled along the road to Viterbo.

Suddenly Laura pointed and cried out that she could see
houses ahead of them. They pulled up to look, and there sure
enough on the horizon was the town of Viterbo.

'It will not be very long now,' cried Giulia. 'More than half
the journey is done. I shall write to His Holiness when we reach
Viterbo and tell him that we are on the way.'

'Listen!' said Adriana.

'What was that?' asked Giulia.

'I thought I heard the sound of horses' hoofs.'

They waited. They could hear nothing, and Giulia laughed
at her mother-in-law. 'You are nervous. Did you imagine
Orsino was galloping after us to take us back by force?'

Laura began to cry at the thought. 'I want to see my father.'

'And so you shall, my darling. Have no fear. We shall be
with him shortly. Come, let us waste no more time but ride
with all speed into Viterbo.'

They started off, but this time it was Giulia who fancied she
heard the sound of galloping horses.

They stopped again. This time there was no mistake. Giulia
looked fearfully at her little party, mostly women.

'Let us go on with all speed,' she said. 'We do not know
whom we might meet on these roads at such times.'

They put spurs to their horses but it was not long before one
of the women cried out that cavalry were advancing upon them.

They rode desperately on but nearer and nearer came their
pursuers, and they were almost a mile from Viterbo when they
were surrounded.

Adriana's lips moved in silent prayer; Giulia was horrified
when she recognized the uniform of the French invaders.

It was a desperate moment as they were forced to stop while the men surrounded them, and Giulia felt several pairs of eyes fixed upon her, knowing too well what those looks meant.

'Fair lady,' said the commander, 'whither do you go in such a hurry?'

He spoke in French, and Giulia did not understand him very well. She turned to Adriana who was so terrified that she could only murmur prayers almost involuntarily while her mind ran on, visualizing the horrible things which could happen to the women at the hands of the invaders.

Laura, who was riding with her mother, suddenly cried out and flung her arms about Giulia as though to protect her from the strangers.

'By the saints,' said one man, 'she's a beauty!'

'Keep your eyes from her,' answered another. 'She'll be for the Captain. If you're wise you'll look more closely at one of the other girls – and be satisfied.'

Giulia said imperiously: 'I am Giulia Farnese, wife of Orsino Orsini. You would be wise to allow me to pass. The Pope is my friend.'

One of the men pushed his way through to her and touched her golden hair wonderingly. She slapped his hand aside, and the man growled ominously.

Then someone said: 'Look out. Here comes the Captain.'

A tall handsome man came riding up, and Giulia's spirits rose at the sight of him, for he had an air of natural nobility about him, and there was a certain gentleness in his face which was very comforting at such a time.

'What have we here?' he cried.

The men, who had been handling some of the women, dropped back.

'A party of women and their servants, sir,' said the man who had led the band. 'One's a real beauty, sir.'

The commanding officer looked at Giulia and said slowly: 'So I perceive.' Then he bowed and spoke in fluent Italian, with the faintest trace of a French accent.

'My lady, forgive my men's roughness. I trust they have not insulted you.'

'But they have,' said Giulia. 'And I would have you know that I am Giulia Farnese, the wife of Orsino Orsini. You have doubtless heard of me.'

He bowed again. 'Who has not heard of the most beautiful woman in Italy? I see now that rumours have not lied. Madame La Bella, accept my apologies for what has passed. My name is Yves d'Allegre, at your service.'

'I am pleased to see you here, Monsieur d'Allegre,' said Giulia. 'And now I am sure you will tell your men not to be foolish. We are in a hurry.'

'Alas, alas,' sighed Yves d'Allegre. 'These roads are unsafe for beautiful ladies.'

'Then accompany us to Viterbo, and there perhaps it can be arranged that we shall have soldiers to protect us. A message to His Holiness the Pope telling him of our plight will call forth an immediate response.'

'I am sure it would,' said the Frenchman, his gaze taking in the beauty of her exquisite figure. 'There is not a man in Italy or in France who would not serve you.'

Giulia's fear was rapidly disappearing. The man was so charming. The French were notoriously gallant and the Captain had even more than French gallantry to offer. She was beginning to enjoy the adventure.

'Alas,' he went on, 'your beauty is such, Madame, that it may so madden those who behold it that they forget the respect and honour due to a lady of your rank. I shall ask you to allow me to ride beside you into Montefiascone, when I shall protect you with my sword.'

'I thank you,' said Giulia. 'But it is to Viterbo that we wish to go.'

'Alas, I am a soldier, with duties to perform. What a hard taskmistress duty is when she conflicts with pleasure! A thousand apologies, but I must take you and your party into Montefiascone.'

Giulia shrugged her shoulders. 'Well then, when we are there, will you do this for me? Will you have a message sent to His Holiness to tell him what has befallen us?'

Yves bowed and said that he would certainly do that.

So, taking Giulia's horse by the bridle and placing it at the head of the little band, with her beside him he led the party towards Montefiascone.

Montefiascone was already in the hands of the French and, as they approached the place, soldiers hurried out to look at them. There were shouts of delight when they saw the women, and many eyes were on Giulia. But Yves d'Allegre shouted stern orders. His prisoner was no ordinary woman. Any laying hands on her or her party would suffer immediate and drastic punishment.

The men fell back. They thought they understood. The Captain had selected the beautiful captive for himself.

Giulia herself believed this to be so and, as she looked at the handsome man riding beside her, she shivered, not without a certain pleasure, wondering what lay before her.

Yves rode with her into the town and, after he had had a short conversation with his superior officers, Giulia and her party were received with the greatest respect and lodged in one of the most comfortable houses of the town.

Giulia sent Laura to rest in the care of her nurse, and went to the room which had been allotted to her. She took off her cloak and shook her hair out of its net. She lay on the bed, thinking of all the strange things which had befallen her since she left Rome. Her mind went with distaste to the episode with Orsino; she told herself that she had been forced to participate in that affair, and was glad it had come to an ignoble end.

This . . . this would also be *force majeure*. The man was so charming, so handsome. . . .

But she waited in vain for the coming of Yves d'Allegre, for, while she was waiting, he was penning a note to the Pope telling him that La Bella Giulia was a captive in the hands of the French and that a ransom of 3,000 scudi was demanded for her safe conduct to Rome.

When Alexander heard the news he became frantic with anxiety that some ill might befall his mistress. He hastily collected the money, which was despatched at once. Then, trembling with anticipation, he found he could not wait patiently in the Vatican for the return of Giulia.

He must go to meet her. No matter if the French were at his

gate; no matter if the whole world were laughing at an old man's passion (and that man a Pope) for a young woman, he could not remain in the Vatican. He must ride out to greet her. He was like a man of twenty. He ordered that fine clothes be brought to him. He wore a black doublet with a border of gold brocade; about his waist was a beautiful belt of Spanish leather, in which was a jewelled sword and dagger. On his feet were Spanish boots, and he wore his velvet beret at a jaunty angle.

Thus he rode out to greet Giulia and bring her back to Rome.

Giulia was delighted to see him. She now felt humiliated by her encounter with Orsino and piqued by that with Yves d'Allegre, but here was Alexander, the most important man in Italy – despite all the evil rumours of late – and he was her passionate and most devoted lover.

'Giulia, my darling!' cried the Pope.

'Most Holy Lord!' murmured Giulia submissively.

And if there was laughter throughout Rome because the Holy Father, dressed as a Spanish grandee, had behaved like a young man of twenty with his mistress, little Alexander cared. His position was precarious, the French were almost in Rome, he had his crown to fight for – but that seemed little to a man of his immense genius for statecraft. His mistress was delighted to be back, turning away from younger lovers to be with him.

There remained one other thing necessary to his complete content. Lucrezia must be brought back to Rome.

Alone in her husband's palace at Pesaro, Lucrezia eagerly waited for news. Sometimes a wandering friar would come begging for food and a night's lodging; sometimes a messenger would arrive with letters from her father; Lucrezia welcomed such visitors warmly, and listened eagerly to all they had to tell, for she felt shut away from the world behind the hills which encircled Pesaro.

She heard that the conflict was growing, that Charles of France was on his way to Rome; she heard of Giulia's capture and release, and of the ransom which the Pope had gladly paid. She heard that her father had ridden out to meet his mistress dressed like a young man, a gallant Spanish grandee, and how happy he was to have Giulia with him once more.

Others might sneer at her father's behaviour. Lucrezia did not. She would sit at her window, looking out across the sea envying Giulia the affection and passion she inspired in the Pope, and thinking how different Alexander was from the cold man she had married.

But when she heard that the French were almost at the gates of Rome she trembled for her father.

There was no one in Rome who remained calmer than Alexander, as he considered the little King with his magnificent army, and the Italians who were eager to dress up and play at soldiers, but who were not so anxious to fight.

Cesare was with him at this time, sardonic because he had been denied the pleasure of defeating the French, losing no opportunity to point out to his father that had he been in charge of his *condotta* there would have been at least one company ready to hold back the invader.

He laughed scornfully and beat his fists against his chest.

'Oh, no! I must stay in the Church. I . . . who might have saved Rome, who might have saved Italy and would certainly have saved you from your present humiliating position, am not allowed to fight.'

'My dear son,' chid the Pope, 'you are too impetuous. Let us not be so hasty. The battle is not over yet.'

'Is Your Holiness aware,' said Cesare, 'that the French have stormed Civita Vecchia and that in a day or so they will be at the very gates of Rome?'

'I know it,' replied the Pope.

'And you intend to remain here so that the King can make you his prisoner and present you with his terms, to which you will have to agree?'

'You go too fast, my son. I am not yet little Charles's prisoner. And I have no intention of being so. Wait awhile. See who, in a few months' time, is the victor of the campaign. Do not, I pray you, make the mistake of placing yourself among my enemies who, from the moment the first French foot stepped onto Italian soil, have been telling themselves and each other that I am a defeated man.'

The calmness of Alexander had a soothing effect, even on Cesare.

But when the Pope saw the vanguard of the French army camping on Monte Mario, he knew that he must immediately, with his family, take refuge in the fortress of St Angelo.

The entry into Rome of the French King was spectacular. It was growing dark when he and his army came marching into the City, and in the twilight they seemed more terrifying than they would by day. They came by the light of a thousand torches, and the Romans shivered to behold them. The Germans and Swiss, who earned their livelihood by fighting other people's wars, were all stalwart men, strong and rough, as was to be expected. The French were fine soldiers and so far they had met nothing but easy victory. There were numerous noblemen accompanying the soldiers, and these were decked out with many a glittering jewel, mostly plunder, which had been picked up on the way to Rome. The Army took six hours to march past; there were the archers from Gascony and d'Aubigny's Scotsmen whose pipers played stirring music as they marched; there were the macebearers and crossbowmen, and thirty-six bronze cannon. With the procession came the King, the least awe-inspiring of any. Surrounded by his victorious army, the deformed and stunted Charles looked pathetic in his golden armour.

Through the Via Lata went the column to the Palace of Saint Mark, where the King was to have his lodging; and the cannon were formidably drawn up in the piazza.

From his fortress Alexander and his entourage heard the shouts in the city of 'Francia! Rovere!'

Cesare stood beside his father, clenching and unclenching his fists. He knew, as Alexander knew, that when night fell it would go hard with the citizens of Rome. There were tempting treasures in the houses – gold and silver plate, ornaments of majolica and pewter. And there were the women.

Rome, the eternal city, was about to be sacked.

And as they waited they heard the shouts, the screams, and the thousand tortured cries of a ravished city.

'There is my mother's house,' said Cesare in a low voice.

'Grieve not for a house,' said the Pope. 'Your mother will not be in it.'

'Where is my mother?' cried Cesare.

'Have no fear.   I arranged that she should leave Rome with her husband some days ago.'

How could he be so calm? Cesare wondered. The fate of the Borgias was in danger; yet he who had made the name great could stand there listening to the sounds of horror, serene, as though this was nothing but a passing thunder-storm.

Cesare cried: 'I will have my revenge on those brutes who enter my mother's house.'

'I doubt not that you will,' said Alexander quietly.

'But what are you doing? Oh my father, how *can* you remain so calm?'

'There is nothing else to be done,' said Alexander. 'We must wait for a propitious moment to make terms with *il Re Petito*.'

Cesare was astounded, for it seemed to him almost as though Alexander did not understand what was happening. But Alexander was thinking of another crisis in his life. Then his uncle had lain dying and the whole of Rome was crying out against the friends of Calixtus. Alexander's brother, Pedro Luis, had fled from Rome and consequently had never realized his great ambitions. Alexander had stayed, counting on his dignity and bold strategy; and Alexander had lived to succeed in his ambitions.

This was what he would do again.

In the Borgia apartments of the Vatican the little French King fidgeted. He paced up and down looking out of the windows across the gardens, beyond the orange trees and pines to Monte Mario.

He felt somewhat aggrieved. He came as a conqueror. Should he be expected to wait for the conquered? But this was no ordinary victim of a conquering army. This was the Holy Father himself, the head of the Catholic Church throughout the world. Charles was Catholic, his country was devoutly so; and Charles would never be able to cast aside the respect he felt for the Holy Father.

At last the Pope had agreed to discuss terms. What else

could he do? The north of Italy was conquered; Charles was in command of Rome, ready to fight his way south to Naples and achieve his country's great ambition.

The Pope had been forced to make terms. He had been besieged in Castle St Angelo, but when a bullet had pierced the walls of that seemingly impregnable fortress, he had felt it was time to come out and talk peace terms. And those terms, decided the French King, would be *his* terms, for the Holy Father, a prisoner in his own city, would be forced to agree to them.

The January sun was shining on the gold and enamel of Pinturicchio's murals, as yet not completed, and here portrayed were members of the Borgia family. Charles was studying them when he heard a movement in the room and turning saw a splendid figure in a golden mantle. For a moment he thought he was in the presence of a supernatural being and that one of the paintings on the walls had come to life. It was Alexander who had entered through a low and narrow doorway, and as the Pope advanced into the room, Charles fell to his knees immediately conscious of that great dignity.

Alexander bade him rise; his manner was paternal and benign.

'So, my son,' he said, 'we meet.'

And from that moment he was in command; Charles could not think of himself as the conqueror in this presence; he could only speak with the utmost respect to the Holy Father who spoke to his son, as though bidding him take courage in spite of the predicament in which he found himself.

It was quite ridiculous, but nevertheless Charles stammered that he wished free passage through the Papal States, and that he had come to demand it.

The Pope's eyebrows shot up at the word demand, but even as Charles was speaking he heard sounds of looting in the streets below and was brought back to reality, remembering that he was a conqueror and that the Pope was in his power.

'So you would ask for free passage,' mused the Pope. He looked beyond the French King, and he was smiling serenely as though he were looking into the future.

'Yes, Holiness.'

'Well, my son, we will grant you that, if you and your soldiers will leave Rome immediately.'

The King looked at one of his men who had stepped forward – a bold soldier who would not be impressed by his surroundings or the majestic personality of Alexander.

'The hostages, Sire,' he said.

'Ah yes, Most Holy Father,' said the King, 'we should need hostages if we left you free in Rome.'

'Hostages. It seems a just demand.'

'Right glad I am that Your Holiness agrees on this. We have decided on Cesare Borgia and the Turkish Prince Djem.'

The Pope was silent for a while. Prince Djem, yes. They were welcome to him. But Cesare!

Outside he heard the piteous wails of women; he could smell smoke. Rome was being ravished. She was in flames and crying out to her Holy Father in her agony. He must save Rome through Cesare and Djem.

Looking out over the beautiful Adriatic Sea, Lucrezia felt her uneasiness growing. She knew that Giovanni was in a desperate situation; he was in the pay of the Pope and the Neapolitans, and was working for Milan. How could she blame him? Nothing would have induced her to work against her own family, so how could she blame Giovanni for what he was doing? Lucrezia characteristically tried not to think of her husband; he was an unpleasant subject.

But to brood on the affairs of her family seemed even more so. What was happening to the Borgias? When travellers arrived at the Sforza palace Lucrezia had them brought immediately to her; she would give them food and shelter and implore them to tell her what was happening to her father.

She tried to visualize the situation. The French in Rome; her mother's house pillaged; her father forced to receive the little King of France and listen to his terms. And Cesare – proud Cesare – to be forced to ride out of Rome, a hostage of the conquerors. That was the worst thing that could have happened. She pictured his rage, and as she sat brooding, trying to turn her mind from unpleasantness, working a little with her needle, idly playing her lute, she was aware of disturbance below and, putting aside her work, she hurried down in case it should be messengers with news.

The arrival turned out to be that of a friar, humble and hungry, who was calling on the Lady of Pesaro to tell her the news – great news from Rome.

Lucrezia found it difficult to show him how delighted she was. She clapped her hands for slaves to bring him water with which to wash his tired feet; they brought wine and food for him; but before he was refreshed Lucrezia insisted on his telling her whether the news was good or bad.

'Good, lady,' he cried. 'The best of good news. As you know, the French conqueror had audience with the Holy Father in the Vatican, and there it was necessary for his Holiness to come to terms.'

Lucrezia nodded. 'And I know the terms included the giving of hostages, and that one of these was my brother Cesare.'

''Tis so, Madonna. They rode out of Rome with the conquerors. The Cardinal Borgia and the Turkish Prince.'

'How was my brother? Tell me that. Angry I know he must have been since his pride was brought so low.'

'No, Madonna. The Cardinal was serene. All those who watched him marvelled – not only at his calmness but also at that of the Holy Father who could watch his son depart with what seemed like indifference. We did not understand then. The Cardinal took with him much baggage. There were seventeen wagons all covered with velvet, and this caused much amusement among the French. "What sort of a Cardinal is this," they asked each other, "to be so concerned with his possessions!" And, as you will guess, Madonna, the Turkish Prince travelled with equal splendour.'

'So he rode out to the jeers of our enemies,' said Lucrezia, 'yet he rode with serenity and dignity. Oh, but how angry he must have been.'

'He surprised them when the soldiers encamped at the end of the first day. I have heard that it was a sight to behold when he threw off his Cardinal's robes and, stripped to the waist, wrestled with them and threw their champions.'

Lucrezia clasped her hands and laughed. 'That would have delighted him. I know it.'

'They were astonished that a Cardinal should behave thus, Madonna. But the next night he had a greater surprise for them.'

'Tell me quickly, I beg of you. I cannot endure the suspense of waiting.'

'The second night they halted at Velletri, on the edge of the Pontine Marshes. All was quiet and none noticed when one of the muleteers rose and moved silently among the foreign soldiers. That muleteer made his way to a tavern in the town and there he found a servant waiting with horses. The muleteer mounted a horse, and he and the servant rode hotfoot to Rome.'

'It was Cesare, my brother!'

'It was the Cardinal himself, Madonna. He has rejoined the Holy Father in Rome, and I heard that there is much laughter and merrymaking in the Vatican on this account.'

Lucrezia laughed with pleasure.

'It is the best news I have heard for a long time. How he would have enjoyed that! And poor fat Djem, he did not escape?'

'Nay, the Prince remains with his captors. It is said that he lacked the stamina of His Eminence. He could not wrestle with the French; nor could he have managed to escape. He stays behind. But they have only one hostage where they wished for two; and the more important of the two – the Pope's own son – has escaped them.'

Lucrezia rose to her feet and there before the friar danced a few steps of a Spanish dance.

The friar watched in astonishment, but Lucrezia only threw back her head and laughed as she whirled round and round until she was breathless.

Then she paused and explained: 'I am carried away with joy. This is an omen. My brother has made a laughing stock of the French. It is a beginning. My father will rid Italy of the conquerors, and all men throughout the land will be grateful to him. This is the beginning, I tell you. Come! Now you shall eat your fill of the best we have in this palace. You shall drink the best wine. You must be merry. This night there shall be a banquet in the palace and you shall be our guest of honour.'

'Madonna, you rejoice too soon,' murmured the friar. 'This

is but the escape of a hostage. So much of Italy lies in the hands of the conqueror.'

'My father will save all Italy,' said Lucrezia solemnly.

But she was solemn only for a moment. Now she was calling to her slaves and attendants. She wanted them to prepare a banquet; there would be dancing and revelry in the palace this day.

Cesare had triumphed, and Cesare's triumphs were as important to her as her own.

Lucrezia was right. That was the beginning of brighter prospects. The French were furious at the hoax played on them by Cesare, but there was nothing they could do about it. A protest to Alexander made him shake his head sorrowfully. 'The Cardinal has behaved badly, very badly,' he murmured; and had to retire hastily to give vent to the laughter which shook him.

Fat little Djem could not stand up to the rigours of life with an army; he was stricken with fever and died. Thus in a short while the French were robbed of both their hostages.

However, they went marching on to Naples, where Alfonso, the King, hearing of their approach, hurried to Sicily leaving his kingdom in the hands of his son Ferrandino. But Ferrandino proved to be no soldier, and when he saw the French armies approaching, followed his father's example – choosing the island of Ischia for his refuge, whither he went with his court – leaving Naples open to the invaders.

This seemed good luck for Charles, but the French King had reckoned without the climate and the indolence of his soldiers. Italy lay behind them, a conquered country, and they were encamped in sunny Naples. The women were luscious, the brothels were numerous, and the soldiers determined to enjoy a rest from the march.

Meanwhile Alexander had not been idle. Messengers had been riding hard back and forth between the Vatican and Venice, to Milan, to the King of Spain and to the Emperor Maximilian.

Alexander pointed out that unless they quickly became his allies, Italy would fall completely under the dominion of the

French, and that this would be to the advantage of none of
them.

When the French King heard of the alliances which were
being formed he became alarmed. His soldiers were in a debili-
tated condition; moreover they were becoming insubordinate,
and many of them were sick. Charles was about to receive the
crown of Naples, when it occurred to him that this crown
would be of little use to him if he was to wear it but for a week
or so before his enemies overcame him.

There was only one way out of his difficulty. He must leave
Italy with all speed. But on his way he would see the Pope,
whom he rightly suspected of organizing his, Charles's, enemies
against him, and he would demand from him the investiture of
Naples.

Charles left Naples and started the march northward, but
Alexander, hearing of his approach, immediately left Rome for
Perugia, so that when Charles reached Rome he found the
Vatican deserted.

Fuming with anger, he could do nothing but continue his
march.

He was bewildered. He had conquered the land with his
victorious armies, and the rulers of states had fallen before him;
then he had come to Rome, believing that the Borgia Pope was
as much his vassal as those heads of states who had stood aside
for him. It had seemed so. And yet . . . it was not so.

Charles went marching on, cursing the wily fox of the
Vatican.

Alexander found life amusing at Perugia. Once again he had
proved his strategy to be sound. It was as it had been at the
time of the death of Calixtus. He had waited then, as now,
serene, accommodating; and now, as then, his enemies had
played into his hands.

With him were Giulia and Cesare; but there was one whom
he sadly missed; his dearest daughter.

'Lucrezia must come to us here,' he told Cesare. 'She has
been parted from us too long.'

Cesare smiled at the prospect of seeing his sister again. He
was feeling happier. His father had been highly amused by his

adventure. Was he beginning to see what an asset Cesare would be as a commander of the armies? It was not like a Cardinal to wrestle, as he had, with soldiers, and to accomplish such a spectacular escape.

Cesare was twenty; he was growing in stature; and the Pope, for all his miraculous virility, was sixty-four years of age.

Cesare began to think of the day when his father would turn to him for advice, and when he, Cesare, would make the decisions.

Now they were in perfect accord, for they had both determined that Lucrezia should come to them at Perugia.

Giovanni Sforza, who was back in Pesaro, was not pleased by the message from the Pope.

He stormed into Lucrezia's apartment where she was giving orders as to the packing of her baggage.

'You shall not go,' he said.

'Not go?' The light eyes were wide with incredulity. 'But these are orders from my father.'

'I am your husband. It is I who shall say where you may go.'

'Giovanni, you cannot refuse to allow me to go.'

'I can and I will.'

He was bold; that was because he was thinking of the miles between Perugia and Pesaro. Poor Giovanni! thought Lucrezia. He is not a bold man.

But almost immediately she was alarmed, for she too remembered the distance between Pesaro and Perugia.

Giovanni was a weak man and as such he was always eager to show his strength when he thought he had a chance of doing so. Now he turned to her servants. 'Take out the Countess's gowns,' he said. 'Put them back where they belong.'

Then he turned and left her.

Lucrezia did not storm or rage. She was like her father and was aware of the efficacy of diplomacy. She was convinced that after a short delay, she would be on her way to Perugia. So she smiled regretfully and sat down to pen a letter to her father.

Giovanni had his price. He was learning the necessity of bargaining. He was kept poor and of no importance, but the

Borgias must remember that although his wife was the Pope's daughter, as her husband he, Giovanni, had some control over her. Since she was so precious to them, they must show some respect to her husband. He wanted to be freed from the invidious position into which they had thrust him. He wanted a new command; and since the Pope had made an alliance with Venice, why should he not be enrolled as a Captain in the Venetian army? The Pope could easily arrange this for his son-in-law; let him do it and, for such services, Giovanni Sforza would place no restrictions on his wife's movements.

When the Pope heard of Sforza's aspirations, he laughed aloud.

'Why,' he said to Cesare, 'there is some spirit in the poor thing after all. I will see what can be arranged with the Doge.'

Cesare was scornful of his brother-in-law. He would have hated him, whoever he was, simply because he was Lucrezia's husband, but it seemed humiliating to him that his sister should have had to accept such a man.

' 'Tis a pity,' he said to his father, 'that we cannot find some means of ridding Lucrezia of Sforza.'

The Pope's gaze shifted a little. 'Mayhap . . .' he murmured. 'Sometime. . . . At the moment we will pass him to the Doge.'

Giovanni stormed up and down his wife's apartments.

'So,' he cried, 'I am tò have a *condotta* in the Venetian army!'

'And you are glad, are you not?' asked Lucrezia lightly. 'Was not that what you wanted?'

'I should have equal treatment with your brother,' shouted Giovanni.

'Is that not what you have? Giovanni Sforza and Giovanni Borgia both have commands in the Doge's army. Is that not so?'

'Yes, it is so. We both have commands. But there is a difference. Your father has seen to that. I am to get four thousand ducats . . . your brother thirty-one thousand!'

'But Giovanni,' soothed Lucrezia, 'if you had not heard what my brother was to have, you would have been happy with your four thousand.'

'But I *have* heard!' Giovanni's veins stood out at the temples. 'I am treated thus to show that I am of no importance beside your brother. Your father deliberately insults me. I shall not let you go.'

Lucrezia was silent for a few seconds; then she said demurely: 'If you do not, then even the four thousand ducats will not be yours.'

Giovanni clenched his fists and stamped his foot. He looked as though he would burst into tears.

Lucrezia watched him dispassionately. She thought: Soon we shall set out for Perugia and when he has taken me there he will leave us.

She gave herself up to the pleasure of contemplating reunion with her father and Cesare.

CESARE

LUCREZIA WAS EMBRACED by her father and Cesare, and how warm, how passionate were those embraces!

'I cannot understand how we managed to live without you,' declared the Pope.

'We have missed you more than we can tell,' Cesare murmured.

She turned from one to the other, taking their hands and kissing them. 'Oh my father, oh my brother!' she cried. 'Why is it that all other men seem small and insignificant beside you?'

They made her turn about as they studied each detail of her appearance. She had changed, declared Cesare; and temporarily his brow darkened; he was remembering that her marriage had now been consummated.

'Our little one grows up,' murmured the Pope. 'I reproach myself. It would have been possible to have kept you with me, my dearest, through all the troubles.'

'There were many uneasy moments,' mused Cesare, 'I think we should have suffered agonies of anxiety, Holiness, if our beloved one had been exposed to danger.'

'You are right, my son. And why should we grieve over what is past. Let there be a banquet to welcome my dearest child, and let me see you two dance and sing together.'

Cesare had taken her hand. 'And what say you sister?'

'I long to dance with you. I long to show everyone how happy I am that we are re-united.'

Cesare had taken her face in his hands and was studying it intently. 'How have you changed, sister?'

'I am a little older, nothing more.'

'More learned in the ways of the world,' said the Pope fondly and almost archly.

Cesare kissed her. 'I trust, dearest sister, your ordeal has not been too tedious?'

She knew what he meant, and she laughed. 'No, it was well enough.'

The Pope, watching them, laid his hand on Cesare's shoulder. 'Let her go now. Let her women dress her for our banquet. Then I shall see you two dancing together and I shall feel so happy because I have two of my dear ones under the same roof as myself.'

Lucrezia kissed her father's hand and both men watched her as she left them.

'How enchanting she is!' said Cesare.

'I am beginning to believe she is the loveliest girl in Italy,' replied the Pope.

'I am sure of it,' Cesare said.

He looked at his father quickly. Giulia was losing her hold on the Pope, for he had not forgiven her since she had lived with her husband. He had made the grand gesture of riding out to greet her when he had paid her ransom, but Cesare was fully aware that Giulia was no longer the Pope's favourite mistress, and he was glad. He had always been irritated by the rise to power of the Farnese family.

While he appeared to take frivolous pleasure in the revelries which were going on about him, Alexander was planning ahead. He now said to Cesare: 'I hope it will not be long before we return to Rome. There is much we have to do if we are going to prevent near disasters arising such as that through which we have now passed. Cesare, we must concentrate on destroying the power of the barons who proved themselves to be so weak and feeble at the approach of the invader. I visualize a strong Italy.'

'A strong Italy under the Papacy,' agreed Cesare. 'You need a strong army, Father, and good generals.'

'You are right, my son.'

Alexander saw the request rising to Cesare's lips: Release me. See what a general I will make.

It was not the time, Alexander realized, to tell Cesare that as soon as he was in Rome he intended to bring back Giovanni from Spain. Giovanni should have charge of the Pope's armies and he should go out and do battle against the Orsinis, who during the French invasion had shown themselves to be traitors to the Pope's interest. When he had subdued them, rival families would see how powerful the Pope had become; they would conform to the wishes of the Borgia Pope or suffer likewise.

He would have enjoyed talking of these matters with Cesare, but clearly they could only lead to one subject: the recall from Spain of Giovanni.

It was so pleasant to have his dear Lucrezia with him; it made him happy to see Cesare's delight in her and hers in him. Alexander did not want anything to spoil that pleasure, so deftly changed the subject.

'Our little Lucrezia . . .' he murmured. 'I would we had found a husband more worthy of her.'

'It maddens me to think of that oaf . . . that provincial boor . . . near my sister.'

'We will arrange it so that he does not enjoy Perugia,' suggested the Pope.

Cesare was smiling again. 'We must send him with all speed to the Doge,' he said. 'Can it be arranged?'

'We must put our heads together, my son. Then we shall have Lucrezia to ourselves.'

Lucrezia lay on her bed, her hair damp about her. She felt a strange excitement as she recalled the pleasures of the previous night. It had been a grand banquet in the palace of Gian-paolo Baglioni, who as a fief-holder of the Church had deemed it his duty and pleasure to entertain the Holy Father.

Baglioni was a fascinating man, handsome and bold. There were stories in circulation about his cruelty, and his slaves and servants trembled at a stern look from him. Cesare had told her as they danced that in the dungeons below the palace those who offended Baglioni were tortured without mercy.

It seemed hard to believe that such a fascinating man could be cruel; he had shown nothing but kindness to Lucrezia. If she had seen anyone tortured at his command she would have hated him; but the dungeons were a long way from the banqueting hall, and the cries of victims could not reach the revellers.

Baglioni had watched her and Cesare as they danced, and

his eyes were full of malicious amusement. So were those of others.

'The Spanish dances, Cesare,' she had whispered. 'Our father would like to see us dance them.'

And they had danced, she and Cesare together, danced as she had danced with her brother Giovanni at her wedding. She had recalled those wedding dances, but had not referred to them; she did not want to make Cesare angry on such a night.

Baglioni had danced with a very beautiful woman, his mistress.

He was tender towards her and, watching them, Lucrezia whispered to Cesare: 'How gentle he is! Yet they say that he inflicts terrible torture on those who offend him.'

Then Cesare had drawn her to him. 'What has his gentleness towards her to do with his cruelty towards others?'

'Merely that it is difficult to believe that one who can be so gentle could also be so cruel.'

'Am I not tender? Am I not cruel?'

'You . . . Cesare . . . you are different from anyone else on Earth.'

That had made him smile; and she had felt his fingers gripping her hand so that she could have cried out in pain; but the pain inflicted by Cesare had always in some strange way delighted her.

'When we return to Rome,' he had told her, and the expression on his face had made her shudder, 'I will do such things to those who violated our mother's house as men will talk of for years to come. I will commit acts to equal those which take place in Baglioni's dungeons. And all the time I shall love you, my sister, with the same fierce yet gentle love which you have had from me since you were a baby in your cradle.'

'Oh Cesare . . . have a care. What good can it do to remember what was done in the heat of war?'

'This is the good it can do, sister. It will show all those who took part that in future they must remember what they risk by daring to insult me or mine. Ah, you are right in saying that Baglioni loves that woman.'

'She is his favourite mistress, I have heard; and there can be no doubt of it.'

'Have you heard aught else concerning her, Lucrezia?'

'Aught else? I think not, Cesare.'

He had laughed suddenly, and his eyes had grown wild. 'She is indeed his beloved,' he had said; 'she is also his sister.'

It was of this Lucrezia was thinking as she lay on her bed.

Her husband came into the room and stood by the bed looking at his wife. Then he waved his hands to the woman who sat close by, stitching at one of Lucrezia's gowns.

Lucrezia studied her husband through half-closed eyes. He seemed smaller, less imposing, here at Perugia than he had at Pesaro. There she had seen him as her husband and, being Lucrezia, she was ready to be contented with what life had given her; she had done her best to love him. It was true she had found him unsatisfying, cold, lacking in ardour. Her desires had been aroused, and she was constantly aware of their remaining unsatisfied.

Here at Perugia she saw him through the eyes of her brother and father; and it was a different man she saw.

'So,' he cried, 'I am to go. I am to leave you here.'

'Is that so, Giovanni?' she asked languidly, making sure that he should not be aware of the faint pleasure which she was feeling.

'You know it!' he stormed. 'It may well be that you have asked to have me removed.'

'I? Giovanni! But you are my husband.'

He came to the bed and took her roughly by the arm. 'Forget it not,' he said.

'How could I forget such a thing?'

'You might well do so now that you are with your family.'

'No, Giovanni. We all talk of you constantly.'

'Talk of how you can rid yourselves of me, eh?'

'Why should we wish to?'

That made him laugh.

'What fine bracelets you are wearing! Whence came they? Do not tell me – I'll guess: A present from the Holy Father. What fine presents for a father to give his daughter! He lavished nothing better on Madonna Giulia at the height of his passion for her. And your brother, he is equally attentive. He rivals his father, one might say.'

She lowered her eyes; she let her long slender fingers play with the jewelled ornaments on her wrists.

She remembered her father's putting them there; the solemn kisses, the words of love.

'They do not want me here,' shouted Giovanni. 'I am an encumbrance. I am a nuisance. Am I not your husband?'

'I pray you, Giovanni, do not make such scenes,' she said. 'My brother might hear you.'

She looked at him then, and saw the lights of fear come into his eyes. The mention of Cesare's name did that to many people, she knew.

His clenched fists had dropped to his sides. He took one look at the beautiful and seductive girl on the bed; then he turned away.

She was the decoy. He must be careful. He was like a careless fly who had flown into the Borgia web. The safest thing he could do was to escape while he had time. At the moment he was a mild irritation to them. Who knew what he might become?

He thought of her gentleness and of the first weeks in Pesaro when she had truly become his wife. She was young and seemingly innocent; she was also very beautiful, very responsive; indeed, perhaps too responsive; with his natural fear he had been a little afraid of something which had warned him of pent-up passion within that exquisitely formed yet frail body.

He wanted to say to her: Come away with me. Come secretly. Do not let them know, because they will never allow you to escape them.

But if she came with him, what would happen to the pair of them? They would never be allowed to escape. He understood that. He realized now why they would not let her go.

The knowledge came to him when he had seen Baglioni and his mistress at their banquet. The Pope had blessed them both, Baglioni and his mistress, and the Pope had known about them.

Giovanni Sforza hesitated. Take her with you, urged a voice within him; she is your wife. As yet she is undefiled; she is gentle and there is kindness in her. They have not yet made her one of them . . . but they will. And she is your wife . . . yours to mould, yours to keep for ever.

But he was a meek man. He had watched the look in her father's eyes as they had rested on her; he had seen the fierce possessiveness in those of her brother.

But Giovanni dared not, for he was a frightened man.

'I am to go,' he cried out in sudden anger. 'And you will stay. They are saying in Rome that there is ample shelter for you beneath the apostolic robe!'

She seemed to have forgotten he was there.

She was thinking of herself dancing with Cesare, and of Baglioni, sitting at the table caressing his beautiful sister.

Cesare had been right when he had said she had grown up. There were many things which she was now beginning to understand.

Lucrezia's slaves were combing her long hair. Freshly washed, it gleamed golden as it fell over her shoulders. She was growing more beautiful. Her face still wore the innocent look which was perhaps largely due to her receding chin and wide eyes; but in those eyes there was now an expectancy.

She was back in Rome after a brief visit to Pesaro, and her husband Giovanni was with her again, but soon he would be going away. He must return to his *condotta*. She was glad he was going. She was weary of Giovanni and his continual insinuations. At the same time she was conscious of her father's growing dislike of her husband, and of Cesare's firm hatred.

Cesare was the most important person in her life, yet still she retained her fear of him – that exquisite terror which he aroused in her and which she was beginning to understand.

Her life with Giovanni had taught her what she could expect from men, and it might have been that, because she now knew herself to be capable of passion even as were her father and brothers, she was eagerly waiting for what the future would bring her. From Giovanni she expected nothing; yet, because he was a coward, and because he was continually worried by his lack of dignity and the lack of respect paid to him, she was sorry for him; and she would be glad when he had left, because not only was she sorry for him, she was afraid for him.

Her women had fixed the jewelled net over her hair and she was ready for the banquet.

This was to be in honour of the conqueror of Fornovo, and her father had insisted that Gonzaga should be entertained at the Palace of Santa Maria in Portico, that all Rome might know in what esteem he held his beautiful daughter.

So she was indeed growing up. This night would be gathered in her house all the most notable people in Rome, and she was to be their hostess.

Giovanni Sforza would be angry, for it would be clearly shown that he was of little importance. He would be in the background and no one would take any notice of him; and when Gonzaga rode away, Giovanni would ride with him and there would be a brief respite from his company once more.

She was very lovely as she went to greet her guests, her tiny negress holding the train of her dress which was of rich brocade and stiff with jewels. She had the gift of looking both younger and older'than her sixteen years – at one moment an innocent child, at another a woman.

There assembled were her father, brother and members of the Papal Court, and among them the retinue of Francesco Gonzaga, the Marquis of Mantua.

The Marquis himself stood before her, a man of striking appearance and personality. He was very tall, thin and very dark; and his body, though graceful in the extreme, suggested an immense strength and virility. His dark eyes were brilliant, deep set, and their hooded lids gave them the appearance of being constantly half-closed; his lips were full and sensuous; he was clearly a man who had enjoyed many adventures – both in love and war.

He bowed graciously before the daughter of the Pope.

'I have heard much of your charms, Madonna,' he said in a voice which held a note of tenderness; 'it gives me the greatest pleasure to kiss your hand.'

'We have heard much of you here,' murmured Lucrezia. 'The story of your valour has travelled before you.'

He sat beside her and told her of the battle, of how he reproached himself because the French King had escaped.

'He left behind him many prisoners,' said Lucrezia, 'so we

have heard here, with many of the treasures which he had taken from the people of Italy.'

It was true, agreed Gonzaga, and he went on to explain more details of the campaign, amazed at himself for talking thus to a beautiful girl. But this was merely a child. She was sixteen years old, but to him she seemed much younger.

As for Lucrezia, she wished this attractive man would talk of himself, which she knew would interest her far more than details of his battles.

They danced, and she felt a tingle of excitement run through her as their hands touched. She thought: If Giovanni Sforza had been such a man, how differently I could have felt towards him.

She lifted her eyes and smiled at him, but he still saw her as a child.

The Pope and Cesare watched them as they danced.

'A handsome pair,' said the Pope.

Cesare looked uneasy. 'Gonzaga is notorious for his attractiveness to women. He should not think that Lucrezia is for his taking before he passes on to the next conquest.'

'Rest assured he does not,' murmured Alexander. 'He sees her as a pretty child.'

There was another matter which Alexander would have to broach soon to Cesare, and he wished to choose the right moment for doing so. Giovanni Borgia would receive his father's letter very soon, and he had no doubt that the young Duke of Gandia would lose little time in returning to Rome.

And when he came, Alexander was going to put him in charge of his armies, which would infuriate Cesare.

They are my sons, pondered Alexander; is it not for me to command them?

Perhaps. But, as he looked at the glowering face beside him, he was uneasy. That dark and brooding side of Cesare's nature had become more pronounced of late. Cesare had had great devotion showered upon him; he had enjoyed many privileges. When he was at the universities the wealth and power of his father had enabled him to assemble a little court of his own, a court of which he was the despotic ruler. There were disquieting rumours regarding Cesare's powers and the methods he employed for ridding himself of his enemies.

Alexander would not believe that he, the all-powerful Pope, who had recently triumphed over his enemies, was afraid of his own son.

Yet now he hesitated to tell him that there was little doubt that his brother would soon be in Rome.

Instead he spoke of Goffredo, that younger son, whom he had also recalled.

'It is time,' he said, 'that Goffredo and Sanchia were with us. The rumours concerning that woman grow more and more interesting.'

That made Cesare laugh; and there was nothing Alexander liked so much as to enjoy a little light-hearted gossip with the members of his family. It seemed very amusing to them both to contemplate little Goffredo with this wife of his, who was notorious for her amours.

'Such a woman,' said Cesare lightly, 'will be an interesting addition to Your Beatitude's household.'

Lucrezia stood with her father and Cesare on the balcony, watching the departure of Francesco Gonzaga. He rode at the head of that procession, the man who had stirred some feeling of regret within her because Giovanni Sforza was not such a man. Now Francesco was making his way to Naples and, as he passed through Italy, everywhere he would be honoured as the man who, with the Holy Father, had done more than any to drive the invader from the land.

He had the appearance of a conqueror. The crowds shouted their acclaim; they strewed flowers in his path and the eyes of the women were for him alone in the vast procession.

Graciously he acknowledged the acclaim, his dark eyes lighting as they fell on some girl or woman outstanding for her beauty. A smile of admiration for the beauty, regret that he was but passing by, would touch his face momentarily changing its expression.

He turned and smiled his last farewell to the group on the balcony, and his eyes rested briefly on the daughter of the Pope, for she was such a pretty child with her glistening golden hair, but if the thought occurred to him that in a few years' time she would be worthy of a closer acquaintance, it was quickly forgotten. There was one other who rode in the procession and who turned to take a last look at the assembly on the balcony: this was Giovanni Sforza. He felt angry as his eyes rested on the golden-haired girl. There she stood between father and brother, and it seemed to Giovanni that she was their captive. They would take her from him; they would make her one of them, and very soon it would be impossible to recognize the docile girl who had been his wife during those months at Pesaro. He felt regretful for those months, for he knew that he would never again live in such harmony with his gentle Lucrezia.

Already she was changing. She was a young girl still, but she was a Borgia, and they had determined to stamp her with the mark of the Borgia. In a few years' time – perhaps less – she would be as they were ... that charming innocence lost, her sensuality enlarged so that she, too, would be ready to appease it at no matter what cost; they would tarnish that tenderness in her; they would supplant it with indifference.

He longed to turn back, to storm into the palace, to force her to leave them and come with him back to Pesaro where they would live away from the conflict of politics and the shadow of her scheming and unscrupulous family.

But who was he to dream such dreams? He was a small man; he was a coward who had always been afraid of someone or something, always trying to shake off the memory of humiliation.

No. It was too late. They had taken her from him and already she was estranged; already he had lost her.

Mists of anger danced before his eyes.

Francesco had turned to him.

'It grieves you,' he said, 'to leave the Lady Lucrezia.'

Sforza laughed bitterly. 'It does not grieve her,' he said. 'She is happy enough to settle under the apostolic mantle.'

Francesco was looking at him oddly. Sforza, remembering past slights, could not stop himself from muttering savagely: 'His Holiness is eager to be rid of me. He wishes to have the complete care of his daughter ... he wishes to be husband as well as father.'

There was silence. Francesco was looking ahead of him; the cavalcade rode on.

On the balcony the Pope was looking fondly at his daughter.

'So Gonzaga rides away,' he said. 'Now, my dearest, you must make preparations to greet your brother Goffredo and your sister-in-law Sanchia. It will not be long now before they are with us.'

SANCHIA OF ARAGON

THE VOLUPTUOUS SANCHIA lay on her bed nibbling sweetmeats. Sprawling on the bed, helping themselves now and then from the dish were her three favourite ladies-in-waiting: Loysella, Francesca and Bernardina.

Sanchia was telling them about last night's lover, for she enjoyed recounting details of her various love affairs, declaring that thus she acquired a double pleasure – first in actuality, then in memory.

Sanchia was strikingly beautiful, and one of her greatest attractions was the contrast between her dark hair, dark brows, olive skin and her startling blue eyes. Her features were bold, her nose aquiline and beautifully shaped; her mouth was soft and sensual. To look at Sanchia was to be reminded immediately of erotic pleasures; Sanchia knew this, and the frank sensuality of her smile suggested that she had made discoveries which were unknown to all others but which she would be delighted to impart to those at whom she was smiling, that they and they alone might share this secret.

Sanchia had had lovers for as long as she could remember and she knew that she would go on taking them until she died.

'I do not anticipate the journey with much pleasure,' she was saying now. 'But what fun it will be when we arrive in Rome. I am halfway in love with Cesare Borgia already, and I have not even seen him. Oh, what a great passion awaits us!'

'You will make the Pope jealous of his own son,' suggested Francesca.

'I think not. I think not. I shall leave his Holiness to you, Loysella, or perhaps to little Bernardina. Together mayhap you will compensate him for his weariness of Madonna Giulia – she who is known as La Bella.'

Loysella said: 'Madonna, you should not talk thus of the Holy Father.'

'He is but a man, my child. And do not look so shocked. It is not as though I suggest you should be bedfellow to that mad monk Savonarola.'

Loysella shivered, but Sanchia's eyes were speculative. 'I have never had a lover who was a monk,' she mused. 'Perhaps on our journey we shall pass by some monastery....'

'Oh, you are wicked, Madonna,' said Francesca with a giggle. 'Are you not afraid to talk thus?'

'I am afraid of nothing,' retorted Sanchia. 'I confess and I do my penances. When I am old I shall reform my ways and doubtless enter a nunnery.'

'It will have to be a monastery for you, wicked one,' said Loysella.

'Nay, nay, although I would try a monk, it would be but for once. I do not ask for monk night after night ... day after day.'

'Hush!' said Francesca. 'If our conversation were reported ...'

'It matters not. No one attempts to make me change my ways. My father the King knew how I love men, yet what did he do? He said: "She is one of us. You cannot grow oranges on pear trees." My brother shakes his head and agrees; and even my old grandmother knew it was useless to try to reform me.'

'His Holiness will reform you. It is for this reason that he sends for you.'

Sanchia smiled wickedly. 'From what I hear of His Holiness it is not to *reform* me that he invites me to Rome.'

Loysella pretended to stop her ears because she would not listen to such profanity, but Sanchia merely laughed and bade Francesca bring out the necklace of gold and rubies which her latest lover had brought her.

She leaped up and putting on the necklace paraded before them.

'He said: "Only the best is worthy to adorn that perfect body."'

She grimaced and looked at the necklace. 'I hope it is of the best,' she said.

'The workmanship is exquisite,' Francesca cried, examining it.

'You may try it on,' said Sanchia. 'All of you. Ah,' she went on, 'last night was wonderful. To-night perhaps will be as exciting, but perhaps not. It is the voyage of discovery which enchants me. The second night is like crossing a sea which has already been traversed. Not the same surprises . . . not the same discoveries. How I wish I had been here when the French soldiers were in Naples!'

Francesca pretended to shiver. 'There have been such tales. You would not have escaped. They would have seized on you.'

'That would have been exciting. And they say the French are good lovers, and so chivalrous, so gallant. To think that while we were cowering on that dull, dull island of Ischia, such exciting things were going on in Naples.'

'You might have hated it,' suggested Bernardina. 'There was one woman who, pursued by soldiers, killed herself by leaping from the roof of her house.'

'I can think of better resting places than the courtyard stones,' said Sanchia. 'Oh yes, I wish I had been here to meet the gallant French. I was angry . . . quite angry when we were hustled away to live in exile. That is why I must take so many lovers now. There is much time to be made up. You understand?'

'Our lady makes up for lost time very creditably,' Loysella murmured.

'At least,' said Sanchia, 'the rumours have not lied. His Holiness writes to my father that accounts of my conduct, which have reached him in Rome, have most seriously disturbed him.'

'Madonna . . . Sanchia, take care . . . take care when you reach Rome.'

'Take care! Nay, I'll take Cesare instead.'

'I have heard much talk of Cesare,' said Loysella.

'Strange talk,' put in Francesca.

'It is said,' went on Loysella, 'that when he casts his eyes on a woman and says "Come hither", she dare not disobey. If she does, she is taken by force and punished for having dared delay in obeying the lord Cardinal.'

'I have heard,' added Bernardina, 'that he roams the streets looking for suitable virgins to fill his harem. I have heard that any who stand in his way die mysteriously; none knows how.'

Sanchia clasped her hands at the back of her neck, threw back her rippling black hair and laughed. 'He sounds more exciting than any man I have ever met. I long to see him face to face.'

'Take care, Sanchia,' begged Bernardina. 'Take care when you come face to face with Cesare Borgia.'

'I would have you take care,' said Sanchia with a laugh. 'I pray you keep my little Goffredo busy this evening. I do not want him strolling into my bedchamber when I am entertaining visitors. It is bad for the dear little creature's morals.'

The girls laughed.

'Dear Goffredo. He's a darling, and so pretty. I long to pet him,' declared Francesca.

'You may pet him all you wish,' Sanchia promised her. 'But I pray you keep him from my bedchamber. Where is he now? Let us have him come to us and tell us about his brother. After all, he knows more of Cesare Borgia than any one of us.'

They helped Sanchia into her gown, and she was lying back on her pillows when Goffredo came in.

He was very pretty and looked younger than his years, for he was nearly fourteen.

He ran to the bed and threw himself down beside his wife. She put out an arm and held him against her while she stroked his beautiful hair, which was touched with tints of copper. His long-lashed eyes looked at his wife with admiration. He knew that he had married a woman who was said to be the most lovely in all Italy. He had heard her beauty compared with that of his sister, Lucrezia, and his father's mistress, Giulia; and most of those who had seen the three beauties declared that Sanchia had beauty to equal the others and something more – there was a witchery about Sanchia, something which made her unique. She was insatiably sensual; she scattered promises of undreamed-of delight on all those of the opposite sex who came near her. Thus, although the golden beauty of Lucrezia and Giulia was admired, the dark beauty of Sanchia was more than admired; it was never forgotten.

'And what has my little husband been doing this day?' asked Sanchia.

He put up his face to kiss the firm white chin. 'I have been riding,' he said. 'What a pretty necklace!'

'It was given me last night.'

'I did not see you last night. Loysella said I must not disturb you.'

'Wicked Loysella,' said Sanchia lightly.

'You had a lover with you,' stated Goffredo. 'Was he pleasing?'

She kissed his head absently, thinking of last night's lover.

'I have known worse, and I have known better,' she pronounced judgment.

Goffredo laughed and lifted his shoulder slightly, as a child does in pleasure. He turned to Loysella and said: 'My wife has had more lovers than any other woman in Naples – except courtesans of course. You cannot include courtesans, you will agree.'

'Agreed,' said Francesca.

'Now,' demanded Sanchia, 'tell us about your brother. Tell us about the famous Cesare Borgia.'

'You will never have known a man like my brother Cesare.'

'All that we have heard leads us to believe it,' Sanchia answered.

'My father loves him dearly,' boasted Goffredo, 'and no woman has ever said no to him.'

'We have heard that women are punished for saying no to him,' said Loysella. 'How can that be, if none ever do?'

'Because they know he would punish them if they said no. They would be afraid to say it. Therefore they do not say no, but yes . . . yes . . . yes.'

'It's logic,' said Sanchia. 'So must we all prepare ourselves to say yes . . . yes . . . yes.'

She popped a sweetmeat into Goffredo's mouth; he lay back against her, sucking contentedly.

'Francesca,' commanded Sanchia, 'comb my little husband's hair. It is such pretty hair. When it is brushed it glows like copper.'

Francesca obeyed; the other two girls stretched themselves

out at the foot of the bed. Sanchia lay back sleepily, her arm about Goffredo. Occasionally she would reach for a sweetmeat and nibble a piece before putting it into Goffredo's mouth.

Goffredo, well contented, began to boast.

He boasted about Cesare – Cesare's prowess, Cesare's cruelty.

Goffredo did not know for whom his admiration was the greater: for his brother at whose name everyone in Rome trembled, or for his wife who had taken more lovers than any woman in Naples, except of course courtesans – which was an unfair comparison.

The cavalcade which made its way towards Rome was a merry one, for in its centre rode the lovely Sanchia with her little husband and her three devoted ladies-in-waiting. Sanchia had the bearing of a queen; it might have been because she was the illegitimate daughter of the King of Naples that in public she assumed an air of royalty; this enhanced her startling attractiveness because, underlying the air of royalty, was that look of promise which was directed towards any personable young men she encountered, no matter if they were no more than grooms.

Her ladies-in-waiting laughed at her promiscuity; they themselves were far from prudish; lighthearted in their love affairs as butterflies on a sunny day, they flitted from lover to lover: but they lacked the stamina of Sanchia.

Sanchia had ceased to regret that she had not stayed behind in Naples during the French invasion. She had ceased to care because she had not been allowed to meet the French King. Cesare Borgia, she felt sure, would be a more amusing and exciting lover than poor little Charles.

In any case Sanchia was not one to repine. Life was too full of pleasure for such as she was; *her* kingdom was within her reach. Sad and terrible things might happen to those about her. Her father had been driven to exile and to madness. Poor Father! He had been heartbroken when the French took his kingdom.

Knowing of his anguish, Sanchia was determined not to set store on such treasures as those which delighted her father.

When she had heard that they were to marry her to a little boy – a Pope's bastard and not even a favourite bastard at that – she had at first been piqued. That was because the proposed marriage had shown her clearly that she was not of the same importance as her half-sister who was the legitimate daughter of King Alfonso.

Goffredo Borgia, the son of Vannozza Catanei and possibly the Borgia Pope – and possibly not! She knew that there had been suspicions as to her little husband's birth and that at times even the Pope had declared the boy to be no son of his. Should Sanchia, daughter of the King of Naples – illegitimate though she might be – be given in marriage to such as Goffredo?

But they had explained to her: Whether or not he is the Pope's bastard, the Pope accepts him, and that is all that matters.

They were right. The Pope sought alliance with Naples and it was for this reason that the marriage was arranged. But suppose there should be a time when the Pope fell out with Naples and no longer considered the marriage could bring him good?

She had heard how Giovanni Sforza had fallen out of favour with the Pope, and how shabbily he was treated in Vatican circles.

But that was different. Sforza was a man, not very attractive, not prepossessing, and of a nature which could not be called charming. Sanchia would know how to take care of herself, as poor Giovanni Sforza had not.

So she had become reconciled to her marriage, and she had grown fond of the little boy they had brought to her; she had joined in the sly jokes about the marriage and there had been many, for the whole Court knew that she had her lovers, and they could not hide their amusement at the thought of their experienced and accomplished Princess with this young boy.

Such a pretty little boy he had been when they had brought him to her. And, when they had been put to bed and he had been a little frightened by those who had crowded about them with their crude jokes and lewd gestures, she had answered them with dignity; and when she was alone with her husband she had taken him in her arms, wiped away his tears and told

him not to fret. There was nothing he need worry about.
Being Sanchia she had been glad of such a husband. It was
so simple to leave him in the care of those devoted ladies of hers
while she entertained her lovers.

Thus it was with Sanchia. Life would always be merry. Lovers
came into her life and passed out of it; her reputation was
known throughout Italy; and she believed there were few men
who would not have been delighted to become the lover of
Madonna Sanchia.

And so to Rome to become a member of that strange family
regarding whom there were so many rumours.

In her baggage were the gowns she would wear when she
visited the Pope in the Vatican; there was the gown in which
she would make her entry. She must be beautiful for that
because, if accounts could be relied upon, she had a rival in her
sister-in-law, Lucrezia.

Rome was in a fever of excitement. All through the night the
citizens had been congregating to line the streets. It would be a
brilliant procession; the people were sure of that, for the Pope's
youngest son was bringing his bride to Rome, and one of the
greatest accomplishments of the Borgias was their ability to
organize brilliant pageants.

In the Vatican the Pope waited with obvious eagerness. It
was noted that he was absent-minded concerning his duties,
but that he was deeply interested in the preparations which
were being made for the reception of his daughter-in-law.

Cesare was also eagerly awaiting the arrival, although he did
not express his joy as openly as did his father.

In the Palace of Santa Maria in Portico, Lucrezia was more
anxious than any, as she was a little afraid of all she had heard
concerning her sister-in-law.

Sanchia was beautiful. How beautiful? Lucrezia studied
herself anxiously in her mirrors. Was her hair as golden as it
had been? It was a pity Giulia was scarcely seen nowadays;
being no longer in favour she was a rare visitor at the Vatican
and at Santa Maria. Giulia would have offered comfort at a
time like this. Lucrezia was aware of a slight feeling of anger,
which was alien to her nature, when she thought of how

Cesare and her father talked constantly of Madonna Sanchia. 'The most beautiful woman in Italy!' She had heard that again and again. 'She has but to look at a man and he is her slave. It is witchcraft, so they say.'

Now Lucrezia was beginning to know herself. She was envious of Sanchia. She herself wished to be known as the most beautiful woman in Italy; she wished men to look at her and become *her* slaves; and she longed to be suspected of witchcraft because of her extraordinary powers.

And she was jealous . . . deeply jealous because of the attention Cesare and her father had given to this woman.

Now the day had arrived. Very soon Sanchia of Aragon would be riding up the Appian Way. Very soon Lucrezia would see whether rumour had lied.

She felt vaguely unhappy. She had not wanted to go to meet her sister-in-law, but her father had insisted: 'But of course, my dearest, you must go to meet her. It is the respect due to your sister. And what a pleasant picture you will make – you and your ladies, she and hers. You two must be the most lovely creatures in the country.'

'I have heard it said that she is. Do you not think that she will put me in the shade?'

The Pope pinched his daughter's cheek affectionately, murmuring: 'Impossible! Impossible!'

But his eyes were gleaming and she, who had observed his absorption in Giulia at the beginning, knew that his thoughts were with Sanchia, not with his daughter.

Lucrezia wanted to stamp her foot, to shout at him: 'You go and meet her, since you're so eager for her arrival.' But being Lucrezia she merely bowed her head and suppressed her feelings.

So now she was preparing herself.

She stood in her apartment while her green and gold brocade dress was slipped over her head. There was a murmur of admiration from her women.

'Never, never, Madonna, have you looked so lovely,' she was told.

'Yes, yes,' she said, 'here in the apartment among you all who are dressed without splendour. But how shall I look when we meet at the Lateran Gate? Suppose she is dressed more splendidly? How shall I look then, for they say she is the most beautiful woman in Italy, and that means in the world?'

'How can that be, Madonna, when you hold that title?'

Characteristically she allowed herself to be soothed; and indeed, when she looked at herself in green and gold, when her eyes went to the feathered bonnet which so became her, when she looked at her glistening golden hair, she was appeased. Nobody had hair like hers, except Giulia, and Giulia was out of favour.

Her train was ready and she had selected it with care. There were twelve girls in beautiful dresses – not beautiful girls but beautiful dresses; one did not want too much competition – and her pages wore mantles of red and gold brocade.

Lucrezia did not feel that she was going out to meet a sister-in-law, but a rival. She knew that while she murmured polite welcoming words she would really be thinking, Is she more beautiful than I? Are my father and my brother going to give all their attention to this newcomer and forget Lucrezia?

In the May sunshine, the retinues of the Cardinals were waiting for her, all splendidly clad, all glittering in the clear bright air; the ambassadors were present, and the palace guards were on duty.

The people cried out in admiration as Lucrezia with her twelve girls appeared. She certainly looked charming, her fair hair rippling about her shoulders beneath the feathered hat, and the green and gold brocade sparkling with jewels. But as they approached the Lateran Gate Lucrezia caught sight of the girl who had caused her so many jealous thoughts, and she realized that Sanchia was indeed a formidable rival.

Surrounded by the retinue which, as Princess of Squillace, Sanchia had brought with her – her halberdiers and equerries, her women and men, her slaves, her jesters – she rode with Goffredo at her side.

A quick look was enough to tell Lucrezia that Goffredo, although he had grown up a little, was still a boy. People might admire his pretty looks and his beautiful auburn hair, but it was towards the woman who rode beside him that every eye would be turned.

This was Sanchia, dressed solemnly in black – as was Goffredo – to remind all who beheld them that they were Spanish. Sanchia's dress was heavily embroidered and her sleeves were wide; her blue-black hair rippled over her shoulders and her eyes were brilliantly blue in contrast.

Suddenly the green and gold brocade seemed girlish – pretty enough, but lacking the elegance of an embroidered black Spanish gown.

Sanchia's dark eyebrows had been plucked a little, after the fashion, but they were still plentiful and her face was heavily painted; there were murmurings in the crowd that she looked older than nineteen.

Her manner was both royal and insolent. It was haughty, and yet as always there was that look of promise in her expression for every personable young man who caught her eye.

Lucrezia had drawn up her horse before that of her brother and sister-in-law, and their greeting was affectionate enough to satisfy all who beheld them.

Then they turned their horses and rode together towards the Vatican.

'I rejoice that we meet at last,' said Sanchia.

'I also rejoice,' answered Lucrezia.

'I am sure we shall be friends.'

'It is my ardent wish.'

'I have long desired to meet the members of my new family.'

'Particularly Cesare,' put in Goffredo. 'Sanchia has asked endless questions about our brother.'

'He is as eager to see you. Reports of you have reached us here in Rome.'

Had she been alone with Lucrezia, Sanchia would have burst into loud laughter. As it was, she said: 'Tales of you all have reached me. What beautiful hair you have, sister!'

'I must say the same of yours.'

'I have never seen hair so golden.'

'You will see it often now. The women of Rome are having silken wigs made, and we see them walking in the streets wearing them.'

'In honour of you, dear sister.'

'They are mostly courtesans.'

'Beauty is their business, and they try to look like you.'

Lucrezia smiled faintly but she was unable to hide the apprehension this young woman aroused in her.

She did not hear the whispers behind her.

'Madonna Lucrezia does not like to have a rival in the Vatican.'

'And what a rival!'

Alexander had been unable to wait with the Cardinals to greet the procession, as formality demanded. He had been in a room which overlooked the piazza, impatiently looking out, so eager was he for the first glimpse of this girl who was reputed to be more beautiful than any woman in Italy and as free with her favours as any courtesan.

Now as he saw her at the head of the procession, and riding beside her his golden-haired daughter – raven-haired and golden-haired – the sight enchanted him. How beautiful they were – both of them! What a contrast, a delightful contrast!

He must hurry down to be in his place to greet them when they arrived. He was all impatience to embrace the beautiful creature.

He stood beneath the golden vault, on which was depicted the story of Isis, as he waited for his daughter-in-law to come to him. About him were ranged the Cardinals, and Alexander knew a moment of great content. He revelled in all the pageantry, the ceremony, which as Holy Father he encountered at every hour of his daily life; he loved life; it had everything to offer him for which he craved and he was one of those rare beings who could be satisfied with each moment as it came. He was a happy man; and never happier than at moments such as this.

She was approaching now – beautiful, dark-haired, and so bold; her eyes were downcast, but she could not hide her boldness. She had all the arrogance of a woman who knows herself to be desired; she had all the charm of her sex for a man such as himself.

He was in a fever of excitement as she, with little Goffredo beside her, knelt to kiss his toe.

Now she had stepped back and the others came forward, those ladies of hers – all delicious, all worthy to be her handmaidens, thought Alexander. He studied them all in turn, and he felt anew his pleasure in having them with him.

Now they had taken their places; Goffredo was standing by Cesare, and Cesare had his speculative eyes on his brother's bride; and on the steps of the throne, kneeling on two red velvet cushions, were Lucrezia and Sanchia.

Oh, this is a happy moment, thought Alexander; and he wished quickly to dispense with solemn ceremony that he might talk with his daughter-in-law, make her laugh, make her understand that, although he was her father-in-law and head of the Church, he was none the less a merry man and one who knew how to be gallant to the ladies.

One of the Cardinals who watched turned to another and said: 'Brother and father have eyes on Goffredo's wife.'

Another whispered: 'All have eyes on Goffredo's wife.'

The answer came back: 'Mark my words, Madonna Sanchia will bring trouble to the Vatican.'

Sanchia came into Lucrezia's apartment and with her were her three handmaidens.

Lucrezia was a little startled by the intrusion. It was Whit Sunday, two days after the arrival of Sanchia and Goffredo, and Lucrezia was being dressed for the service at St Peter's.

Sanchia had begun by ignoring all rules of etiquette and Lucrezia saw that she was determined to behave here in Rome as though she were at the lax court of Naples.

Sanchia's dress was black, but she looked far from demure; the blue eyes were almost cynical, thought Lucrezia; it was as though Sanchia was weaving plans, secret subtle plans.

'And how is my dear sister this day?' asked Sanchia. 'Ready for the ceremony? I hear we are to listen to a Spanish prelate.' She grimaced. 'Spanish prelates are apt to be over-devout and therefore to deliver over-long sermons.'

'But we must attend,' Lucrezia explained. 'My father will

be present, and so will all the dignitaries of the Papal Court. It is an important occasion and . . .'

'Oh yes . . . oh yes . . . we must attend.'

Sanchia, putting her arm about Lucrezia and drawing her to a mirror, looked at their reflections. 'I do not look as though I am about to attend a solemn service, do I? And, when I look closer, nor do you. Oh Lucrezia, how innocent you look with your lovely light eyes and your golden hair? But are you innocent, Lucrezia? Are you?'

'Innocent of what?' asked Lucrezia.

'Oh, life . . . of what you will. Oh Lucrezia, thoughts go on inside that golden head, of which you say nothing. You look startled. But I am right, am I not? One as lovely as you are cannot be so remote from . . . from all that makes the world so interesting.'

'I am afraid I do not understand.'

'Are you such a child then? What of Cesare? He will be at this solemn service. Do you know, sister, I have longed to meet you all, and you are the only one with whom so far I have been alone.'

'There have been so many ceremonies,' murmured Lucrezia, uncertain of the girl who was so outspoken and who therefore said those things which embarrassed and would have been so much better left unsaid.

'Oh yes. Later I shall know you all very well, I doubt not. Cesare is not exactly as I would have imagined him. He is as handsome in person as rumour says he is. But there is a strangeness about him, a brooding resentment. . . .'

'My brother wished to be a great soldier.'

'I see. I see. He does not take kindly to the robes of the Church.'

Lucrezia looked uneasily about her. She said to her servants: 'That will be enough. Leave us now.'

She looked at Sanchia, expecting her to dismiss her women.

'They are my friends,' said Sanchia. 'I hope they will be yours. They admire you. Do you not?' she demanded of the trio.

'We all agree that Madonna Lucrezia is quite lovely,' said Loysella.

'Now tell me about Cesare,' insisted Sanchia. 'He is angry
.. a very angry man. I know it.'

'Cesare will always succeed in the end,' said Lucrezia. 'He
will always do what he sets out to do.'

'You are very fond of your brother?'

'It is impossible not to admire him more than anyone on
Earth, as he excels all others.'

Sanchia smiled knowledgeably. Now she understood. There
was something in these rumours she had heard, of the strange
and passionate attachments which existed in the Borgia
family.

She knew that Lucrezia was suspicious of her, jealous
because she feared Sanchia might attract the Pope and Cesare
so that they ceased to be so eager for Lucrezia's company. It
was a novel situation and one which appealed to Sanchia.

Moreover it was comforting to think that Cesare Borgia did
not have all his own way. He hated the robes of the Church yet
he was forced to wear them, and that was why she had seen that
smouldering anger in his eyes. She, as the illegitimate daughter
of the King of Naples, forced to take second place to her half-
sister, understood his feelings. It drew her closer to Cesare,
and his vulnerability intrigued her.

As they set out for St Peter's she felt almost recklessly gay;
she put her arm lovingly through Lucrezia's as they entered the
church. How long the ceremony was! There was the Holy
Father, seeming quite a different person from the jovial father
who had been so affectionate during last night's banquet. She
had been right about the Spanish prelate; his sermon went on
and on.

'I am tired,' she whispered to Lucrezia.

Lucrezia's pale face turned slightly pink. The Princess from
Naples seemed to have no understanding as to how to conduct
herself during a solemn ceremony.

Lucrezia said nothing.

'Will the man never end?'

Loysella smothered a giggle, and Bernardina whispered:
'For the love of the saints, Madonna, be quiet!'

'But it is too long to stand,' complained Sanchia. 'Why
should we not be seated? Look, there are empty pews.'

Lucrezia said in an agonized whisper: 'They are for canons when they sing the gospel.'

'They shall be for us now,' said Sanchia.

Several heads turned on account of the whispering voices, so many saw this beautiful young woman climb into the pews with a rustling of silk and the exposure of very shapely legs. Loysella, Francesca and Bernardina, who followed their mistress in all things, did not hesitate. Where Sanchia went, so did they.

Lucrezia, watching them for a second, was aware of a rising excitement within her. She knew that these girls lived colourful lives, and she herself longed for the sort of adventures which she knew to be theirs; she wanted to identify herself with them.

Without hesitation, she followed, climbing into the pews, settling down beside them with a rustle of garments, an unusually mischievous smile on her lips, the laughter rising within her.

They had settled down in their pews and Sanchia had forced a look of mock piety on to her face. Loysella dropped her head hurriedly to hide her mirth, and Lucrezia needed all her willpower to stop herself breaking into hysterical laughter.

They had shocked the Papal Court.

Never, complained the Cardinals, had such behaviour been seen during a solemn service. The woman from Naples was clearly nothing more than a Court harlot. The glances she distributed confirmed the reputation which had preceded her.

Girolamo Savonarola declaimed long and loudly from the pulpit of San Marco in Florence that the Papal Court was a disgrace to the world, and the Pope's women behaved with great impropriety and were the disgrace and scandal of the people.

The Cardinals tentatively approached the Holy Father.

'Your Holiness will have suffered great sadness,' said one. 'The spectacle of those young women's behaviour during the Whitsuntide ceremonies horrified all who beheld it.'

'Is that so?' said Alexander. 'I noticed many an eye glistened as it turned in their direction.'

'With disgust, Holiness.'

'I saw no disgust, but I did see some delight.'

The Cardinals looked grim. 'Your Holiness will doubtless deal adequately with the offenders?'

'Oh come, come, what offence is there in the pranks of girls? Young girls are by nature high-spirited. I for one would not have them otherwise. And who among you was not a little bored by our worthy preacher?'

'Nevertheless, to bring the manners of Naples to Rome!'

The Pope nodded placatingly. He would speak to the girls.

He did. He put an arm about Sanchia and another about Lucrezia, and composed his features into an expression of mock reproach. He kissed them tenderly and smiled benignly at Loysella, Bernardina and Francesca who stood before him, their heads bowed – but not so low as to prevent their glancing upwards occasionally at the Holy Father.

'You have shocked the community,' he said, 'and if you were not so beautiful, I should be forced to scold you, and so I am sure bore you as thoroughly as did your Spanish prelate.'

'But you understand, Most Holy Lord,' said Sanchia, looking at him from under her dark lashes with those bluest of blue eyes.

'I understand this,' said the Pope, giving her a passionate look. 'It gives me the greatest pleasure in the world to see so much brightness and beauty at my Court; and should I as much as frown on you I should be the most ungrateful man on Earth.'

Whereupon they all laughed, and Sanchia said they would sing for him, for he was not only their Holy Father but their greatly beloved one.

So Sanchia sang to the accompaniment of Lucrezia's lute, and the girls ranged themselves about him, Loysella, Bernardina, Francesca on stools at his feet, raising wondering and admiring eyes, while Sanchia and Lucrezia leaned against his knees.

Scold these lovely creatures! thought Alexander. Never! Their little pranks could only amuse such a benevolent father.

That night Sanchia danced with Cesare. His eyes held hers and she was conscious of that smouldering resentment against the world which had afflicted herself. She was of a different temperament, and it was because of this that she had been able to shrug aside the slights and enjoy her life. But there was a bond between them.

For all his demonstrations of affection the Pope had not assigned to her that position at the Papal Court for which she longed. She was merely the wife of Goffredo, himself suspected of having a father other than Alexander; it would have been different had she been the wife of Cesare.

But her sensuous nature made it possible for her to forget all else in the pursuit of sexual satisfaction. That satisfaction dominated her life. It was not so with Cesare. He craved carnal pleasures but he had other desires as insistent. His love of power was greater than his desire for women.

She, who had known so many men that she read them easily, was aware of this, and she determined now to make Cesare forget his ambitions in his pursuit of her. They were both experienced, and they would find great pleasure in surprising each other by their accomplishments. Each was aware of this as they danced; and each was asking: Why delay longer? Delay was something which neither of them would tolerate.

'You are all that I heard you were,' Sanchia told him.

'You are all that I hoped you would be,' he answered her.

'I wondered when you and I would be able to talk together. This is the first time it has happened, and all eyes are on us now.'

'They were right,' said Cesare, 'when they said you were the most beautiful woman in the world.'

'They were right when they said there was something terrifying about you.'

'Do you find me terrifying?'

She laughed. 'No man terrifies me.'

'Have they always been so kind?'

'Always,' she said. 'From the time I was able to talk, men have been kind to me.'

'Are you not weary of my sex, since you know it so well?'

'Each man is different from all others. That is what I have found. Perhaps that is why I have always discovered them to be so fascinating. And none that I have ever known has been remotely like you, Cesare Borgia; you stand apart.'

'And you like this strangeness in me?'

'So much that I would know it so well that it ceases to be strangeness and is familiar to me.'

'What tales have you heard of me?'

'That you are a man who will never take no for an answer, that men fear your frown, and that when you beckon a woman she must obey, in fear if not in desire. I have heard that those who displease you meet ill fortune, that some have been discovered in alleys, suffocated or with knives in their bodies. I have heard that some have drunk wine at your table and have felt themselves to be merely intoxicated, only to learn that they are dying. These are the things which I have heard of you, Cesare Borgia. What have you heard of me?'

'That you practise witchcraft so that all men whom you desire fall under your spell, and that having once been your lover none can ever forget you.'

'And do you believe these tales of me?'

'And do you believe the tales of me?'

She looked into his eyes and the flame of desire in hers was matched by that in his.

'I do not know,' she said, 'but I am determined to discover.'

'Nor do I know,' he answered; 'and I think I am as eager to make my discoveries as you are.'

His hand tightened on hers.

'Sanchia,' he said, 'this night?'

And she closed her eyes and nodded.

They were watched.

The Pope smiled affectionately. It was inevitable. How could it have been otherwise? Cesare and Sanchia! They were well matched, and from the moment Cesare had heard of her he had determined it should be so.

Now we shall have the tiresome scandalmongers whispering, mused Alexander, now we shall have the Cardinals raising shocked hands and voices; and Savonarola will be thundering from his pulpit of the vice which goes on at the Papal Court.

The Pope sighed, faintly envious of his son, laughing slyly to himself; he would prevail upon Cesare to give him a full account of the affair.

Goffredo watched delightedly. How handsome they looked dancing together. My wife and my brother. They are the two most distinguished people in the ballroom. All watch them. And they find each other delightful.

Cesare, great Cesare, will be grateful to me because I have brought him Sanchia. And Sanchia, she is clearly delighted to meet Cesare. All her lovers must seem so unworthy when she compares them with him!

Lucrezia watched.

So, she thought, Goffredo's wife has now determined to take Cesare as her lover. She knows how to lure him, how to please him.

Lucrezia wanted to bury her face in her hands and sob; and fervently she wished that Sanchia had never come to Rome.

They lay together on Sanchia's bed.

Sanchia was smiling, glancing sideways at her lover. It is true, she thought exultantly, he is as no other man. He has the virility of two men; he is skilled and yet eager to discover; he is ardent and yet aloof, passionate and yet cold. In all her experience she had never known a lover such as Cesare Borgia.

She turned to him and said languidly: 'They should have married me to you . . . not to Goffredo.'

She saw the change creep into his face; the slack sensuality disappeared and in its place was sudden anger so intense that it shocked her even in her present mood of indolence.

He clenched his fists and she realized that he was fighting with himself to hold back his anger.

'My father,' he said, 'saw fit to send me to the Church.'

'It is incomprehensible,' she answered soothingly, and she laid her hand on his arm to draw him to her, once more to court desire.

But he was not to be seduced from his anger.

'I have two brothers,' he said, 'and yet I was the chosen one.'

'You will be Pope,' she told him; 'and that need not prevent your enjoying adventures such as this, Cesare.'

'I wish to command the armies,' he said. 'I wish to have sons . . . legitimate sons. I wish to cast aside my Cardinal's robe. I loathe the thing and all connected with it.'

She sat up in bed, her long hair falling about her nakedness. Her blue eyes shone. She wanted now to turn him from his anger, to bring him back to making love. It was a challenge. Is his anger more important to him than I am? What sort of man is this to talk of his ambitions while he lies in bed with me?

She took his hands and smiled at him.

'I doubt not all that you desire will be yours, Cesare Borgia.'

'Are you a witch?' he asked.

She nodded slowly and laughed showing her red tongue.

'I am a witch, Cesare Borgia, and I promise you this . . . a soldier's uniform, a wife and legitimate offspring.'

He was looking at her intently; at least she had focussed his attention on herself, even if it was the possible power of prophecy, rather than her body, which attracted him.

Her eyes were wide. 'One of the family must go into the Church,' she went on. 'It should have been little Goffredo. Why should it not be Goffredo?'

He knelt on the bed beside her; he took her by the shoulders and looked into her wild blue eyes.

'Yes,' she said. 'Here is the answer. There should be a divorce. Little Goffredo should wear the Cardinal's robes and Sanchia and Cesare should be man and wife.'

'By the saints!' cried Cesare, 'it is a good plan.'

Then he seized her and kissed her wildly.

She laughed. 'I trust my lord likes me no less because I might one day be his bride. They say the gentlemen of Rome find the mistresses they discover for themselves more to their liking than the wives who are found for them.'

'Have done,' he said fiercely.

'First,' she cried, 'you must declare that you wish to be my husband. . . .'

She fell back laughing, and they struggled for a while.

'Cesare,' she murmured blissfully, 'you have the strength of ten men.'

Lucrezia begged audience of her father.

Alexander studied his daughter anxiously. She looked pale and unhappy.

'What is it, my dearest?' he asked.

She lowered her eyes. She hated lying to him, yet she could not bring herself to tell him the truth.

'I feel unwell, dearest Father,' she said. 'There is plague in the air of Rome, and I think it affects me. I have suffered from a slight fever these last days and nights.'

His cool jewelled hands were on her forehead.

'My blessed one,' he murmured.

'I crave your pardon,' said Lucrezia, 'because I am going to ask something which I know you will not be anxious to grant me. I feel I need a change of air, and I would go for a short while to Pesaro.'

There was silence.

Her husband would be there, thought the Pope; and he was becoming increasingly dissatisfied with his daughter's marriage. But Lucrezia looked wan, and he longed to make her happy.

She let her eyes linger on the red velvet cushion on which she knelt.

She felt that she was a strangely bewildered girl, who did not understand herself. She hated Sanchia – Sanchia with her bright blue eyes, wild laughter and deep, deep knowledge.

Sanchia treated Lucrezia as a child, and Lucrezia knew that in worldly matters she would remain a child while her emotions were such as she did not understand. She only knew that she could not bear to see Sanchia and Cesare together; that she hated the complaisance of Goffredo, the giggling of those three women who served Sanchia.

Often she had thought of Pesaro during the last weeks, when she had gone to Sanchia's apartments because she knew that Cesare would be there and that if she did not go she would miss seeing him that day.

Pesaro, that quiet little town with the hills which formed a semi-circle about it and the blue sea washing its shores, Pesaro, where she could live with her husband and behave as a normal wife. In Pesaro she had felt herself to be as other women, and that was how she wanted to be.

Her father's fingers were caressing her hair; she heard his

voice, very gentle and tender, as though he understood: 'My dearest, if it is your wish that you should go to Pesaro, then to Pesaro shall you go.'

Alexander met his son in the Papal apartments.

'I have news for you, Cesare,' he said.

Alexander was uneasy, but the news had to be broken soon, and Cesare was deep in a love affair with Sanchia which was proving to be an absorbing one. Alexander had no doubt of that. Therefore with Cesare satisfied, this was a good moment to tell him that which he had long wished to tell and which could not much longer be kept a secret from him.

Cesare answered: 'Yes, Most Holy Father?'

'Giovanni is coming home.'

Alexander quickly slipped his arm through that of his son; he did not want to see the blood rush into Cesare's cheeks; he did not want to see the angry red in his eyes.

'Yes, yes,' said Alexander, walking towards the window and gently pulling Cesare with him. 'I am growing old and I shall be a happy man to have all my family about me once more.'

Cesare was silent.

No need yet, thought Alexander, to tell Cesare that Giovanni was being brought home to conduct a campaign against the Orsini who must be punished for going over to the French without a fight during the invasion. No need to say, When Giovanni comes I shall make him commander of the Papal forces. Cesare would have to know . . . but later.

'When he returns,' said Alexander lightly, 'we must recall little Lucrezia. I long for the day when I have every member of my beloved family sitting at my table, that I may feast my eyes upon them.'

Still Cesare did not answer. His fingers twitched as he pulled at his Cardinal's robes. He did not see the piazza beyond the window; he was unaware of Alexander, standing beside him.

All he could think of was that Giovanni, the envied, the hated one, was coming home.

ROMAN CARNIVAL

THE TWO BROTHERS met at the Porta Portuense. Cesare, as tradition and his father insisted, set out at the head of that procession which was made up of the Cardinals and their splendid households, to greet the brother whom he hated more than anyone in the world.

They faced each other. Giovanni had changed a little since he had gone to Spain. He was more arrogant, more magnificent and the lines of cruelty about his mouth had deepened. Dissipation had marked his features, but he was very handsome still. His dress was more grand than anything Cesare had ever seen him wear before. His red velvet cape was decorated with pearls, and his waistcoat of the same material in a light shade of brown was ablaze with pearls and glistening jewels of all colours. Even his horse was made brilliant by golden ornaments and silver bells. Giovanni was a dazzling sight as he entered the city of Rome, and the citizens were astonished to behold him.

As they rode side by side to the Apostolic Palace, which was to be the Duke's home, Giovanni could not help taking sly glances at his brother, letting him know that he was fully aware of the enmity which existed between them and that, now he was a great Duke with a son and another child shortly expected, now that he came home at their father's request to command their father's forces, he realized that Cesare's envy was not likely to have abated in the smallest degree.

The Pope could not contain his joy at the sight of his best-loved son.

He embraced him and wept, while Cesare watched, standing apart, clenching his hands and grinding his teeth, saying to himself, Why should it be so? What has he that I lack?

Alexander looking towards Cesare guessed his feelings and, as he knew that Cesare must certainly feel still more angry when he understood in full the glory which was to be

Giovanni's, he stretched out his hand to Cesare and said tenderly: 'My two sons! It is rarely nowadays that I know the pleasure of having you both with me at the same time.'

When Cesare ignored the hand, and strolled to the window, Alexander was uneasy. It was the first time Cesare had openly rebuffed him, and that it should have happened in the presence of a third party was doubly disturbing. He decided that the best thing he could do was to ignore the gesture.

Cesare said without turning his head: 'There are crowds below. They wait, hoping to catch further glimpses of the splendid Duke of Gandia.'

Giovanni strode to the window; he turned to Cesare, smiling that insolent smile. 'They shall not be disappointed,' he said, looking down at his bejewelled garments and back at Cesare. 'A pity,' he went on, 'that the comparatively sombre garments of the Church are all you have to show them, brother.'

'Then you understand,' Cesare answered lightly, 'that it is not the Duke whom they applaud, but the Duke's jewelled doublet.'

Alexander had insinuated himself between them, putting an arm about each.

'You will be interested to meet Goffredo's wife, my dear Giovanni,' he said.

Giovanni laughed. 'I have heard of her. Her fame has travelled even to Spain. Some of my more prudish relatives speak her name in whispers.'

The Pope burst into laughter. 'We are more tolerant in Rome, eh, Cesare?'

Giovanni looked at his brother. 'I have heard,' he said, 'that Sanchia of Aragon is a generous woman. So generous indeed that all she has to bestow cannot be given to one husband.'

'Our Cesare here, he is a fascinating fellow,' said Alexander placatingly.

'I doubt it not,' laughed Giovanni.

Determination was in his eyes. Cesare was looking at him challengingly, and whenever a challenge had been issued by one brother to the other it had always been taken up.

Giovanni Sforza rode towards Pesaro.

How thankful he was to be home. How tired he was of the conflicts raging about him. In Naples he was treated as an alien, which he was; he was suspected of spying for the Milanese, which he had. The last year had brought nothing to enhance his opinion of himself. He was more afraid, and of more people, than he had ever been in his life.

Only behind the hills of Pesaro could he be at peace. He indulged in a pleasant daydream as he rode homewards. It was that he might ride to Rome, take his wife and bring her back with him to Pesaro – defying the Pope and her brother Cesare. He heard himself saying: 'She is my wife. Try to take her from me if you dare!'

But they were dreams. As if it were possible to say such things to the Pope and Cesare Borgia! The tolerance which the Pope would display towards one who he would believe had lost his senses, the sneers of Cesare towards one whom he knew to be a coward parading as a brave man – they were more than Giovanni Sforza could endure.

So he could only dream.

He rode slowly along by the Foglia River, in no hurry now that Pesaro was in sight. When he reached home he would find it dreary; life would not be the same as it had been during those months when he had lived there with Lucrezia.

Lucrezia! At first during those months before the marriage had been consummated, she had seemed but a shy bewildered child. But how different he had discovered her to be! He wanted to take her away, make her his completely and gradually purge her of all that she had inherited from her strange family.

He could see the castle – strong, seeming impregnable.

There, he thought, I could live with Lucrezia, happy, secure, all the days of our lives. We should have children and find peace in our stronghold between the mountains and the sea.

His retainers were running out to greet him.

'Our Lord has come home.' He felt grand and important, he the Lord of Pesaro, as he rode forward. Pesaro might have been a great dominion; these few people might have been a multitude.

He accepted the homage, dismounted and entered the palace.

It was a dazzling manifestation of his dream, for she stood there, the sun shining on her golden hair which fell loose about her shoulders, and lighting the few discreet jewels she wore – as became the lady of a minor castle.

'Lucrezia!' he cried.

She smiled that fascinating smile which still held a child-like quality.

'Giovanni,' she answered him, 'I was weary of Rome. I came to Pesaro that I might be here to greet you on your return.'

He laid his hands on her shoulders and kissed her forehead, then her cheeks, before he lightly touched her lips with his.

He believed in that moment that the Giovanni Sforza whom he had seen in his dreams might have existence in reality.

But Giovanni Sforza could not believe in his happiness. He must torture himself – and Lucrezia.

He was continually discovering new ornaments in her jewel cases.

'And whence came this trinket?' he would ask.

'My father gave it to me,' would invariably be the answer. Or: 'It is a gift from my brother.'

Then Giovanni would throw it back into the box, stalk from the room or regard her with glowering eyes.

'The behaviour at the Papal Court is shocking the world!' he declared. 'It is worse since the woman from Naples came.'

This made Lucrezia unhappy; she thought of Sanchia and Cesare together, of Goffredo's delight that his wife should so please his brother, of Alexander's amusement and her own jealousy.

We are indeed a strange family, she thought.

She would look across the sea, and there was a hope in her eyes, a hope that she might conform with the standards of goodness set up by such men as Savonarola, that she might live quietly with her own husband in their mountain stronghold, that she might curb this desire to be with her own disturbing family.

But although Giovanni had no help to offer her, and only gave her continual reproaches, she was determined to be patient; so she listened quietly to his angry outbursts and only mildly tried to assure him of her innocence. And there were occasions when Giovanni would throw himself at her feet and declare that she was good at heart and he was a brute to upbraid her continually. He could not explain to her that always he saw himself as a poor creature, despised by all, and that the conduct of her family and the rumours concerning them made him seem ever poorer, even more contemptible.

There were times when she thought, I can endure this no longer. Perhaps I will hide myself in a convent. There in the solitude of a cell I might begin to understand myself, to discover a way in which I can escape from all that I know I should.

Yet how could she endure life in a convent? When letters came from her father, her heart would race and her hands tremble as she seized on them. Reading what he had written made her feel as though he were with her, talking to her; and then she realized how happy she was when she was in the heart of her family, and that only then could she be completely content.

She must find a compensation for this overpowering love which she bore towards her family. Was a convent the answer?

Alexander was begging her to return. Her brother Giovanni, he pointed out, was in Rome, even more handsome, more charming than he had been when he went away. Each day he asked about his beloved sister and when she was coming home. Lucrezia must return at once.

She wrote that her husband wished her to remain in Pesaro, where he had certain duties.

The answer to that came promptly.

Her brother Giovanni was about to set out on a military campaign which was to be directed first against the Orsini, and which was calculated later to subdue all the barons who had proved themselves to be helpless against the invader. The rich lands and possessions of these barons would fall into the Pope's hands. Lucrezia knew that this was the first step on that road along which Alexander had long planned to go.

Now, his dear son-in-law, Giovanni Sforza, could show his mettle and win great honours for himself. Let him collect his forces and join the Duke of Gandia. Lucrezia would not wish to stay on at Pesaro alone, so she must return to Rome where her family would prepare a great welcome for her.

When Giovanni Sforza read this letter he was furious.

'What am I?' he cried. 'Nothing but a piece on a chequer-board to be moved this way and that. I will *not* join the Duke of Gandia. I have my duties here.'

So he stormed and raged before Lucrezia, yet he knew – and she knew also – that he went in fear of the Pope.

However, on this occasion he determined to try compromise. He gathered together his men but, instead of leaving with them, he wrote to the Pope and explained that his duties in his own dominion prevented his leaving at this time.

He and Lucrezia waited for the command to obey, the expressions of angry reproach.

There was a long silence; then from the Vatican came a soothing reply. His Holiness fully understood Giovanni Sforza's reasons; he no longer insisted that he should join the Duke of Gandia. At the same time he would like to remind his son-in-law that it was long since he had seen him in Rome, and it would give him the utmost pleasure to embrace Giovanni and Lucrezia once more.

The letter made Lucrezia very happy. 'I feared,' she told her husband, 'that your refusal to join my brother would have angered my father. But how benevolent he is! He understands, you see.'

'The greater your father's benevolence, the more I fear him,' growled Giovanni.

'You do not understand him. He loves us. He wishes to have us in Rome.'

'He wishes you to be in Rome. I do not know what he wishes for me.'

And Lucrezia looked at her husband and shivered imperceptibly. There were times when she felt there was no escape from the destiny which her family was preparing for her.

Cesare had rarely been so happy in the whole of his life as he was at this time.

His brother Giovanni was helping to prove all that he, Cesare had been at such pains to make their father realize. How angry he had been at that ceremony when Giovanni had been invested with the standard, richly embroidered, and the sword, richly jewelled, of Captain General of the Church! How the fury had welled up within him to see his father's eyes shining with pride as he beheld his favourite son!

'Fool!' Cesare had wanted to cry. 'Do you not see that he will bring disgrace on your armies and the name of Borgia?'

And Cesare's prophecies were coming true. That was what gave him this great pleasure. Now surely his father must see the folly of investing his son Giovanni with military honours which he could not uphold, and the crass stupidity of preventing the brave bold Cesare from taking over the command which, in a fond father's folly, had been given to Giovanni.

Everything was in Giovanni's favour. The wealth and might of the Pope was behind him. The great Captain Virginio Orsini was still a prisoner in Naples and could not take part in his family's defence. To any with an ounce of military knowledge, so reasoned Cesare, the campaign should have been swift and victorious.

And at first it seemed as though it would be so, for, with Virginio a prisoner, the Orsinis appeared to have no heart for the fight, and one by one surrendered to Giovanni's forces as they had to the French. Castle after castle threw open its gates, and in marched the conqueror without the shedding of one drop of blood.

In the Vatican the Pope rejoiced; even in Cesare's presence, knowing how galling it was to his eldest son, he could not hide his pride.

That was why the new turn of events was so gratifying to Cesare.

The Orsini clan were not so easily overcome as the brash young Duke of Gandia and his doting father had believed. They had gathered in full force at the family castle of Bracciano under the leadership of the sister of Virginio. Bartolommea Orsini was a brave woman. She had been brought up in a military tradition and she was not going to submit without a fight. In this she was helped by her husband and other members of the family.

Giovanni Borgia was startled to come up against resistance. He had had no experience of war, and his methods of breaking the siege at Bracciano seemed to the experienced warriors on both sides, both childish and foolish. He had no wish to fight, for Giovanni was a soldier who had more affection for jewelled sword and white stick of office than for battle. He therefore sent messages to the defenders of the castle, first wheedling, then threatening, telling them that their wisest plan would be to surrender. It was uncomfortable, camping outside the castle; the weather was bad; and Giovanni's gorgeous apparel unsuited to it. His most able captain, Guidobaldo of Montefeltro, the Duke of Urbino, was badly wounded and forced to retire, which meant that Giovanni had lost his best adviser.

Time passed and Giovanni remained outside the stronghold ·of Bracciano. He was tired of the war, and he had heard that the whole of Italy was laughing at the Commander of the Pope's forces, and moreover he guessed how his brother was enjoying this turn of events.

The people of Rome whispered about the grand Captain: 'How fares he now? Does he look quite so gorgeous as he did when he set out? The rain and wind will not be good for all that velvet and brocade.'

Alexander was filled with anxiety, and declared he would sell his tiara if necessary to bring the war to a satisfactory conclusion. He could not bear the company of his elder son Cesare, for Cesare did not attempt to hide his delight at the way things were going. This hatred of brother for brother, thought Alexander, was folly of the first order. Had Cesare and Giovanni not yet learned that strength was in unity?

Cesare was with him when the news came to him that Giovanni was still waiting outside the castle and that Urbino had been wounded.

He watched the red blood flood his father's face and, as he stood there, exulting, Alexander swayed and would have fallen had not Cesare rushed forward to catch him.

Looking at his father, whose face was dark with rich purple blood, the whites of his eyes showing red, and the veins knotted at his temples, Cesare had a sudden terrible fear of a future in which there would be no Alexander to protect his family.

Then did he realize how much they owed to this man – this man who hitherto had been renowned for his vitality, this man who surely must possess true genius.

'Father!' cried Cesare aghast. 'Oh, my beloved father!'

The Pope opened his eyes and became aware of his son's anxiety.

'Dear son,' he said. 'Fear not. I am with you still.'

Once again that exceptional vitality showed itself. It was as though Alexander refused to accept the ailments of encroaching age.

'Father,' cried Cesare in anguish, 'you are not ill? You cannot be ill.'

'Help me to my chair,' said Alexander. 'There! That is better. It was a momentary faintness. I felt the blood pounding in my veins, and it seemed that my head would burst with it. It is passing. It was the shock of this news. I must control myself in future. There is no need to fret about that which has not yet happened.'

'You must take greater care, Father,' Cesare warned him.

'Oh my son, my son, do not look so distressed. And yet I feel happy to see that you care so much for me.'

Alexander closed his eyes and lay back in his chair smiling. The astute statesman, always wilfully blind where his family was concerned, allowed himself to believe that it was out of affection for his father that Cesare was alarmed, not because he was aware of the precarious position he, with the rest of his family, would be in if the Pope were no longer there to protect them.

Cesare then begged his father to call his physician, that he might be examined; and this Alexander at length promised he would do. But the Pope's resilience was amazing and, a few hours after the fainting fit, he was making new plans for Giovanni's success.

Alas, eventually even Alexander had to face the fact that Giovanni was no soldier, for this became undeniable when help came to the Orsini from the French, and they were able to attack the besiegers of the castle.

Faced with real battle Giovanni proved himself to be a hopeless leader, and the engagement went badly for the Papal forces;

the only man among them who distinguished himself was the Duke of Urbino who, recovered from his wounds, was taken prisoner by the Orsini. As for Giovanni, he was wounded, but slightly, and realizing that he was in a somewhat ridiculous position, from which above all things he longed to extricate himself, he declared that being wounded he was unable to carry on, and must leave his armies to finish the conflict under a new commander.

Now the whole of Italy was laughing at the adventures of the Pope's son. They remembered the ceremony at which he had been made head of the Papal armies; when he had led his armies out of Rome, he had marched like a conqueror.

This was very amusing to the Romans; and many people were pleased. This should teach the Pope that it was dangerous to his own interests to carry nepotism too far.

Cesare had recovered from his alarm over the Pope's fainting fit, for Alexander was as full of vitality as ever, and Cesare was not going to lose this opportunity of scoring over his brother.

He called his friends to him and together they devised brilliant posters which they set up on various important roads throughout the city.

'Wanted,' ran the words on these posters, 'those who have any news concerning a certain army of the Church. Will anyone having such information impart it at once to the Duke of Gandia.'

Giovanni came home, where he was received with undiminished affection by his father, who immediately began making excuses for his son and assuring everyone that, had Giovanni not had the ill luck to be wounded, there would have been a different tale to tell.

And all who heard marvelled at the dissembling of Alexander who so delighted to deceive himself. But they were soon admiring his diplomacy, for it appeared that the Pope never lost a war. Defeated in battle he might be, but terms followed battle, and from these terms the Pope invariably emerged as the victor.

Cesare went to see his father, and found Giovanni with him.

As Cesare looked at his brother he could not prevent a sneer from curling his lips.

'So,' he cried, 'you have not rejoined your army, General.'

'Cardinal, my army and I have parted company,' said Giovanni lightly. 'We wearied of each other.'

'So I hear.' Cesare laughed. 'All Rome talks of it. There are even posters on the city's walls.'

'It would be interesting to discover who put them there.' Giovanni's eyes gleamed murderously.

'Be at peace, my sons,' put in Alexander. 'What is done is done. We have suffered ill-fortune and we will now make peace.'

'We have to sue for peace!' Cesare's tone was grim. 'A pretty pass.'

'We'll make it a pretty pass in all truth,' mused Alexander. 'The Orsini are in no mood to continue the fight. I have offered my terms to them now and they will be accepted.'

'Your terms, Holiness?'

'My terms and their terms,' said Alexander lightly. 'I shall allow them to buy back their castles. You will see that we shall lose nothing from this war.'

'And Urbino?' asked Cesare. 'He is a prisoner. What ransom will be asked for him?'

The Pope shrugged the question aside. 'Doubtless his family are gathering together the ransom.'

Cesare's eyes narrowed. This brilliant man who was their father was in actuality turning Giovanni's defeat into victory. Giovanni was watching his brother slyly.

He said: 'Being weary of war, I rejoice that to-morrow the carnival begins.'

There was hatred in Giovanni's eyes to match that in Cesare's. You have sought to disparage me in our father's eyes, Cesare Borgia, he was thinking; do not imagine that I shall allow you to attack me with impunity. Have a care, for I will find a way to turn the tables, my lord Cardinal!

It was with Cesare that the Pope discussed the peace terms. Giovanni was too busy contriving his costume for the carnival and planning his own revels. He missed Djem who had always had some bizarre and fantastic suggestion to make at such a time.

There must come a day, Cesare was thinking, when our father realizes that I am the one to stand beside him, to share his ambition. How can a man, so brilliant as he is, continue to risk our position through this blind and foolish trust in one son at the expense of the other?

At such times as this Cesare was almost happy. There was no need now to call attention to Giovanni's shortcomings; they must be perfectly obvious even to the besottedly devoted Alexander.

'My father,' he said now, 'you astonish me. We Borgias have just suffered defeat which would have proved disastrous to many, and you are fast turning that defeat into victory.'

Alexander laughed. 'My son, more is won at the council table than on the battlefield.'

'That, I venture to suggest, Holiness, might depend on the soldiers. Had I been a soldier I would have carried my banner into the enemy stronghold. I would have placed my heel on the enemy's throat, and the terms I made would have been all my terms. Indeed, there would be no terms. I should have been conqueror of their estates and castles.'

'Nobly spoken, my son.'

Cesare was alert. Did he detect a certain speculative light in his father's eyes? Was Alexander going to be reasonable at last?

'But,' went on the Pope, 'we are in a certain position now, and we must extricate ourselves from it. The important point in the present case is speed. If *we* have been humiliated, my son, *they* are exhausted. They dread further fighting; that is why they are ready to make terms.'

Cesare laughed in admiration. 'And you have made them buy back their castles!'

'For 50,000 golden florins.'

'But you would rather have kept the castles, Father; which you would have done had you defeated them completely.'

'We are 50,000 florins the richer.'

'This was to be a beginning. We but started with the Orsini. And now?'

'We shall resort to peace for a while.'

'And the Orsini, when they have recovered from their weakness?'

The Pope looked straight at his son. 'There is one clause in the treaty to which I have had to agree. Virginio Orsini was in prison in Naples during the conflict. . . .'

Cesare snapped his fingers. 'And if he had not been, oh my father, that would have been very unfortunate for us.'

The Pope agreed to this. Cesare was smiling; he was remembering those days long ago when he had left his mother's house and lived for a year in Monte Giordano. He remembered the coming of the great soldier to the Orsini stronghold, and how his young boy's heart had rejoiced in that man; he thought of the long rides, of Virginio's grim yet affectionate way with him. During that year one of the heroes of Cesare's life had been Virginio Orsini. Cesare had been proud when Virginio had wished that he had been his son; and if he had been, he would have made a soldier of him.

'You admire him, I see,' said Alexander.

'He is a great soldier.'

'Not so reliable when the French invaded Italy.'

'Doubtless he had his reasons, Father. The Orsinis have made themselves allies of the French.'

'Against us,' said the Pope. 'But this clause in the treaty. . . . The Orsini demand that Virginio be immediately released from his prison.'

'I see, Father, that you do not wish to release Virginio.'

'You have said yourself that it would have been a different state of affairs had Virginio been at hand to lead his family's forces. They are our enemies still. At this time they are exhausted by the recent conflict; they are without a true leader; but if they had such a leader . . .' The Pope shrugged his shoulders. 'My son, it occurs to me that the Orsini may be so ready to agree to my terms, insisting only that Virginio be free, so that when he is among them again they may band themselves against us. Virginio must not be freed.'

'Yet you say this is the clause they insist on.'

'It is.'

'And you have agreed to it?'

'I have.'

'So Virginio will in a very short time *be free*.'

'He should not leave his prison.'

'Yet you have agreed. . . .'

'We have friends in Naples. There are a few days yet. Cesare, I charge you with this. You have always sought to show me your subtlety. Great commanders must be possessed, not only of courage, but resource.'

'When I was a boy and lived at Monte Giordano I knew him well,' said Cesare slowly.

'That was long ago, my son.'

'Yes,' said Cesare, 'long ago.'

The Pope laid his hand on his son's shoulder.

'You will know how to do what is best for our family,' he said.

It was foolish to harbour sentimental feelings.

Cesare paced up and down his own apartments. It was unlike him to delay when he knew something must be done which would redound to his advantage. And yet, memories would keep recurring. He could see himself riding behind that stalwart figure; he could feel again the admiration he had known.

Virginio Orsini, the man who had made life at Monte Giordano tolerable; Virginio who had wanted to make a soldier of him.

There was no time for delay. A message must be taken at once to Naples. A small quantity of a white powder must be carried there and instructions given.

Virginio Orsini would soon be taking his last meal in the prison.

If it were another I would not hesitate, thought Cesare. I would not give the matter a second thought. But Virginio! Oh nonsense, nonsense! What was a boy's hero-worship?

Yet he had been kind.

Kind! What had kindness to do with Cesare Borgia?

Still he continued to pace up and down his apartment.

'Not Virginio,' he murmured, 'not Virginio Orsini.'

In the streets the Carnival was at its height, and the people of Rome were bent on enjoying themselves. The Pope, with that mental dexterity which amazed all who came into contact with it, had once more brought diplomatic victory out of military defeat with the sleight of hand of a conjuror. The Orsinis had been the victors. But what had they won? A cessation of hostilities merely. They had paid heavily to regain their castles; and the head of their family, Virginio Orsini, although the Pope had granted his release, had died suddenly a few hours before he was due to leave his prison.

The people laughed at the wily ways of the Holy Father as they gave themselves up to enjoying themselves.

Men and women in masks and fancy dress filled the streets. Processions passed along, among which some carried grotesque figures held high over the heads of the revellers; others manipulated fantastic bizarre figures, puppets which performed lewd gestures to the immense amusement of the crowd. There was music, dancing and general revelry, and wars and political intrigue seemed far away.

From his apartment Cesare looked out on the revellers in the square and was angry with himself because he could not erase the memory of Virginio Orsini from his mind; when he slept he would awake startled, imagining that the tall stern figure stood at his bedside watching him reproachfully.

It was foolish, unlike him. He wanted entertainment. He wished Lucrezia was in Rome. He and his father must bring her back, and they must free her from that provincial boor, Giovanni Sforza. He hated the fellow. There was comfort in hating.

Now he would go along to Sanchia's apartment. He would indulge with her in such an orgy of sensuality that he would forget all the shadows which hung over him, the thought of Sforza and Lucrezia, the memory of Virginio Orsini.

He found Loysella alone in Sanchia's apartment and demanded to know where her mistress was.

'My lord,' answered Loysella, throwing glances at him from under lowered lids, 'the Princess went out some time since with Francesca and Bernardina to look at the carnival. Your lordship should not be dismayed. They were masked.'

He was not dismayed; only slightly irritated.

He was in no mood to go out into that seething crowd to search for her.

He looked at Loysella; Loysella was hopeful.

Then suddenly he turned away in disgust. It was as though

he were a boy again, and Virginio stood beside him, reproaching him for some breach of manners.

Abruptly he left the apartment; he went to his own and in vain tried to shut out the sounds of carnival.

Sanchia's mask only partially concealed her beauty. Through it her blue eyes regarded the scene about her. Her black hair escaped from the hood of her cloak.

Francesca and Bernardina were similarly masked; and they were giggling because they knew that as they left the palace they were being followed.

'What excitement! What a grand carnival!' breathed Francesca. 'There were never such carnivals in Naples.'

'Let us wait here and watch the crowds go by,' suggested Sanchia, knowing that the three men were standing behind them.

She glanced over her shoulder and a pair of brilliant eyes beneath a mask met hers and held them.

'I think,' she said, 'that we were unwise to come out alone, unescorted by any gentlemen. Why, anything . . . just anything might happen to us.'

Some passing revellers halted as they saw three girls, for there was that in their bearing which attracted immediate attention.

One young man, carnival-bold, approached Sanchia and seized her hand. 'There is a very fair lady cowering beneath that mask, I'll swear,' he said. 'Come, fair one . . . join us.'

Sanchia said: 'I do not wish it.'

'This is carnival, lady, and such as you must not stand aloof.'

She screamed as he took her arm, and one of the men who had been standing behind her cried out: 'Dispatch the insolent dog.'

The young man who had first spoken to her turned pale under his mask as one of the trio stepped forward, his sword in his hand. The young man stammered: ''Tis carnival time. No harm was meant. . . .' Then as the other raised his sword and pricked his arm, he cried out and ran, followed by the members of his party.

'Shall I give pursuit, my lord?' asked he who had drawn his sword.

'Nay,' said a languid voice. 'It is enough.'

Sanchia turned to him. 'I thank you, my lord,' she said. 'I shudder to think what might have befallen me and my women had you not been at hand to save us.'

'It is our great pleasure to save such as you,' said the man. He kissed her hand.

She knew him and she was fully aware that he knew her also. But this was a pleasant game they were playing; it had begun with his return from the wars. She was also aware that it was partly due to his hatred of Cesare that he was determined to pursue her; and although she had no intention of allowing herself to become a symbol between them, she was determined to make Cesare's brother her lover.

He was handsome – in his way handsomer than Cesare; his reputation was as evil but in a different way. She was going to teach the Duke of Gandia a lesson; she was going to show him that his need of Sanchia of Aragon would exceed his desire for revenge on his brother. That need was going to be the most important thing in his life.

But at the moment it pleased them to pretend, masked as they were, that they were unaware of each other's identities.

He kept her hand in his.

'Shall we join the revellers?'

'I am not sure that it would be fitting for us to do that,' replied Sanchia. 'We merely came out to watch from a distance.'

'Impossible to watch carnival from a distance as you have learnt from the conduct of those insolent dogs. Come, let me show you the carnival. You need have no fear. I am here to protect you.'

'We must keep together – my ladies and I,' she murmured. 'I should never forgive myself if aught happened to them.'

She was smiling slyly. What she meant was: I do not trust to your protection, Giovanni. Were there danger, you might run away. But with your attendants close at hand I shall be happier.

'We will keep with our little party,' said Giovanni. He signed to the two men, one of whom immediately took Francesca's hand the other Bernardina's. 'Now,' he went on, 'whither shall we go? To the Colosseum? There will be great revelry there. Or to see the racing in the Corso?'

'Escort us whither you will,' said Sanchia.

'Then may I suggest, my lord,' put in one of the men, 'that we find our way out of the crowd. These delicate ladies are in danger of being trampled underfoot by the plebs.'

'You speak wisely,' said Giovanni.

'There is a little *albergo* near the Via Serpenti. A place where we can be free of the clamour of the common people.'

'Then to it,' said Giovanni.

Sanchia turned to Francesca and Bernardina. 'No,' she said, 'I do not think I and my ladies should accompany you to this inn. If you will take us to St Peter's Square, we shall be safe enough and . . .'

'Come,' said Giovanni, his eyes shining through his mask. 'put yourself in my hands, fair lady. You will regret nothing.'

Sanchia pretended to shiver. 'I am a little uneasy. . . .'

But Giovanni had his arm about her and started off at a run, taking her with him. She looked fearfully over her shoulder, but Francesca and Bernardina were being similarly treated. They gave little shrieks of feigned horror, but their cavaliers ignored them as they followed Giovanni and Sanchia.

'Make way! Make way!' shouted Giovanni as he forced his way through the crowds. Many called after him; some attempted to stop him. Spirits and tempers ran high in carnival time.

But always those two men would be close to Giovanni, and was it something they said, or were they known? However, it was apparent every time that those who challenged them soon slunk away in fear.

Then Sanchia noticed that Giovanni's cloak was caught together by a brooch on which was emblazoned the grazing bull. His men carried the emblem too, one in his hat, the other on his doublet. Sanchia laughed inwardly. Giovanni would not venture into the streets masked at any time without some indication of who he was, prominently displayed on his person. There might be many to attack a young braggart who made himself unpleasant, but who would dare to raise an arm against a Borgia?

She was enjoying her evening. Cesare was to be taught a

lesson. He had been far more interested in his brother's humiliation than in her, and such slights must be paid for. She knew of a way which would infuriate him more than any. That was the way in which Cesare should pay for the slights he had given her.

There had been understanding glances between herself and Giovanni during the last few days; but this was the most amusing way to allow those little innuendoes to reach their climax.

When they reached the Via Serpenti they hurriedly slipped through a maze of alleys. The noise of the merrymakers seemed muted now as one of Giovanni's men pushed open the door of an inn and they all went in.

Giovanni shouted: 'Bring food. Bring wine . . . plenty of it.'

The innkeeper came running to them. He bowed low and looked very frightened as his eyes rested on the brooch which Giovanni was wearing.

'Good sirs,' he began.

'You heard us ask for wine and food. Bring it quickly,' said Giovanni.

'With the greatest speed, my lord.'

Giovanni sat on a couch and pulled Sanchia down beside him.

'I am determined,' he whispered, 'that you shall enjoy the hospitality . . . all the hospitality . . . which the innkeeper can offer.'

Sanchia said: 'My lord, I think I should tell you that I am no humble woman to be seized in carnival time.'

'Your voice, your manner betray you,' he said. 'But women who venture into the streets at carnival time ask to be seized.'

His men laughed, and applauded everything he said.

'We will drink wine with you and then we shall leave you here,' declared Sanchia.

'We are eager to enjoy *all* the pleasures that the carnival can offer,' ventured one of the men, keeping his eyes on Giovanni.

'*All*,' echoed Giovanni.

The innkeeper came hurrying in with wine.

'Is this the best you have?' demanded Giovanni.

'The very best, my lord.'

'Then it should be good, and if it is not I may grow angry.'

The innkeeper was visibly trembling.

'Now,' cried Giovanni, 'bolt all doors. We would be alone . . . completely alone, you understand me?'

'Yes, my lord.'

'As for food, do not bring it after all. I find I am not hungry. Wine will suffice. You have some comfortable rooms in your inn?'

'I can vouch for them,' said one of the men with a snigger, 'having already used them.'

'Now leave us, fellow,' said Giovanni. And turning to the ladies: 'We will drink to the joy this day will bring us all.'

Sanchia had risen.

'My lord . . .' she began. Giovanni put his arms about her and embraced her. She struggled, but Giovanni was fully aware that her struggling was feigned, that she knew who he was and that she had been as determined that this should happen as he was.

He put down his goblet and said: 'At such a time, I have no need of wine.' He picked up Sanchia in his arms shouting: 'Landlord! Take me to the best of your chambers . . . and delay not, for I am in a hurry.'

Sanchia kicked prettily and ineffectually. Bernardina and Francesca clung together while their two prospective lovers seized them and Sanchia and Giovanni disappeared.

The room was small; its ceiling low; but it was as clean as could be expected.

'Not the couch I would have chosen for you, my Princess,' said Giovanni. 'But it will suffice.'

'You should know who I am,' Sanchia told him.

He took off her mask. 'I was as wise before,' he answered, 'as you were. Why, sweet Sanchia, did you wish me to stage this pretty little show of rape? Mutual agreement to meet the inevitable would have been so much more comfortable.'

'Considerably less amusing,' she said.

'I have a notion,' he challenged, 'that you are afraid of Cesare.'

'Why should I be?'

'Because you have been his mistress since you came into Rome, and he is reputed to be a jealous lover.'

'I am afraid of no man.'

'Cesare is unlike other men. Sanchia ... insatiable Sanchia. You cannot look at a man without wishing to know him. I saw your looks ... I saw your speculation. At the moment we first met I saw it. You were determined that we should be together thus, but you thought to play safe. "Let Giovanni take all the blame," you said. "Therefore let it be rape." '

'Do you think I care what my old lovers think?'

'Even you are afraid of Cesare.'

'I will be dictated to by none.'

'There you are mistaken. In this room, the door locked behind us, I shall be your dictator.'

'You forget that a moment ago you accused me of arranging this.'

'Let us not argue about that. Sanchia ... Sanchia!'

She laughed. 'How masterful you are! Why, if you had shown the same determination against the Orsini as you do towards three defenceless women ...'

He caught her by the shoulders and shook her, temporarily angered. Then he laughed at her. 'You do not want a gentle lover, Madonna Sanchia. I understand.'

'I am thinking of Francesca and Bernardina.'

'They will be in their lovers' arms by now. They have been watching each other for days; ever since you decided that you would change brothers, those four people have been waiting for this day. Come, why procrastinate?'

'Why, indeed!' she murmured.

Cesare was furious, for it was not long before his spies brought news to him that Sanchia and Giovanni were constantly together.

He went to Sanchia's apartments while her women were combing her hair. Bursting in upon them he found them giggling over their adventures with their lovers. He strode to Sanchia, swept the dish of sweetmeats from the table and, waving his arms, shouted to her women: 'Get out!'

They left her fearfully, for they thought they saw murder in Cesare's eyes.

'So you harlot,' he said, 'I hear that you are my brother's mistress.'

Sanchia lifted her shoulders reflectively. 'And does that surprise you?'

'That you give yourself to any who asks, no! But that you dare to arouse my anger, yes!'

'It surprises me that you have time to be angry with me . . . you who waste so much of it being jealous of Giovanni's dukedom, and Giovanni's favour with your father.'

'Be silent. Do you think I shall allow you to insult and degrade me in this way?'

'I cannot see, Cesare, that you can do very much about it.'

She had turned and was smiling at him, her blue eyes blazing with desire for him. When he had this mad rage upon him she found him more interesting than she did when he was an affectionate lover.

'You will see, Sanchia,' he said. 'I only ask you to have patience.'

'I am not a very patient person.'

'You are a harlot, I know, the most notorious harlot in Rome. One brother's wife, and mistress of the other two. Do you know that the whole of the city talks of your behaviour?'

'And of yours, dear brother . . . and of Giovanni's . . . and of the Holy Father's. Yes, and even of Lucrezia's.'

'Lucrezia is innocent of all scandal,' he said sharply.

'Is that so?' she asked lightly.

Cesare strode to her and gave her a stinging blow on the side of her face, she caught his hand and dug her teeth into it, watching the blood spurt while she put her hand to her burning cheek.

It was as though the sight of blood maddened him. Anger leaped into his eyes as he caught her by the wrist, and she cried out in pain. 'Do not think,' he said, 'that you can treat me as you may have treated others.'

'Cesare, take your hands from me. You are causing me pain.'

'It delights me to hear it. It is exactly what I intend.' Again those sharp teeth were dug into his hand; he caught her by the shoulder and, as his grip on her wrist was released, she scratched his face. The excitement of battle was on them both. He tried to grasp her hands again; but she had him by the ear and was twisting it.

In a few moments they were rolling on the floor together, and inevitably, with two such people, desire and brutality mingled.

She resisted; not because she wished to resist but because she wished to prolong the battle. He called her bastard, harlot, every name that he could think of which would hurt one as proud as she. She retaliated. Was he not a bastard? she screamed. 'Brute! Cardinal!' she sneered.

She lay panting on the floor, her eyes wild, her clothes torn, while she thought of fresh insults to hurl at him.

'All Rome knows of your jealousy of your brother. You . . . the Cardinal! You with your fine clothes and your mistresses. . . . I hate Your Eminence. I hate you, Cardinal Borgia.'

He bore down on her; she kicked him; he cursed her; and after a while they were silent together.

She laughed afterwards, rising from the floor to stare at her appearance in the polished metal of her mirror.

'We look like two beggars on the Corso,' she said. 'How shall I hide these scratches, these bruises you have given me, you brute? Ah, but you are well marked too. It was worth it though, was it not? I begin to think that the floor is as good a bed as any.'

He was looking at her with hatred. But she liked his hatred. It was more stimulating than affection.

'Now,' he said, 'perhaps you will be more wary when you next meet my brother.'

'Why so?' she asked.

'Because you have discovered that I am a man of some temper.'

'I adore your temper, Cesare. You cannot ask me to forgo the pleasure of rousing it.'

'You mean then that you will not give him up?'

She appeared to be considering. 'We find such pleasure in each other,' she said almost plaintively, longing to arouse him to a fresh frenzy.

But he had grown cold.

He said: 'If you prefer one at whom all Italians are jeering, then continue to enjoy him.'

And he went out, leaving her stimulated but a little disappointed.

The Pope watched the growing antagonism between the two brothers with uneasiness.

Little Goffredo was bewildered. He had been delighted that both his brothers found his wife so attractive; but when he discovered that their admiration for his beautiful wife caused dissention between them which was greater than anything ever had before, he began to be worried.

Giovanni rarely left Sanchia's side. He liked to ride out with her through the streets of Rome; he did his best to circulate rumours concerning their relationship and was very eager that they should reach Cesare's ears.

Then suddenly Cesare seemed to lose interest in Sanchia.

His father sent for him because Alexander had some matter of importance to discuss, and he was finding that it was with Cesare rather than with his cherished Giovanni that he wished to discuss matters of policy.

'My dear son,' said Alexander, taking Cesare into his arms and kissing him, 'there is a matter of some importance which I wish to discuss with you.'

It delighted the Pope to see the frown on his son's face fade at such words.

'It is of Lucrezia's husband, this man Sforza that I wish to speak,' said the Pope.

Cesare's lip curled in disgust and Alexander went on: 'Your opinion of the man coincides with my own.'

'It has caused me great grief,' replied Cesare, 'to think of my sister's spending her days in that remote town, far away from us all . . . and Your Holiness giving him orders which he does not obey. I would that we could rid Lucrezia of the oaf.'

'It is to discuss this matter that I have called you to me now. Cesare, I wish this to be a closely guarded secret.'

'Between us two?' asked Cesare eagerly.

'Between us two.'

'And Giovanni?'

'No, Cesare, no. I would not even trust Giovanni with this. Giovanni is light-hearted and not as serious minded as you are, Cesare. I wish this to be a matter closely guarded, so that is why I choose to confide in you.'

'Thank you, Most Holy Lord.'

'My dearest son, I am determined to rid my daughter of that man.'

'And the means?'

'There is divorce, but divorce is not beloved of the Church; and as the Head of the Church I am expected to frown on it except in special circumstances.'

'Your Holiness would prefer another method?'

Alexander nodded.

'It should not be impossible,' said Cesare, his eyes shining. He was thinking, it had been sad to know that Virginio must die, but there would be no such sadness where Giovanni Sforza was concerned.

'Our first move,' said the Pope, 'would be to recall him to Rome.'

'Then let us make it.'

'Easier said than done, my son. The provincial lord entertains certain suspicions regarding us.'

'My poor Lucrezia, how she must suffer!'

'I am not sure of that, Cesare. Her letters would seem to grow more distant. Sometimes I feel that the Lord of Pesaro is taking our Lucrezia away from us, that she is becoming more of a wife to him than a daughter to me or a sister to you.'

'It shall not be. He will rob her of her charm. He will make her dull . . . insipid as he is. We must bring her back, Father.'

The Pope nodded. 'And Sforza with her. And when they come . . .' The Pope hesitated, and Cesare prompted him: 'And when they come, Holiness?'

'We will disarm him with our friendship. That will be the first step, Cesare. We will tell him by our words, gestures and deeds that we are no longer estranged from him. He is the spouse of our dearest one, and as such we will love him.'

' 'Twill be a hard task,' said Cesare grimly.

'Not when you remember to what it is leading us.'

'When we have his confidence, we will ask him to a banquet,' mused Cesare. 'He will not die at once. His shall be a lingering death.'

'You shall introduce him to the embrace of cantarella.'

'With the utmost pleasure,' said Cesare.

So to Rome came Lucrezia and with her rode her husband. Giovanni Sforza was reluctant; he grumbled continually throughout the journey.

'What do your family plan now? Why have they become so friendly towards me? I do not trust them.'

'Oh, Giovanni, you are too distrustful. It is because they have so much regard for me, because they are delighted to see me as a happy wife, that they offer you their friendship.'

'I warn you I shall be wary,' declared Giovanni.

He was surprised by his reception.

The Pope embraced him, called him his beloved son, and said that as the husband of Lucrezia he was entitled to a high position at the Papal Court. Never had Giovanni enjoyed such prestige as he did during those weeks. He began to lose his fears. When all is considered, he told himself, I am Lucrezia's husband, and Lucrezia is well satisfied with me.

He confided in a certain retainer of his whom he liked to take with him wherever he went, for he felt that Giacomino, his handsome young chamberlain, was one of the few people whom he could trust.

'My lord,' said Giacomino, 'it appears that you are well received here, but have a care, oh my lord. They say that it is unwise to eat rashly at the Borgia table.'

'I have heard such rumours.'

'Remember the sudden death of Virginio Orsini, my lord.'

'I think of it.'

'My lord, it would please me if you ate food prepared only by me.'

That made Giovanni laugh; but there were few people who had such a true affection for him as Giacomino had, and he knew it; he laid an affectionate arm about his servant's shoulders.

'Fret not, Giacomino,' he said. 'I can take good care of myself.'

He told Lucrezia of Giacomino's anxieties.

'They are groundless,' Lucrezia assured him. 'My father has taken you into the family circle. He knows that you and I can be happy together. But Giacomino is a good fellow, Giovanni; and I am glad he feels so deeply for you.'

And in the weeks which followed, Giovanni Sforza acquired a new air of confidence.

I can make Lucrezia happy, he thought; and the Pope loves his daughter so dearly that he is ready to bless any who can do that. He began to believe that he had exaggerated rumour and that the Borgias were merely a family who, with the exception of Giovanni and Cesare, were particularly devoted to one another.

Carnival time came round again, and the Borgias found the revels irresistible. The Pope, watching the scenes from his balcony, called his applause for the lewdness, and gave his blessing at the same time. There had never been a man who was able to mingle his love for the lewd and the pious so happily together; there was never a man more ready to take his religion in a merry way. At carnival times, more than any other, the people were satisfied with their Holy Father.

Giovanni Sforza disliked the carnival, was embarrassed by the lewd scenes which were enacted and, finding no pleasure in the coarse jokes, he was already homesick for Pesaro.

He did not want to go out and mingle with the crowds in the streets, so Lucrezia went with her brothers and Sanchia, some of their men and Sanchia's and Lucrezia's women.

It was Giovanni Borgia's idea that they should dress as mummers and mingle more freely with the crowds.

This seemed great fun to Lucrezia who, unlike her husband, delighted in the gaiety of Rome and certainly did not sigh for quiet Pesaro.

Sanchia had decided to give her attention to Giovanni in order to arouse Cesare's anger, and Giovanni was nothing loth; in their mummers' dresses, masks hiding their faces, they danced through the streets, Sanchia and Giovanni leading the troupe, dancing in the Spanish manner, suggestively, and going through the motions of courtship to an end which seemed inevitable.

But Cesare was not thinking of Sanchia at this moment; he had plans which concerned Giovanni, but he was shelving those, for more pressing ones concerning another Giovanni obsessed him at this moment. Moreover Lucrezia was with him, and his lust for Sanchia had never been as great as his love for his little sister.

He could lash himself into a fury now, not because Sanchia was behaving amorously with Giovanni, but by thinking of Lucrezia's life with Sforza.

'Lucrezia, little one,' he said, 'you love the carnival.'

'Oh brother, yes. Did I not always? Do you remember how we used to watch from the loggia of our mother's house and long to be among the revellers?'

'I remember how you clapped your hands and danced there on the loggia.'

'And sometimes you lifted me, so that I could see better.'

'We share many happy memories, beloved. When I think of the times we have been parted, I feel murderous towards those who parted us.'

'Do not talk of murderous feelings on such a night as this, Cesare.'

'It is such a night that takes my thoughts back to those weary separations. That husband of yours has deliberately kept you from us too long.'

She smiled gently. 'He is Lord of Pesaro, Cesare, and as such has his duties to Pesaro.'

'And what think you, Lucrezia – will he soon be carrying you back to his dreary home?'

'I think that ere long he will be impatient to return.'

'And you want to leave us?'

'Cesare! How can you say so? Do you not realize that I miss you all so sadly that I can never be happy away from you?'

He drew a deep breath. 'Ah! That is what I wished to hear you say.' He put his arm about her and held her close to him. 'Dearest sister,' he whispered, 'have no fear. It will not be long now before you are free of that man.'

'Cesare?' She spoke his name in the form of a question.

The excitement of the dance was upon him. His hatred of Sanchia and his brother was overlaid by his love for this little sister. He felt a great longing to protect her from all unhappiness and, believing that she despised her husband, even as he and their father did, he could not lose another moment before telling her that she would soon be free of him.

'It will not be long, sweet sister,' went on Cesare.

'Divorce?' she asked breathlessly.

'Divorce! Holy Church abhors it. Have no fear, Lucrezia. There are other ways of ridding oneself of an undesirable partner.'

'You cannot mean . . .' she cried.

But he silenced her.

'Listen, my dearest. We'll not talk of these matters here in the streets. I have plans concerning your husband, and I can promise you that before next carnival time you will have forgotten his very existence. There, does that please you?'

Lucrezia felt sick with horror. She did not love Giovanni Sforza, but she had tried to; when she was in Pesaro she had done her best to be the sort of wife he wished for, and she had not been unhappy in her efforts. He was not the lover of whom she had dreamed, but he was her husband. He had feelings, aspirations; and if he was full of self-pity, she too had pity for him. He had been unfortunate so many times.

'Cesare,' she said, 'I am afraid. . . .'

His lips were close to her ear. 'People watch us,' he said. 'We are not dancing with the others as we should. I will come to your apartment to-morrow in the afternoon. We will make sure that we are neither overlooked nor overheard. Then I will explain my plans to you.'

Lucrezia nodded mutely.

She began to dance, but now there was no gaiety in her. Those words of Cesare's kept drumming in her ears. They are going to murder Giovanni Sforza, she told herself.

Afraid and unsure, that night she was sleepless, and next day disturbed.

Never in her life had she felt so closely bound to her family; never had she had to face such an important decision.

To her father and her brother she believed she owed complete loyalty. To betray their confidences would be to commit an unforgivable act. And yet to stand aside and allow them to murder her husband – how could she do that?

Lucrezia discovered that she had a conscience.

She was aware of her youth and inexperience of life. She realized that like her father she longed for harmony all about her; and unlike him she could not achieve it ruthlessly. She did not love Sforza; she understood now that she would not greatly care if she never saw him again; but what horrified her was that he should be led to violent death or even quiet death, and that she would be among those who led him there, which she must be if she did not warn him.

She was faced with two alternatives. She could remain loyal to her father and brother and let Sforza go to his death or she could warn Sforza and betray her family.

It was a terrible decision which she had to make. All her love and devotion was at war with her sense of rightness.

Murder! It was a hideous thing and she wanted none of it.

If I let him to go his death the memory of my betrayal would haunt me all my life, she thought.

And if she betrayed Cesare and her father! They would never trust her again; she would be shut out from the trinity of love and devotion on which she had come to rely.

So she lay, sleepless, asking herself what she must do, rising and going to the Madonna's shrine, falling on her knees and praying for help.

There was no help. What she did must be her own decision.

Cesare was coming in the afternoon to tell her of his plans, and she knew that before that time she must have decided which course she was to take.

She sent one of her women for Giacomino, Sforza's chamberlain.

As Giacomino stood before her she thought how handsome he was; there was an honesty in him which was apparent, and she knew that he was her husband's most faithful servant.

'Giacomino,' said Lucrezia, 'I have sent for you that I may talk to you for a while.'

Lucrezia was aware of the little lights of alarm which had sprung into the young man's eyes. He believed that she found him attractive, for doubtless many women did, and she felt that she was making matters very difficult; but this was her plan and she must carry it out, since she saw no other way out of her dilemma. Giacomino stood before her with bowed head.

'Do you long to return to Pesaro, Giacomino?'

'I am happy to be where my lord is, Madonna.'

'Yet if you could choose, Giacomino?'

'Pesaro is my home, Madonna, and one has an affection for home.'

She nodded and went on to talk of Pesaro. She was thinking, He is bewildered, this good Giacomino, and I must go on talking, even though he may believe that I am seeking to make him my lover.

Giacomino had taken the stool she had indicated. He seemed to grow more miserable with every passing moment, as though he were already wondering how he, his master's most loyal servant, was going to repulse her. But at length she heard the sound for which she was waiting, and greatly relieved, sprang up, crying: 'Giacomino, my brother is on his way here.'

'I must go at once, Madonna,' said the agitated Giacomino.

'But wait. If you leave through the door he will see you, and my brother would not be pleased to see you here, Giacomino.'

What fear Cesare inspired in everyone! The young man had grown pale, his discomfort turning to terror.

'Oh Madonna, what shall I do?' stammered Giacomino.

'I will hide you here. Quick! Get you behind this screen and I will place these draperies over you. If you keep perfectly still you will not be discovered. But I implore you to be as still as you possibly can, for if my brother were to discover you in my apartments . . .'

'I will be still, Madonna.'

'Your teeth are chattering, Giacomino. I see you realize full well the dangerous position in which you find yourself. My brother does not like me to receive young men in friendship. It angers him. Oh, do take care, Giacomino.'

As she spoke she was pushing him behind the screen and

arranging the draperies over him. She looked at her work with satisfaction; the chamberlain was completely hidden.

Then she hurried to her chair and was sitting there assuming a pensive attitude when Cesare came into the room.

'Lucrezia, my dearest.' He took both her hands and kissed them, as he smiled into her face. 'I see you are prepared for me, and have arranged that we should be alone.'

'Yes, Cesare, you have something to say to me?'

'It was dangerous to talk last night in the streets, sister.' He went to the window and looked out. 'Ah, the revelries still continue. The mumming and masquing goes on. Is Giovanni Sforza out there in the streets this day, or is he moping in his apartment dreaming of dear dull Pesaro?'

'Dreaming of Pesaro,' said Lucrezia.

'Let him dream while he may,' cried Cesare grimly. 'There is not much time left to him for dreaming.'

'You refer to the plans you have made for him?'

'I do, sister. Oh, it has maddened me to think of you with that provincial boor. He deserves to die for having presumed to marry my sweet sister.'

'Poor Giovanni, he was forced into it.'

'You yearn for freedom, dearest sister, and because I am the most indulgent brother in the world, I long to give you all you desire.'

'You do, Cesare. I am happy when I am with you.'

Cesare had begun to pace the floor.

'Our father and I have not told you of our plans before. This is because we know you to be young and tender. You were ever one to plead for the meanest slave who was in disgrace, and ask that punishment be averted. It may be, we thought, that you would plead for your husband. But we know that you long to be free of him . . . even as we long to see you free.'

'What do you plan to do, Cesare?' asked Lucrezia slowly.

'To remove him.'

'You mean . . . to kill him?'

'Never mind how we do it, sweet sister. Ere long he will cease to worry you.'

'When do you propose to do this deed?'

'Within the next few days.'

'You will ask him to a banquet or ... will it be that he meets his assassins by night in some dark alley near the Tiber?'

'Our little Sforza is not without friends,' said Cesare. 'I think a banquet would suit him better.'

'Cesare, there is talk of a poison which you use – cantarella. Is it true that the secret is known only to you and to our father, and that you are able not only to kill people but decide on the day and even hour of their death?'

'You have a clever brother, Lucrezia. Does it make you happy to know that he puts all his skill at your disposal?'

'I know that you would do anything in the world for me,' she told him. She moved to the window. 'Oh Cesare,' she went on, 'I long to go out into the streets. I long to mingle with the revellers as we did last night. Let us ride out to Monte Mario as we did in the old days, do you remember? Let us go *now*.'

He came to her and laid his hands on her shoulders. 'You want to feel the air on your face,' he said. 'You want to say to yourself, Freedom is one of the greatest gifts life can offer, and soon it will be mine!'

'How well you know me,' she said. 'Come, let us go now.'

Only when they had left the Palace could she breathe freely. She was astonished at the cleverness with which she had been able to play her part.

Every minute had been fraught with terror that something would betray the presence of a third party in the room; and even more terrifying had been the constant thought: Cesare, my dearest, my beloved, I am betraying you.

Giacomino extricated himself from the draperies and made all haste to his master's apartments. He was breathless and begged Giovanni Sforza to see him privately.

'My lord,' he stammered as soon as they were alone, 'Madonna Lucrezia sent for me, I know not why, unless it was to give me some message to bring to you, but while I was in her apartments Cesare Borgia arrived and Madonna Lucrezia, fearing his anger, forced me to hide behind a screen. There I heard that he and the Pope are planning to murder you.'

Sforza's eyes dilated with terror.

'I suspected it,' he said.

'My lord, there is not a moment to spare. We must leave Rome with all speed.'

'You are right. Go prepare the strongest horses we have. We will set out at once for Pesaro. Only there can I be safe from my murderous relations.'

So Giacomino obeyed, and in less than an hour after the chamberlain had heard Cesare and Lucrezia talking together, he and Sforza were riding at full gallop out of Rome.

SAN SISTO

THE POPE AND Cesare were annoyed by Sforza's flight. Already the news was being whispered throughout Rome that he had fled because he feared the dagger or the poison cup which the Borgias were preparing for him.

'Let him not think to escape,' raged Cesare.

Alexander was serene.

'Calm yourself, my dear son,' he said. 'The only matter which concerns us is his separation from your sister. He is suspicious of our feelings towards him. It would be dangerous now to go the way we planned. There is only one course left open to us. I do not like it. As a Churchman I find it distasteful. The other would have been so much more convenient. I fear, Cesare, that we are left with divorce.'

'Well then, let us set about procuring it as soon as possible. I have promised Lucrezia her freedom and I intend her to have it.'

'Then let us study this matter of divorce. There are two alternatives, as I see it. First we could declare that the marriage was invalid because Lucrezia had never been released from a former entanglement with Gasparo di Procida.'

'I fear, Father, that that would be difficult to prove. Lucrezia was released from that betrothal, and there would be many to point to the proof of this. We should have Ludovico and Ascanio coming to their kinsman's aid if we put forward such a reason.'

'You are right there, my son. That leaves us the other alternative. We will ask for a divorce on the grounds that the marriage has never been consummated.'

'But this is not so.'

'My dear son, who shall say that it has been consummated? Is there a child to confirm it?'

'It is a barren marriage, Father, but consummation has surely taken place.'

'Who shall swear to this?'

'Sforza. He will not wish his impotence to be proclaimed to the world.'

'But Lucrezia will say what we wish her to.'

'Sforza will protest, he will protest vigorously.'

'We will protest with equal vigour.'

'It is the answer. Truly, Father, you have genius.'

'Thank you, my son. Are you beginning to realize that I know how to manage my family's affairs and do what brings my children the most good?'

'You have done much for Giovanni,' said Cesare with a hint of sullenness; 'and now I see that you will do what is best for Lucrezia.'

Alexander patted his son's shoulder affectionately. 'Send for the sweet creature,' he said. 'Let us tell her of the joy we are preparing for her.'

Lucrezia came to them. She was full of fears but, because she was growing up and learning the art of dissimulation which they practised so expertly, she managed to hide the state of her mind from their searching eyes.

'My dearest,' said the Pope embracing her, 'Cesare and I could not resist the pleasure of bringing you here. We have great news for you. You are to be freed from Sforza.'

'In what way, Father?'

'There will be a divorce. We do not like divorce, but there are times when it is necessary. So we shall use it to free you from Sforza.'

A feeling of relief swept over her. So they had abandoned their plans to murder him, and she had saved him.

The men noticed this relief and they smiled at one another. Their dear Lucrezia would be very grateful to them.

'Unfortunately,' declared the Pope, 'the Church is opposed to divorce, and my Cardinals will demand a very good reason if we are to grant it.'

'It will be a simple matter,' added Cesare, 'as the marriage has not been consummated.'

Lucrezia said quickly: 'But it *has* been consummated.'

'No, my child,' contradicted the Pope, 'it has not.'

'Father, we have shared the same bed on countless occasions.'

'Sharing a bed is not necessarily tantamount to consummation. My dear sweet innocent child, there is much you do not know. The marriage has not been consummated.'

'But Father, I swear it has.'

The Pope looked uneasily about him.

'All is well,' whispered Cesare. 'No one would dare remain within hearing when I have given orders that they should not.'

'My child,' went on the Pope, 'consummation is not what you think.'

'I know full well,' persisted Lucrezia, 'that my marriage has been consummated.'

The Pope patted her cheek. 'They may insist,' he said to Cesare, 'on an examination of the child. They are full of doubts and suspicions.'

'Father, I must assure you that I . . .'

'Have no fear, my child,' whispered the Pope. 'Such examinations have taken place before. It is so easy. The virgin, veiled on account of modesty. You understand. You yourself need not submit. We shall find a suitable virgin, and all will be well. All you would have to do would be to swear before the jurists and Cardinals of a commission.'

'Father, I could not so swear.'

The Pope smiled. 'You fret too much, my child. There are times when it is necessary for us to diverge from the truth, if not for the sake of ourselves, for the happiness of others.'

She was aghast. She looked from one to the other of these two men whom she loved beyond all others in the world. She knew that whatever the future held she must continue to love them, that they must mean more to her than anyone else, that she was bound to them in more ways than she understood; she belonged to them, and they to her; she was bound to them by bonds of affection and a family feeling which was stronger than any other she had known; and she knew them to be dissemblers, treacherous liars and murderers.

She could not endure any more. She said: 'Father, I pray you give me leave to retire. I would consider this matter.'

They kissed her tenderly, brother and father; and she left them, talking together of their plans to overcome any opposition.

As to Lucrezia, they did not expect any trouble from her.

She would not sign the monstrous document. It was a lie, a blatant lie.

Her father and Cesare pleaded with her. She must throw aside her scruples; she must remember what was at stake. Her brother Giovanni joined his pleas to those of Cesare and Alexander. It was degrading, he declared, that Lucrezia Borgia should remain married to such a man as Giovanni Sforza. Certainly her family wished to bring about her release. She was foolish to hesitate. What was the mere signing of a document?

'But it is a lie . . . a lie,' cried Lucrezia.

The Pope was gentle in his explanations, but astonished, he said, that his little daughter – the best loved of all his children – should so grieve her father.

'It is not the lie, so much, Father,' she tried to explain, 'but the hurt it will give to my husband. He will be branded as impotent, and you know what humiliation that will cause him.'

'You must not worry so much on account of others, my child. He will be free to marry again and prove himself.'

'But who will wish to marry a man who, it is declared, cannot give children?'

'This is a little foolish, my child. Sign the document. It is so simple. Your name here . . . and in a short time all will be well.'

But again and again she refused.

Meanwhile Giovanni Sforza, enraged at the terms on which the Pope intended to procure a divorce, protested loudly and vigorously.

It was a lie to say that the marriage had not been consummated, he declared. It had been consummated a thousand-fold.

He decided that there was only one place to which he could go for help. He would ride with all speed to Milan and seek the aid of his Sforza cousins. They had not shown themselves very eager to help in the past, but surely a family must stand together when one of its members was so insulted.

Having his own worries Ludovico was not very pleased to see his cousin. It might be that the French would return to Italy, and if they did Milan would be one of their first targets. If such circumstances arose, Ludovico would need the help of Alexander; and for what could he hope if he opposed the Pope in this matter? Ludovico obviously could offer little help to poor Giovanni Sforza.

'My dear cousin,' said Ludovico, 'why do you not agree to the divorce? It would be quickly over and there would be an end to the matter.'

'Do you not understand this monstrous suggestion?'

'I see that the Pope will allow you to retain Lucrezia's dowry if you agree. He also says you shall keep his goodwill.'

'Dowry! Goodwill! I am to retain these if I allow him to bruit it abroad that I am impotent!'

'It was a handsome dowry, and Papal goodwill is not to be despised.'

'Cousin, I ask you this: Had such a slur been thrown on *your* virility, how would you act?'

Ludovico was thoughtful for a few seconds, then he said: 'Well, Giovanni, my cousin, there is a way in which you could prove the Borgia's allegations to be wrong.'

'How so?' asked Giovanni eagerly.

'Prove it without doubt in the presence of our ambassador and the Papal Legate. Lucrezia could come to the castle of Nepi, and there you could show us publicly that you are capable of being a good husband.'

Giovanni shrank from his cousin in horror at the suggestion.

'But my dear cousin,' said Ludovico mildly, 'it has been done before. And if Lucrezia refuses to come, why then I could arrange for several courtesans to be in attendance. You could take your choice, and I can assure you that our Milanese women are as desirable as any they have in Rome.'

'It would be quite impossible.'

'I have made the suggestion,' said Ludovico, shrugging his shoulders. 'If you refuse to consider it, then people will draw their own conclusions.'

'I refuse to make a public spectacle of myself.'

'It seems to me the only way to counter this charge.'

'In the presence of the Milanese ambassador and the Papal Legate!' cried the outraged Giovanni. 'And who is the Papal Legate? Another Giovanni Borgia, a nephew of His Holiness. Why, I doubt not that, whatever I did in his presence, he would swear I was impotent. He is another example of the incessant nepotism of the Pope! And the Milanese ambassador! Doubtless he would be bribed to speak against me, or threatened if he refused.'

Ludovico looked at his relative sadly, but there was no other advice he could offer. Giovanni Sforza was an unlucky man; he had aroused the contempt and dislike of the Borgias. He was also a foolish man; because the Borgias wished to be rid of him, and he was making it difficult for them.

Lucrezia knew that she must sign. She could not hold out against them any longer. Each day they visited her or she was summoned to the Pope's presence. They all assured her that she must sign. There was her father, benevolent still but giving the faintest hints of losing patience; Cesare, growing angry with her now and then as he had never been before; Giovanni, telling her she was a stupid little girl who did not know what was good for her.

She did not know where her husband was. At first she had considered leaving Rome by stealth and fleeing to Pesaro, but when she had heard of the cruel things which Giovanni had said about her she no longer wanted to do that; for Giovanni Sforza, humiliated and angry, had declared that the Pope was eager for a divorce because he wanted his daughter to live in his immediate circle that he might take the place of her husband.

This was the first time that Lucrezia had heard this evil rumour concerning herself, and she shrank from the man who could spread it.

She had never felt so much alone as she did at that time. She longed to have someone like Giulia to confide in, but she never saw Giulia now; Sanchia was too immersed in her own affairs and the battle between Cesare and Giovanni for her favours which she was engendering.

And so there came the day when she signed the document

which they had prepared for her, in which she declared that, owing to her husband's impotence, she was still *virgo intacta*.

There was laughter in Rome.

A member of the most notorious family in Europe had declared her innocence. It was the best joke that had been heard in the streets for many years.

Even the servants, amongst themselves, could not refrain from sly titters. They had witnessed the passionate rivalry of the brothers for Lucrezia's affection; they had seen her embraced by the Pope. And there were many who could swear that Giovanni Sforza and Lucrezia had lived as husband and wife.

They did not do so, of course. They had no wish to be taken to some dark dungeon and return minus their tongues. They did not care to risk being set upon one dark night, tied in sacks and thrown into the river. They had no wish to drink of a certain wine and so step into eternity.

But at that time one of the most unhappy people in Rome was Lucrezia. She was filled with shame for what she had done, and she felt that she could no longer endure the daily routine of her life.

She thought longingly of those days of her childhood when she had lived so happily with the nuns of San Sisto, and everything within the convent walls had seemed to offer peace; and, very soon after she had signed that document, she left her palace for the convent of San Sisto.

There she begged to be taken to the Prioress and, when Sister Girolama Pichi came to her, she fell on her knees and cried: 'Oh, Sister Girolama, I pray you give me refuge within these quiet walls, for I am sorely oppressed and need the comfort this place has to offer me.'

Sister Girolama, recognizing the Pope's daughter, embraced her warmly and told her that the convent of San Sisto was her home for as long as she wished it to be so.

Lucrezia asked that she might see her old friends, Sister Cherubina and Sister Speranza, who so long ago, it seemed, had undertaken her religious teaching. The Prioress sent for them and, when Lucrezia saw them, she wept afresh and Sister Girolama told them to take Lucrezia to a cell where she might pray, and that they might stay with her as long as she needed their comfort.

When he discovered that Lucrezia had gone to the convent, Cesare was angry, but the Pope soothed him and begged him not to let any know how concerned they were at this unexpected move.

'If any should know that she had run away from us they would ask the reason,' said the Pope, 'and there would be many to question whether she had willingly put her name to our document.'

'They will know soon enough that she has fled to the nuns to seek refuge from us.'

'That must not be. This day I will send men-at-arms to bring her back to us.'

'And if she will not come?'

'Lucrezia will obey my wishes.' The Pope smiled grimly. 'Moreover the nuns of San Sisto will not wish to arouse Papal displeasure.'

The men-at-arms were dispatched. Lucrezia was with four of the nuns when she heard them at the gates.

She turned startled eyes to her companions and wished she were one of them, serene and far removed from all trouble. Oh, she thought, what would I not give to change places with Serafina or Cherubina, with Paulina or Speranza?

The Prioress came to her and said: 'There are men of the Papal entourage below. They have come to take you back, Madonna Lucrezia.'

'Holy Mother,' said Lucrezia, falling on her knees and burying her face in the voluminous black habit, 'I beg you do not let them take me away.'

'My daughter, is it your wish that you should renounce all worldly things and stay here with us all the days of your life?'

Lucrezia's lovely eyes were full of bewilderment. 'They will not permit it, Holy Mother,' she said; 'but let me stay awhile. I pray you let me stay. I am afraid of so much outside. Here I find solitude and I can pray as I cannot in my palace. Here in my cell I am alone with God. That is how I feel, and I believe that if you will but give me refuge for a little longer I shall know whether I must give up all outside these walls and become one of you. Holy Mother, I implore you, give me that refuge.'

'We would deny it to none,' said Girolama.

One of the nuns came hurrying to them to report that men were at the gates demanding to see the Prioress. 'They are soldiers, Holy Mother. They are heavily armed and look fierce.'

'They have come for me,' said Lucrezia. 'Holy Mother, do not let them take me.'

The Prioress went boldly to the gates and faced the soldiers, who told her they were in a hurry, and had come, on the orders of His Holiness, to take Madonna Lucrezia with them.

'She has sought refuge here,' said the Prioress.

'Now listen, Holy Mother, this is an order from the Pope.'

'I regret it. But it is a rule of this house that none who asks for refuge shall be denied it.'

'This is no ordinary visitor. Would you be so foolish as to offend His Holiness? The Borgia Pope and his sons do not love those who oppose them.'

The soldiers meant to be kind; they were warning the Prioress that if she were a wise woman she would heed the Pope's request. But if Girolama Pichi was not a wise woman she was a brave one.

'You cannot enter my house,' she said. 'If you do, you commit an act of profanity.'

The soldiers lowered their eyes; they had no wish to desecrate a holy convent, but at the same time they had their orders.

Girolama faced them unflinching. 'Go back to His Holiness,' she said. 'Tell him that as long as his daughter craves refuge, I shall give it, even though His Holiness commands me to release her.'

The men-at-arms turned away, abashed by the courage of the woman.

In the Vatican, the Pope and his two sons chafed in quiet anger.

They knew that in the streets it was whispered that Madonna Lucrezia had entered a nunnery, and that the reason was that her family was trying to force her to do something which was against her will.

Alexander came to one of his quick and brilliant decisions. 'We will leave your sister in her convent,' he said, 'and make no more attempts to bring her out. They cause gossip and scandal, and until the divorce is completed we wish to avoid that. We will let it be known that Madonna Lucrezia has been sent to San Sisto by ourselves, our wish being that she should live in quiet retirement until she is free of Giovanni Sforza.'

So Lucrezia was left in peace; but meanwhile the Pope and her brothers redoubled their efforts to obtain her divorce.

Life for Lucrezia was now regulated by the bells of San Sisto, and she was happy in the convent where she was treated as a very special guest.

No one brought her news so she did not know that Romans continued to mock at what they called the farce of the divorce. She had never been fully aware of the scandals which had circulated about herself and her family, and she had no notion that verses and epigrams were now being written on the walls.

Alexander went serenely about his daily life, ignoring the insinuations. His one aim was to bring about the divorce as quickly as possible.

He was in constant communication with the convent, but he made no attempt to persuade his daughter to leave her sanctuary. He allowed the rumour, that she intended to take the veil, to persist, realizing that the image of a saintly Lucrezia was the best answer to all the foul things which were being said of her.

He selected a member of his household to take letters to his daughter and, as he was planning that after the divorce he would send her to Spain for a while in the company of her brother the Duke of Gandia, he chose as messenger a young Spaniard who was his favourite chamberlain.

Pedro Caldes was young and handsome and eager to serve the Pope. His Spanish nationality was on his side as Alexander was particularly gracious to Spaniards; his charm of manner was a delight to the Pope, who was anxious that Lucrezia should not become too enamoured of the nuns and their way of life.

'My son,' said Alexander to his handsome chamberlain, 'you will take this letter to my daughter and deliver it to her personally. Now that the Prioress knows that my daughter is in the Convent of San Sisto with my consent, you will be admitted to my daughter's presence.' Alexander smiled charmingly. 'You are to be not merely a messenger; I would have you know that. You will talk to my daughter of the glories of your native land. I want you to inspire within her a desire to visit Spain.'

'I will do all in my power, Most Holy Lord.'

'I know you will. Discover whether she is leading the life of a nun. I do not wish my little daughter to live so rigorously. Ask her if she would like me to send a companion to her – some charming girl of her own age. Assure her of my constant love and tell her that she is always in my thoughts. Now go, and when you return come and tell me how you found her.'

So Pedro set out for the convent determined to make a success of his mission. He was delighted with it; he had often seen Madonna Lucrezia and had greatly admired her. She was the most beautiful of all the women, he thought, preferring her serene youthfulness to the more bold beauty of Madonna Giulia; as for the Princess of Squillace she was not to his taste at all, being nothing more than a brazen courtesan. It seemed to Pedro that, compared with such women, Lucrezia was wonderful.

He stood before the convent, at the foot of the Aventine, and looked up at the building. He felt then that this was a fateful moment in his life; he was to have a chance to win the friendship of Lucrezia, a chance which he had never thought would be his.

He was allowed to enter, and the nuns who passed him in the corridors hurried along with downcast eyes, scarcely looking at the stranger. He was conducted to a small room. How quiet it was!

He looked about him at the stone floor and the bare walls on which there was nothing but a crucifix. The furniture in the room consisted of a rough bench and a few stools. Outside the brilliant sun seemed far away for it was so cool behind those thick walls.

And suddenly Lucrezia came and stood before him. She was dressed in a long black robe, such as the nuns wore, but there was no covering on her head, and her golden hair streamed down her back. It was symbolic, thought Pedro. The display of all that golden beauty meant that she had not yet decided to take the veil. He would know when she had, because then he would not be allowed to see her golden hair.

He bowed; she held out her hand and he kissed it.

'I come from the Holy Father,' he said.

'You have brought letters?'

'Yes, Madonna. And I hope to take a reply back to him.'

'You are welcome.' He noticed how eagerly she took the letters.

He hesitated, then said: 'Madonna, it is the wish of His Holiness that I should linger awhile and talk with you, that you might ask me for news of the Vatican.'

'That is kind of him,' said Lucrezia with a dazzling smile. 'I pray you sit down. I would offer you refreshment, but . . .'

He lifted a hand. 'I want none, Madonna. And I could not sit in your presence unless you sat first.'

She laughed and sat down facing him. She had laid the letters on the bench, but kept her hands on them as though her fingers were longing to open them.

'Tell me your name,' she said.

'It is Pedro Caldes.'

'I have seen you often. You are one of my father's chamberlains, and you come from Spain.'

'I am honoured to have been noticed by the lady Lucrezia.'

'I notice those who serve my father well.'

The young man flushed with pleasure.

'It is a double delight for me to be here,' he said, 'for not only has His Holiness entrusted me with the mission, but it is the pleasantest I ever undertook.'

Lucrezia laughed suddenly. 'It pleases me to hear a compliment again.'

'There are rumours which have greatly disturbed your eminent father, Madonna. Some are hinting that it is your

intention to remain here for the rest of your life.' She was
silent, and there was alarm in Pedro's eyes as he went on:
'Madonna Lucrezia, that would be wrong . . . wrong!'

He paused, waiting to be dismissed for his insolence, but
there was nothing arrogant about Lucrezia. She merely smiled
and said: 'So you think it would be wrong. Tell me why?'

'Because,' he said, 'you are too beautiful.'

She laughed with pleasure. 'There are some beautiful nuns.'

'But you should be gracing your father's Court. You should
not hide your beauty in a convent.'

'Did my father tell you to say that?'

'No, but he would be deeply wounded if you made such a
decision.'

'It is pleasant to talk to someone who cares what I do. You
see, I came here for refuge and I found it. I wanted to shut
myself away from . . . so many things. I do not regret coming
here to dear Sister Girolama.'

'It was a pleasant refuge, Madonna, but a temporary one.
May I tell His Holiness that you are looking forward to the day
when you will be reunited with your family?'

'No, I do not think you may. I am as yet undecided. There
are times when the peace of this place overwhelms me, and I
think how wonderful it is to rise early in the morning, and to
wait for the bells to tell me what to do. Life here is simple and
I sometimes long to live the simple life.'

'Forgive me, Madonna, but you would deny your destiny
were you to stay here.'

She said: 'Talk of other things, not of me. I am weary of
my problems. How fares my father?'

'He is lonely because you are not with him.'

'I miss him too. I long for his letters.' She glanced at them.

'Would you wish me to leave you that you might read them
in peace?'

She hesitated. 'No,' she said. 'I will keep them. They will
be something to look forward to when you have left. How are
my brothers?'

Again Pedro hesitated. 'All is much as it was when you left
them.'

She nodded sadly, thinking of them and their passion for

Sanchia of which they were making another issue on which to build their hatred.

'Will you return to Spain one day?'

'I hope so, Madonna.'

'You are homesick?'

'As all must be who belong to Spain and leave her.'

'I fancy I should feel the same if I were forced to leave Italy.'

'You would love my country, Madonna.'

'Tell me of it.'

'Of what shall I tell you – of Toledo which is set on a horse's shoe of granite, of the Tagus and the mighty mountains? Of Seville where the roses bloom all through the winter, of the lovely olive groves, of the wine they make there? It is said, Madonna, that those whom God loves live in Seville. I should like to show you the Moorish palaces, the narrow streets; and never did oranges and palms grow so lush as they do in Seville.'

'You are a poet, I believe.'

'I am inspired.'

'By your beautiful country?'

'No, Madonna. By you.'

Lucrezia was smiling. It was useless to pretend that she did not enjoy the young man's company, that she did not feel revived by this breath of the outside world; she felt as though she had slept long and deep when she needed sleep, but now the sounds of life were stirring about her and she wanted to wake.

'I long to see your country.'

'His Holiness hinted that when the Duke of Gandia returns to Spain he might take you with him.'

To Spain! To escape the gossip, the shame of divorce! It seemed a pleasant prospect.

'I should enjoy it . . . for a while.'

'It would be for a while, Madonna. His Holiness would never allow you to stray long from his side.'

'I know it.'

'And so solicitous is he for your happiness that he is concerned to think of you here. He asks: "Is your bed hard? Do you find the food tasteless? Do the convent rules irk you?" And he wonders who combs your hair and washes it for you. He says he would like to send you a companion, someone

whom he would choose for you. She would be young, a friend
as well as a servant. He asks me to bring him word as to whether
you would like him to do this.'

Lucrezia hesitated. Then she said: 'I pray you convey my
deep devotion to my father. Tell him that the love he bears me
is no more than that I bear him. Tell him that I pray each
night and morning that I may be worthy of his regard. And
tell him too that I am happy here, but that I have enjoyed your
visit and look forward to receiving one whom he will send me
to be my servant and companion.'

'And now, Madonna, you would wish me to retire and leave
you with your letters?'

'How kind you are,' she said. 'How thoughtful!'

She extended her hand and he kissed it.

His lips lingered on her hand and she was pleased that this
should be so. The nuns were her good friends, but Lucrezia
bloomed under admiration.

She was still safe in her refuge; but she had enjoyed that
breath of air from the outside world.

The Pope sent for the girl whom he had chosen to be
Lucrezia's companion in the Convent of San Sisto.

She was charming, very pretty and small, with brilliant dark
eyes and a dainty figure. Alexander had thought her charming
when he first saw her. He still thought so, but at the moment he
admired red hair such as that of his favourite mistress.

He held out his arms as the girl approached. 'Pantisilea,' he
said, 'my dear child, I have a mission for you.'

Pantisilea lowered those wonderful eyes and waited. She
was afraid that the Holy Father was going to send her away.
She had been dreading this. She had known that their relationship could not continue indefinitely; the Pope's love affairs
were fleeting, and even that with Giulia Farnese had not lasted
for ever.

Pantisilea had had dreams. Who in her place would not?
She had pictured herself as a lady of substance like Vannozza
Catanei or Giulia Farnese.

Now she was beginning to understand that she had been
lightly selected to charm a weary hour or two.

'You are trembling, my child,' said Alexander kindly.

'It is in terror, Holy Lord, of being sent away from you.'

Alexander smiled kindly. He was always kind to women. He fondled the dark curls absentmindedly; he was thinking of his red-headed mistress.

'You shall not go far from us, my dear; and, when you hear for what mission I have selected you, you will rejoice, knowing that I could give this task – not only to one I loved, but one whom I respected and trusted.'

'Yes, Holiness.'

'You are going to the Convent of San Sisto, there to attend my daughter Lucrezia.'

Pantisilea's relief was obvious. The lady Lucrezia was a gentle mistress, and all those who served her considered themselves fortunate to do so.

'There,' said the Pope. 'You are delighted, for you are aware of the honour I do you.'

'Yes, Holiness.'

'You must be prepared to leave this day. My daughter is lonely, and I want you to comfort her, and be her friend.' He pinched the girl's soft cheek tenderly. 'And at the same time, my sweet child, you will constantly let her know how grieved her father is because he does not have her with him. You will wash her hair for her and take some of her fine clothes and jewels with you. You will persuade her to wear them. Pantisilea, my dear, it is said that my daughter wishes to become a nun. I know this to be but talk; but my daughter is young and impressionable. It is your task to remind her of all the joys outside a convent walls. Girls' chatter, gossip, fine clothes! My Lucrezia loved them all. See, my child, that she does not lose that love. The sooner you bring her from that place, the greater will be your reward.'

'Holy Father, my ambition is to serve you.'

'You are a good child. You are beautiful too.'

The Pope took her into his arms in a farewell embrace which was one of mingled approval and passion.

Lucrezia was ready to be very fond of Pantisilea. She was excited to have someone who laughed readily, and enjoyed

gossiping. Serafina and the others were too sober, believing
that there was something sinful in laughter.

Pantisilea opened trunks and showed Lucrezia the dresses
she had brought with her.

'These become you far more than that black habit, Madonna.'

'I have no heart for them in this quiet place,' Lucrezia
explained. 'They would look incongruous here, Pantisilea.'

Pantisilea appeared bitterly disappointed. 'And your hair,
Madonna!' she persisted. 'It is not as golden as it used to
be.'

Lucrezia looked slightly alarmed. It was sinful to care for
worldly matters such as the adornment of her person, the
sisters had told her; and she had tried not to regret that her
hair was left unwashed.

She explained to Pantisilea that the sisters would not have
approved of her washing her hair as often as had been her
custom. They would accuse her of vanity.

'Madonna,' said Pantisilea slyly, 'they have not golden hair
like yours. I pray you let me wash it, only to remind you how
it will shine.'

What harm was there in washing her hair? She allowed
Pantisilea to do so.

When it was dry, Pantisilea laughed with pleasure, took
strands of it in her hands and cried: 'But look, Madonna, it is
pure gold again. It is the colour of the gold in your green
and gold brocade gown. Madonna, I have the dress here. Put
it on.'

Lucrezia smiled at the girl. 'To please you, little Pantisilea.'

So the green and gold dress was put on and, as Lucrezia
stood with her golden hair about her shoulders, one of the nuns
came to tell her that Pedro Caldes had arrived at the convent
with letters from the Pope.

Lucrezia received him in the cold bare room.

He stared at her, and she watched the slow flush creep up
from his neck to the roots of his hair. He could not speak, but
could only stare at her.

She said: 'Why, Pedro Caldes, is aught wrong?'

He stammered: 'Madonna, it would seem that I am in the
presence of a goddess.'

It was so pleasant to be wearing beautiful clothes again, and to sense the admiration of this young man. He was personable and she had been too long without admiration.

After that she did not wear her black habit again and her hair was always gleaming like gold.

She could never be sure when Pedro would call, bringing messages from her family; and she was determined that this young man, who so admired her, should always see her at her best.

Pantisilea was a merry companion, and Lucrezia wondered how she had endured the long days before the coming of this bright girl.

They would sit together in rooms allotted to them and work at a piece of embroidery, although Pantisilea liked better to sing to the accompaniment of Lucrezia's lute. Pantisilea had brought the lute with her; she had also had some tapestry sent so that the bare walls were hung with this and it no longer seemed like a cell. She continually talked of the outside world. She was amusing and a little indiscreet; and perhaps, thought Lucrezia, that was what made her company so exciting; she felt now that she would go to sleep in that of the kindly but sombre sisters.

Pantisilea, delightedly shocked, gossiped about Cesare's anger against his brother and how Sanchia was alternately the mistress of each. There had never been anyone at the Papal Court like Sanchia, she declared. The brothers visited her openly, and the whole of Rome knew that they were her lovers. And there was little Goffredo too, delighted that his wife should be causing so much controversy, and helping his brother Cesare prevail over his brother Giovanni.

She had a story to tell of a lovely girl from Ferrara who was betrothed.

'His lordship of Gandia set eyes on her and greatly coveted her,' said Pantisilea; 'but her father was determined on her marriage, for it was a good one. She had a big dowry and that together with her beauty, was irresistible. But the Duke of Gandia was determined to make her his mistress.

It is all very secret, Madonna; but now the marriage has
been postponed and there are some who say that the masked
companion who is seen often with the Duke of Gandia is this
lady.'

'My brothers are alike in that what they want they are
determined to have.'

'Indeed it is so, and there is much gossip throughout Rome
concerning the Duke's mysterious love affair.'

'And the masked one is this girl?'

'No one can be sure. All that is known is that in the company of the Duke of Gandia there is invariably a masked figure.
They ride together – sometimes pillion. The clothes worn by
the Duke's companion are all-concealing, so that it is impossible to say whether it is man or woman.'

'How like Giovanni to attract attention to himself thus. And
my brother Cesare? Has he a masked mistress?'

'No, my lady. The Lord Cardinal has not been seen except
at the church ceremonies. There is talk that he no longer cares
for Madonna Sanchia, and that because of this, harmony has
been restored between the two brothers.'

'I trust it is so.'

'They have been seen, walking together, arms linked like
true friends.'

'It does me good to hear it.'

'And, Madonna, what will you wear? The green velvet with
the pink lace is becoming to your beauty.'

'I am well enough as I am.'

'Madonna, what if Pedro Caldes should come?'

'What if he should?'

'It would be wonderful for him to see you in the green velvet
and pink lace.'

'Why so?'

Pantisilea laughed her merry laugh. 'Madonna, Pedro Caldes
loves you. It is there in his eyes for anyone to see – but perhaps
not for anyone. Not for Sister Cherubino.' Pantisilea made a
wry face that was a fair imitation of the good sister. 'No, she
would not recognize the signs. But I do. I know that Pedro
Caldes is passionately but hopelessly in love with you, Madonna.'

'What nonsense you talk!' said Lucrezia.

He *was* in love with her.

She knew that Pantisilea was right. It was in every gesture, in the very tone of his voice. Poor Pedro Caldes! What hope was there for him?

But she looked forward to his visits, and was taking as much interest in her appearance as she ever had.

The merry serving-maid was an intrigante. Frivolous and sentimental, it seemed to her inevitable that Lucrezia should indulge in a love affair. Continually she talked of Pedro – of his handsome looks, of his courtly manners.

'Oh, what a tragedy if the Holy Father decided to employ another messenger!' she cried.

Lucrezia laughed at her. 'I believe you are in love with this young man.'

'I should be, were it of any use,' declared Pantisilea. 'But his love is for one and one only.'

Lucrezia found that she enjoyed these conversations. She could grow as excited as Pantisilea, talking of Pedro. There in their little room, which was becoming more and more like a small chamber of one of the palaces, they sat together gossiping and laughing. When Lucrezia heard the bells, when she looked out of her window and saw the nuns passing to the chapel, and when she heard their singing of Complines, sometimes she would start guiltily out of her reverie. Yet the sanctified atmosphere of the convent made the visits of Pedro seem more exciting.

One day when she went into the cold bare room to receive him, she noticed that he was quiet, and she asked him if anything had happened to sadden him.

'Madonna,' he said earnestly, 'I am sad indeed, so sad that I fear I can never be happy again.'

'Something very tragic has happened to you, Pedro?'

'The most tragic thing that could happen to me.'

She was at his side, touching his sleeve with gentle and tender fingers. 'You could tell me, Pedro. You know that I would do all in my power to help.'

He looked down at her hand resting on his sleeve, and

suddenly he took that hand and covered it with kisses; then he fell on his knees and hid his face against her billowing skirts.

'Pedro,' she said softly. 'Pedro, you must tell me of this tragic thing.'

'I can come here no more,' he said.

'Pedro! You are weary of these visits. You have asked my father to send another in your place.' There was reproach in her voice, and he sprang to his feet. She noticed the shine in his eyes and her heart leaped with exultation.

'Weary!' he cried. 'These visits are all that I live for.'

'Then Pedro...'

He had turned away. 'I cannot look at you, Madonna,' he murmured. 'I dare not. I shall ask His Holiness to replace me. I dare not come again.'

'And your tragedy, Pedro?'

'Madonna, it is that I love you . . . the saints preserve me!'

'And it makes you sad? I am sorry, Pedro.'

He had turned to her, his eyes blazing. 'How could it make me anything but sad? To see you as I do . . . to know that one day the order will come, and you will return to the Vatican; and when you are there I shall not dare to speak to you.'

'If I returned to my palace it would make no difference to our friendship, Pedro. I should still ask you to come and see me, to entertain me with your conversation and tales of your beautiful country.'

'Madonna, it is impossible. I crave leave to depart.'

'It is granted, Pedro,' she said. 'But . . . I shall expect you to visit me still, because I should be so unhappy if any other came in your place.'

He fell on his knees and, taking her hands, covered them with kisses.

She smiled down at him, and she noticed with pleasure how the fine dark hair curled on his neck.

'Oh yes, Pedro,' she said. 'I should be very unhappy if you ceased to visit me, I insist that you continue to do so. I command it.'

He rose to his feet.

'My lady is kind,' he murmured. Then he looked at her with

a hunger in his eyes which enthralled her. 'I . . . I dare stay no longer,' he said.

He left her, and when he had gone she marvelled that in this convent of San Sisto she had known some of the happiest hours of her life.

Cesare rode to his mother's house to pay her one of his frequent visits. He was thoughtful, and those about him had noticed that of late there had been a certain brooding quietness in his demeanour.

He had ceased to court Sanchia; he had ceased to brood on his sister's voluntary retreat to the convent; he had become quite friendly with his brother Giovanni.

When Vannozza saw her son approaching, she clapped her hands vigorously and several of her slaves came running to do her bidding.

'Wine, refreshment,' cried Vannozza. 'I see my son, the Cardinal comes this way. Carlo,' she called to her husband, 'come quickly and greet my lord Cardinal.'

Carlo came running to her side. Carlo was well satisfied with his lot, which had brought marriage with the Pope's ex-mistress and mother of his children. Many privileges had come his way, and he was grateful for them. He showed his gratitude by his profound respect for the Pope and the Pope's sons.

Cesare embraced his mother and his stepfather.

'Welcome, welcome, dearest son,' said Vannozza with tears of pride in her eyes. It never ceased to astonish her that these wonderful sons of hers should visit their comparatively humble mother. All her adoration shone in her eyes, and Cesare loved her for that adoration.

'My mother,' murmured Cesare.

Carlo declared: 'It is a great day for us when my lord Cardinal honours our house.'

Cesare was gracious. He sat with his mother and his step-father, and as they drank from the silver goblets which had been hastily taken from the *credenza*, Vannozza was regretting that she had not been warned of her son's coming and had not had time to hang the tapestries on the walls and bring out the majolica and pewter ornaments. They talked of Lucrezia and of the impending divorce.

'Your father will do what is best for you all,' said Vannozza. 'Oh, my son, I would that I were not such a humble woman and could do more for you.'

Cesare laid his hand over hers and smiled at her; and when Cesare smiled his face was beautiful. It was real affection which he had for his mother; and Vannozza, because she knew how others feared him, valued that affection the more.

After they had refreshed themselves, Cesare asked that she would show him her flowers, of which she was justly proud, and they went into the gardens.

They wandered among her plants, Cesare's arm about her waist; and since he was so affectionate, Vannozza found courage to tell him how pleased she was that he and his brother Giovanni seemed to be better friends.

'Oh, Mother, how senseless quarrels are! Giovanni and I are brothers. We should be friends.'

'They were merely brotherly quarrels,' soothed Vannozza. 'Now you are growing older you realize the futility of them.'

'It is so, Mother. I want the whole of Rome to know that Giovanni and I are now friends. When you next give a supper party let it be an intimate one . . . for your sons only.'

Vannozza stood still, smiling delightedly. 'I shall give the party at once,' she said. 'For you and Giovanni. It is too hot in the city. It shall be an alfresco supper in my vineyards. What think you, Cesare, of that idea?'

'It is excellent. Make it soon, dearest Mother.'

'Say when you wish it to be, oh my beloved, and it shall be then.'

'Tomorrow is too soon. The day after that?'

'It shall be so.'

'Mother, you are my very good friend.'

'And should I not be, my best beloved son who has cherished and honoured me at all times?'

She closed her eyes and remembered what Cesare had done to all those who, he had been able to discover, had taken part in the raiding of her house during the French invasion. He had been brutal and many had suffered, and Vannozza was a woman who did not care to see great suffering; but this showed the measure of Cesare's love for her. 'Nothing,' he had cried, 'nothing . . . is too severe for those who sought to dishonour my mother by desecrating her house.'

'You will be glad to see Giovanni with me at your supper party,' said Cesare. 'You love him too, remember. It is a pity Lucrezia will not be with us.'

'I should take great pleasure in seeing my daughter, and I agree that I shall be happy to have Giovanni with me. But, my son, of all my children there is one who delights me as none other could. It is you, my dearest.'

He kissed her hand with that extravagant show of love which the family displayed towards each other.

'I know you speak truth, dear Mother. I swear to you here and now that no harm shall ever come your way while there is power in this body to prevent it. I will inflict torture and death on any who dare whisper a word against you.'

'My dearest, do not be so vehement on my poor account. I need nothing to make me happy but to see you often. Bless me with your presence as frequently as is possible – although I know that you have your destiny, and I must not let my selfish love interfere with that – and I shall be the happiest woman on Earth.'

He held her against him, and then they continued their walk among the flowers, planning the supper party.

Cesare walked through the streets, his cloak concealing his fine clothes, his mask hiding his features, so that none would have guessed his identity. Reaching the Ponte district he sauntered into a narrow street, slipped into another and paused before a house. Looking about him to make sure that he was not followed, he walked through the open door shutting it behind him, and descending the stone steps to a room with wooden panelling and flagstone floor, clapped his hands as he did so.

A servant appeared, and when Cesare removed his mask the man bowed low.

'Your mistress is here?' asked Cesare.

'Yes, my lord.'

'Conduct me to her at once.'

He was led to a room which was typical of many such rooms, furnished with a canopied bed, wooden chairs with carved backs, and the statue of the Madonna with the lamp burning before it.

A very beautiful young girl, tall and slender, who had risen at Cesare's entry, fell on her knees before him.

'My lord,' she murmured.

'Rise,' said Cesare impatiently. 'My brother is not here?'

'No, my lord. He comes two hours from now.'

Cesare nodded.

'The time has come for you to fulfil your duty,' he said.

'Yes, my lord?'

Cesare looked at her shrewdly. 'You are beloved by my brother. What are your feelings for him?'

'I serve one master,' she said.

His fingers closed about her ear. It was a gesture both tender and threatening. 'Remember it,' he said. 'I reward those from whom I demand service, and the reward depends on the nature of their service.'

The girl shivered, but she repeated firmly: 'I serve one master.'

'That is well,' said Cesare. 'I will tell you quickly what is required of you. You will present yourself at the vineyard of Vannozza Catanei at midnight on a date which I shall give you. You will be cloaked and masked as usual when you ride with my brother. You will leap on to his horse and ride away with him.'

'Is that all, my lord?'

Cesare nodded. 'Except this one thing. You will insist on taking him to an inn which you have discovered, and where you will tell him you have planned to stay until morning.'

'And this inn?'

'I will give you its name. It is in the Jewish quarter.'

'We are to ride there after midnight!'

'You have nothing to fear if you obey my instructions.' He took her face in his hands and kissed her lingeringly. 'If you do not, my beautiful one . . .' He laughed. 'But you will remember, will you not, that you serve one master.'

Vannozza, still a very beautiful woman, greeted her guests in

her vineyard on the summit of the Esquiline. The table was
heavily laden with good food, and the wine was of the best.
Carlo Canale was beside her to do honour to the distinguished
guests.

'You think we shall be merry enough with only your
sons' cousin, the Cardinal of Monreale, and a few other relations?'

'When my sons come to me they like to escape from all the
pomp which usually surrounds their daily life.'

Canale kept sipping the wine to assure himself that it was of
the very best; Vannozza nervously surveyed her table and
shouted continually to the slaves; but when the guests arrived
she gave all her attention to them.

'My dearest sons,' she murmured, embracing them; but the
embrace she gave Cesare was longer than that she had for
Giovanni, and Cesare would notice this.

The warm summer night was enchanting; they could look
down on the city, while the cool sweet air and the scent of
flowers from the meadows about the Colosseum wafted up to
them.

A perfect night, thought Vannozza.

Conversation about the table was merry. Cesare teased
Giovanni in the pleasantest way.

'Why, brother,' he cried, 'you expose yourself to danger. I
have heard that you ride among desperadoes with none but a
groom to protect you – you and your masked friend.'

'None dare harm my father's son,' said Giovanni lightly.

'Nay, but you should take care.'

'I have taken most things in my life,' laughed Giovanni, 'but
rarely that.'

'Yes, my son,' said Vannozza, 'I beg of you take greater
care. Do not go to those parts of the city where danger
lurks.'

'Mother, I am a baby no longer.'

'I have heard,' said Cesare, 'that he was seen riding in the
Jewish quarter late one night. That is foolish of him.'

'Foolish indeed, my son,' scolded Vannozza.

Giovanni laughed and turned to Canale. 'More wine, Father.
'Tis good, this wine of yours.'

Canale, delighted, filled his stepson's goblet, and the conversation turned to other matters.

It was past midnight, and they were preparing to leave when Cesare said: 'Why look, who is that lurking among the trees?'

The company turned and looking saw that cowering in a clump of bushes was a slender masked figure.

'It would appear that your friend has called for you,' said Cesare.

'It would appear so,' answered Giovanni, and he seemed to be well pleased.

'Must your friend come even to our mother's house?' asked Cesare.

'Perhaps,' laughed Giovanni.

'This friend is very eager for your company,' said Cesare. 'Come, we will not delay you. Farewell, dear Mother. It has been a night I shall long remember.'

Vannozza embraced her sons and watched them mount their horses. When Giovanni was in his saddle, the masked creature sprang up behind him in order to ride pillion.

Cesare was laughing and calling to the few attendants, whom he had brought with him, to follow him: and he broke into a song, in which the others all joined, as they rode down the hillside and into the city.

When they reached the Ponte district Giovanni drew up and told his brother that he would be leaving him there. He called to one of his grooms: 'Hi, fellow, you come with me. The rest of you . . . go to your beds.'

'Whither are you bound, brother?' asked Cesare. 'You are surely not going into the Jewish quarter?'

'My destination,' retorted Giovanni arrogantly, 'is my own concern.'

Cesare lifted his shoulders with an indifference which was unusual.

'Come,' he said to his followers and to those of Giovanni's servants who had not been commanded to accompany him, 'home to the Borgo.'

So they left Giovanni, who, with the masked figure riding behind him, and the groom a little distance in the rear, went on into the narrow streets of the Jewish quarter.

That was the last time Cesare saw Giovanni alive.

The next day, Alexander, waiting to receive his beloved son, was disappointed by his continued absence. All that day he waited, but still Giovanni did not put in an appearance. He sent to Giovanni's household. No one had seen him. He had not visited Sanchia.

Alexander chuckled. 'I doubt not that he has spent the night in the house of some woman, and he fears to compromise her by leaving in daylight.'

'Then he is showing himself unusually discreet,' said Cesare grimly.

But that day brought no news of Giovanni, and towards the end of it, a messenger hurried to the Pope to tell him that the young Duke's groom, who had been seen to accompany him, was found stabbed to death in the Piazza degli Ebrei.

All Alexander's serenity vanished. He was frantic with anguish.

'Send out search parties,' he cried. 'Examine every street ... every house ... I shall not rest until I hold my son in my arms.'

When the search had gone on for several days and there was no news of Giovanni, the Pope grew desperate, but he would not believe any harm had come to his son.

'It is a prank of his, Cesare,' he kept repeating. 'You will see, he will come bounding in on us, laughing at us because he so duped us. Depend upon it.'

'It is a prank of his,' agreed Cesare.

Then there was brought before the Pope a Dalmatian boatman who said that he had something to say, and he would say it only to the Holy Father because he believed it concerned the missing Duke of Gandia.

Alexander could scarcely wait to see the man, and he was immediately brought before the Pope who, with Cesare and several high officials of the Court, waited eagerly for him.

His name, he said, was Giorgio and he slept in his boat which was tied up on the shores of the Tiber.

'My duty, Holiness,' he said, 'is to guard the wood pile near the church of San Gerolamo degli Schiavoni close to the Ripetta bridge.'

'Yes, yes,' said the Pope impatiently. 'But do not waste time. Tell me what you know of my son.'

'I know this, Holiness, that on the night when the Duke of Gandia disappeared I saw a man riding a white horse, and on this horse he carried what could well be the body of a man. There were two other men, holding the body as the horse came down to the river's edge. When the horse came to the water the rider turned so that the horse's tail was to the river; then the two men pulled off that which could well be a body, Holiness, and it fell into the river.'

'Can we trust this man?' demanded the Pope. He was fearful. He did not want to believe him. While the man had spoken he had visualized that limp body on the horse, and it was the body of his beloved son.

'We have no reason to doubt him, Most Holy Lord,' was the answer.

'Holiness,' said Giorgio. 'I can tell you more. The body slipped into the water, and it was held up by what seemed to be his cloak, so that it floated and began to drift down stream. Then the man on the horse said something to the others and they began throwing stones at the floating cloak. They pitched the stones on to it again and again until it sank with the weight and disappeared. Holiness, they stood watching for some time and then they rode away.'

'You saw this happen,' said Cesare, 'and you told no one! Why not?'

'Why, bless Your Eminence, I live by the river, and living there see countless bodies thrown into the water. There seemed nothing especial to report about this one, save that it happened on the night about which the gentlemen were asking.'

The Pope could bear no more. A terrible melancholy had come to him.

He muttered: 'There is nothing to do but drag the river.'

Thus they found Giovanni. There were wounds in his throat, on his face and his body; the mud of the river clung to his fine clothes on which the jewels still remained; his purse was full of

ducats, and his rings, brooches and necklace, worth a fortune
had not been taken.

When Alexander was told he went out and stopped those
who carried the corpse as it was brought into the castle of St
Angelo. He threw himself on to the body, tore his hair and beat
his chest, while he cried out in his grief.

'To those who have dealt thus with him, so they shall be
dealt with!' he cried. 'Nothing shall be too bitter for them to
endure. I'll not rest, beloved son, most beloved of all, until I
have brought your murderer to justice.'

Then he turned to those who carried the ghastly corpse and
said to them: 'Take my beloved, wash him, perfume him, put
on his ducal robes; and thus he shall be buried. Oh Giovanni,
oh my beloved son, who has done this cruel deed to you . . .
and to me?'

He was washed and dressed in his ducal robes, and at night
by the light of one hundred and twenty flares he was carried
from Castle St Angelo to Santa Maria del Popolo.

The Pope did not accompany him, and as he sat at the
window of Castle St Angelo, looking down on the winding
cortège lit by those flares, he could not contain his grief.

'Oh Giovanni, Giovanni,' he moaned, 'best loved of all, my
dearest, my beloved, why have they done this to thee and me?'

Pedro Caldes came to the convent to see Lucrezia. He was
very agitated when she received him, falling on his knees and
kissing her hands.

'There is news, terrible news. You will hear of it ere long, but
I wished to break it gently. I know how you cared for him.
Your brother . . .'

'Cesare!' she cried.

'No. Your brother Giovanni.'

'He is ill?'

'He disappeared, and now they have discovered his body. It
was in the Tiber.'

'Giovanni . . . dead!'

She swayed uncertainly, and Pedro put his arms about her.

'Madonna,' he murmured, 'dearest Madonna.'

She sat down and leaned against Pedro.

She lifted her eyes to his face; they were bewildered and filled with misery. 'My brother Giovanni . . . but he was so young, so full of health.'

'He was murdered, Madonna.'

'Who . . .?'

'None knows.'

She covered her face with her hands. Giovanni, she thought. Not you. It is not possible. She saw him strutting about the nursery, asserting his rights, fighting with Cesare. Fighting with Cesare!

Not Cesare, she told herself. It could not be Cesare who murdered him.

Such thoughts must not be spoken.

Pedro kept his arms about her. He told her the story, beginning with the supper party at Vannozza's vineyard, while Lucrezia stared blankly before her, picturing it all.

Cesare had been there, and the masked person had lurked in the bushes. Evil thoughts kept coming into her mind. Who was the masked person?

'Did they discover the masked one?' she asked.

'No. None knows who it was.'

'And my father?'

'He is overwhelmed with grief. None has ever seen him so distressed, so unlike himself.'

'And . . . my brother, my brother Cesare?'

'He does all he can to soothe your father.'

'Oh Pedro, Pedro,' she cried, 'what will become of us?'

'Madonna, do not weep. I would die rather than see you unhappy.'

She touched his face lightly. 'Sweet Pedro,' she murmured. 'Sweet and gentle Pedro.'

He took the fingers which caressed his cheek, and kissed them frantically.

'Pedro, stay with me,' she begged. 'Stay here and comfort me.'

'Madonna, I am unworthy.'

'There was never one more gentle and kind to me and therefore more worthy. Oh Pedro, I thank the saints that you came

to me, that you will help me bear my sorrows, that you wil
help stay my fear, for Pedro, I am desperately afraid.'

'Of what, Madonna?'

'I know not, I only know I am afraid. But when you pu
your arms about me, dear Pedro, I am less afraid. So . . . do no
talk of leaving me. Talk only of staying with me, of helping me
to forget these evil things which happen all about me. Pedro
sweet Pedro, talk no more of unworthiness. Stay with me
Pedro. Love me . . . for I love you too.'

He kissed her lips this time, wonderingly, marvelling, and
she returned his kisses.

There was a wildness about her.

'Pedro, I keep seeing it. The pictures come to me. The part
. . . the masked figure . . . and my brother . . . and the
Giovanni. Oh Pedro, I must shut them out. I cannot bear them
I am frightened, Pedro. Help me . . . help me, my loved one
to forget.'

Alexander had given orders that a search was to be made to
find the murderers of his son, that they might be brought to
justice, and there were rumours implicating various people, fo
Giovanni had had a host of enemies.

It was said that Giovanni Sforza had planned the murder
that he resented the affection between his wife and her family
and Giovanni Borgia had shared that affection with her brothe
Cesare and her father.

Giovanni Sforza and other suspects quickly established thei
innocence; there was one name, however, which none dared
utter.

The Pope was too unhappy to voice his fears; nor would h
face them. He was shut in his rooms alone because he feared
someone might give voice to the terrible suspicion which a
this time he was unable to face, even in his own thoughts.

This was the greatest tragedy of Alexander's life and when
a few days after Giovanni's body had been discovered, h
stood before the Consistory, he mourned openly for the deat
of his beloved son.

'A worse blow could not have fallen upon us,' he declared
'since we loved the Duke of Gandia above all others. W

would give most willingly seven tiaras if we could bring him back. We have been punished by God for our sins, for the Duke did not merit this terrible death.'

To the astonishment of all present, Alexander went on to declare that the way of life at the Vatican should be reformed and there should be no more pandering to worldly interests. He would renounce nepotism and begin the reforms in his own household.

The Cardinals were aghast. Never had they thought to hear Alexander make such utterances. He was a changed man.

Cesare sought audience with his father afterwards, and looking at that stricken face he was filled with sharp jealousy as he asked himself: Would he have felt such grief for me?

'Father,' said Cesare, 'what meant you by those words you spoke before the Cardinals?'

'We meant exactly what we said,' replied the Pope.

Cesare felt as though icy hands were gripping his body, realizing that his father would not meet his eyes.

'Then,' pursued Cesare, who could not leave this subject, once he had started it, 'do you mean that you will do nothing to help me, to help Goffredo, Lucrezia and the rest of our family?'

The Pope was silent.

'Father, I beg of you, tell me what is in your mind.'

The Pope lifted his eyes to his son's face, and Cesare saw there what he had dreaded to find. They held an accusation.

He suspects! thought Cesare. He knows.

Then he remembered those words which the Pope had spoken when he heard of Giovanni's death. 'To those who have dealt death to him so shall they be dealt with. Nothing shall be too bitter for them to endure.'

'Father,' said Cesare, 'we must stand together after a tragedy such as this. We must not forget that, whatever happens to any of us, the family must go on.'

'We would be alone,' said the Pope. 'Go from us now.'

Cesare went uneasily.

He sought out Sanchia. 'I would Lucrezia were here,' he said. 'She might comfort our father. But he did not ask even for her. He does not seem to want any of us now. He thinks of nothing but Giovanni.'

But Cesare could find no peace with Sanchia. He must go to his father once more. He must know whether he had read aright the accusation in those eyes.

He went to the Pope's apartments, taking Sanchia and Goffredo with him, and after a long delay they were admitted.

Sanchia knelt at Alexander's feet and lifted her beautiful blue eyes to his face. 'Father, be comforted,' she said; 'it is double grief to your children to see you so.'

The Pope looked at her with cold eyes. He said: 'They quarrelled over you – he and his brother. Go from me. I am arranging that you shall leave Rome. You will be departing shortly, with your husband, for Squillace.'

'But Father,' began Sanchia, 'we would comfort you in your bitter loss.'

'You comfort me most by removing yourself from my presence.'

It was the first time Cesare had seen his father unmoved by beauty.

'Please go now, you and Goffredo,' he said to Sanchia. Then, turning to Cesare, he went on: 'I would have you stay.'

When they were alone they looked at each other, and there was no mistaking the meaning in Alexander's eyes.

His voice broke as he said: 'They shall search no more. I would not have them discover my son's murderer now. I could bear no further misery.'

Cesare knelt and would have taken his father's hand, but Alexander removed it. It was as though he could not bear to be touched by the hand which had slain Giovanni.

'I wish you to go to Naples,' he said. 'You are appointed Cardinal Legate for the coronation of the new King.'

'Father, another could go,' protested Cesare.

'It is our wish that you should go,' said the Pope firmly. 'Now, I pray you leave me. I would be alone with my grief.'

Pedro presented himself daily at the convent. When Sister Girolama suggested his visits were too frequent he had his explanations: His Holiness was prostrate with grief; his one comfort was derived from his daughter's messages. He did not wish her to return to the Vatican which was deep in mourning, but to stay where she was that he might write to her and she to him. He wished to hear details of her daily life. That was why Pedro called so frequently at the convent.

This was not true, but it was a good enough excuse. It might have been that the sisters had realized that the beautiful girl would never be one of them. Perhaps they sensed her innate worldliness and made no effort to combat it.

Lucrezia lived in her cells which she had converted into comfortable rooms, and if Pedro visited her there instead of in the cold bare room at first assigned to them, that was a matter between the Pope's daughter and her visitor. Her maid would act as chaperone and, although the maid was a very frivolous creature, she was one who had been selected for the post by the Holy Father, and it was not for the Prioress to complain.

Lucrezia had changed, but the nuns were not conscious of physical appearances, and it was left to Pantisilea to tell her that her eyes were brighter and that she was a hundred times lovelier than she had been when she, Pantisilea, had first come to attend her.

'It is love,' said Pantisilea.

'It is such a hopeless love,' murmured Lucrezia. 'Sometimes I wonder where it can lead us.'

But when Pedro was with her she ceased to ask herself such practical questions. All that mattered to Lucrezia was the fulfilment of her love, for she was fully alive now to her own sensuality.

That love had begun in sorrow. She remembered well the day when the terrible shock of Giovanni's death had made her turn to Pedro. It was then, when he had put his arms about her, that she had realized how deeply in love with him she was.

Love! It was a precious thing. It was worth facing danger for the sake of love; and she had discovered this about herself: She would never again be one to deny love.

Love filled her life, filled the cell at the convent, touching austerity with a roseate light.

Sorrow passed, she found, for news came that even the Pope

had come out of retirement, that he was no longer heard weeping and calling for Giovanni.

On the day when Pedro brought the news that the Pope had taken a mistress, they were all very lighthearted in Lucrezia's room. Only Pantisilea was a little regretful, wishing she had been the one chosen to comfort the Pope. But her place was with Lucrezia whom she hoped never to leave. Nor should she; Lucrezia had promised her that.

'You shall always be with me, dear Pantisilea,' Lucrezia told her. 'When I leave this place you shall come with me. No matter where I go I shall take you with me.'

Pantisilea could be happy, for when they left this place she would still live close to His Holiness, and there was always hope that he might notice her again.

Weeks passed. The Pope seemed to have forgotten his grief completely. Cesare was on his way home from Naples, and Alexander was preparing a welcome for him.

Giovanni, the beloved son, was dead, but that was in the past, and the Borgias did not grieve for ever.

Cesare stood before his father, and now the Pope looked full into his son's eyes.

'My son,' he said brokenly.

Cesare kissed his father's hands; then turned his appealing eyes upon him.

Alexander had been too long alone, and having lost one son he did not intend to lose another.

Already, because he was Alexander, to him Giovanni had become a shadowy figure, and Cesare was here beside him, young, ambitious, strong.

He is the stronger of the two, mused Alexander. He will do great deeds before he dies. With him at its head, the house of Borgia will prosper.

'Welcome home, my son. Welcome home, Cesare,' said the Pope.

And Cesare exulted, for all that he had done, he now knew, had not been in vain.

Lucrezia and Pantisilea were working on a piece of em-

roidery when Lucrezia dropped the work and let her hands
lie idly in her lap.

'Does aught ail you, Madonna?' asked Pantisilea.

'What should you think?' asked Lucrezia sharply.

'I thought you seemed . . . over-pensive, Madonna. I have
noticed it of late.'

Lucrezia was silent. Pantisilea was looking at her in some
alarm.

'You have guessed,' said Lucrezia.

'It cannot be, Madonna. It must not be.'

'It is so. I am to have a child.'

'Madonna!'

'Why do you look so shocked? You know that it can easily
happen when one has a lover.'

'But you and Pedro! What will your father say? What will
your brother do?'

'I dare not think, Pantisilea.'

'How long?'

'It is three months.'

'Three months, Madonna! So it happened in the beginning.'

'It would seem so.'

'June, July, August,' counted Pantisilea. 'And it is now the
beginning of September. Madonna, what shall we do?'

'I do not know, Pantisilea. I think mayhap I shall go away
somewhere in secret. These things have happened before. Perhaps Pedro will come with me.' Lucrezia flung herself into the
arms of Pantisilea. 'Lucky one!' she cried. 'If you loved you
might marry; you might live with your husband and children,
happy for the rest of your life. But for one such as I am there
is nothing but the marriage which will bring advantage to my
family. They betrothed me twice and then they married me to
Giovanni Sforza.' Now that she loved Pedro she shuddered at
the memory of Giovanni Sforza.

'They will soon divorce you from him,' soothed Pantisilea.
'Mayhap then you will marry Pedro.'

'Would they allow it?' asked Lucrezia, and all the melancholy had left her face.

'Who knows . . . if there is a child? Children make so much
difference.'

'Oh Pantisilea, how you comfort me! Then I shall marry Pedro and we shall go away from Rome; we shall have a house like my mother's and I shall have my *credenza* in which I shall store my silver goblets, my majolica. Pantisilea, how happy we shall be!'

'You will take me with you, Madonna?'

'How could I manage without you? You shall be there, and mayhap I'll find a husband for you. No, I shall not find you one. You shall find your own and you must love him as I love Pedro. That is the only way to marry, Pantisilea, if you would live happily.'

Pantisilea nodded, but she was apprehensive.

Lucrezia had yet to be divorced, and she was to be divorced because she was *virgo intacta* on account of her husband's being unable to consummate the marriage. Pantisilea believed that Lucrezia would have to appear before the Cardinals, perhaps submit to an examination. 'Holy Mother of God,' thought Pantisilea, 'protect us.'

But she loved Lucrezia – how she loved her! No one had ever been so kind to her before. She would lie for Lucrezia; she would do anything to make her happy. To be with Lucrezia was to share her philosophy of life, to believe that everything must come right and that there was really nothing about which to worry oneself. It was a delightful philosophy. Pantisilea planned to live with it for the rest of her life.

'Pantisilea, should I go to my father, should I tell him that I am to have Pedro's child? Shall I tell him that Pedro is my husband in all but name and that he must let us marry?'

When Lucrezia talked thus, Pantisilea felt herself jerked roughly into reality.

'His Holiness has had a shock, Madonna. The death of your brother is but three months away. Let him recover from one shock before he is presented with another.'

'This should mean happiness for him. He loves children and he longs for us to have them.'

'Not the children of chamberlains, Madonna. I beg of you, take the advice of Pantisilea. Wait awhile. Choose the right moment to tell His Holiness. There is time yet.'

'But, people will notice.'

'The sisters? They are not very observant. I will make you
dress with voluminous petticoats. In such a dress your child
uld be about to be born and none know it.'

'It is strange, Pantisilea, but I am so happy.'

'Dearest Madonna, you were meant to have children.'

'I think that is so. When I think of holding this child in my
ms, of showing him to Pedro, I am so happy, Pantisilea, that I
rget all my troubles. I forget Giovanni. I forget my father's
ief, and I forget Cesare and . . . But no matter. It is wrong
me to feel so happy.'

'Nay, it is always right to be happy. Happiness is the true
eaning of life.'

'But my brother so recently murdered, my father bowed
wn with grief, and myself a wife already to another man!'

'The time passes and the grief of His Holiness with it. And
iovanni Sforza is no husband to you and never was . . . so
e Pope would have it.'

Pantisilea did not press that subject. She knew that Lucrezia
ould have to appear before the gathering of Cardinals and
clare herself a virgin. The petticoats would have to be very
ide.

The Pope and his elder son were often together now. It was
id in the Vatican: 'His Holiness has already forgotten his vow
end nepotism; he has forgotten his son Giovanni, and all the
ffection he had for him is now given to Cesare.'

There was a new relationship between Alexander and Cesare;
e shock of Giovanni's death had shaken Alexander; Cesare
as exultant because he believed that his father would never
e the same again, that their positions had shifted, very slightly
was true; but there was an indication of what they would one
ay be to each other.

Alexander had lost a little of his authority; Cesare had
ained that little. At the time of his great grief Alexander had
eemed like an old man; he had recovered, but he had never
egained that air of a man in his prime.

Cesare had learned something of great importance: I may do
hat I will and it makes no difference. There is nothing I can-
ot do, and he will help me to achieve my ambitions.

Now the Pope said to him: 'My son, this divorce of you sister is long delayed. I think we should arrange for her t appear before the assembly.'

'Yes, Father. She cannot be too quickly freed from the man.

'You were not idle while you were in Naples, Cesare? Yo sounded the King on the question of a possible husband fo your sister?'

'I did, Holiness. Alfonso, the Duke of Bisceglie was sug gested.'

The Pope murmured: 'Illegitimate.'

Cesare shrugged his shoulders.

'And,' went on Alexander, 'Sanchia's brother.'

'He is like his sister in appearance only,' Cesare said.

The Pope nodded. He could forgive Cesare for bringin about the death of Giovanni, because he was a Borgia and hi son; but he found it harder to forgive Sanchia for being on of the causes of jealousy between Cesare and Giovanni.

He considered the marriage. Alliance with Naples would b good at this juncture; and if the marriage became irksom there were always ways of ending it.

'I have been approached by the Prince of Salerno on accoun of his son Sanseverino.'

'I doubt not that the King of Naples had heard of it, and tha is why he was so anxious for you to consider Alfonso o Bisceglie. He would not wish to see such a firm ally of th French joined with us by such a marriage.'

'Francesco Orsini is another; and there is the Lord o Piombino and Ottaviano Riario.'

'Dear Lucrezia – although she is not yet rid of one husband she has many waiting for her. Fortunate Lucrezia!'

'You are thinking that you are denied marriage, my son.

Cesare's eyes were now alight with eagerness. 'Oh my father,' he said, 'Carlotta of Aragon, the King's *legitimat* daughter who is being educated at the Court of France, i marriageable. It was hinted that were I free she might be my wife.'

There was a brief silence. This seemed to Cesare one of th most important moments of his life, for it was as though th Pope were struggling to regain his old supremacy.

Then, after what seemed a long time to Cesare, Alexander spoke. He said slowly: 'Such a marriage would be advantageous, my son.'

Cesare knelt in sudden emotion. He took his father's hand and kissed it passionately.

In this son, thought Alexander, I shall forget all my grief. He shall achieve such greatness that in time I shall cease to regret the loss of his brother.

Life for Lucrezia in the Convent of San Sisto had been an alternation of joy and terror.

She and Pedro indulged in feverish pleasure which was the more intense because they both knew that it could not last. They were two people who must snatch at every moment of happiness, savouring it, cherishing it because they could not know when it would be their last together.

Pantisilea watched them, sharing vicariously their joys and sorrow; her pillows were often wet at night when she lay awake trying to look into the future.

There came that day when Pedro brought an inevitable message from the Pope. Lucrezia was to prepare herself to appear before an assembly of Envoys and Cardinals at the Vatican. There she should be declared *virgo intacta*.

Lucrezia was terrified.

'But what can I do?' she demanded of Pantisilea.

The little maid tried to comfort her. She should try on the dress Pantisilea had made for her. It was winter-time and she would be expected to wear many petticoats, as it was cold in the convent. She would hold her head high and impress them all with her innocent appearance. She must.

'How can I do it, Pantisilea?' she cried. 'How can I stand before those holy men and act this lie?'

'You *must* do it, Madonna dearest. The Holy Father commands it, and it is necessary that you should be freed from Giovanni Sforza. On what other grounds could you be divorced?'

Lucrezia began to laugh hysterically.

'Pantisilea, why do you look so solemn? Do you not see what a joke this is? I am six months pregnant, and I am to go before the assembly and swear that I am *virgo intacta*. It is like a tale told by Giovanni Boccaccio. It is a joke . . . or it would be if it were not so serious . . . if it might not end tragically.'

'Dear Madonna, we will not let it end tragically. You will do what your father asks of you, and when you are free you will marry Pedro and go away to some place where all will be peace and happiness for you.'

'If only that could be so!'

'Remember it when you stand before those men, and that will give you courage. If you act this lie convincingly you will gain your freedom; and it is, after all, not the child of Giovanni Sforza that you carry. Your happiness – and that of Pedro – depend on how you act before the assembly. Remember that, Madonna.'

'I will remember it,' said Lucrezia firmly.

Pantisilea dressed her with care. Cunningly she arranged the velvet flounces, and when she had finished she was pleased with her work.

'None will guess . . . I swear it. But, Madonna, how pale you are!'

'I feel the child moving within me as though to reproach me for denying it.'

'Nay you are not denying it. You are making a happy life for it. Do not think of the past, Madonna. Look to the future. Look to happiness with Pedro, and all that will come out of this day.'

'Pantisilea, my dear little maid, what should I have done without you?'

'Oh Madonna, none ever had a sweeter mistress. If I could not serve you, life would be dull for me Anything I have done for you has been repaid a thousandfold.'

They clung together, two frightened girls.

And so she came to the Vatican, and there in the presence of her father and the members of the assembly she listened to the reading by one of the Cardinals of the document which declared that her marriage to Giovanni Sforza had not been consummated and that as a result Lucrezia was *virgo intacta*. This being no true marriage they were gathered together to pronounce its annulment.

She stood before them and never had her innocent looks served her so well.

The Cardinals and Envoys were impressed by her beauty and her youthful appearance; they needed no other proof of her virginity.

She was told that she was no longer married to Giovanni Sforza, and she answered with a speech of thanks which was so disarming that all present were charmed with her.

There was a moment when, feeling the child move within her, she felt dizzy and swayed slightly.

'Poor child!' murmured one of the Cardinals. 'What an ordeal for one so young and innocent to endure!'

The Pope was waiting for her in his private apartments; Cesare was with him.

'My dearest,' said the Pope, embracing her warmly, 'at last I hold you in my arms again. This has been a trying time for us all.'

'Yes, Father.'

Cesare added: 'And to have you shut away from us . . . that has been the most trying of all.'

'I needed the refuge,' she answered, not daring to meet their eyes.

'I trust,' said the Pope, 'that you found little Pantisilea a good servant?'

Lucrezia replied passionately: 'I love the girl. I do not know what I should have done without her. Thank you a thousand times, Father, for sending her to me.'

'I knew she would serve you well,' answered Alexander.

'The time has come for you to begin a new life, dear sister,' Cesare murmured. 'Now that you are rid of Sforza you will find life sweet again.'

She did not answer. Desperately she was seeking for courage to tell them of her condition, to explain why they must put aside all thought of a grand marriage for her, how she loved Pedro and that he was the father of the child she carried.

She had imagined herself telling them, again and again as she lay in her converted cell and, although it had seemed a great ordeal which lay before her, it had not seemed impossible. Facing them, she found that she had underestimated the fear and awe in which she held them, the power which they held over her.

Alexander's smile was almost roguish. 'There are many clamouring for your hand, daughter.'

'Father . . . I do not wish to think of them.'

Cesare had moved swiftly towards her and put an arm about her. 'What ails you, Lucrezia? You look ill. I fear you have suffered privation in your convent.'

'No . . . no. I have been comforted there.'

'It is no place for such as you are.'

'But you are pale and you look exhausted,' said the Pope.

'Let me sit down a moment,' Lucrezia begged.

Both men watched her intently. Only Alexander realized how frightened she was, and he motioned her to a stool.

Cesare told her of the men who were eager to marry her. 'Francesco Orsini . . . Ottaviano Riario . . . and there is Sanchia's brother, the little Duke of Bisceglie.'

Alexander said suddenly: 'This has been an ordeal for the child. She needs rest now. Your apartments have been prepared for you, my dear. You shall go to them at once.'

Cesare was about to protest, but the Pope was his old firm self. He was clapping his hands and slaves were appearing.

'Madonna Lucrezia's women should conduct her to her apartments,' he said.

When he was alone, Alexander stood before the shrine in his apartments. He was not praying; he was staring at it, and there were furrows in his brow and the rich purple blood stained his face, while in his temples a pulse throbbed visibly.

It was impossible. But it was not impossible at all. What had been happening in the convent all these months? He had heard stories of what could and did happen in convents. But not that of San Sisto.

He had not dared voice his supicions before Cesare. Oh yes, he was afraid of his son. If Cesare had guessed what was in his mind he might have done anything, however reckless. Cesare must not know yet . . . if it were true. But this monstrous thing which he suspected must not be true.

He thanked the saints that Cesare's mind was so constantly on his own affairs that he had failed to be as perceptive as his father. Cesare had been dreaming of release from the Church and marriage to Carlotta of Naples, even as Lucrezia stood before them, and he had not noticed how complete was the change in Lucrezia. Could all those months of quiet life at San Sisto's have wrought such a change? Not they alone.

But he must be careful. He must remember his fainting fits. It would not do for him to be ill now, because if what he suspected were true he would need all his wits to deal with it.

He must wait. He must recover his equanimity; he must remind himself that he was Alexander, who had emerged triumphant after the death of Calixtus – Alexander who on every occasion turned defeat into victory.

At length he made his way to his daughter's apartment.

Lucrezia was lying on her bed, and only Pantisilea sat beside her. There were tears on Lucrezia's cheeks, and the sight of them filled Alexander's heart with tenderness.

'Leave us, my dear,' he said to Pantisilea; and the girl's dark eyes were fearful and yet adoring as they met his. It was as though she implored him, out of his great tenderness, his power and understanding, to save her dear mistress.

'Father!' Lucrezia would have risen, but Alexander put a hand on her shoulder and gently forced her back on to the pillows.

'What have you to tell me, my child?' he asked.

She looked at him appealingly, but she could not speak.

'You must tell me,' he said gently. 'Only if you do, can I help you.'

'Father, I am afraid.'

'Afraid of me? Have I not always been benevolent to you?'

'The kindest father in the world, Most Holy Lord.'

He took her hand and kissed it.

'Who is he?' he asked.

Her eyes opened wide and she shrank against her pillows.

'Do you not trust me, child?'

She sprang up suddenly and threw herself into his arms; she began to sob wildly; never had he seen his serene little Lucrezia so moved.

'My dearest, my dearest,' he murmured, 'you may tell me. You may tell me all. I shall not scold you whatever you have to tell. Do I not love you beyond all else in the world? Is not your happiness my most constant purpose?'

'I thank the saints for you,' sobbed Lucrezia.

'Will you not tell me? Then must I tell you. You are to have a child. When, Lucrezia?'

'It should be in March.'

The Pope was astounded. 'That is but three months hence. So soon! I should not have believed it.'

'Pantisilea has been so clever . . . oh, such a comfort, Father. Thank you for sending her. I could not have had a dearer friend. I shall always love her . . . as long as I live.'

'She is a dear creature,' said the Pope. 'I am glad that she comforted you. But tell me, who is the father of your child?'

'I love him, Father. You will permit our marriage?'

'It is difficult for me to deny my daughter anything.'

'Oh Father, beloved Father, would I had come to you before. How foolish I was! I was afraid. When you were not with me, I did not see you as you really are. I saw you as the powerful Pope determined to make a politically advantageous marriage for me. I had forgotten that the Holy Father of us all was first my own dear father.'

'Then it is time we were together again. The name of the man?'

'It is your chamberlain, Pedro Caldes.'

The Pope rocked her to and fro in his arms.

'Pedro Caldes,' he repeated. 'A handsome boy. One of my favourite chamberlains. And he visited you in your convent, of course.'

'It was when he brought me news of Giovanni's death, Father, and I was so unhappy. He comforted me.'

The Pope held her fiercely against him; for a moment his face was distorted with rage and anguish. My beloved

Giovanni murdered, he was thinking; my daughter pregnant
with the child of a chamberlain!

But when Lucrezia looked at him, his face wore its habitual
expression of tenderness and benignity.

'My dear child,' he said, 'I will confess that I am startled.'

She took his hands and covered them with kisses. How
appealing she was, looking at him with those adoring yet
frightened eyes; she reminded him of her mother at the height
of their passion.

'Father, you will help me?'

'Do you doubt it . . . for one moment? Shame, Lucrezia! But
we must be cautious. You have been divorced in the belief that
your husband is impotent and you are a virgin.' In spite of the
Pope's horror at the situation with which he was confronted he
he could not refrain from smiling. It was a situation which, in
any circumstances, must seem to him essentially humorous.
'What will our good Cardinals say, think you, if they discover
that the charming innocent young virgin, who appeared before
them so decorously, was six months pregnant? Oh Lucrezia,
my clever one, my subtle one, it would not do at all. We might
even have Sforza claiming the child and swearing it was his.
Then where would be our divorce? We have to act now with
the utmost caution. The matter must be kept secret. Who
knows of it?'

'None but Pedro and Pantisilea.'

The Pope nodded.

'None must know, my child.'

'And Father, I may marry Pedro? We want to go away from
Rome to live quietly and happily somewhere together, where
no one concerns themselves with us and what we do; where we
can live peaceful happy lives, as ordinary people may.'

The Pope smoothed her hair from her hot face. 'My beloved,' he said, 'you must leave this matter in my hands. The
world shall know that the ordeal through which you have passed
has been a trying one. You will stay in your apartments at
Santa Maria in Portico and, until you have regained your
health, none shall wait on you but the faithful Pantisilea. In
the meantime we will discover what can be done to make you
happy.'

Lucrezia lay back on her pillows, and the tears slowly ran down her cheeks.

'In truth,' she said, 'Alexander VI, you are not a man; you are a god.'

Madonna Lucrezia was ill. For two months since she had left the convent she had been confined to her apartments, and only her maid Pantisilea and the members of her family were allowed to see her.

The citizens of Rome laughed among themselves. What did this mean? What had Madonna Lucrezia been doing during her stay in the convent? They remembered that she was after all a Borgia. In a few months' time would there be a child at the Vatican, a little infant whom the Pope in his benevolence had decided to adopt?

Cesare heard the rumours, and declared he would be revenged on those who repeated them.

He went to his father's presence and told him what was being said.

'It is inevitable,' said the Pope. 'There are always such stories concerning us. The people need them as they need their carnivals.'

'I'll not have such things said of Lucrezia. She must come out of her seclusion. She must show herself.'

'Cesare, how could she do that?'

The Pope was looking at his son, marvelling at the egoism of Cesare, who was waiting for that day when he would be released from the Church to marry Carlotta of Naples and take charge of the Papal armies. That image in his mind was so big that it obscured all others. Thus it must have been when he arranged for the murder of Giovanni. The grief of his father was as nothing beside his own grandiose ambitions. Even Lucrezia's predicament was not known to him, which seemed fantastic because, had he given the matter a moment's thought, it would surely have been obvious.

'By appearing among them,' Cesare replied.

It was time he realized the true state of affairs. At the end of the month, or the beginning of next, Lucrezia's child would be born. He would have to know.

'That,' said Alexander, 'would be but to confirm the
umours.'

Now Cesare was really startled. The Pope watched the hot
blood rush into his handsome face.

''Tis true enough,' went on Alexander. 'Lucrezia is with
child. Moreover the birth is imminent. Cesare, I wonder you
did not realize this.'

Alexander frowned. He understood how terrified Lucrezia
would be of Cesare's discovering her condition. She and little
Pantisilea would have been doubly careful when Cesare visited
her.

'Lucrezia . . . to have a child!'

The Pope lifted his shoulders. 'These things happen,' he
said lightly.

'While she was in the convent!' Cesare clenched his fists.
'So that was why she was so contented there. Who is the
father?'

'My son, let not our tempers run high. This is a matter
wherein we need all our cunning, all our calm. It is unfortunate,
but if this marriage we are planning for Lucrezia is to be
brought about, it will not help us if it should be known that,
while she stood before the Cardinals declaring herself *virgo
intacta*, she was in fact six months pregnant. This must be
our little secret matter.'

'Who is the father?' repeated Cesare.

The Pope went on as though he had not spoken. 'Listen to
my plan. None shall attend her but Pantisilea. When the child
is born it shall be taken away immediately. I have already been
in contact with some good people who will take it and care for
it. I shall reward them well, for remember, this is my grandchild, a Borgia, and we have need of Borgias. Mayhap in a few
years' time I will have the child brought to the Vatican. Mayhap I will watch over its upbringing. But for a few years it must
be as though there was no child.'

'I wish to know the name of this man,' insisted Cesare.

'You are too angry, Cesare. I must warn you, my son, that
anger is the greatest enemy of those who allow it to conquer
them. Keep your anger in chains. It was what I learned to do at
an early age. Show no anger against this young man. I shall not.

I understand what made him act as he did. Come, Cesare, would not you and I in similar circumstances behave in exactly the same manner? We cannot blame him.' The Pope's expression changed very slightly. 'But we shall know how to deal with him when the time comes.'

'He shall die,' cried Cesare.

'All in good time,' murmured the Pope. 'At the moment . . . let all be peaceful. There is my little Pantisilea.' The Pope's tone was regretful, and his smile tender. 'She knows a great deal. Poor child, such knowledge is not good for her.'

'Father, you are wise. You know how to deal with matters like this, but I must know this man's name. I cannot rest until I do.'

'Do nothing rash, my son. His name is Pedro Caldes.'

'Is he not one of your chamberlains?'

The Pope nodded.

Cesare was shaking with rage. 'How dare he! A chamberlain, a servant . . . and my sister!'

The Pope laid a hand on his son's shoulder, and was alarmed by the tremors which shook Cesare.

'Your pride is great, my son. But remember . . . caution! We shall know how to settle this matter, you and I. But at the moment our best method is caution.'

Caution! It was not in Cesare's nature to be cautious. The rages which had come to him in boyhood were more frequent as he grew older, and he found it becoming more and more difficult to control them.

His mind was dominated now by one picture: His sister with the chamberlain. He was obsessed by jealousy and hatred, and there was murder in his heart.

The Pope had urged caution, but he no longer obeyed the Pope. After the death of his brother he had learned his father's weakness. Alexander did not remember to mourn for long. He forgot the misdeeds of his family; he ceased to regret the dead and gave all his attention to the living. The great affection of which he was capable—evanescent though it might be—was intense while it lasted; and it had to be directed towards some one. Cesare had taken the affection his father had given to

Giovanni, as though it were a title or estate. Cesare knew he need not fear the loss of his father's affection, no matter what he did. That was the great discovery he had made. That was why he felt powerful, invincible. Alexander was lord of Italy, and Alexander would bend to the will of his son.

So when Alexander said Caution, why should Cesare heed that warning unless he wished to?

One day he came face to face with Pedro Caldes in one of the ante-rooms leading to the Papal apartments, and Cesare's anger flared up to such an extent that he was drained of all memories of his father's warning.

'Caldes, halt!' cried Cesare.

'My lord . . .' began the startled chamberlain, 'what would you have of me?'

'Your life,' said Cesare, and he drew his sword.

The startled young man turned and fled towards the Pope's apartments. Cesare, grasping his sword, followed.

Pedro, breathless and terrified, could hear the cruel laughter of Cesare close behind him; once Cesare's sword touched his thigh and he felt the hot blood run down his leg.

'You waste time in running,' Cesare cried. 'You shall die for what you have dared do to my sister.'

Fainting with fear, Pedro reached the Papal throne, on which Alexander was sitting; with him were two of his chamberlains and one of the Cardinals.

Pedro cried: 'Holy Father, save me . . . save me ere I die!' And he flung himself at Alexander's feet.

Cesare was upon him. Alexander had risen, his expression horrified and full of warning.

'My son, my son, desist,' he cried. 'Put away your sword.'

But Cesare merely laughed and thrust at the chamberlain, as Alexander stooped forward to protect him, so that the blood spurted up and stained the Pope's robes, and even splashed his face.

Those who had been with the Pope stood back aghast, while Alexander put his arms about Pedro and looked up into his son's glowering face.

'Put away your sword,' he said sternly, and there was a return of the Alexander who, benevolent as he was, had always

known how to quell his sons. 'Bring not your quarrels to o~
sacred throne.'

Cesare laughed again, but he felt once more that awe of h~
father which he was surprised to discover he had not qui~
overcome.

He obeyed as he said truculently: 'Let him not think th~
this is the end of our quarrel.'

Then he turned and strode out of the apartment.

Alexander murmured: 'The hot blood of youth! He does n~
mean to be so rash. But who of us was not rash in youth? Ha~
this young man's wounds attended to and . . . for his ow~
safety let him be kept under guard.'

Pantisilea leaned over the bed.

Lucrezia murmured: 'It is beginning, Pantisilea.'

'Lie down, Madonna. I will send a message to the Ho~
Father.'

Lucrezia nodded. 'He will take care of everything.'

Pantisilea despatched a slave to the Vatican with a sign~
ring which the Pope had given her and which was to be a sig~
between them that Lucrezia was in need of a midwife. In th~
affair, the Pope had decided, no word should be written. Whe~
he received the ring he would know its purpose, and for n~
other reason must it be sent to him.

'How blessed I am in such a father,' murmured Lucrezi~
'Oh, Pantisilea, why did I not go to him at once? If I ha~
Pedro and I might have been married now. How long it is sin~
I saw Pedro! He should be close to me now. How happy ~
should be if he were! I shall ask my father to bring him to me~

'Yes, Madonna, yes,' soothed Pantisilea.

She was a little uneasy. She had heard rumours concernin~
the disappearance of Pedro Caldes, but she had not tol~
Lucrezia of this. It would upset her with her confinement s~
near.

'I dream, you know,' said Lucrezia. 'I dream all the tim~
We shall have to leave Rome. That will be necessary for ~
while, I doubt not. We shall live quietly for a few years in som~
remote place – even more remote than Pesaro; but I do n~
think my father will allow us to be away from him for ever. H~

ill visit us; and how he will love his grandchild! Pantisilea, do
ou think it will be a boy?'

'Who can say, Madonna? Let us not pray for a boy or a girl,
ut that it will bring you great happiness.'

'You speak like a sage, Pantisilea. And look, your cheeks are
et. You are crying. Why are you crying?'

'Because . . . because it is so beautiful. A new life about to
egin . . . the fruit of your love. It is beautiful and it makes me
eep.'

'Dear Pantisilea! But there are the pains to be endured first,
nd I confess I am frightened.'

'You should not be, Madonna. The pains come and then . . .
ere is the blessing.'

'Stay with me, Pantisilea. All the time stay with me. Promise.'

'If it is permitted.'

'And when the child is born, when we have our little home,
ou will be with us. You must not make the baby love you too
uch, Pantisilea, or I shall be jealous.'

Pantisilea's answer was to burst into stormy tears.

'It is because it is so beautiful,' she repeated. 'Almost too
eautiful to be true.'

The midwife came. She was masked and accompanied by
wo men, also masked. They waited outside the door of
ucrezia's room and the midwife came to the bed.

She examined Lucrezia and gave orders to Pantisilea. The
wo men remained outside the door during Lucrezia's labour.

Lucrezia awoke from exhaustion, and asked for the child. It
as placed in her arms.

'A little boy,' said Pantisilea.

'I feel I shall die of happiness,' murmured Lucrezia. 'My
wn child. I would that Pedro were here. He should be eager
o see his son, should he not? Pantisilea, I want you to bring
edro to me.'

Pantisilea nodded.

'I want you to bring him at once.'

The midwife had come to the bed. She said: 'The Madonna
weary and needs to rest.'

'I want to hold my baby in my arms,' said Lucrezia, 'and

when his father is here with me I shall feel completely at rest.

'Your maid shall be sent at once for the child's father. It has been arranged,' said the midwife. She turned to Pantisilea. 'Put on your cloak, and prepare to go at once.'

'I do not know where to find him,' began Pantisilea.

'You will be taken to him.'

Lucrezia smiled at Pantisilea, and the little maid's eyes were wide with joy.

'I will not delay a moment,' she cried. 'I will go at once.'

'You will be conducted there. You will find your guide waiting at the door.'

'I shall not be long, Madonna,' said Pantisilea; and she knelt by the bed and kissed Lucrezia's hand.

'Go, Pantisilea,' murmured Lucrezia. 'Go with all speed.'

Lucrezia's eyes followed Pantisilea to the door. Then the midwife stooped over the bed.

'Madonna, I will take the baby from you now. He must sleep in his cradle. You need rest. I have a draught here which will send you to sleep. Take it and sleep long and deep, for you will have need of your strength.'

Lucrezia took the draught, kissed the child's fair head, gave him to the midwife and lay back on her pillows. In a few minutes she was asleep.

One of the men who had been waiting outside the door of Lucrezia's apartment stepped forward as Pantisilea came out.

'Follow me,' he said, and together they went out of the palace to the courtyard, where a horse was waiting for them.

It was evening and there was only moonshine to light the streets as Pantisilea rode pillion with her guide away from the palace. They went from the populous quarter and down to the river.

When they were near the bank, the horseman stopped.

He said: ''Tis a beautiful night, Pantisilea.'

She looked at the pale moonlight on the water and thought it wonderful. All the world looked beautiful because she was happy. Her mistress safely delivered of a fine boy, herself on the way to bring Pedro to Lucrezia. She had been thinking of their future as they rode along.

'Yes,' she said, 'it is beautiful. But let us not tarry. My
istress longs to see Pedro Caldes.'

'There is no hurry,' said the man. 'Your mistress will have
long sleep. She is exhausted.'

'I would rather proceed at once to our destination.'

'Very well, Pantisilea.'

He leaped down from his horse.

'Whither are you going?' she asked.

His answer was to lift her from the horse. She looked about
er for some dwelling where Pedro might be sheltering, but she
uld see none.

The man said: 'How small you are, Pantisilea, and so
ung.'

He bent his head and kissed her lips.

She was astonished, but not displeased. It was long since a
an had caressed her.

She laughed softly and said: 'It is not the time. I wish to be
ken at once to Pedro Caldes.'

'You have spoken, Pantisilea,' said the man.

He put his hands tenderly on her head and moved them slowly
own to her ears, caressing them. She looked up into his face;
e was not looking at her; he seemed to be staring at the moon-
t river. His eyes were fixed and glassy, and suddenly a terrible
ar took hold of Pantisilea.

For in a moment of blinding understanding she knew, even
fore it happened.

Then she felt the hands slide down to her throat.

Lucrezia awoke. It was daylight.

She had been dreaming. She was in a beautiful garden in the
untry; her baby boy lay in his cradle, and she and his father
ere bending over it looking at the child.

A happy dream, but only a dream. And here was the day,
d she was awake.

She was not alone in her room; a man sat on either side of her
d, and she was conscious of the dull thudding of her heart.
edro had been promised her; and he had not come; and where
as Pantisilea?

She struggled up.

'You should rest,' said Alexander. 'You need your strength my dear.'

'Father,' she murmured; and then she turned to that other figure. 'And Cesare,' she added.

'We have come to tell you that all is well,' said Cesare. He spoke in stern clipped tones, and she knew that he was angry. She shrank from him towards her father. Alexander's voice had been as kind and tender as it ever was.

'I want my child,' she said. 'Father, it is a boy. You will love him.'

'Yes,' said the Pope. 'In a few years he shall be with us.'

She smiled. 'Oh, Father, I knew I could rely on you to look after me.'

The beautiful white hand patted hers. 'My little one,' murmured Alexander. 'My wise little one.'

She took his hand and kissed it.

'Now,' said Alexander briskly, 'there is nothing to worry about. Everything has been settled. You will in a short while resume your normal life, and this little affair, although there have been some ugly rumours, will have been forgotten.'

'Father, Pedro . . .'

'Do not speak his name,' said Cesare harshly.

'Cesare, dearest brother, understand me. I love Pedro. He is the father of my child and soon to be my husband. Our father has arranged that it shall be so.'

'My dearest,' said the Pope, 'alas, that cannot be.'

She struggled up in her alarm.

'My dear daughter,' murmured the Pope. 'It is time you knew the truth.'

'But I love him, Father, and you said . . .'

Alexander had turned away and put a kerchief to his eyes.

Cesare said almost viciously: 'Pedro Caldes' body was recovered from the Tiber yesterday. You have lost your lover, sister; lost him to death.'

She fell back on her pillows, her eyes closed. The Pope leaned over her lovingly. 'It was too sudden,' he said. 'My sweet, sweet child, I would I could bear your pains for you.'

A smile of sarcasm twisted Cesare's lips as he looked at his father.

He wanted to shout: 'At whose orders was the chamberlain murdered? At mine and yours. Rightly so. Has she not disgraced our name enough by consorting with servants!'

Instead he said: 'There is another who has joined him there . . . your maid Pantisilea. You will never see her face again.'

Lucrezia covered her face with her hands; she wanted to shut out the sight of this room and the men who sat on either side of her. They were her guardians; they were her jailors. She had no life which was not designed by them. She could not take a step without them; if she attempted to do so, they arranged that she should meet only disaster.

Pedro in the river! She thought of him with the wounds on his body or perhaps the bruises on his throat; perhaps neither. Perhaps they had poisoned him before they had given him to the river.

Pedro, the handsome boy. What had he done but love Lucrezia?

And little Pantisilea. Never to see her again. She could not endure it. There was a limit to the sorrow one could suffer.

'Go . . . go from me,' she stammered. 'Have my child brought to me . . . and go . . . go, I say.'

There was silence in the room. Neither Cesare nor Alexander moved.

Then Alexander spoke, still in those gentle soothing tones. 'The child is being well looked after, Lucrezia. You have nothing to fear on his account.'

'I want my son,' she cried. 'I want my baby. I want him here . . . in my arms. You have murdered the man I love. You have murdered my friend. There is nothing I want now of you but to give me my child. I will go away. I will live alone with my child . . . I want never to see this place again. . . .'

Cesare said: 'Is this Lucrezia speaking? Is this Lucrezia Borgia?'

'Yes,' she cried. 'It is I, and no other.'

'We have been wrong,' said Alexander quickly. 'We have broken this news too sharply. Believe me, dearest daughter, there are times when one sharp cut of the knife is best. Then the healing can begin at once. It was wrong of you – a Borgia, our own beloved daughter – so to conduct yourself with a servant. And that there should be a child, was ... criminal. But we love you dearly and we understand your emotions. We forgive them as we would forgive all your sins. We are weak and we love you tenderly. We have saved you from disgrace and disaster, as we always should. You are our dearest treasure and we love you as we love none other. I and your brother feel thus towards you, and together we have saved you from the consequences of great sin and folly. Those who shared this adventure are no more; so there is no danger of their betraying you. As for the child, he is a beautiful boy and already I love him. But you must say goodbye to him – oh, only for a short while. As soon as it can be arranged I shall have him brought back to us. He is a Borgia. He kicked and screamed at me. Bless him. He is in the best of hands; he has a worthy foster-mother. She will tend him as her own – nay better. She'll not dare let any harm come to our little Borgia. And this I promise you, Lucrezia: in four years ... nay, in three, we'll have him with us, we'll adopt our lusty boy, and thus none will be able to point a finger at him and say, "There is the bastard of Lucrezia and a poor chamberlain." '

She was silent. The dream had disappeared; she could not grasp the reality. Not yet. But she knew she would. She knew that she could do no other.

Cesare had taken her hand, and she felt his lips touch it.

'Dearest,' he said, 'we shall arrange a grand marriage for you.'

She shivered.

'It is too soon to talk of such things,' reproved Alexander. 'That comes later.'

Still she did not speak.

They continued to sit there. Each held one of her hands and now and then would stoop to kiss it.

She felt bereaved of all happiness; and yet she was conscious of a vague comfort which came to her through those kisses.

She was growing aware of the inevitability of what had happened. She was beginning to realize how foolish her dreams had been.

THE SECOND BRIDEGROOM

UCREZIA WAS BEING dressed for her wedding. Her women
stood about her, admiring the dress, heavy with golden
mbroidery and sewn with pearls. Rubies glittered about her
eck, and the design on the dress was the mingling arms of
ragon and the Borgias.

It was but a few months since she had given birth to her son,
et now she had recovered her outward placidity; and as she
tood in her apartment while she was dressed in her finery, she
ppeared to have no thought for anything but the ceremony
bout to take place.

Sanchia was with her.

Lucrezia turned slowly and smiled at her sister-in-law. Who
ould have thought that it should be Sanchia who would bring
uch comfort in her misery?

It was Sanchia who had talked of her numerous love affairs,
ho had explained that in the beginning one felt so intensely.
)id not one remember one's first ball, one's first jewels? Thus
was with love affairs. Did not Sanchia know? Was not
anchia a connoisseur of love?

Sanchia had talked of her little brother. He was gentle; he
as beautiful; and all loved him. Lucrezia would bless the day
iat she had taken Sanchia's brother, Alfonso Duke of
isceglie, to husband.

Sanchia was excited at the prospect of her brother's arrival in
ome, and inspired Lucrezia with that enthusiasm. Oh,
iought Lucrezia, how glad I am to have Sanchia with me at
iis time!

She was a Borgia. She must not forget it. Everywhere she
ooked she was confronted by the emblem of the grazing bull.
Ve must not dream of simple love and marriage, she told her-
:lf. That is for simple people, people without a great destiny.

She was the beloved of her father and brother. It was as
iough they had forgotten she had ever attempted to defy them.

Somewhere in Rome – perhaps not even in Rome – a little boy was being brought up by his foster-parents, and in a few years he would come to the Vatican. He was all that remained of that brief idyll which had given him life and brought such suffering to his mother, and death to two who had loved her dearly.

As a Borgia one did not brood. The past was as nothing, the present and the future all-important.

She was ready now to go to her bridegroom.

F
PLA

Plaidy, Jean

Madonna of the
seven hills

DATE			